Bone China

Bone China

Kristen Cornwall

Paintwater Press

ISBN-13: 9798992818543

Cover design and photography: Kristen Cornwall
Linnea Borealis Art: Mary Delaney (1700-1788)
Library of Congress Control Number: 2025904883
Printed in the United States of America

For the ashes and the bones. You've been an inspiration.

1.

Berkshires, October 2014

The sweet scent of decomposing foliage bloomed under the impact of Linnea's feet. The tips of large rocks peeked through the fallen leaves lining the trail, but posed no threat. She ran Miller's loop most mornings as the sun arrived, often starting in low light, and she knew where to place her steps.

Burning tones fluttered down from the trees, muted against the backdrop of impending rain. Linn estimated having time to finish her run before the sky opened up.

Running had a way of transporting her, and not just in the literal sense. The act was primal and meditative, the repetitive motion like kneading clay, or grinding bone. She rarely encountered anyone on a dry day with full sun at the hour she ran. The rare birder crossed her path, and a woman who must start at the other end of the loop, passing with a silent nod.

With breath mellowed to a steady rhythm, the softened metronome of ocean waves passed through her, in and out. And where her respirations kept time within, her feet shared a tempo with the twenty-eight small ceramic beads threaded on her necklace. She didn't wear them often, keeping them instead with others in a grey bowl in her living room; a memorial, a reminder of loss, potential, communion.

After about an hour and a half, roughly three quarters through with her loop, Linn's eyes fixed on a shadow in the distance. The black seemed too concentrated; the shape too contrived, like a small steppe pyramid about the size of a milk crate. The object stood on her side of a fallen tree to the right of the trail. The shape was soft, topped in mauve. Perhaps a jacket had been left behind by a distracted runner who'd tied it round their waist. It wouldn't be the first thing she'd transported back to the trailhead.

The anomaly came into focus as Linn neared, her steady pace slowing as she made out sneakers stacked neatly atop a folded fleece, clothes, phone coiled in the thin white cord of a set of ear-buds.

Fighting her body's urge to gasp for air, Linnea urged her lungs to remain silent, stopping all but her racing heart. Stepping cautiously, she listened to the forest for anything: a rustle, snapped twig, some animal response to a predator on behalf of the chipmunks and birds. But her surroundings remained as they had been, pensive, waiting.

She moved forward, her focus on the sneakers, until a burst of color came from the other side of the fallen tree. A swath of pink caught her eye, stark against the bright green moss growing atop the decomposing wood. A swath of pink, from the woman lying among the leaves like spring lost in autumn.

The victim wore only her deep green sports bra and underwear the color of coneflowers. Swatches of fabric had been removed, exposing skin and hair, and her arms had been posed, rounded over her head, legs together.

Linnea pulled out her phone, instinct to begin resuscitation not triggered in the slightest, as the woman was well past time of death. She swiped the screen, stared at the keypad a moment, then slid the phone back in her pocket.

Leave everything as it is, she thought, wholly aware of the steps she'd taken to arrive where she stood, of the stone that had supported her for five years, the milestone that had sustained her. Linn crouched beside the unknown woman, the one she'd nodded to dozens of times, the white jeep woman. Fully aware this wasn't her path forward; Linn couldn't help taking a moment for herself.

Not a fiber. She isn't yours.

Tiny drops of rain began to fall, so sparse and gentle that their touch seemed personal, the sound intimate. *The rain will wash a great deal away.*

She hovered over the stranger's relaxed mouth. Was there something in there?

The smell of roses wafted up as Linnea moved closer, then her memories seeped in, bringing something stronger with them: the scent of gin and gasoline, blood and clay, rosemary, fire, and inspiration.

2.

Berkshires, August 1986

Linnea woke to darkness and sheets that felt different. Either of those things could have set her heart racing, or perhaps it was the dream. She heard her heart beating, heard someone else breathing. Instinct compelled her to remain still, but she fought it, and turned.

Seeing her brother asleep in his bed, Linnea exhaled, temporarily relieved. She and Lars were staying with their dad at Grandma Grace and Papa's house while their Mom was on a work trip. They'd even brought their cat, Barny, with them, but where *was* she?

The agony of being the only one awake weighed down that fear on her chest; but she wouldn't be alone if Lars woke...

Linnea blew air forcefully through her nose, eyes wide, assessing Lars for any reaction to the noise while also completely aware of the darkness in the room, of the possibility that she'd disturbed something.

Lars was still asleep.

Linnea felt around under the covers, her arms and hands safely separated from the dark room and thus moving freely without consequence. She found the stuffed brown bear, which provided her little comfort other than for the opportunity it provided. Taking another chance, she pushed the bear up and out from the blankets, exposing her limb just enough…

She chucked the stuffy at her brother, rousing him with brilliant success.

"Lars," she whisper-shouted. "Can I come in?"

"You have to go pee first," he said.

Linnea knew she could get from her bed to his, but out to the *bathroom*… He might as well be telling her to go to the basement. It was too far.

"I don't need to go."

"You're supposed to pee if you wake up, Linn. It's just across the hall. Where's Barny?"

"Probably with a mouse."

Linnea didn't think they had mice back home, and imagined their cat was fulfilling some duty, destiny, or both now that they were at their grandparents' house.

"I'll stay awake while you go," Lars offered. "Step one: put your feet on the floor."

Steps was something their father told them to do; said he'd learned it from GG. He used steps to help them with big projects, like getting dressed, cleaning up, or putting a sandwich together. *Break it down into steps,* he'd say. Then you weren't thinking about the whole overwhelming thing. You focused on the step you were on, knowing the next would come when you were ready.

Linnea put her feet on the floor and stood. The wood almost felt cool beneath her, the tips of her toes brushing at the rug between the two beds. "Step one," she whispered.

Her brother wouldn't be awake much longer, and once he was dreaming, she'd be alone again. *Step two*… She moved swiftly to the doorway and peaked into the hall. She heard breathing, loud and rough, but not close. It had to be Papa, because her house didn't sound like that at night, and she didn't think GG would snore. It wouldn't be like her grandmother to make that kind of noise.

In the corner across from where Linnea stood, the bathroom glowed slightly. They were on the second floor, and she needed to cross in front of the downstairs steps to get to dad's room, then turn left and go all the way down to the end of that hall to get there… She'd be fast. She'd be *so* fast, then crawl into Lars's bed when she got back.

Linnea took a deep breath and began to move on the exhale, swift on her feet like something was behind her, but she did *not* let her mind wander there, she had too much concern for what was in front of her. Her feet were swift over the creaking floor and old carpet, until her toes touched down against tiny black and white tiles.

After making quick work of why she'd come, Linnea made the return journey. Soft on her feet, and with a little more caution, she tiptoed back. Rounding the corner by her dad's room, she couldn't help but look down the stairs.

Panic and relief flooded her startled heart.

Grandma Grace looked up at her from the bottom of the steps with what might have been a smile. The darkness challenged her eyes, but Linnea could see GG wore her apron with the paisley block print, had the long ropes of her greying hair twisted in a bun atop her head. The shadows made everything soft, a different soft than during the day, when the wooden banister and floorboards were a warm brown and GG's skin was like cocoa and cinnamon. This was a softness of reality, of whether or not things were there.

GG motioned with her hand, inviting.

Linnea looked toward her room, where Lars had probably been sleeping since she set foot in the hall. Turning back to GG, she dropped a tentative toe down to the first step, eliciting a loud creak.

"Don't worry about the noise," GG said, waving her hand to dispel concern. "Come on down."

Movement in the darkness at GG's feet caught Linnea's eye. Barny, black as the shadows surrounding her. She wondered briefly where the cat had been, if she'd made it outside to visit her namesake behind the neighbor's house. Linnea had been about two, when Cap and his wife, Missy, had showed them the kittens in his barn next door. He'd been a captain in the navy, then he had the farm where she and Lars went to pick pumpkins for Halloween.

Linnea lifted her hand to the banister, and brought her other foot forward. Though too dark to see her path, she took the steps one at a time, until Barny's cheek brushed against her leg and GG's warm arm wrapped around her shoulders. Earlier in the day Grandma Grace had smelled like cookies and blue dish soap, but in the dark, GG carried the scent of clay, and something like the garden.

GG guided her to the kitchen, where Linnea saw what dim glow the moon and stars offered, streaming through the window above the sink. The light was grey, almost white, and there wasn't very much of it. The only other source was an orange coil hiding under a saucepan on the stove.

"Do you want a snack?" GG asked.

Linnea thought for a moment, then shook her head. "I'd have to brush my teeth again," she said softly. "What are you doing down here with the lights off?"

"I was working out in the studio, and came in to make some tea," GG said, tilting her head toward the saucepan on the stove where water was starting to bubble. "Then I heard little feet, far too big for a mouse. Barny and I were curious, so we investigated."

"Why didn't you use the tea kettle?"

"Whistle's too loud."

Linnea nodded with understanding. "I had to be quiet waking Lars. I was too scared to be loud, so I threw my bear at him."

"Were you scared you'd wake someone else?"

It felt like that almost, like she was scared of rousing something other than her family, and bringing attention to herself. Linnea shook her head, not knowing how to put it into words.

"The dark?" GG asked.

Linnea nodded, relieved, but aware that what she'd been afraid of still loomed all around them. She was safe with GG, and Barny, obviously, but some instinct wouldn't release her mind completely.

"Oh, Honey," her grandmother said, pulling Linnea into her warmth, rubbing her back. "It's been a long time since I've felt that. GG forgets. I could just *tell* you there's nothing to fear, but what we really need is to work together out in the studio."

"*Now?*"

"Mmmhmm," GG replied, releasing Linnea with another rub to her back. "It has to be made during the night," she added, turning off the stove and pouring water into a mug.

With one hand on GG's apron, Linnea went through the kitchen door and into the studio. GG made all kinds of things in there, like delicate tea cups and saucers, big mugs and large plates, teapots, and things Linnea didn't have names for. The space was filled with wonder during the day, all turned to secrets at night.

Tables, shelves, and a cold wood stove down back were lit vaguely by moonbeams streaming through skylights. Everything in the room seemed reduced to their shapes, blending together, all ranging from silver to black, like GG's hair.

Barny pressed against Linnea's leg again, then slipped back into shadow.

Grandma Grace tied Linnea's hair up into a bun and picked up the white shirt off the back of a chair. She threaded it over Linnea's head and arms, hem falling almost to her knees. It was one of Lars's shirts. GG said they didn't have an apron her size when she'd helped in the studio earlier, so Lars had given her a shirt to cover up her clothes. He said he didn't mind and she could have one, but Linnea still offered to pick blackberries for him from the bushes at the edge of the yard. He accepted.

"Go ahead and have a seat, Honey."

GG took a few steps away toward the desk against the wall, where she disappeared into the dark, becoming only sounds. Linnea heard the sip of tea and the mug settling back down.

"I have some clay wedged," GG said, walking back into the moonlight, holding her fisted hands about seven inches apart. She brought them in toward the dark blob at the center of the table where Linnea sat and, while her hands maintained their distance, a piece of the clay form separated.

"How did you *do* that?" Linnea whispered with wonderment.

"Wire," GG said with a smile in her voice. Linnea felt her grandmother's hand against hers, the cold, damp metal string she pressed against her palm, then something wooden. "The wire has handles on each side so you don't hurt yourself. It can put quite a strain on the hands when you're slicing through a larger piece, but it cuts through clean."

GG replaced the wood and wire with a cool, wet mound of clay about the size of a baseball, if the baseball had melted a little.

"Are you going to put on the light?" Linnea asked.

"Oh, no, Honey; this needs to be done in the dark."

Linnea watched GG's form weaving about through the studio, apron and locked hair losing definition the deeper she moved into the dark, gathering up what they needed. She brought the unknown supplies over to one of the spinning wheels where she made her cups and things, and patted one of two chairs.

"Come, sit with me, and bring that clay with you," she said. "We're going to work the darkness into it, and the best way to do that is with the lights off. Moon shouldn't be a problem."

Linnea dug her fingers in under the sticky lump and peeled it from the wooden surface. She sat down beside GG and, with her grandmother's hands guiding hers, placed the clay on the wheel's center, scooped water and let it trickle over.

GG called it *slip* when the clay and the water were mixed together like a milkshake. Grandma Grace let Linnea help her in the studio sometimes, pouring slip into plaster molds to make her bone cups.

"Are there bones in this one?" she asked.

"No, you need to use your hands for this project, and bone china slip is too thin. It's weak when wet, but the bone makes it strong once it's fired."

"Will my cup be strong?"

"Of course it will, Honey. You're putting your strength into it."

GG placed her large hands-on top of Linnea's, and the wheel began to spin with a soft hum. She pushed Linnea's palms against the clay with hers, pressing down in the center.

"Slow down a little, Honey," her grandmother said, that smile in her voice. "Slow and steady. Trickle the water on."

Linnea did as she was instructed, adding water, then pushing down flat on the top, from the sides, fingers pressing in, pulling up until there was an inside.

"God's first creation here was done in darkness, just as we're doing now," GG said gently over the soft hum of the wheel. "More water, Honey."

God, Linnea thought curiously. She'd heard her father use the word, but she wasn't quite sure what God *was.* And hadn't her father said, *he?*

"Is God a man?" Linnea asked.

"I don't suppose there'd be much reason for God to be either man or woman," her grandmother said. "But I think it's hard for people to think that way. It's written that we were made in God's image, but I think God is powerful enough to change into any form. It's my suspicion that God left a piece of their self inside us when we were made, the part that knows right from wrong, the part driven to create things."

GG pulled their hands away, and pressed something into Linnea's palm.

"This has a blade on the end we'll use it to trim the top off," she said, guiding Linnea's hand in trimming a ribbon of clay from the top.

After adding more water, Linnea's hands seemed to move away from her creation of their own accord, allowing the vessel to end its dance without interference as the wheel began to slow, and the hum

"I think it's come out rather nicely," GG whispered. "If darkness had a body, bones, or blood, we could have added them, but there's no need. The dark is here, surrounding us like a womb, and you're going to conquer your fear with every sip you take."

Linnea could almost feel the water on her tongue. She liked the idea of drinking from the shadows that Barny slipped into, from the feeling of something she couldn't see.

"Is it done?" she whispered back.

"This part is, but it needs to dry a little before we can add a handle. It will need to be *completely* dry before we put it in the kiln, but that won't happen until after you've gone back home with Lars and your Dad."

Linnea looked up toward the windows in the ceiling. "Will the sun get it?"

"No, we've worked enough of the night in, but I'll tuck your cup away where the light won't reach, just in case. First, we need to set it free. Come, take this."

Grandma Grace pressed something into each of Linnea's palms, then pushed her hands apart, stretching taught what couldn't be seen.

"The wire!" Linnea whispered, delighted.

"Indeed," GG said, guiding her hands, wiggling the metal thread under the cup.

Once separated, they moved the piece to a cabinet beside GG's desk, then Linnea followed her over to the big sink to rinse her hands.

"Leave what's under your nails, and bring what we've done into your dreams" her grandmother said. "Do you need me to walk you back?"

Linnea shook her head, then paused. "Maybe just to the stairs."

Though the path was unseen, she had a sense of the way, and her bare feet always found the next step waiting. Linnea looked back down when she reached the top, lifting her fingers to send a silent wave through the darkness. She didn't want to disturb the quiet, not out of fear, but a sense of respect.

The rhythmic tide of Lars's breath greeted her as she entered their room. Her feet fell quietly against the rug and the wooden floor, her body gliding between the sheets of her bed. She smiled and slid a hand up toward her face, fingernails pressed beneath her nose as she inhaled new memories, made new dreams.

*

Linnea woke with a breath so deep, it felt like her first in hours.

Grandma Grace's grey rope hair brushed over the sheets and against Linnea's shoulder.

"It's time we got back to work," she whispered.

GG had a different schedule than Linnea's parents, or Papa. Some nights GG stayed up late, other nights, she went to bed early with Papa and got up before the sun to *greet the morning.*

"I wanted you to witness the dawn," GG said as they passed through the kitchen. The house was soft, but the dark felt more familiar. "A gift that unfolds every day, yet unobserved by so many, drunk on their dreams. You'll see."

Grandma Grace said things like that, deeper than Linnea knew, but she drank each word, her roots reaching down to soak up every drop.

Together they fashioned a handle from clay, attached it to Linnea's cup. After returning the piece to the darkness of the cabinet, the two passed through the kitchen for tea, then headed outside.

The slate patio came through in shades of steel and silver, moss between the stones like a network of black veins. The large wooden table where she'd eaten dinner had all but disappeared into shadow under the pergola, grape vines growing thick overtop and down posts to the ground. She breathed in honeysuckle, the scent coming from the arched arbor that created a passageway to Cap and Missy's yard. Flowers wove through the structure, their fragrance seeping into her like a dream.

The driftwood and hammered spoons of GG's windchimes were quiet, but Linnea heard music upon passing over the threshold, a song that seemed not to match the stars still hanging overhead. Birds, singing and chattering throughout the surrounding trees.

"It sounds like daytime," Linnea marveled, nearly walking into the table. GG's guiding hand prevented the collision, allowing her to continue on, mesmerized. "It's *more* than daytime, I think."

Grandma Grace nodded as she sat down, taking a sip and setting her mug on the table.

"Are they singing for the sun?" Linnea asked.

"That is a lovely thought, but no. I think the birds are calling out in the darkness for one who'll be just the right match for them. To anyone else, their song is a declaration of territory, a warning." GG paused, taking another sip from her cup. "Instinct and ferocity. Nature is beautiful," she smiled.

*

It may have been a jostling movement that woke Linnea next. She was in Papa's car, Lars staring out the window beside her. The back seat smelled like the pond. They'd all been night fishing while GG stayed home to work.

"Where's Dad and Papa?" She asked, unsure where they were, or why they'd stopped, seeing there was no one up front.

"Flat tire," Lars said, working hard to roll down his window. "Dad wanted to drive the rest of the way home since we're so close, but Papa said we'd damage the rim, and that it's his car so we're pulling over. You were sleeping."

"I was up early with GG and the birds," she said defensively.

"And you need more sleep, that's why you nap."

"I don't take naps."

"You don't do it on purpose, but it happens. You fell asleep today after lunch when we were looking at marbles."

It was true. They had been in the study, and she'd been looking at marbles Papa kept in a glass dish. She'd been on the small couch while her brother sat on the floor, but then Barny was there asleep by her legs, and Lars was gone. When she'd stretched, she'd found one of the marbles and two of GG's tools between the couch cushions. Lars called it *couch fishing* when they found things in the furniture. At home, they found pencils, coins, crumbs, and a lot of their own toys. At GG and Papa's, they found GG's tools instead of the toys.

"If you need help, you could ask GG to wake me next time too one night," Lars said.

Then their dad shouted, "I want you two out on the grass! I need to jack up the car!"

"Get out on my side," Lars said, opening his door. "Yours is on the street."

Without question, she followed him, sliding across the seat, out the door, and into the night. The darkness was speckled with stars and a few lit windows along

the street, but the houses were few and far between, set back enough to feel distant.

Another light danced on the pavement, peeking out from under the car. When Linnea investigated, she found Papa holding a flashlight over where her dad was crouched, trying to place the jack.

"If you had a coal miner's helmet, you wouldn't need a flashlight helper," Lars said.

"Well, I wouldn't need a flashlight helper if it were daytime…" Their father said. "But your Papa likes an adventure, especially when I'm the one breaking a sweat…"

"It'll be daylight tomorrow when you patch it," Their papa said. "Then you can help me in the hallway afterwards."

The hallway was a project Papa had been working on, connecting the new garage he built to the house. GG had her studio in the old one, and he said he was tired of cleaning snow from their car in winter.

Their dad grunted as he pumped the jack. "I want you two off the street. Go sit by one of those trees, listen for crickets and see if you can catch one."

Linnea and Lars wandered a little past a big maple, settling against the next tree they came to. Leaning into the bark, and a little against each other, they listened. They listened, and they watched the light move under the car, until another light moved toward them. As it got closer, Linnea realized it was a headlight; one where two should have been.

The sound of the impact was abrupt and paralyzing. Crushed by a truck against the first maple they'd passed, Papa's car breathed fire, flames reaching up, illuminating the green leaves so they looked like autumn.

"Dad!"

Linnea didn't know if it was her voice or Lars's screaming, but her mouth was open, eyes wide.

The truck door was pounding, creaking open.

"Dad!"

There hadn't been a body in the street before.

"Lars, where's Dad and Papa?"

Lars pushed her against the tree trunk where they'd been sitting. "Stay here. Don't move." And then he was running to see who occupied the road.

She didn't want to be alone, though, and a man was stepping out of the truck. Half his face was bloody, and she couldn't see his eye on the red side. Like the headlight on the truck, it was just gone somehow.

Linnea raced toward Lars where he'd stopped in the road, hands on his knees, breathing weird. The body beneath him had her dad's pants on, and his shirt, but everything else was wrong. She crouched, her heart racing, fingers outstretched, his shirt wet against her hands.

"Linn," her brother said, his arm at her waist.

"It's Dad's shirt," she said, loud, but not meaning to shout. Everything was *wrong.*

"Linn, that's Dad!" Lars shouted, *real* shouting, as he pulled at her. "That's Dad!"

How could he know? How could he know when there wasn't a face? She held on tight, gripping the wet shirt. Some part of her thought maybe she could still get at him, that he could be in there somewhere, inside the clothes she'd seen him wearing all day, at dinner, and fishing. If she burrowed in, like Barny did with blankets, she could find him still, smooth him out like crumpled paper.

"We have to get out of the street. We have to find Papa!" Lars cried, wrenching her toward him. She released the scarecrow to the ground, blood smeared on her hands like slip.

They turned, and the red-faced man was there, walking with a stumble and a limp. He was tall, and he was awful.

Linnea screamed, not with fear, but with fury. She looked into his eye with both of hers, and she roared. Then he brought a hand to her mouth as if to cover it, smearing blood across her face as she shook her head, her fingers clawing at his missing eye. He smelled like meat, rubbing alcohol, and Christmas trees.

Lars. Lars was there, arms flailing, fists pounding. The man pushed him off into her, sending both she and her brother scrambling up and across the street. She barely registered the small squares of light popping on, windows waking.

Running, she held Lars's hand tight, though she knew he wouldn't let go. She stumbled in vines of squash, the valley's between. Lars said Cap's farm was near GG's, and they were close.

They passed over a rock wall, turning to see the fire behind them flash with red and blue up at the tops of the maple trees in the distance. Standing on GG's street, they looked left and right over and over. The houses didn't have color, but they had shape, and she could see the sign for the farm stand at the end of Cap's driveway.

"Cap's!" she shouted, knowing her grandparents lived right next door.

They rounded the old garage at GG's to the back patio, panting at the rear kitchen door. It was usually open, but with both kids grabbing for the knob with urgency, it felt locked. Finally bursting through, they saw Grandma Grace leaning against the counter, the pockets of her paisley apron heavy with those little wooden tools. One of her hands clutched a pencil, the other pressed a phone to her ear, long cord trailing toward the wall.

A look of wild relief flashed and settled on GG's face as the pencil fell from her hand, arm outstretched.

"Dad's not ok!" Lars wailed as they collapsed into her, crying against the crusted clay of their grandmother's clothes. "It was a car accident. We couldn't find Papa, and I think Dad is *dead!*"

"They're here," GG sighed into the phone. Her voice sounded like she was sick. "I've gotta go, Noreen. Tell them the kids are here… No, I can't drive like this. Call Cap and Missy, send them over… Alright."

Linnea hadn't noticed before, the way her breath cut on its way down to her lungs, sharp. Her body felt like it was still running, pounding in her feet and up her legs. Her heart was still running, too, running down a hill and about to tumble off a cliff.

GG's hand pressed against the back of Linnea's head, and Lars's arm was around her waist, part of her shirt worked into his fist.

"Let's get you two cleaned up a little before Cap and Missy get here," GG said, her voice calm, but still sounding sick. "Do you need a drink of water?" She asked, looking into Linnea's frantic eyes.

Linnea nodded, catching sight of Barny emerging from the studio door, carrying an idea with her, and into Linnea's mind. GG reached up into the cabinet, but Linnea shook her head, unable to form words.

Lars, somehow calm, looked right into her eyes. His voice was soft, but textured from use, and he spoke like it was just the two of them there. "What do you need?"

"I need my cup," she said, flat between breaths, hoping her grandmother would understand. "I need my cup."

GG paused, considering. "It's firm enough that you could take a sip, but the water will soften the insides a little. Just a sip, then you drink from a glass. Can you walk?"

Linnea nodded, and took a step, then, one after the other, her feet kept moving her toward the studio.

When GG reached for the light switch, Linnea shouted, "No," and Lars reached up to stop GG's hand.

Grandma Grace nodded, and they continued on, Barny nudging their legs, pressing his face against Linnea as she waited for the cabinet to open. This time GG reached in, rustling plastic as she pulled out the mug, its handle still fresh. Linnea took a few steps and turned on the sink, spray and droplets of water splashing up and onto her chest, arms, and her hands… but Grandma Grace shook her head in the moonlight.

"The force from the sink might be too strong. Here," she said, pouring a bit of liquid from a teacup on her desk into Linnea's mug. Handing the vessel to her granddaughter, she added, "Gentle, like an egg."

Linnea took the clay in her hands, coating it in blood reconstituted from the spray of sink water. She drank, tasting the garden in Grandma Grace's cold tea mixing with something like dirty coins, and the clay... slippery sediment that left a smooth grit on her tongue and between her teeth. She swallowed the tea, the blood, and the darkness, that they would become a part of her she wouldn't fear. Then, she handed the cup to Lars, and he drank what was left, careful not to disturb the handprints she left behind.

Linnea learned later that blood would burn off in the kiln, but like the darkness, it became a part of the clay, a part of the story that she couldn't see, but she knew was there.

3.

Berkshires, August 1997

A single flame lit the workspace, warm light dancing out from atop a thick pillar of beeswax. Linnea sat beside GG, with the moon overhead and only about an hour before dawn crept into the sky.

When asked about the need for a candle, GG simply replied, "This is a time for fire."

Linnea had eleven beads on a necklace, eleven small, round, blue years, but this would be her first time helping Grandma Grace make them.

As Linnea's eyes explored the materials before her, it became obvious it was only the glazing they'd be working on. The beads were formed and firm, having been fired once already, each speared by wire and suspended from a bead rack. The one in front of Linnea held four beads for the memory of her father. She would get one, as would her mother, GG, and Lars. Linnea's beads were always dark blue with a little tap of crimson, and the one's for Papa were deep red, like bricks at night, but both had a melted, crackling appearance. The rack by GG had a single bead for Papa's memory, one, just for her.

GG brought over two stone bowls, glaze, brushes, and two glass jars. Each jar had a thin layer of white at the bottom, then the rest was filled about three quarters with something dark and difficult to identify. It didn't look like powder, so she didn't think it was meant for the glaze, but she'd learned not to assume with her grandmother…

After painting the surface of all four beads blue, and adding the tap of crimson, Linnea looked to the bowls and the jars, to GG who had been waiting for her to finish.

"Open your jar," her grandmother said.

Linnea unscrewed the metal lid, paused to look at the indecipherable contents, and reached in. She felt a rough substance at her fingers, something soft and frayed like fabric, but firm in places.

"Take out two pieces," her grandmother instructed, doing the same with the other jar, but it seemed she'd only removed one of whatever it was.

Linnea pinched and removed something about the size of a quarter, placed it in her hand, then took out another and pushed the two pieces of what appeared to be old fabric around on her palm.

"The lid, Honey."

Linnea squeezed the fabric in her palm, screwed the lid back on, and waited.

"What we put into the work is part of the creation, our intentions, the darkness, the fire," GG started, gesturing behind her, then to the flame. "When your father and Papa died, I was offered their belongings, after the bodies were brought in. I discarded some, but their shirts… I kept the shirts, saturated as they were. The blood dried, and I cut them up into pieces, put salt at the bottom of the jars to help keep them dry, to preserve them."

The irregularly shaped patches of cloth in her palm had come from her father's shirt. What caused the firm texture of the larger piece, had been inside him. Linnea tried to see the details of what she held, tried to match it to her memory, to know how to dress the distorted figure that had been her father in the road.

"Place them in the bowl when you're ready."

Linnea looked up from her hand to see that GG held scissors in one hand, while the other positioned the tip of a black and grey dreadlock between the blades.

"I've been growing these since your father was a boy," she said. "And I have a lifetime of memories stored here."

Sheers sliced, and a pinch of hair was sprinkled over each bowl. Then GG sat still, waiting.

I'm ready, Linnea thought, as she offered the pieces of her father, dropping them into her vessel.

"From that moment, their bodies, and from their history, mine, carried through ash…"

GG held two thin wooden sticks, each about the length of Linnea's forearm. Matches. Long matches. She handed one to Linnea, then dipped hers into the flame until a bright burst sprayed at the tip, and sulfur pinched at her nose. Linnea mimicked her grandmother's actions, carrying fire to her stone vessel.

"You might need to tilt it a little," GG said, demonstrating how she tipped her bowl to better manage.

So, Linnea tilted her bowl, watching the hairs smolder and spark, watching the edges of her father's shirt take the orange light, drawing it inward. It was not lost on her that she was performing a sacred act. She felt connected, powerful, *purposeful* as she transformed the items with which she'd been entrusted.

When what remained in her bowl was black and gritty, Linnea ground the contents with a pestle, then rolled her four beads around the concave stone.

"A bit of saliva on the finger helps the ash to stick," GG advised. "I wouldn't go so far as to touch the glaze to my tongue, though. I breathe enough chemical content in the studio, I don't need to start eating it."

Linnea took the four beads into her palm, feeling the powdered remains of blood, fiber, and memory coating her skin. What she'd done felt like prayer, like *magic.*

Threading her beads back onto the Nichrome wire, Linnea let out a breath, inhaled. "I feel like, like I'm two different people sometimes. Back home and at school, I have field hockey, and my friends… I don't think they would understand the part of me that makes things in the dark." She said, feeling the ashes between her fingers.

"And should you be just one thing, like a Halloween costume?" GG asked, the visual carrying intended absurdity.

"No," Linnea smiled.

"No. When God took the form of a burning bush and spoke to Moses, Moses asked what he should tell the Israelites when they asked for God's name. Who are you?" GG asked, without waiting for an answer. "God didn't list hobbies or accomplishments. God didn't even give a *name* when answering Moses. I AM. To represent their identity, God simply said, *I am.*" She paused, letting the last two words resonate. "You can be all the things, Honey, you don't have to pick, and there doesn't need to be a word for what you are."

*

The smell of honeysuckle came through the screen door, entering Linnea before she stepped outside. She'd dressed for a run, wearing sneakers, blue Adidas shorts, and a black *Joy Division* band shirt that fell loose enough over her to provide a little air flow.

Under the pergola, grapes ripening above him, Lars sat with a glass of lemonade on ice. He wore athletic shorts and a Bonnie Raitt t-shirt he'd scored at a thrift store, probably exhausted as she was after staying up most of the night.

Linn thought about asking him to go running with her, but judging by the sweat coming through his clothes, he'd already gone. Usually she went alone, but Lars could be present without making a fuss about it; could be all the way quiet.

He lifted a finger to his mouth as she approached, then tapped his ear, and tilted his head toward the honeysuckle where Grandma Grace stood talking with Cap. Their words were distant, but close enough to catch.

"Business is doing pretty well, considering," Cap said. "It's only been a year though..."

"Been doing well because she's been running it," GG huffed. "And with his name still on everything..."

Linnea squinted her eyes at Lars. Who were they talking about?

He dragged his thumb over one closed eye, down his face in a vertical line, and she knew. Bill West. The last time she saw him, half his face had been bloody, his eye on that side indiscernible. The eye, as it turned out, had lost function, so mangled he'd needed a prosthetic. After killing her father and Papa, he served ten years while his sister took the helm at West Landscaping, then he came right back, picking up things where he left off. Missy had been friends with Mrs. Sarah Preston, Bill's sister. She and Missy had known each other since junior high, and attended the Stockbridge School of Agriculture together. By Missy's account, Sarah was delightful and a skilled horticulturist, but the brother had always been trouble. This was all information GG could have ascertained from Missy, but there was something off-putting about it, something like asking Missy to break a trust between friends. So, Cap related any news on West to Grandma Grace, the buffer seeming enough for the two of them.

While Cap and GG spoke with the casual demeanor of two friends engaged in neighborhood gossip, Linnea and her brother listened with eager ears, warring between the potential relief of letting go, and that other thing, the need to dig deep into the dirt, blood, and bones of it all. To scrape until their fingernails were black and they'd uncovered some sense of closure. The conversations they overheard, words stolen, fed that need to know anything more.

Cap nodded. "She's just managing the nursery now, but Missy says she prefers it that way. The responsibility while Bill was gone, it was too much stress, and her health... She's had heart surgery, a couple toes taken off from the diabetes, but I think they're going back for part of the foot."

"Jesus."

"Younger than me," he said. "Both of us."

"Age isn't everything," GG sighed. "Has the boy seen him?"

Cap shook his head. "Sarah said he comes by her place when he can, same as always, works in the garden when he visits, helps with her son, poor kid."

"But he hasn't seen West."

Cap shook his head again.

The man had a kid, apparently. He'd been thirteen or fourteen at the time, she couldn't remember, but he'd gone to live with Mrs. Preston after the accident because his mom had taken off when he was young, and there were no grandparents.

Grandma Grace and Cap's conversation transitioned to her arthritis and Cap's suspicion he was coming down with it. As their words drifted away from gossip, so did Linnea and her brother's attention to what was being said.

Several breaths passed, and Lars drank his lemonade down past the ice. He'd arrived the night before after returning home from Ecuador on a medical mission with their mom, an operating room nurse, and their stepfather, Don, an anesthesiologist she met on a mission about a year after Linn's father had died. She was eight when Don relocated from New York to Boston after taking a job at MGH, and she was nine when he finally moved in with them. She initially received him with all the warmth a man dating her mother deserved, giving him ice-cold scrutiny and skepticism. Well versed in human potential, she searched him for *ugliness*. She searched for the shadow part of him, but Don seemed not to have one. He just fit. He fit her mother, and he fit their family.

From then on, it was the four of them packing medical equipment into suitcases the night before the annual trip to Ecuador. It was strange that first year, though, to have someone else present during what had been a private, family ritual. But Don had become family, and where anyone else would have felt like an intruder, he seemed to belong, and perhaps that's what was strange. Her parents, for that's how she began to collectively refer to them, were fortunate to have found each other. Linnea was twelve when they got married. Her mom joked that she went through with it because she was tired of doing taxes, and if they made things legal, she could just have Don file once for the both of them. Their togetherness was a reminder that, while Linnea might experiment, she would never form a partnership with someone who didn't fit.

Linn and Lars had always stayed with GG when their parents were away, but with Lars entering his sophomore year studying nursing at Boston College and a plan for med school after, the trip was a great experience for him. He worked part time in admin for the non-profit over the summer, but after his second year at school he'd probably get a job as a nursing assistant.

Though fatigued from travel, Lars had stayed up late into the night listening to Linnea talk about her week while they lounged on the living room couch. He drank in the details of fabric, blood, fire, and stone as she described glazing their dad's beads with GG, then they'd made popcorn and checked the couch cushions for treasure. Their bounty consisted of eighty-seven cents, a charcoal pencil, dried orange peels, and one of GG's clay tools.

After returning to the kitchen for hot chocolate and marshmallows, they settled in again on the couch. Lars painted a picture with his words, of mountains and an excursion to the Papallacta hot springs. When he reclined, Barny curled onto his chest and purred, listening as Lars described how one of the docs had molded an ear for a child. Together, he and Linnea had wondered if the surgeon sculpted with clay when not sculpting with flesh.

"How many miles are you gonna put in?" Lars asked, sipping his lemonade and nodding toward her field hockey stick on the table.

"Eh, it's hot and I'm still tired. I was thinking I'd do twenty-five minutes out and turn around. Looks like you got yours in already," she said, gesturing to the sweat seeping through his shirt.

He raised his brows and tucked his chin. "That was a warmup."

"Lars," Cap hollered from the honeysuckle. "You up for some shooting before you two head back home? Never too early to plan for November."

"I was taught to start getting ready in January," Lars quipped with a smile.

Cap grinned. "Wise words. Your teacher must be *magnificent*."

Lars had run cross country in fall, wrestled in winter, and ran track in spring during high school, but it was cross country that he continued at Boston College. The sport took up too much time during bow season, but shotgun he could manage.

"It'll be a few hours."

"Why don't you guys come over for lunch?" Cap suggested.

"I was thinking of making a crisp," Grandma Grace chimed in.

"I like the sound of that," Cap grinned. "I'll go pick up some cold cuts; the deli has a good potato salad too, they put bacon in it."

Linnea stood, grabbing her stick. "You two work on the menu and we'll help when we get back."

"*Menu*," Cap huffed, shaking his head with a smile.

Linnea paused to regard Lars as he turned for the kitchen door instead of heading around the house with her.

He held up his glass. "I'll meet you out front. Gonna put a couple lemonades in the freezer. They'll be slushy with an ice crust on top by the time we get back."

"*Yesss*," she said with a slow nod, raising her free hand for a high-five before they went their separate ways.

*

Slowing to a trot, Linnea entered the driveway, then walked a bit, taking long, controlled breaths. Lars's footsteps were light behind her. She turned to see the back of his sweat-soaked shirt as passed her and kept going up the front steps.

"I'm not stopping until cold air from the freezer hits my face," he said. "I'll meet you out back with our slushies."

She nodded, hearing the back door to the kitchen open and close as she rounded the house, the scent of honeysuckle wafting on a welcome breeze, chilling her wet shirt.

Barny was there on the grass, poised at attention a few paces in front of Grandma Grace, who seemed to be staring at the tree line. Linnea's eyes followed GG's to some wheat-colored movement, a dog loping toward them, but not a dog, a coyote. The scraggly animal picked up speed, jaw slung open as if in a smile. Barny, black and patient, waited like a bullfighter hiding her sword, fearless in her power. GG waved her arm, shouting as she put a foot forward, as if to protect the cat.

Linnea's legs were already churning with energy, propelling her forward, bursts of primal energy flowing through her body like lightning. The stick swung as an extension of her arm, GG was screaming, and then curved wood connected with hair covered muscle and bone. The animal's head took the impact, front legs buckling as it stumbled, stunned enough for Linnea to dive onto the creature. She snaked her right arm around the front of its neck to grab the inside of her opposite elbow, her other forearm coming around the back of its neck, left hand gripping her right arm as she *squeezed.*

The kitchen door thwacked shut, Lars's body a blur as he approached, but she felt no hands on her, no fingers grabbing to pull her off.

"You got this?" He asked, vibrant, ready to step in or remain on standby.

The animal's neck was small and strong, wild strong, but not enough to pump blood past the pressure put on its arteries. Fury, like fire, required oxygen.

"Yeah," she ground out, and that was all he needed.

The coyote's bludgeoned head thrashed, jaws snapped, smearing blood from Linnea's chest to her chin, but her arms were relentless. Coarse hair rubbed against her skin, against her thighs, combining a fetid musk with the scent of honeysuckle, engulfing her in a heady perfume. Claws scraped at her legs as the coyote pushed, tilting its head back in an attempt to slide through her grip, but Linnea held firm.

And then the creature went limp, limbs unresponsive, dead weight beneath her. As consciousness slipped from the animal, Linnea remained steadfast, though with a sense of relief, and some other feeling of release flooding through her in an almost euphoric calm.

I'm a creator, she thought. *I'm human, I'm an animal, and I am more. I am all the things. I am. I* am.

Missy came tearing through the arbor, stopping beside Grandma Grace, jaw slack and eyes wide.

"Don't let go," Lars commanded. Linn's head turned up, his eyes catching hers. "If you release too soon, it'll just get back up. Give it a few minutes," he added, checking his watch, keeping time.

Linnea nodded, using the time to slow her breathing, her heart, to come down.

"What *happened?*" Missy called out in panic. "Jesus. Is she *okay?*"

Linnea had no intention of speaking until she got up. There was an intimacy to what had happened between her and the animal. To have Lars, and maybe even GG present was tolerable, but Missy suddenly felt foreign, not unwelcome so much as out of place, seeing too much.

"She's alright," Grandma Grace reassured.

"A little longer," said Lars. "You're doing good."

"Just *good?*" Linnea breathed with a smile.

"Do you need me to detail how impressive your takedown was? A coyote with your bare hands?"

"I started with a stick, to be fair," she panted.

"Noted," he said flatly, then there was relative silence save for the birds, the breeze, and the smell of the animal mixing with honeysuckle. "Wish I'd seen that swing," he added quietly.

Gravel crunched in the distance. A car, no, a truck. The engine cut, door closed.

"Cap!" Missy yelled.

Around the house came Cap, not quite running but he was moving fast, paper grocery bag in his arms. He slowed as he approached the three standing, seeing Linnea wasn't in danger, then he stopped, looked at the animal, the field hockey stick on the ground, the blood. He looked at Linnea, saw her, saw *everything*.

"That's time," Lars said. "Four minutes down should be enough."

She slid her arms from around the coyote's neck, bracing herself on her hands and knees before standing, feeling an odd combination of buzzed, calm, and spent.

"We're not letting that thing back up," Cap said, then looking to Linnea he asked, "You get bit? Scratched?" His eyes traveled over her body. "Shit."

Linnea looked down about the time everyone else did, past the dirt on her knees, to the scrapes on her legs from the animal's back claws.

"I'll give Doug a call down at the vet, see if he wants the whole thing or just the head."

"The head?" Linnea asked.

"They use the brain to check for rabies, and it needs to be done. It's not the blood, but the saliva you need to be concerned with, and it can get in through a bite, or scratches."

Linnea looked down at herself again, blood and scrapes on her legs, dirt thick at her knees, the chest of her shirt covered in blood and hair.

Grandma Grace caught Linnea's eyes, holding them in a way that kept that ball of potential inside her from rolling downhill, toward panic. "Honey, there's nothing you can change, and nothing you need to do for several hours."

Lars's arm came around her waist, over the blood, hair, sweat, and dirt.

Missy took the paper bag from Cap. "I bet a nice hot shower will feel good, then come on over for lunch after."

Despite the heat and humidity, a hot shower did sound right.

"Go ahead in and get cleaned up, Linn," Cap said with calm authority. "We'll take it from here."

She nodded, her smile returning. "Alright," then she shook her head and laughed. "I can't believe that just happened."

Cap huffed and smiled, "Yeah, you and the rest of us."

The kitchen was warm, deep with the scent of apples, vanilla, and brown sugar. Lars held a slushy glass of lemonade beside her mouth, straw against her lips. Ice cold.

After washing her hands, Linnea opened the second drawer beside the sink and pulled out a freezer bag, handing it to Lars.

"Can you hold that?" she asked, opening the top drawer and retrieving a pair of scissors. She tried to look down at her shirt, then glancing back to her brother she asked, "The collar has blood on it, right?"

He nodded, "Yeah, there's blood and hair on your neck, the shirt collar…"

"Okay, I want you to cut the collar off, just go around the ring," she said, holding out the scissors.

"You can't just cut up one of my shirts like that, a *good* shirt. One wash and it'll be fine. It's mostly black, besides, anything left over would be like battle scars, totally badass."

"This hasn't been your shirt in years, and I'm not cutting the whole thing up, just the collar. It will have a wide neck, which will look cute while retaining the badassary."

He stood there, looking over her face, the shirt. "You're going to make something."

She nodded.

"Like with the beads, burning the shirt for glaze."

Linnea nodded again.

Lars put the plastic bag down, took the scissors in his hand, and said, "Lift your hair."

4.

Berkshires, August 1998.

"The kiln out back is *massive*," Lars said, dipping his head to catch a mini marshmallow Linn sailed toward his mouth. "Were they still building it when Mom dropped you off?"

The two of them sat in the living room in the dim light of late evening, eating popcorn and marshmallows. Lars had arrived late after returning from another medical mission with their mom and Don, this one to Bhutan.

"No," she answered, a smile coming to her face. "It sounds like it was a real party, though."

GG had built the outdoor kiln with students and another professor as part of a summer class she ran. In the end, when they'd run it with greenware, it had taken days to fire the clay. Students stayed over in tents out back, taking shifts.

"Made anything?" he asked.

"Not like last summer," she grinned, but with it came a wistful feeling as she recalled the work she'd done: making glaze with the bloody neck of her shirt, coyote ash on her hands while she molded clay into two bowls... Linnea had felt a rush of purpose and creative calling, a sense of that dark place within her waking. But now it waited; *she* waited.

"Hard to top that," Lars said. "So, what *have* you been working on?"

"Slip casting china. GG has a commission for a tea set."

It hadn't been Linnea's first time slip-casting, pouring the liquid clay into molds, then draining the excess out so a thin layer remained in the shape of a tea cup, or dish. The special formulation of bone china, made the substance nearly impossible to throw on a potter's wheel, so molds were typically used. She'd heard of people hand-building with bone china, but it wasn't something GG had taught her, nor was she interested. Slip casting had her attention, and while there wasn't a rush, like with the coyote ceramics, there was a sense of promise when she worked, a sense that she was on a path toward something she could sink into, deep.

"I'll show you studio things in the morning; tell me about Bhutan! Ugh," she sighed. "You guys are like rockstar astronauts."

Linn had a passion and perhaps a gift for ceramics, but knew she'd end up working in healthcare. Aside from job security, the prospect of joining a medical mission team was a major selling point for Linnea when she considered nursing a potential career option. Her mom and Don, now Lars too, they were real-life explorers as far as she was concerned. The stories and pictures they brought home were thrilling, and Linnea listened to them knowing her family hadn't just been on vacation, they'd been useful. They weren't some ragtag group of travelers, they were an organized team performing surgery on kids.

"Yeah, I feel like a rockstar… smoking out my tent to try and keep away leeches," Lars laughed.

"Stop. You *what?*"

"I Brought you something."

"Heck yeah, you did. The earrings you got me from Quito last year are still my favorite."

"Yeah, there's some earrings, prayer flags, and traditional clothing back at the house... I brought something else with me," he said, then popped up off the couch and trotted over to a backpack by the mudroom door.

After digging around, Lars pulled out a rolled-up t-shirt, and brought it back to the couch with him. He unraveled the parcel, removed a plastic bag, then from the bag, he carefully extracted two terracotta-colored objects, each about the size of a goose egg and the shape of a pear. They appeared to have been constructed with red clay.

Lars placed one in her hand and, with the rounded bottom in her palm, Linn lifted it to examine the markings on the half. Rows of repeating indentations encircled the cone up to its tip, the edges softened by time. Sediment coated her skin where she handled the object, grit like fine salt scraping between her thumb and forefinger.

"What are these?" She asked.

"Tsa Tsas. We found hundreds and hundreds of them in a structure we visited in the mountains. I thought of you and GG when I first saw them, but it wasn't until our guide later told us what they are, that I thought they could give some inspiration..." He smiled, pausing intentionally.

"Oh my gosh, Lars, what *are* they!" She grinned, pushing her leg into his.

"Offerings left at holy places. The act of making and offering them is a way to increase positive and decrease negative in one's life. They are very sacred, made with clay from special sites, mixed with herbs, and pressed into the mold."

GG had taught Linnea to feel for what was hidden, for what had been carefully kneaded and folded, tucked into life like magic. Some secrets stay silent and dark, unseen, while others whisper, barely more than sound above breath, like the scent of a flower through that of an old forest, an awareness of something unnamed inside oneself. Some secrets are small enough for one to hold, warm in one's palm as if still beating, others large enough to stand within.

"This hasn't been fired," she observed.

"No, they're dried in the sun. A scroll with a mantra can be placed inside with ink made from a sacred source," Lars continued. "The paper, everything that becomes a part of the tsa tsa is meaningful."

Ideas trickled like water into Linnea's mind, thoughts of tucking things *inside* her work. The paper would burn off, but would the air pocket pose a problem? If it were hollow…

"The clay is often mixed with cremated remains from a funeral pyre," he added, his eyes waiting for her.

Ice. Whatever water had flowed in from Lars's words had turned cold as it ran through Linnea's arteries.

"Ashes from the dead?" Linnea asked, glancing back down to the umber and ochre sediment lining her hands.

"Yes."

"Does mom know?"

"Yeah… She didn't know I'd taken them until it was too late to bring them back. Then we found out what they were and she was *pissed*. She doesn't want them in the house, so… They're yours but we're gonna need to leave them here."

Linnea nodded. "She'll understand."

*

Linnea sat shaded under the grape arbor, eyeing the outdoor kiln while taking the last bites of cereal from her coyote bowl. Lars thought her rendering looked like a fox, but knew as well as she did what was painted there, and what the glaze had been made from.

She had wanted to get her run in early, but she and Lars had stayed up late talking until sometime between three and four in the morning. He'd still been sleeping when she got up, but Linnea could hear him inside through the kitchen window, talking with GG until the phone rang.   Linnea walked in through the back and placed her bowl in the sink.

"No, she's here, she's fine," GG said to the phone at her ear while looking at Linnea, her face a bit puzzled. Then her expression changed, distorted.

"I'm headed out for my run," she whispered to her grandmother, miming an exaggerated jog as she headed for the door. To Lars she said, "I'll keep it short, then we can do a long run after you fuel up. Not too late, though, it's already getting gross out."

"You got it," he said.

The sound of her brother pouring dry cereal followed her through the screen door. Linnea thought of Lars at the counter, his bowl a mirror of her own, decorated with a blonde animal that wasn't a fox or a wolf. It had felt right to make him one of his own. He'd been there. He knew.

"Bring your stick," GG hollered out the window, her voice shaky, almost frantic.

"She doesn't need it," Lars laughed. "Or don't you remember? No, take it though," he shouted, and Linnea turned to see his face nearly pressed against the screen above the sink. "It doesn't hurt to start with one." Then he quickly turned away.

She was at the end of the driveway stretching when Lars caught up with her, field hockey stick in hand.

"I'm coming with you, take this," he said, attempting to pass it to her, his face serious.

"My shoulder's being weird," she grumbled. "I was just going to leave it."

"Then I'll carry it this time, but if I'm not with you, take the stick. For now, anyway. There's a thing…" he said vaguely, trailing off. "We'll talk about it later, let's just run."

Linnea tried to get a read on her brother's expression as he ran beside her, through light conversation and silence. He'd met her in the driveway mere minutes after going in to eat, but he couldn't have finished that fast. No, she'd seen him eat, he was capable… But she suspected something had happened in the kitchen to make him join her early, and she knew he'd tell her later.

Later came after her run, and after a shower, under the grape arbor with GG and Lars. GG had a pitcher of iced mint lemonade waiting, three glasses, and a story to tell.

"Some local kids had a party out in the woods last night, you know how kids do," she started, glancing sideways at Lars. "They think we don't know… every generation believes they've invented drinking in the woods… If I had less to say, I might mention a memory or two from when your father was your age, but I'll save that for another time," she sighed, threads of something bittersweet in the sound of her voice.

"I spoke with Noreen earlier," she continued, then took a sip from her glass. "George had phoned to check in with her after getting called into work. They found a body, a girl. He didn't say who she was, only what had happened to her, and that she was about your age, Linn."

"Oh," Linn breathed with understanding, glancing from Lars back to GG. "The stick. I'm fine, really. I run during the day, without a bunch of drunk kids around me making bad choices."

"Her friends went looking for her at sun up, they didn't know who she'd gone off with. When they found her, she was dead. Some of her hair and clothes were gone, and she had what they think is pollen rubbed over her skin. This was more than some drunk kids and bad choices, Honey. That poor girl had flower petals arranged all around her." Grandma Grace looked into Linnea's eyes, holding. "Arranged all around her, like a portrait."

Linnea played with the condensation on her glass, collecting water, clearing space, then she brought the vessel to her lips. Frida Kahlo flashed into her mind, framed by flowers and symbolism, every brush-stroke a purposeful movement. She thought about her own work…

"What happened to that girl was an act of creation directed through a warped lens," GG said. "Compulsion like that can't be stopped willingly."

"You think they'll kill someone else?"

"It was an act of creation, Honey. How would you feel if you couldn't make art anymore?"

Lars huffed out a breath beside her. The question was almost absurd.

"I'd find a way," Linn said. "Even if it wasn't on purpose. Some of the coolest stuff I've made has been by accident, or unplanned, I guess. Well, it starts unplanned maybe? I don't know, but I don't think I could be kept from it, do you? No. No, I'd find a way…"

"Damn right you would," Lars agreed.

"God put a piece of themselves in all of us, Honey," GG said. "And the piece you got is *powerful*, divine, and capable of greatness. No one on this earth can stop that. You'd find a way, and so will whoever did that to that poor girl in the woods. There's a piece of god inside them too, but what they got became twisted and wrong somehow. The force of it is still there, though. The *need*. What they did is more than killing, and until they're caught, I want you running with a stick."

"Okay," Linnea whispered across the table, under the grapes and the bird song.

GG nodded and took another drink from her lemonade, swallowed, breathed deep, slow. She took on a distant, but focused look in her eyes.

"I'd grind their bones to make my bread," she said, low, and final.

Lars refilled her glass, and Linn felt the weight of her necklace. Twelve beads. Twelve years. She gazed at the new kiln, with echoes of slip dripping down her arms, ochre dust from The Himalayas coating her hands. She glanced at GG, then met her brother's eyes.

"I'd grind their bones to make my clay."

5.

Berkshires, June 2000

Sweat trickled down the valleys of Linnea's torso, front and back. She stood in front of two pots on an open fire stove GG had set up by the outdoor kiln. Taking a few steps back, she leaned against one of the pergola's posts in an attempt to escape the heat and catch a breeze.

"What's cookin'?"

Linn turned to see Cap coming through the honeysuckle in faded jeans, a fitted navy t-shirt, and camo hat nearly as worn as his pants. She looked down at the bits of meat and hair undulating in the boiling water around the larger, partially intact bodies they'd separated from.

"Well," she started as he approached. "I'm working on a project. It's a little bit science, a little bit art. There's a type of clay that uses bone, and usually folks who use that type get the ash from the store…"

Cap leaned over the pots, gave his head a tilt. "Rabbits?"

"Yeah, the one on the left has rabbits, the one on the right has voles and mice. Got them from Barny."

Cap nodded thoughtfully. "You know, I made a European mount once. November, eighty… six?"

"What's a European mount…?"

"Deer skull up on the wall in the den."

"You made that?"

"Sure did. Same as what you're doing here, pretty much. I removed the hair and quite a bit of meat first, but I suppose that's hard to do with such small animals. I boiled the skull a few hours, power washed it, and used some small tools to get some little bits from inside the nasal cavity. Might be work cleaning all those tiny bones; let me know if you need a hand. You could spread them out on the table under the grapes. I can come over with Missy after dinner and, better yet, we'll bring desert and paper plates. No cleanup. Then, after we eat, we can spread the bones out and work off all that butter and sugar I'm hoping Missy bakes into whatever it is she makes for us," he smiled.

It was a generous offer, but Linnea wondered if she wanted help, or if she should accept it. Would it dilute what she put into the work by having too many hands involved? Maybe, but there was a part of her that liked what it added to the story, the togetherness of it.

"I'm having a hard time saying no to that offer," she grinned.

*

On the table beneath the grape pergola, a plastic tablecloth had been laid down and separated into four sections with masking tape, each labeled by animal with permanent marker. Tooth brushes, tooth picks, and sandpaper were available in each area. The setup had Linnea thinking of eating crabs. She'd seen pictures of people going to a restaurant and ordering a pile of crabs, the table littered with exoskeletons and meat, diners working with mallets. It wasn't something Linnea had ever done, but, while she was probably too young to have a bucket list, if she had one, the whole crab-restaurant thing would be on there. Lobsters, though, those she was familiar with.

"We'll need some bowls to put the cleaned-up bones in," GG said, shifting to rise from the table.

"No, I'll get them," Linnea smiled as she popped up, full of energy and the family feel, the feel of her project *happening*.

She rummaged around the kitchen, warring between her desire to get back out there and her need to pick the right bowls. Ceramic would be heavy and not flip over accidentally, but the plastic wouldn't be missed, and she was using four of them…

Through the kitchen window she heard GG, Missy, and Cap talking as Barny slid around her ankles then padded toward the door.

"What happened with bringing one of the barn kittens over?" she heard GG ask.

Cap scoffed, "What Sarah *doesn't* need is something else to trip over. Woman's got half a foot on one side from the diabetes, and a house full of stairs."

Linnea suspected either Missy, or GG, or both had rolled their eyes.

"I mean no disrespect," Cap continued. "Getting old isn't for the faint of heart. My fingers have started aching in the morning… I should clarify that it started years ago."

"I was thinking about a cat for the *kid*," GG said. "But I've got a salve for the hands, helps a little. My arthritis is more advanced than yours, I've had time to experiment."

"Arthritis aside, a cat brings companionship," Missy added. "Thank god she has work at the nursery; it gives her more sense of purpose. If things get too bad with her health… Well, I can't imagine her brother taking over. I don't know how he manages the landscaping business while back on the bottle. Sorry, Grace. Anyway, I've brought three kittens over there through the years. Sarah hasn't been able to keep one, and she doesn't want to try anymore."

Linnea decided on the ceramic and opened the door, letting Barny into the evening. She imagined the cat creeping along through dusky grass, listening for something deep, becoming unexpected. Perhaps she could smell the rain coming.

"Barn cats are fiercely independent creatures," GG said, her head ticking toward Barny's shadowy figure in her periphery, though her eyes lingered on Linnea a moment before she added, "There's something about them still very much connected to the wild."

As the table emptied and the bowls filled, Missy said, "It seems like a lot of work when you could just buy this already ground up at the store. Putting the work in makes it that much yours, I suppose."

"Like your embroidery…" Cap winked, tucking his chin with a smile and a nod toward Missy. "Sits for hours, sewing her pictures, content as when she's baking, or reading her stories."

"Moreso," Missy added, expertly working a tiny bone in her hand with a small tool. "I do like to sit by the fire or out in the sun, listening to the birds or crackling logs, sewing, or reading. I love it," she said.

"Have you considered using something with bigger bones, though," Cap teased dryly, holding up an example from the snake section. It didn't need to be cleaned, but he made a point she was not unfamiliar with.

"Barny's a little old for hunting *bear*, Cap…" Linnea sighed. "But it certainly would be nice to have bigger bones, more material to work with. As it is, I'll be scraping by with what I have from all this."

"You can use whatever's left from what I take down in November for deer season." He offered.

Linnea nodded. "Thank you," she started, initially thinking she'd politely decline, but it *would* be good to have material to supplement with. "I'll have school, but maybe you could bag the bones for GG to freeze?"

"I might have actual food to put in my freezer," GG pointed out, fingers working, smile teasing her lips.

"You have plenty of room now that we've cleaned all this out of there," Linnea said, pointing at her grandmother with a toothbrush, then paused for a moment before continuing. "I'd really wanted to harvest the bones myself for my next project, take the pressure off Barny."

Missy remained focused on her work, Cap grinned, but GG eyed Linnea with a density to her thoughts, little escaping her.

"I can take you out," Cap offered. "I took Lars for years. It might not be too late to get you a hunter safety course for this season."

"I'll have school, though, in the fall."

"Yes, but you could come out on the weekends. I'd be more than happy to take you. Start practicing with the bow while you're here. My archery days are numbered, though. It's not that I don't have the muscle," he said, flexing a pronounced bicep, then wiggling his fingers. "It's these, and my wrist, even with the confounded trigger release... I have another couple years left. You see me when you're ready."

"I'd like that," Linnea sighed. "To start practicing with the bow, I mean. Maybe I can come by Monday, sometime after dinner?"

"Sure, or check in tomorrow. I'm right next door," he smiled.

"Speaking of right next door, I can't wait to see the kiln up and running again. It's like having fireworks all night. We can see the flames coming out the chimney from our house."

"And it shaves about a year off my life every time," GG added. "What with all the work, and having the kids all over the backyard in their tents," she smiled. "It's fun though, and I don't mind staying up. You know me, I'm a night owl."

Hours later, after the bones had been cleaned and laid to rest in their clay bowls, after the outdoor kiln had been loaded with wood and set ablaze, Linnea crept effortlessly out the back kitchen door. The fire needed to be fed.

Wet grass met her feet after the first few steps over a damp patio, following the only light she could see. The deep orange flickering through the small portal in the kiln glowed like a window into the soul of a burning eye. Crackling fire blended with the pattering of water that surrounded her. Rain sparkled cold on her skin, on her face as she tilted up toward the dark sky falling. Night had a way of closing the eyes, of letting sound into the heart like a drum, of calling the hairs on her arms upward. Darkness pulled ideas outward to collect and run down her body like rain, down to her fingertips, that she could give them form with her hands.

*

When powdered bone had been turned to clay, made firm with fire, and painted with skill, Linnea held the first vessel she pulled from the depths. Its body was white, translucent, and wore the story of its origin… She cradled it gently in her palm like a sleeping kitten, like a delicate dream, luminant with morning light passing through the glass wall of the studio.

"Survived its last firing," GG smiled beside her.

It had been nearly painful waiting for the studio kiln to cool…

"I'm proud of you, Linnea. I'm always proud," her grandmother continued. "You are like a fire burning low and constant with brilliance, but this, this is a log thrown on, a log coated with birchbark, and coated with magnesium," she chuckled.

Beautiful, Linnea thought, examining her work. The cup was so delicate, and yet strong from the bone making up half of what she held. And the story… The story was more than anything she'd created, told on the inside of the vessel as well as the surface. With the careful strokes of her brush, she'd painted Barny's prowess with great care, and it showed.

She ran her finger over the cat's image, then the bird. The animals used were a sacrifice, an offering. Linnea was thankful, but there was a great yearning bubbling inside her, something that had been there and surfaced.

"The coyote," she whispered, brushing against memories of a time when she'd been the hunter, when *she* had fought, conquered, and earned. Then, a little louder, she said, "Cap buried it out back?"

Grandma Grace's eyes became steady, and with a look of stern caution and stillness, she said, "No."

Still cradling the teacup, Linnea lowered her hands. "He did *something* with it. The vet only needed part... I swear he buried the rest."

"It's buried out there, but my answer is *no*. I will not have you digging up the corpses of rabid animals and boiling them out back."

"It won't have rabies anymore, it's been years. It's probably just bones anyway."

"Slow down, Honey."

"I've been working with bones from the butcher, and the bones from Barny's offerings, but I still feel removed, and I don't know what the next step is. With the coyote I was present, there was a sense of, of *communion*..."

"I'm not in charge of you, Linn, I'm only your guide. I can't make you do anything, but it is my strong advice that you don't walk down the path of exhuming the dead and buried. You had a chance before we put the animal in the ground, and you got more than one souvenir from the encounter."

The bowls and the shirt… Though Linnea had washed the shirt, memories were still embedded.

She sighed. Yes, there was a sacred transition back to the earth that all living things made, even, in a sense, the erosion of nonliving things, but after life had passed, to Linnea, they became materials to harvest. Grandma Grace, though, was truly bothered by the idea of disturbing the dead once they'd been *laid to rest*.

"It would be like digging up stones, or artifacts, or *carrots*. Archeologists dig up bones, GG. I just don't see the harm in at least checking to see if they're even still there. Do you think they'd have decomposed with the soft parts of the body?"

"One would need to have experience to know something like that, and I have no business with what's been put to rest under the soil."

"I'll leave the coyote, and try to get out with Cap in the fall," Linnea sighed." It was a logical next step that she hoped would be enough.

With her uncanny way of knowing things, GG softened, her arms wrapping around Linnea and pulling her in. "There's a path forward, you just can't see it yet. Look behind you, everything you've done, Honey, and have faith that you won't fall forward. Smooth stones will rise from the ground, stepping stones rising up to meet you. But for now, I think the best thing to do would be to set the table," GG said conspiratorially. "Mint tea?"

"Perfect. Very *summer*." Linnea smiled, heart warm, weight mostly lifted, though she felt something deep down, tucked into dormancy like a child into bed, or a bear in torpor.

"And blueberry scones, I think. I'll make some up while you start on the dining room."

"Do you want to pick your teacup?" she asked as GG ascended the studio steps.

"Oh, no, Honey. You surprise me."

Linnea examined what she still held in her hands, what she had *made* from her hands, had pulled from the darkness like the earth and the ocean before. She had the spark of creation in her, something great, and undeniable. She would find a balance, but the thing in her that called the sky down as rain, that told stories from bone, would not be denied.

6.

Berkshires, December 2009

The house, lit primarily by candlelight for Winter Solstice, was fragrant with the smell of pot roast, flavored with rosemary, wine, and onions turning sweet in the oven. The fresh evergreen scent from the Christmas tree couldn't compete with GG's cooking.

"A little to the left," Grandma Grace advised, her dry humor almost undetectable.

Lars's chuckling beside her, however, was less subtle.

Linnea rolled her eyes from atop the chair she stood on, and nudged one of the two tsa tsas a millimeter in the requested direction. GG moved the clay memorials seasonally to provide a change of scenery, trying to keep them at elevated locations.

"They look good up there," Lars said, Giving Linn a hand as she hopped down.

"I'd thought about bringing them out for a fire later," GG started, "But I don't want to forget them out there. I like to take them out on summer mornings and listen to the birds. I think it's what I would want. You know," she went on with a tilt of her head. "I might like to have my ashes mixed with clay. It would be fitting, wouldn't it?"

"No tea set?" Linnea teased, only half joking, perhaps less.

"There are rules here, where we live, about what can be done with a human's body when they die. Not like your creatures, Honey, not like Barny."

Their beloved cat had met her end quietly a few years prior. GG had found her curled under Papa's old desk in the study, cocooned in a soft shadow. Linnea had seen to it that another set of cups and saucers were fired and painted, embedded with Barney's story.

"They won't let you separate my bones out," GG continued. "You'll have to burn the whole of me. Bury some beside Papa and your father, but take some for yourself. Make one of these little cones," she said, nodding up to the tsa tsas. "Bring me out with the others to listen to birds. Not my hair, though." She looked between her two grandchildren, a hand reaching up to the ropes of grey hair coiled on her head like a crown. "You keep those memories as they are, and cut my locks off at the root. I won't care if I'm bald when I'm powder."

"Of course," Linnea said with a weak smile. "You can sit with me while I sip mint lemonade and make lists. I'll even heckle Cap a bit from our side of the honeysuckle." Her voice was light, but the weight she felt… it was a dark cloud over her, in her chest. A stone. That she would be denied access to something sacred, her divine right. *The body is our own, ours to decide what to do with,* she thought. *Ours by birth to care for, to tend to, to issue.*

"Tell her she has to make two, GG," Lars grinned, dusting his hands on his pants and giving GG's shoulders a squeeze. "I'm going to put you in my pocket."

Linnea laughed with her family, but found herself moving into the kitchen under the pretense of starting boiling water for egg noodles to have with the roast.

"Alright," GG said, her footsteps moving down the hall, "but for now I'll be content to have you set the table."

Linnea felt her grandmother's hand on her shoulder as she filled a pot at the sink. The hand was warm, weighted with understanding, with love.

"It'll be fine," GG whispered. "I have miles to go before I sleep, and who knows what changes will come in that time. People are already talking about natural burials and such."

"It's just…" Linnea sighed, unsure how to start when there was so much… "I'm not saying I thought you'd be next, like I had your name on a list…" she paused, putting the pot on the stove, turning on the burner. "After Barny…"

"Your work with her was beautiful, Linn. *Remarkable.*"

"Thanks, GG," she said, unable to hide the sparkle she felt at her grandmother's praise. "I just thought, well, I felt a next step coming, like waiting for a stone to rise under my feet. I've been waiting, and some part of me thought-"

"You thought you were going to make me into a tea set?" GG asked, her small smile sympathetic.

"Don't belittle the work by saying it like that, GG. It's more than craft that goes into what comes from the dark through my hands."

GG raised a finger, slowing time. "I've taught you since you were no taller than my knee. There's a piece of god inside you, a strong and powerful creator, but I'm not the next step in your journey."

Linnea breathed in and out, deep. Her grandmother's words… GG understood her, and the relief of that alone was a weight heavier than the stone waiting inside her, a weight lifted.

Grandma Grace turned off the oven, but before she opened it, her arms came around. GG encircled Linnea with her body, and a whisper.

"It won't be my bones rising to meet your foot, Honey, but the next step will come, and you will be ready."

*

Belly still digesting her grandmother's stew, rich with rosemary and meat turned magic, Linnea reached into the cabinet she'd been rummaging through. Inspecting a plastic bag half-filled with sticky, white lumps, she said, "GG, are these the only marshmallows you have?"

"Shit," was her grandmother's hushed reply, said under her breath as she loaded plates from dinner into the dishwasher.

"I'm too full," Lars groaned loudly from the living room.

"These ones are all stuck together, like, *fused*," Linnea continued. "And there's something yellowish happening. They look too moist. I'm going to check the pantry."

"Don't bother," GG sighed as she turned round. "I just have those from last year, and they belong in the garbage."

"I'll just run out and get some more," Linnea sighed, not *wanting* to go, but her desire for roasting marshmallows was stronger than the pull to stay put.

"We have the cake," GG said, tilting her head toward the black cake soaked in overproof rum, still housed in the Royal Dansk cookie tin she'd baked it in. "You can't bring it near the flame, though."

"It's not just about the dessert, it's about transforming something in the fire."

"And you can't roast apple slices? The fire transforms the wood we feed it, that can't be enough?"

"G.G…"

"*Fine*," she said, her face serious with unspilled humor. "We'd better go now, though. That cake's too strong to eat before getting behind the wheel."

Joy burst through Linnea like glistening water in the sun. Going together felt more like fun than a chore. Lars would join them, of course.

"Cap and Missy are coming over still, right?" She asked, heading into the living room with GG behind her.

"When they see fire, they'll come."

"I'm too full for marshmallows," Lars sighed as Linnea and GG came through. "I think I have meat sweats."

"You can sweat in the car," Linnea said. "Come on."

"You're going too, GG?" Lars asked, his feigned condition vanishing as he sat up and stretched.

"I'm not missing a moment under the moon with you two while you're here. There's a waxing crescent tonight, though I think it's tucking in early, leaving the longest night at its darkest."

If Linnea had been capable of lifting one eyebrow, she would have as she saw Lars flash a devious smirk, like he'd won something and sat waiting for his prize.

Slowly, from between the cushions, he pulled out a thin, wooden cylinder suspended by a length of wire, the addition of a fettling knife in his palm. "You still offering rewards for couch harvests?" He asked.

"You're too old to collect a fee for finding something I would have discovered on my own," GG scolded, putting her hand out for her clay cutting and carving tools.

"But I've still got med school loans, and an almost wedding," Lars laughed, relinquishing his find.

"And I'd like your almost-*wife* to come out here for Solstice next year, no excuses," she said sternly, taking the blade, wire, and wood, and tucking them into her apron pocket. "No more of this *she's on call* nonsense."

With Lars an anesthesiologist and Linn a nurse, both working in Boston hospitals, rotating schedules made coordinating national holidays tricky. For Linnea, having Christmas Day off meant working Christmas Eve, but there were never conflicts about requesting a couple days for Solstice.

"Keys," Lars said as GG closed the front door behind them.

"Nope," Linnea called back, pulling on fingerless gloves as she got into the driver's seat. "You've got meat sweats."

GG sat shotgun because neither of them would allow her to sit in the back. Lars sat behind Linnea, claiming he needed to keep her on her toes. When she asked for clarification, he flicked her ear.

Once they'd purchased the marshmallows and started back toward GG's, Lars opened the bag, and extended the parcel forward.

"They smell so *good*," Linnea sighed. "I don't care what they're made of."

"Have one," GG suggested.

"No," Lars said with comic seriousness. "She needs to stay strong and wait for the fire."

"Well, it might be a little while," GG said, face tilted toward the window. "I want to see if we can find the moon. I think it's setting early tonight." She followed by giving them directions to a set of farm fields to drive between where the expanse of land met the heavens low in the distance all around them.

Claiming she couldn't adequately enjoy the skyscape while driving, Linnea pulled to the edge of a ditch that ran like a seam between the road and the fields. They idled briefly, then she turned the car off, and they all got out.

Cold air flowed into Linnea's body as she exited the vehicle, crisp all the way down into the branches of her bronchi. Firm soil crunched under her feet as she descended into the ditch, worked her way back up to the edge of the dormant field. Ice and crusted snow muffled by shadow. None of them spoke once they'd crested the ditch and settled in. They moved just enough to meet the needs of their bodies and their curiosity. Breath in and out, Linnea's eyes scanned the horizon, the sky… Her eyes closed.

A distant sound captured her attention, like white noise building, increasing in volume.

"Truck?" Linnea whispered as the trio stood there, observing the blackened object move slowly toward them. No, rapidly. Dark, because it was night, and the moon had set. Dark because they stood between two farm fields. Dark because the headlights were off.

The mass of moving metal was upon them, the vehicle suddenly swerving away in an attempt to avoid hitting their car, then correcting drastically… Linnea's feet pressed against the frozen ground as she, Lars, and GG scattered, but GG slipped in the ditch, disappearing beneath the front end of the truck as it made impact, embedded in snow and soil.

Everything was loud.

And then everything was quiet, and Linnea was a child again.

A flood of numbness and clarity ran through her with awe inspiring speed. Feet pounding, *heart* pounding, she traversed the hard packed earth and snow, arms out, lungs bleeding for all she knew because the frigid air sliced through her with every breath.

Down the sloping earth they went, Linnea and Lars, approaching the wreckage. They took no notice of the equipment that had spilled from the bed of the truck, to the logo, barely visible, painted on the side. They were unconcerned with the status of the body within.

"GG!" Linnea called out, hearing the same name in Lars's voice create a grotesque harmony, deep and guttural.

She dove onto her knees behind him, scrambling to his side, seeing her grandmother's legs disappear beneath the wheel and crumpled metal that had once been the truck's front end.

"GG," She called out into the darkness beneath the engine, frantically pulling at a mass that should have been her grandmother. "Does she have a pulse?"

Lars had their grandmother's boot in his hands, already pulling her sock off. He blew out a breath, closed his eyes, and felt her feet for a dorsalis pedis pulse at the top of her foot, shuffling on his knees to reach up her leg behind her knee for the popliteal. "Nothing. Can you reach her hands? Wrist? GG!?"

Linnea put her body against the ground, moving against her grandmother like a child drawing nearer to see the illustrations in a bedtime story. She reached upward through the strong smell of oil and gasoline, following GG's torso, feeling hair… Her memories.

Lars pulled at Linnea's jacket. "It's not safe," he said.

Linnea managed to push up her grandmother's coat, the apron, and sweater, sliding her hand up under, against GG's chest. She felt for movement from heart or breath, some sign that life had not leaked out into the snow and air. But there was nothing, just the lingering heat of a body not yet cooled to the temperature of its surroundings.

Linnea had come to think of birth as a transformation, she'd seen it in school, how there could be five people in a closed room, then suddenly six as new life entered. Pregnancy transformed cells into a human, a woman into a mother, a body into a portal. And death. She'd known death as a child, had fingerpainted with it onto clay. She'd seen the way an infant tears into the world from the darkness, with blood, and force, and promise, a vessel for the seed god planted. Birth is a powerful passage, and death…

Head swiveling slow on her neck, Linnea turned back to Lars, then her eyes flicked to the white glass that was a windshield. With an unspeakable humming inside her, she stood, Lars at her side. If there were survivors, they'd need to be pulled free before the truck exploded. It would only take a spark.

Ignoring the words on the door of the vehicle, Lars opened it.

"Nine-one-one," he said, pulling out his phone, voice unwavering as he prepared to dial.

Linnea's thoughts began to clear as her pounding heart steadied, reaching for the knife in her coat pocket, thinking they might need to cut a seatbelt, cut someone free.

Lars paused, his body going still, lit by the glow from the undialed phone clutched in his lowering hand. He stepped back, making way for Linnea to take his place. She knew people could react differently in the field compared to the hospital, where patients were cleaned up and diagnosed, already extracted from the environment of their trauma. Whatever had triggered Lars to freeze up, Linnea decided to let him manage it while she took over with the driver and… No, it was just a driver, she observed, taking her own phone out and turning on the flashlight. He was male, older, judging by the amount of grey under the blood.

"Sir!" She shouted as she attempted to assess him. "Sir, can you hear me? We need to get you out of here! Lars," she said, her voice lowering. "Lars, I need you to hold the light."

The man was slumped over into the passenger's side, most of his body on the floor. She tucked the keys back into her pocket. No need for the knife; the driver hadn't been belted in. *Lucky to be alive,* she thought as she watched him move slightly.

The man sputtered as he tried to shift, blood spraying out from his mouth like he was literally blowing raspberries. "He... *Hell...*" he began, words garbled and syrupy. Something stuck out of his abdomen, a spike of some kind, another in his upper chest by the look of it. He reached up to his face, his other arm unmoving. His shirt was red-soaked, no jacket. "Call her and… tell him I'm getting patched up. I know when he's over there, instead of with his old man. I can't reach the bottle," he slurred. "Check under the seat."

Linnea surveyed the cab of the truck, holding her phone high, passing light over what she could. There was no one else. "Who?" She asked, raising her voice.

"There's a bottle under the seat. I need a drink before you pull this shit out." His good hand wandered past his abdomen, reaching up toward the wooden spike protruding from his upper chest, though it could have been his shoulder.

"Don't touch it," she scolded. "You pull that and you'll bleed out through it."

Turning, she observed Lars where he still stood staring, phone dark at his side. His eyes flicked up to her, his face molded with the type of anguish that comes with knowledge.

What did he know?

Her head swiveled and she took a good, hard look at the driver's face, seeing through the blood and hair. A scar ran down from his brow, over his eye…his open, glass eye. Another wave of heat and numbness rushed out from the center of her heart as the scent of gin, like Christmas, came cutting through the oil and gasoline. Memories chased the adrenaline working through her, flames licking the images in her mind. *Dad!* The children echoed internally. What should have been her father, the mangled mess of a body wearing his clothes, the blood that smeared on her hands like warm slip…

But that was all inside her. Where she stood, there was no fire, no light, only a waxing crescent that had given way to the longest night.

She took a step back into Lars, his hands coming around her.

"His name is on the truck," he whispered. "Bill West." The man who'd killed their dad, their papa, and their grandmother. Lars held on strong as she nodded her head, breathing.

"He's been impaled twice by wooden spikes," she said, steady. "One in his abdomen and one in his left upper chest or shoulder. He spit blood, unclear if from the abdominal injury or facial trauma."

"Survivable."

"With immediate intervention," she nodded in agreement.

Lars shifted, keeping his arms around her while he moved, until her eyes caught his. He held her there a moment, not with force, but with connection.

"We pull what's impaling him, drag him out, then call it in."

A death sentence.

The landscape remained darkened, the same field and sky that had called Linnea, Lars, and GG to rest a moment under a moon they couldn't see. No lights. There'd been the brief sound of the crash, and then silence. No houses nearby to disturb.

"We have time," her brother said with urgency.

"Agreed," she said, then moved quickly around the vehicle, the metaphorical sand ever falling.

Climbing in, she put her weight on West's legs, reaching for handholds as she looked over his body, eyeing the affected limb under the light of Lars's phone. The spike went up through his armpit. It wouldn't take much effort to just…

And then she froze, feeling the stone rising into place, waiting. Somewhere within her, Linnea released a cathartic sigh, and took the next step.

Lars caught her eyes from where he stood at the door. "What do you need?"

"I want his arm," she said with startling clarity.

West turned up toward her, confused, injured, drunk.

"I'm taking his arm," she said, a little louder, seeing that her brother understood. He always had.

"You'll need to get it now," he said. "Trauma post mortem looks different. I don't think anyone's going to look this thing over with a fine-tooth comb, but whatever you do, it can't be obvious. No cut marks in the bone."

He took a step forward, leaned in, examining what they had to work with.

"Somebody better pull this thing or I'm doing it myself," the man slurred, then spit more blood onto the floor.

Lars stilled with disdain, no words.

"Not just yet, Mr. West," Linnea said pleasantly, her nurse voice. "We can't let you bleed out until after we get your arm sorted."

They could maybe just work that wooden spike and pull his limb at the same time, or if they had a rope, or a wire…

"Check GG's pockets," she said with a spark in her voice. "Her apron, she's still wearing it. Not the knife, get the wire you found in the couch."

Lars paused, an instant or less, and he was gone, the sound of his footsteps fading, then growing louder behind her, movement under the front of the truck.

Linnea leaned in, the grotesque face beneath the blood coming closer to hers as she lowered herself down. She pressed gently against his cheek with her hand, nudging the flesh with her palm until he caught her eyes with the one he had left.

"I'm going to drink from your bones," she breathed.

Impaired as he was, the man recoiled.

"Got it," Lars said, reaching in from the darkness through the open door. Linnea looked up, seeing the interior light she could have switched on, and took the clay cutting tool from her brother.

"Mr. West," Linnea started in her nurse voice, "I know how much you'd like these uncomfortable wooden spikes out, but we're going to get started with the arm first."

He eyed her warily. "About fucking time," he sputtered, and then his eye closed, as if to rest.

With a solid idea and tools in place, Linnea leaned down one last time.

"Mr. West, we're going to drag you out of the cab, because it isn't safe to leave you here. Your damaged arm is going to become caught, and detach as we pull your body free. You'll exsanguinate before first responders arrive, I know this, because, if you're not dead when we get you to the ground, I'm going to keep one hand on your pulse as you bleed out into the snow, and I won't call them in until your heart stops beating."

He recoiled again, but before he could do much more than thrash once beneath her, Linnea pulled, and so did Lars.

She'd disjointed animals before, after cooking in the house to eat, and outdoors for her work. Bones just seemed to slide apart after the connective tissue had been softened, meat falling off. West's arm had taken significantly more effort, and she preferred it that way. There was something about the tightening of her grip, the exertion… the *feel* of it. It's work that reaps reward, work that causes transformation. Blood. Sweat. *Labor.* Release.

Lars had gone back to their car for a plastic bag and the lighter they'd bought with the marshmallows. She had a couple canvas totes in the trunk, but the arm would need to be wrapped in something first or it would leak everywhere. The limb was still over there, under the dangling remains leaking out from the passenger's seat. They'd not needed to pull him further… Detaching the arm and extracting the torso about halfway had been enough to see him expire, resulting in a more convenient positioning for what would come next.

Tears welled in Linnea's eyes as she sat there on the cold earth, feeling the small, rounded bit of glass in her palm. She'd taken what she needed, but it was by no means an exchange. Her heart ached, red marrow imprinting anguish into new cells as they formed. She worked her thumb against the concave surface of the eye like a worry stone. The shape was right, but she would've preferred a piece of GG in her palm to soak the sorrow flooding out from her, to receive her shaking breath vibrating through the otherwise silent surroundings.

Would there be enough of GG left, that her ashes could be recovered? Linnea's hope felt heavy, sinking down into her chest. She would have faithfully executed her grandmother's plan for her ashes… her memories…

Cold air rushed into Linnea's lungs like knives, cutting loose the lines that had held her hope tethered. *Her memories,* she repeated, glass eye nearly slipping through her fingertips as she slid it into her pocket, and pulled out her keys. Bursting with intention, Linnea's breath came quick as she pulled the knife from her pocket and moved towards GG's legs. Crouching low, then bringing her body to the ground, she slithered against her grandmother for the last time.

A car door closed, footsteps. Lars.

"Linn," he shouted, movement hurried, ground crunching, both muffled and sharp. "Linn, it's not safe." He was already behind her, a hand on her leg.

"I need to get some of her hair," she explained from under the twisted metal and dripping fluid. "You heard what she said. I have to try."

He squeezed her calves, but didn't pull, just held his hands there. *I'm here,* she felt him say. *I'm here with you, and I won't let go.*

With arms raised, Linnea felt for GG's neck, followed the slope upward, and with a ready blade, began to slice through what she could... *at the root.* Tears flowed at the overwhelming odor of gasoline, not from the fumes themselves, but the way they obstructed the smell of pot roast and clay she knew lingered somewhere in the fibers surrounding her grandmother.

She pulled a fistful of hair free, then another, stuffing the ropes of her grandmother's memories down the collar of her shirt, the locks scratchy against her skin. Then, reaching back to GG's throat, Linnea worked at the beaded necklace.

Lars's hands pulsed pressure on her legs.

"Got it!" she shouted back, closing the blade. Fisting the string of beads, she wriggled toward her brother, sucking air as she emerged that it might cleanse the fumes saturating her lungs.

And then they cried together. Lars's arms came around her once more, her hands holding the string of beads embedded with their papa's and father's blood, the hair holding GG's memories against her skin. Their family between them, she and Lars pressed their foreheads together.

The breath that Lars hauled into himself was ragged, an overture for the words to follow. "We'll mourn when it's finished," he said.

When it's finished.

Lars would call in the accident, but not before setting the truck ablaze, blurring the edges a bit. It wouldn't be the last fire they'd light that Solstice. Somewhere, beyond the darkened sky, a waxing crescent watched over them, and the longest night of the year far from over.

7.

Berkshires, October 2014

Water has a way of leaking in, like a memory, or a feeling.

Linnea stood inside room three, eyes open, closed to everything other than the rain running down the glass and seeping through the seams around the edges of the window. Three wasn't the only room where rain leaked though… twelve and fourteen had towels rolled up along their window ledges as well, soaking up what had forced its way in, an inconvenient deluge.

Though she stood dry, Linnea felt flecks of water on her skin like cool sparks when each drop made contact, sliding over her as gravity called them down, rolling around her lips as they parted.

And while autumn rain fell around her, something emerged within, something like water breaking the surface to quench desert sand. Linnea had the sensation of being so whole, her body couldn't contain what she was.

Some leaks are a nuisance, others an oasis, but it was hardly time to drink from the latter.

The phone in her pocket buzzed, a message from Erik asking if she was at work…

Linnea's eyes cut back over to the bed.

"You'll want to keep the tube clamped until your syringe is in place," she said, observing Gabby's work. The nurse Linnea was training had scanned and crushed Mrs. Moore's pills, mixed them with water, and held her thumb hovering over the G-tube clamp in the patient's abdomen. Mrs. Moore remained oblivious to the process, face calm, eyes with a blank stare, hair perfectly combed, nails freshly painted.

"Right," Gabby said, taking a moment to plan her next step in administering Mrs. Moore's medication. With the patient being nonverbal, and almost completely immobile on account of advanced dementia, Linnea didn't think there'd be a *geyser situation*, but as a general rule, you kept that thing clamped until you were ready.

Mr. Moore chuckled from where he sat sipping cola through a straw beside his wife. "I've seen the stuff shoot right out. All she has to do is cough while it's open, and if you think it smells bad *before* it goes in…" He smiled and took a bite of his burger, appetite unflinching. It was true, the tube feed's scent was unpleasant, and the slurry of pulverized pills mixed with water was bitter on top of it. At least it wasn't morning meds with the liquid vitamins…

Linnea's eyes drifted away from Gabby and up to the television mounted to the ceiling.

"Anything good?" She asked.

The tv wasn't often turned on in Mrs. Moore's room. Instead, her husband played old music, or brushed her hair and sang. He read from a book out loud while his voice permitted, to himself when it didn't. But in the early evening, Mr. Moore would go out and get two hamburgers, fries, and a cola. He always returned with a boyish smile and bag in hand; a man on his way to have dinner with his best girl. Then they'd watch the news, or a movie, depending what was on.

"Well, they just found that young woman over in the state forest. Aren't saying much."

A wave of awareness spread through Linnea's body like a flash of heat.

"Was she lost?" Gabby asked, pouring water into the open end of the large syringe, washing down any remaining sediment.

"Haven't said who she is or what she was. They're not saying much, only that she's dead and some poor hiker found her body."

"I wonder if they got to her before the rain did," Gabby said.

"What's that, now?" He asked.

"The rain," she said, raising her voice a bit so Mr. Moore could hear.

It had been raining all afternoon, and the water would wash, would move things. It had started when Linn had been there, kneeling in the moss and leaves.

"Oh, I'm sure they'll manage," Mr. Moore said.

"Linn, can I get a co-sign?"

Alex stood in the doorway holding up a giant syringe of the narcotic Dilauded, PCA keys jingling at his wrist. Alex was tall with dark brown skin. He wore a black fleece vest zipped low over a grey t-shirt that stretched across his broad chest and shoulders. He maintained an impeccable fade, shadow of a beard, and just a hint of black eye liner. He'd been her best friend since she started at Morland Medical, he and Steph.

"Sure thing," Linnea said, heading out to the hall.

"I still don't see it," Alex remarked, tilting his head down toward her.

"Don't see what?"

"Word on the street is you and Gabby look like long lost siblings."

"Word on the street, huh?"

It wasn't a stretch, she supposed. Gabby was fresh out of nursing school and in her early twenties. Linnea was in her early thirties, but wasn't bold in assuming she looked young. She had a few inches on Gabby, but they were both slim, similar in complexion…

"Hailey. She sees that long, dark hair and chai latte skin on the two of you, and she thinks, *same*. Maybe if you had your hair out… But don't you dare. Your mane is too gorgeous for this place. Besides, it's not sanitary… Can you imagine taking down a dressing and finding the last nurse's stray strands in there?"

"Gabby seems to have the ponytail under control. The moment that thing gets near a patient, though, she's wrapping it up or I'm sending her down to the holding room for a hair net."

Linnea's phone buzzed in her pocket. Her mother. She'd seen the news.

It wasn't me, she wrote back. *At work, I'm fine, talk later or in the morning?*

She needed to talk to Lars.

"Where's your PCA, on the moon?" Linnea asked. They'd nearly made it to the double doors separating their unit from another.

"Don't even get me started. Cheryl knows I like cardio, but my spread this shift is insane. I've got room two, my ladies in six, a knee in twelve, and this neurosurge' guy over here in fourteen with the PCA. I better grab a towel," he added, backtracking a few steps to the linen cart. "Rain is already coming through the window."

*

An hour or so later, the gentle sound of bubbling water greeted Linnea and Gabby as they entered room nine. The television had been muted and her patient, Pete, reclined in bed, full focus on his phone, finger tapping and swiping at the screen. His older cousin, William sat in a chair by the window, laptop on a bedside table in front of him. William looked in his mid-forties with short blonde hair and tortoiseshell glasses. He wore his typical tweed blazer over a button-down shirt, bracelet surrounding his left wrist peeking out beyond the cuff just enough for Linnea to catch a hint of color.

"Hey Pete," Linn smiled. "Gabby and I are just going to do your insulin, empty your drains, and check on your chest tube, ok?"

Pete looked up from his game and flashed a broad, honest smile. He was a thirty-nine-year-old male with the mind of a twelve-year-old boy. He'd had a traumatic event of some kind in his youth, but the History and Physical in his chart wasn't specific as to what exactly had happened. Whatever the incident was, it left him delayed and with limited working memory such that he couldn't manage his diabetes or look after himself in general.

"Hi," Pete smiled, looking back and forth between the two nurses. "Are you guys cousins? You look like you could be cousins. Billy's my cousin, but we don't look too much alike, do we Billy? Are you guys sisters?"

"No," Linnea said, her smile never fading. "I'm Linn, and this is Gabby. We're your nurses."

"I think I saw you before," Pete said, eyeing the two of them with curiosity, game paused in his hand. "Billy, were they here before? Checking my blood pressure?"

"Yes," William said, looking up from his work. "They were in not too long ago, but it was the nursing assistant, Marie, who took your vital signs the last time. Good to see you again, Linn."

"Likewise. How's your pain doing, Pete?"

"Oh, just a little sore. I don't even remember what happened. Do you have any grenadine?"

"I don't think so, but I can go check after we're done."

Pete had been brought to the hospital after first responders found him at the bottom of his basement stairs, presumably after having fallen down or off of them. He'd been unable to recall what happened, but his injuries were substantial and included being impaled by a gardening tool. The internal trauma led to fluid, bleeding, swelling. He'd needed surgery and a chest tube to drain fluid from around his lungs, Jackson-Pratt drains in his abdomen to clear out the unwanted fluid there as well.

First responders had also found his mother, deceased, by the washer and dryer amid a pile of partially sorted laundry. Apparently, she'd had a massive heart attack while he was helping her down there. He ran up to the kitchen and called emergency services from a landline, but when the dispatcher asked how his mother was doing, he ran back down to check, and never returned to the call.

Pete would probably have the chest tube and the drains out within a matter of days, but he'd be in for a while, what with his mother gone. He'd need placement somewhere… William was Pete's only living relative, but he'd made it clear he couldn't take on guardianship. Still, he'd promised to come in evenings to sit with him.

"You took a tumble down the stairs at home, and we're helping you get back in shape," Linnea said.

"Oh right," Pete nodded, looking like he was reaching for the memory, but nowhere near finding it. "Did I have dinner yet?"

"Nope," Linnea smiled. "Gabby's going to get you some insulin after emptying your drains. Your blood sugar was one seventy-two. Gabby will dial up two units on the insulin pen, inject them in the back of your arm, then you can have some lasagna, green beans, peaches, a brownie, and we can mix diet ginger ale mixed with cranberry juice the way you like it. I saw the cart coming down the hallway on the way here.

"Wow, that sounds good."

"I'm going to start with meds then do the drains," Gabby said, coming out of the bathroom with the specimen cups to measure the drain output.

Pete returned to the game on his phone.

"How was your morning?" William asked.

"Unexpectedly busy," Linn smiled. "How about you? You mentioned wanting to do some work in your garden, but it must have been a washout with the rain."

"Oh, I'm sure you've heard the saying about there being no such thing as poor weather, only poor clothing choices," William started. "I'm not afraid of rain, though I did get an early start this morning, and moved into the greenhouse before getting wet." Then he held up his right hand, displaying several scratches along the back and over his wrist.

"Cat?" Gabby asked.

"Billy doesn't like cats," Pete said, eyes glued to his phone.

William sighed, smiled, and shook his head. "Roses. A labor of love."

Heat rushed through Linn's chest and prickled under her arms, reverberation of an animal thrashing beneath her, hair grinding into skin... She was no stranger to the garden, or to claws, and she'd withstood the force of a creature struggling to escape her grip. The marks on William's arm were deep and she suspected they'd come from an animal… and he'd enjoyed it.

"Isn't it late for roses?" Gabby asked. "Not that I know anything about flowers."

"Coming to the end of their season, and the right time for transplanting. Early spring is ideal, but Pete's home and gardens have been rather neglected, and I just couldn't wait," he shrugged with a smile. "I spent the rest of my morning in the greenhouse."

"What do you do for work?" Gabby asked, handing Linnea the blue and orange insulin pen. The pen held over three hundred units of insulin and could be dialed up to give as much as sixty units in one dose, though Linnea had never given more than fourteen at once, and that had come with a call to the doctor. The potential for human error was high with nurse-adjusted medications, so two nurses were required to check.

Linnea verified that the dose on the pen matched the amount to be given for Pete's dinnertime blood sugar level, handed it back to Gabby, the words *I just couldn't wait* echoing in her mind as she cosigned her name in the medical record.

"Editor," William said. "Diving into the stories of others, raw and unrefined."

"Oh," Gabby said, surprised. "I figured maybe you were a botanist or something."

"No," he said, almost wistfully. "Flowers are a hobby."

Linnea's heart nodded, feeling as though some part of herself were speaking through him, understanding the pull of something categorized as a pastime.

"Triathlons are another pursuit," he continued, "and I enjoy cooking. I read *outside* of work, occasionally…" William dipped his head slightly and raised his brows. "There must be something you'd rather be doing than this," he said, almost playfully.

"Embroidery and knitting," Gabby blushed. "I know, go figure, right? It started as a family thing but I like it."

"Linn?" He asked, turning the question to her.

"Clay," she said. "Ceramics. I have a space in my garage and do a great deal of work after my shift, so it's late… Sometimes I just get so caught up, usually when I'm the most challenged."

"The more we sweat, so to speak, the more satisfying," William said, holding up his wrist, and wasn't it the truth… She felt well sated when her arms ached, emotions exhausted, remains of her work a taste on her tongue, embedded in the lines of her hands.

"The tube is red," Gabby said of the drain she'd started checking. "And it's leaking into the bulb, but it's stuck to the side kind-of…"

Linnea leaned over the bed to get a better look at the depressed suction bulb at the end of the drain Gabby held. "Yeah, you just need to strip the tube."

Gabby raised her eyebrows and scrunched her nose. She had no idea what that meant.

"Right," Linnea said, taking the tube in her hands. "Blood in the tube sits quite a bit and begins to clot, that's what this ribbon of red is. But that clot can affect the suction, so we help it out by stripping it." She pinched the end of the tube close to Pete between her right thumb and forefinger, then pinched beside them with her left thumb and forefinger and slid them down toward the drain, pulling the ribbon of clotted blood out into the bulb. "Have you ever had lobster?" Linnea asked as she worked. "This reminds me of getting the meat out of the legs: hold one end, then pinch with your teeth and pull."

Gabby looked politely horrified, unable to produce words.

Linn's phone buzzed in her pocket, not stopping. "It can take a little work," she continued. "I'm gonna step out in the hall for a minute, just remember to have one set of fingers as an anchor so you don't pull at the drain site."

Linnea moved to the hall, then to the stockroom, put the phone to her ear.

"It wasn't me," she said.

Lars sighed. "Mom texted an article, and I know you run there."

They both paused for a moment, then Linn whispered, "Your turn, Lars."

"My turn."

"I need to hear you say it."

"Wasn't me, Linn."

She nodded, alone. "I found her."

"You fucking, *what?*"

"I found her on my run. The crime scene. I'm the one who called it in."

"Shit."

"*Yeah*. It was a lot. And… I didn't call it in right away."

"I'm coming over."

"No, I'm at work. But I could use a visit. It was…"

"Stirred some shit."

She nodded, alone. "Yeah. Will you be up later?"

"I'll be up whenever you need me up. Give me a call when you get out; we can chat on your way home."

*

Alex leaned against the med room sink while Linnea pulled meds from the Pyxis machine.

"It's an October night," he started. "I know I'm gonna need red, but I haven't decided if I'm bringing Shiraz or Pinot Noir." Oh, there's Steph," he added, nodding to the rectangular glass panel in the wooden door. Steph was on the other side, punching in the code to unlock it. She turned the handle, pushed… but the door didn't open.

"Has she said what she's bringing?" Alex continued. "Girl will drink from a bottle or a box, but she knows her wine. And this door hates her, apparently."

Punch, punch, punch, pull… Punch, punch, punch, pull…

"Two, One, Seven!" Alex and Linn shouted together.

Punch, punch, punch, pull… And Steph was in.

"Isn't it written on the door jamb?" Linnea asked, stepping back from the Pyxis to lean against the sink with her meds while Alex took his turn logging into the machine.

"There's like three sets of numbers written there," Steph huffed, shaking back the long bangs that didn't fit into her ponytail. While her hair was brown, her highlights fluctuated in color depending on the season. She'd gone blonde over the summer, but transitioned to auburn for autumn. "So, did you go running in the woods this morning?" she asked, focused on Linnea.

"Yeah…"

"The place you always go, right? On Miller's Loop?"

Shit. Linnea nodded. "Miller's to Blue Crest, Long Hill, then I connect back to Miller's."

"Yeah, because I just got a text from Drew saying that he responded to a scene out there where Miller's meets up with the Blue Crest trail. A woman was fucking *murdered* there earlier today. Murdered, Linn.

Shit.

"He said he was surprised you came into work after having such a busy morning."

Alex cocked his head as he turned to look at Linnea, brows raised.

Linnea let out a breath. She knew she'd have to tell them, especially given Steph's husband was the detective she'd spoken to, but she'd wanted to just keep it to herself for a little while.

"I was obviously going to mention it."

"You found a dead body on your morning run, Linn!"

"Post mortem, not in progress, Steph."

"I can't. I mean, are you okay? Don't you need to talk about it? Decompress?"

"Yeah, but it's a lot, and we're at work. I hit the ground running with that guy's chest pain at change of shift. It wasn't the right time."

"I don't like you running alone."

"Steph…"

Steph put up a hand. "You need a dog. I *always* take Benji when I run, even with the kids. I just clip his leash to my fanny pack so I can keep two hands on the stroller."

"But not clipped *to* the stroller," Linnea smirked.

"Never again, oh my god, that was a *disaster*… But really, I told you before I'd go with you, just not so early."

But early was what Linnea liked, when morning stretches its arms, when the forest is loud and quiet at the same time.

"I'm fine, really."

"What if that had been you? It *could* have been you! You were *there*…"

The door opened and Gabby slipped awkwardly inside, Saving Linn from answering as she pressed the room to exceed the number of bodies able to comfortably fit.

"So…" Gabby started. "I spoke to surgical house about the post-op hip I got earlier. It's bleeding a *lot*, and the daughter still won't leave."

"Who answered the page," Linnea asked.

"Dr. Grayer, I think? He asked if you were on, then hung up on me when I said yes. I didn't even get to tell him about the hip…"

The silence hung, all eyes on Linnea.

"Did I do the right thing?" Gabby asked. "I thought I was supposed to call surgical house before the covering doc after hours, right?"

"Yes," Linnea started. "You can always start with the resources you have on the floor, though. Sometimes something might be out of your comfort zone, but still be within normal parameters. One of us could take a look, or the charge nurse. Cheryl is-"

Someone began pounding on the med room door.

Linnea's eyes flicked over Gabby's shoulder to the blue surgical scrubs in the hall, the fist and forearm pressing on the glass window, blocking the face she knew well.

"*Linny,*" Erik called from the other side.

Gabby's eyes went wide. "Who is that?"

"That would be surgical house," Steph said. "He and Linn are… familiar."

"I thought you two resolved your situation," Alex said.

"We're just friends," she replied, reaching for the handle. "It's resolved."

"Not for him it's not…"

"Number's on the door jamb," Linnea said, leading the outpouring of nurses into the hall. Alex probably hadn't finished pulling his meds, but wouldn't leave her to have the conversation alone unless told otherwise.

Erik stood there, tall as Alex, and quietly exasperated. He was in his late thirties with a nearly shaved head and something on his mind.

"I messaged you earlier, Linny. A woman was killed this morning where you run… They haven't released her name. I was worried…"

"Well hello, *Doctor Grey*," Cheryl said as she came down the hall, fanning herself with a clipboard. Cheryl, the charge nurse most evenings, was in her early sixties with a blonde bob and wore a black scrub set, a pattern of fall foliage on the shirt. She wore a smirk as well. Cheryl, Allie, the evening secretary, and another nurse, Judy, were currently reading an erotic novel with their book club.

She stopped beside Erik and took off her reading glasses, letting them hang from the pink beaded strap around her neck.

"It's Dr. Grayer, Cheryl. You're not flirting, are you? That would be *unprofessional*," he teased.

"Doctor, I'm always professional."

"So am I. I even keep a tie in my locker-"

"Fresh!" Cheryl laughed, swatting his shoulder with the clipboard.

Linnea rolled her eyes and smiled. "Cheryl, could you go take a look at a hip with Gabby? She'll explain."

"Sure thing," she said, patting Gabby on the back.

Gabby turned, mouthed, *thank you*, then followed Cheryl to the nurses' station.

"You didn't have to come up," Linnea sighed.

"You ignored my message," Dr Grayer huffed. "Given what's been on the news, yeah, I did."

"I'm not the only one who runs there, Erik."

"Apparently not… Jesus, Linny. I've told you I don't like you running there. I've got a full gym at the house. Just come over in the mornings. I'm not even there half the time."

Linnea offered a blank stare.

"Yeah, I know," he sighed. "I'm just saying… Run on the street where there's people, or, I could go with you."

It was too much to think about on the spot, a way bigger conversation than trail running, and not at all hallway appropriate.

"I have patients, Erik…"

"So do I. Anesthesia's up my ass about an appy ready to go downstairs, but I would've lost my mind in there not knowing. When I got the call from that nurse and she said you were on…" he sighed, taking a few steps back. "Just think about it."

Linnea knew her answer would be no, but she was tired, and he was very much like a couch, a familiar place to rest. She needed more than furniture, though. "I'm not planning on going tomorrow anyway… It'll be too busy over there with crime scene stuff… "I'll think about it, really. Go handle your appendix."

"Call me after report; I'll walk you out," he smiled, then rounded the corner toward the elevators.

The three of them watched him walk away, then Linnea watched Alex and Steph turn back towards her.

"That's a problem," Steph said, pointing behind her to where Erik had disappeared.

Alex nodded. "He's back pedaling, *hard*. We can leave together, or take your chances with the parking lot, but it's sending the wrong message to let him walk you out. He'll start calling, next thing you know he's showing up at Dee Dee's or the grocery store again."

Linnea used to occasionally wind down from her morning run at Dee Dee's Coffee Bar, until Erik started *accidentally* arriving at the same time... So, she'd just stopped going.

"You're fine alone. The parking lot has cameras," Steph added. "Just walk with your keys in your fist, and poke them-"

"I know," Linnea smiled with a bit of a laugh at the notion that she'd be in danger because the sun had gone down, though the thoughtfulness of her friend was appreciated. "I know, Steph... Poke the keys out through my fingers like Wolverine. I'm good, really."

*

Linnea stood alone in front of the elevators, until the stairwell door opened and a hooded man approached, his ominous presence like hot breath on the nape of her neck.

"Erik," she sighed.

"You didn't call."

"I wasn't planning on it."

"I figured as much, so I decided to come up. I'll walk you out."

It would have taken more effort to put him off than just allowing him to walk beside her, so she resolved to tolerate his presence.

"I meant what I said about you trail running. I've always told you it's not worth the risk, Linny, and now you've seen it for yourself," he said, brushing his hand over her arm as they reached her car.

"Fearmongering, Erik? That's so unattractive. And if you think I'm so weak that-"

"It's not that I think you're weak," Erik interrupted, the words like gravel in his throat. "If I thought you were weak, I wouldn't have been interested in the first place. It's just dangerous, and anyone can become a victim when alone and caught off guard."

Her phone buzzed, Lars checking in.

"Wherever your concern comes from," she began, tired and ready to move on. "Thank you, Erik, really. I just want to be sure we're still on the same page about only seeing each other at work."

"And the parking lot," he winked, then turned to head back toward the building.

*

Door closed behind her, Linnea removed her stethoscope and began emptying her pockets into a dish she kept by the mudroom door. She hadn't called Erik to meet her when she left work. Instead, she privately savored the elation of the day's end, the beginning of calm settling in. Her mind usually buzzed a good three quarters of the way home, tapering down toward the stillness she felt when she stood under the night sky in her driveway. Linnea had a garage attached to the right side of the house by a mudroom, the *hallway* her papa had called it. She often chose not to park in the garage, especially on work nights. There was just something about walking through the open air under the sky, a final passage before entering her home.

Alcohol swabs, redcaps, gauze, and a roll of silk tape went into the dish by the door… and Mrs. Kahn's latanoprost eye drops. The glaucoma medication was one of a handful the patient took, but these were only given at night.

Linnea sighed at the discovery, threw her dirty scrubs in the mudroom hamper and headed for the bathroom. Cell phone in hand, she dialed work and asked for the nurse she needed.

"Marr two, this is Chris."

"Hey, it's Linn."

"Hey, what's up?"

The living room to her left and dining room to her right were quiet as Linnea passed them. She'd turned right before entering the kitchen, headed straight into the bathroom and closed the door.

"I have Mrs. Kahn's eyedrops…"

"Ugh… Pharmacy is going to hate me."

"No, it's the latanoprost. I can just throw them in my fridge and bring them when I come in tomorrow."

"Nice. You didn't find Pete's missing Novolog pen, did you?"

"No… I wondered if Gabby took it home and was too nervous to say something. I tried telling her it's no big deal… but it was weird. Day shift said you found the other pen in the room? Gabby must have left it in there."

"I didn't want to put her on-the-spot in report, but yeah, I found his long-acting pen on the bedside table when I was cleaning up all the Shirley Temple cups Friday night…"

"Yikes…"

"When I put it back, I noticed the Novolog pen was gone. You think housekeeping would have snagged it?"

"Maybe? They wouldn't have tossed it though. I don't know. How's Pete doing?"

He'd been anxious at change of shift, they'd had trouble redirecting him, even with the Shirley Temples and his phone.

"He got pretty agitated, so we called William. He offered to come in, but the phone call was enough. They talked for a bit, then Pete went to sleep."

"And he'll dream whatever it was away. Alright, I need to shower."

"You back tomorrow?"

"Sure am."

"Me too. See ya."

Linnea placed the phone down by the edge of the sink. In the dark, she showered, washing away the rest of the skin she'd been wearing, rinsing off what the night air and the silent sky couldn't.

Leaning against her kitchen counter and eating vegetable barley soup in the moonlight, Linnea looked out the window to the garden. She wore soft leggings and a cloudy duster with the sleeves rolled up. The t-shirt underneath had belonged to Lars before she cut the neck, faded black with white words that read *Joy Division* at the top, *Unknown Pleasures* at the bottom, and what she'd once thought was a topographical map between. Her brother had later explained that the image was of a stacked plot of the radio emissions given off by a pulsar, which Linnea had found fascinating.

Angling her bowl toward the window, she took another bite, and admired her work. The top half of the bowl was a light blue-grey, the bottom half matte black with the long body of a coyote etched into it. She'd tried her best to represent the creature's figure, but, she supposed, some might think it a dog or a wolf at first glance. Linnea knew, though, what she'd put there, what was embedded in the glaze.

After eating, she poured the hot water into a modest mug waiting on the counter, a mug that had once been the right size, but had long since become a little small for her hands. The whole of the handled cup was matte black, like it had been dipped in ink, save for the crescent moon etched toward the top on one side. The few dots of red along the bottom seemed almost accidental in appearance, but they were entirely intentional in color and placement.

Mint and lavender scented steam drifted up toward Linnea's face as she slid into her slippers and closed the studio door behind her. Overhead lights illuminated the space where her Grandma Grace had done so much work, taught classes, taught Linn.

Two garage doors down on the left usually stayed closed, then there was the new one she'd had installed to the right. Made entirely of windows, the new door allowed her to see the back garden in autumn, winter, at all hours; a wall she could open during pleasant weather. Two large work tables stood in the center of the room, four pottery wheels. Against the right wall stood a row of shelving, GG's old desk, a huge sink, and a glass cabinet with glass jars, each filled with memories turned to powder in shades of black, white, and grey. It was somewhat cozy over there by the desk, with an old couch separating the area from the rest of the studio, a round Persian style rug and coffee table. An apothecary cabinet took up half the desk, twenty-four tiny drawers, each large enough to fit a grown man's fist, each drawer a secret only she could open.

Linnea descended the steps, anticipation gently rippling through as she eyed the back wall of the studio where two kilns flanked a cold, cast iron wood stove. She set her mug down alongside a marble pestle and mortar at one of the work tables, and picked up an apron with block-printed indigo paisley.

Hot air escaped the kiln as she opened it, warming her skin as she reached for the solitary bowl in the center. Removing the lid, Linnea revealed three small skulls, mouse or vole most likely, along with an assortment of other tiny bones she'd removed from owl pellets she'd found and dissected. The offerings were small, but they added up. There was a time when she'd known the eyes of what remained as bone in her kiln, as she'd known the eyes of the woman in the woods. And while it stirred her blood to remember, it was yet unclear to Linnea what the next step in her path might be... Until then, she would forage, knowing it wouldn't be enough.

Sipping her tea, she sat at the worktable, transferring the calcined remains into the marble mortar, wondering what it meant for a thing to be a labor of love. Her mom and Don used their vacation time performing surgery on kids around the world. Was that it? She supposed, perhaps, it was giving time or energy without reward, but if the sacrifice is rewarding…

That must be the love, she thought. But what of the work Linnea did? She certainly toiled. There were mornings her muscles had been sore from working clay, but she woke satisfied. And while many of the pieces she made brought in money, that's not why she created them. It was the act that sustained her, something which absent would result in her languish. It was labor, and it was deeply pleasurable, and wasn't that love, in a sense?

Mug in hand, Linnea walked to the wall beside the steps, took another sip, and turned out the light. Through shadow and moon, she returned to the table, took up the pestle and began to work.

8.

Berkshires, October 2014

Damp leaves lined the trail, slick from the previous day's rain, and partially concealing rocks Linnea tried to avoid while keeping up her pace. The path was different from her usual route on Miller's Loop, and she found she needed to pay more attention to her footing, though her mind was somewhere else, both clear and drifting.

Alex, Erik, Steph, they'd not wanted Linnea to run alone after what had happened in the woods the day before, Erik and Steph had never liked the idea of it, but she couldn't stay away, not after what had happened. Echoes would fuel the momentum building within her, a wave near cresting. It had been five years since GG's death, since she'd made something *magnificent*, and she wasn't blind to the cycle at work. She'd been existing in the pause between heartbeats, waiting for the next pulse to flood her, and it felt close. She knew it was close.

The movement of her legs, while a part of her body, seemed somewhat disconnected, as though she were traveling both with and without a form, floating through cool greys and golds, through reds and browns, through the muffled chatter of woodland sounds.

The forest had been filled with shadow and cool, blue light when she'd embarked at the trailhead, but with time, sun began to fill the space between the tops of the trees, catching copper and honeyed leaves fluttering down, a final act of glory before they returned to the earth, to *become* earth, again. They'd all been green once, working amongst each other. But things change when the nights grow long. The chlorophyll they wore began to fade, revealing a golden spectrum of carotenoids. What had been there all along comes out of dormancy as darkness creeps in on both sides of the day. And while this amber is a beautiful triumph, something additional happens in some species… A new sugar is produced. Anthocyanins protect their leaves from excess light, and create brilliant, powerful shades of red. The blood rubies of autumn.

As Linnea tapered down to a walk, she lifted her shirt a little to feel the forest's cool breath against the sweat on her abdomen. She wore a black thermal top, blaze orange vest, thick grey leggings, and trail running shoes. She had fingerless gloves on, but held off on wearing a hat, suffering with cold ears in favor of hearing everything around her. The vest had pockets enough for her keys, phone, tin case, and a small water bottle. The blaze wasn't required for hunters until shotgun season in November, but hunters were human, and she wasn't interested in being pierced by an arrow.

While Linnea's steps had become muted, and there was a sense of surrounding peace, the forest was bustling, particularly the rock wall she'd come upon. Chipmunks flitted in and out of the spaces between the stones. In a month's time they'd be silently sleeping in their burrows, heart rates and breathing slowed into a state of torpor, waiting until conditions were right to emerge once more.

She left the trail and followed the stone wall, until a dragonfly caught her attention. Its body was intact, but life gone, an unlikely fortune that the wind hadn't yet taken. She'd have liked finding more owl pellets…

Unable to break down everything they ate, owls regurgitate the bone and hair from their prey in well-formed pellets. The bones were clean, no meat on them, so Linnea only needed to pick them free from the surrounding fur before firing in the kiln. Larger bones would be much easier to work with, but buying them from a butcher… it just didn't feel right. She'd heard of antler sheds, from deer, which would work, but it wasn't the time of year to forage for them, apparently. She'd worked with deer Cap hunted, still had some ash remaining, but the practice had become less than ideal. Hunting her own prey, though… It felt like a logical next step.

She took the small, hinged tin from her vest, tucked the insect inside, and returned it to her pocket. It was about this time that she heard a sound like liquid pouring onto the ground in the distance, a steady stream splashing leaves. As she searched for its source, sure she'd got the direction right, the noise came to a stop. Another sound then, like fabric almost, but it was coming from…

Linnea looked up, up, up, until she found what looked like an elbow leading to a shoulder, a knee leading to a foot, a tree trunk obstructing the rest of her view. She sucked in a breath, and a head swiveled from around the trunk. A man was seated some thirty feet up in the tree, his eyes locking with Linnea's, sending a jolt of liquid light through her body, electricity shooting out from her heart, then retreating back to settle in her chest.

Though he was too distant to make out any details, she observed his short, dark hair, and a beard of some kind. The green of his shirt was the color of balsam fir, pants like worn, grey jeans, dark boots. Cocking his head slightly, he held her eyes with his. He didn't scowl, didn't show much emotion at all, but it may have been the distance.

Linnea raised a hand and offered a soft smile, feeling something hanging in the air between them. As her mouth began to relax, he silently called her to him with a flick of his fingers.

Another burst of electricity zipped through her. She could have turned back, followed the wall to the path she'd been on, jogged to her car and gone home… But Linnea was curious.

Allowing her fingertips to graze the stone beside her as she advanced, Linnea reluctantly took her eyes off the tree-man to monitor the terrain, watching for rocks, roots, and holes. When she looked back up, he seemed to be examining her as she approached from the side, his body still, his expression one of controlled intrigue, eyes never leaving her.

Squinting up at him, she raised a hand to block out some of the ambient sunlight.

Opening day of archery season.

"I didn't notice you were there until I heard a pouring sound, like water," she whispered, knowing her voice would carry.

"It wasn't water," he replied, face unreadable.

Linnea immediately took a step back, looking down around her feet.

"Other side of the tree," he said, voice deep but clear, and with a smile she could hear before she looked back up.

The sky formed a bright halo around him, making her eyes water, but sure enough, the corner of his mouth had raised, tugging at hers to do the same.

"Would you mind holding on to these while I climb down?" He asked, lowering his bow and small pack with a rope.

His gear had reached her arms before she had a chance to answer. As he stood and turned towards the tree, Linnea noticed for the first time that the seat and the footrest of his chair were two separate parts. He loosened a strap around the trunk that appeared attached to a harness he was wearing, then he lifted the chair with his hands, lowered it down, lifted the footrest with his feet, and lowered it down. Slowly he descended the tree, bringing the chair with him, scooting the harness tether along the way, until he reached the forest floor.

"Wow," Linnea began, handing over the cargo in her arms. His eyes were dark, the brown rings almost as black as the holes they surrounded. Her gaze wandered over him, then back up the tree. "I felt a little guilty for disrupting the atmosphere, but I can't say I'm sorry. That must feel amazing, being up there… How early do you come in?"

"Before dawn," he said, appraising her for a moment. She appreciated the stillness he had about him, noting that the pause in words wasn't uncomfortable.

"Do you want to try it?" He asked.

If he'd posed the question right away, she might have thought it rushed. Instead, it seemed thought out, purposeful rather than reactionary. Her inclination should have been to decline, as not to inconvenience him. And while aware that the situation itself was out of the ordinary, Linnea felt no raised hair on her arms, no instinct to flee. She almost felt *comfortable*, but she was too excited for that to be accurate. Perhaps comfortable, with a hint of exhilaration.

"I do," she smiled with a delightful twinge of uncertainty.

His cheeks raised, crinkling his eyes at the corners. "You'll need a harness," he began. "You have the option of not wearing it, but I can't catch you until you reach me, and you could get dinged up along the way. Choice is yours."

"I'd like the harness…" She started, pointing at the one he had on. "I'm guessing you didn't bring an extra?"

"No," he said, placing his bow on the ground, unbuckling his pack, then the clips at his chest and waist. "Don't worry about the size," he went on, stepping out from leg straps so wide she could have fit one around her waist. "It's adjustable."

He crouched, holding out the strap such that she noticed his watch. It was somehow both sleek and chunky, and she suspected it told more than time. Linnea placed a hand on his shoulder, and stepped in.

"I'm Henry," he said, looking up at her as he stood, then down when he'd reached his full height.

"Linnea," she replied, liking the idea of him saying her name.

"Linnea," he repeated, that almost-smile hinting to brighten his face. "I'm going to show you how to tighten this first strap, then you can adjust the others. Okay?"

She nodded, and his hands went to the strap at her waist. Once it had been fastened snug, she nodded again, and took over with the other straps that would have required his sustained contact had he not empowered her to do it herself.

He led Linn to the tree, clipped her harness to the rope tether around the trunk, and gave her a tutorial on how to use the climbing stand.

It was work, but rewarding. When she'd gone about twenty-five to thirty feet up, Linnea stopped and turned. The guardrail brushed against her legs, but still she felt free. Sitting down, she sighed, breathing deep as she surveyed the forest from her new height.

"Close your eyes," he said from below.

And she did.

Close your eyes, his voice echoed in her mind. His voice, deep and low, faded until it was only the sound of the woods surrounding her. With motion she might not have noticed from the ground, Linnea felt the tree sway, felt herself moving with it. Graceful movement, like dancing breath. How lovely it would have been to stay in the place between awake and asleep while in that tree top like a lullaby.

Her eyes opened again to the impressive sight that she'd left upon their closing. *I could lose time up here,* she thought, imagining a day spent observing from her unseen nest. Even while the benevolent stranger stood below her, Linnea felt dangerously close to slipping free of the skin she wore around others, the veil between her thoughts and everything else.

She stood again, turned, and tucked her feet into the platform's foot holds, running through the steps she needed to perform: slip the tether down, lift and lower the platform, lift and lower the seat… slide the tether down… It wasn't until Linnea had nearly reached the forest floor that she took her eyes off the equipment she wielded.

"I probably could have stopped sooner," she said, disconnecting the tether and hopping down from the platform.

Henry seemed mesmerized by her actions, then nodded, still focused on her, though the trance appeared to have been broken.

"I could have taken a nap up there," she went on. "I'd have been too distracted initially by the new vantage point, but I imagined what it would be like while my eyes were closed…"

He nodded again. "I've spent the night in a tree. It's peaceful, blending into the forest. Can get a little stiff, sitting like that, but if you bundle up, it's worth it when the wind blows."

"Yes! The tree movement… It was quite special. Not something I've experienced before."

As excited as she was, a creeping awareness built upon her return to the ground. The idea felt cold in her limbs and hot in her cheeks, the realization that she might be imposing on Henry.

"I should take this off," she said, beginning to loosen the harness straps around her legs, wanting to give him a fighting chance of getting back into it. "You've been remarkably accommodating considering I interrupted… I wish I had something as fantastic as a tree stand experience to offer, unless you need a tiny water bottle, or a dragonfly," she joked, running a mental inventory of what she had on her person.

He raised an eyebrow as she returned the harness, but instead of asking about the aforementioned insect, he said, "You could walk me out? If you don't mind waiting a few minutes while I get the stand packed up…"

Linnea's eyes widened. "Sure… I just… *Really?*" She asked, scrunching up her nose a little. "I hope this isn't because of me. It's still early, and I'm sure the animals will forget you're here once I head back out… You don't need to stop hunting."

"I don't intend to."

His words rang differently in the air, in her ears. She thought of herself, the whole of her, the parts that hid but were never gone.

"It's no trouble," he said, moving toward the tree. "I'm done here for the day."

The tether was loosened and disconnected, then he worked on the seat while Linnea had yet to respond with words. She could turn and leave on her own, but she didn't want to.

"How do you carry it?" She asked.

"Like a backpack."

She watched as he put the seat and the platform together, slipped the padded arm straps she hadn't seen over his shoulders.

She wanted one.

"How much does that weigh?"

"Altogether, about twenty pounds," he said, taking it off again and motioning for her to turn around. "Go ahead."

He held the pack up, allowing Linnea to place her arms through the straps. She could definitely handle that much weight, but for how long?

"Do you mind if I walk with it for a bit?"

"Do I mind if you carry the twenty pounds that would otherwise be on my back?" He smiled. "Lead the way."

"Well, *as you'll recall,* I first saw you from the wall over there," she said, starting back to the way she'd come. "We can just follow the stones to the trail, it's not too far… Did you come in from that way though?" She'd avoided her usual parking location, figuring the area she typically frequented would be occupied, though she hadn't bothered doing a drive-by to check it out.

He shook his head, then with his lips curving up, he said, "Don't worry, I'll get where I need to go."

A comfortable silence grew between them as they walked, one of quiet observation and easy movement, of gestures and body language, of their heads turning together at the sound of rustling leaves, of one pointing so the other could see where a bird had landed, of warm smiles and curiosity. When Linnea noticed a rather tiny clump of fluff to the side of the trail, she slowed, paused, and inspected what turned out to be feathers.

"Kill site," Henry said.

She reached into the fuzzy clump and selected a small, downy feather with red coloring. Then, she took out her tin, and placed the new treasure inside.

"The dragonfly," he observed.

Linnea nodded, took a moment to check in with the weight of the pack she wore and, without a fuss, removed the gear and transferred it back to Henry.

"How did you learn to hunt?" she asked, rolling her shoulders as he strapped the cargo on his back. After nearly an hour of carrying the stand, Linnea felt she'd learned the weight was manageable, but no longer needed to bear it. To his credit, Henry hadn't made a nuisance of questioning her ability to persist, and that trust was refreshing. He'd relied on Linnea to communicate her needs, and she did.

"My dad and older brother in the beginning," he said as they started up walking again. "Hunting has become a solitary activity for me. When we were kids, though, it was educational, and something we did together, my dad and my brothers, and I."

Linnea's eyes drifted like the leaves, her mind floating toward a memory of Lars and her neighbor, Cap, pulling his blue pickup into the driveway next door on a late November afternoon. Lars had been beaming when he took her hand, joy bursting from his smile when Cap opened up the tailgate.

"How many brothers do you have?" She asked.

"Three. One older, two younger."

"*Four* of you? Impressive, I mean, on behalf of your parents. My brother and I kept our mom busy, and it was just the two of us. He's four years older, and I can't believe I didn't ask about sisters. I think four was a larger number than I'd expected, so I assumed there weren't any more."

"One sister, though no longer living. She was the youngest of us. And I want to stop you before you apologize," he said as Linnea sucked in a breath, his smile soft as he continued. "It's okay."

She let out a sigh. "Sorry never feels like the right word. When people are grieving... our vocabulary could be better."

He nodded, and they were silent a while longer.

Ferns turned a warm shade of brown at their tips, trees, chipmunks and leaves, the forest *moved* while Linnea and Henry continued through it. He was fairly quiet when he walked, even with all the equipment he carried, with his height, the wide shoulders and all... Linnea wondered if she was light on her feet as he was, though she didn't seem to disturb things when she was alone. The forest didn't appear to mind Henry, either. Business as usual continued as they walked. Chatter and autumnal preparations for changing weather, all carried on.

Henry's steps slowed, his gaze down. She watched as he focused on the ground and reached...

"For your tin," he said, handing her a red maple leaf so tiny it fit on the pad of her thumb.

Captivated by the thoughtfulness and accuracy of the gesture, Linnea nodded without words, and added the token to the others.

"Do you hunt?" He asked, his low voice not breaking the silence so much as rising from it.

"I had planned to take the classes a few years ago," she sighed, lifting a shoulder. "It was a hectic time, though. I moved out here, to Smithfield, and it just didn't feel right for a while, like I needed to settle in first. My neighbor, Cap, is going to take me out this week. I've been practicing with his wife's old bow all summer. He used to take my brother, Lars out when we were kids. I was always invited, but working with my grandmother in her studio was more appealing to me. I grew up in Boston, but my dad's parents lived out here and we visited quite a bit. GG, my grandmother, was a ceramics teacher with an epic studio in her garage," she sighed. Of course, the garage and the studio had become Linnea's. "My papa was an attorney," she went on. "My dad went into law as well. He worked for my mom's dad, doing some corporate, international, something-or-other law. That's how he met my mom." Linnea searched a moment for more details, then realized she'd forgotten what they were talking about. "I'm giving you my family tree, but there's no way you asked about that," she blushed, eyes still on the trail. "I'm just trying to mentally backtrack and search for what we were talking about…"

"What does your mother's mother do?"

"What?"

"Your maternal grandmother."

Linn turned to see the self-amusement in his expression. He was teasing. "Because you already know what my other grandparents do?"

"Might as well collect the whole set," he smiled.

"She's a pathologist," Linnea grinned, nudging his arm with her shoulder. "Semi-retired, but she still teaches a little I think."

"And your mother?"

"Nurse. Operating room, though she's in perioperative administration now. How about your parents?"

"My dad is an investment something-or-other," he smiled, tipping his head toward her. "And my mom is a lot of things… maybe we all are. She had her hands full with me and my brothers, my sister… Mom's an art historian and owns a gallery in Manhattan."

"Do your parents live in the city?"

"They keep an apartment there, but it's not where they live most of the time. It's a place we all come and go from."

"And how about you? Are you local?" It was entirely possible that he'd just come in for a week, or a long weekend.

"I have a lake house in Ellison."

"How long do you have it for?"

Linnea could see where the trail opened up ahead of them, where her car would be waiting with the rest of her day. The memory of their time together would be tucked away in her memories like a dragonfly, like bones and treasures kept, transformed.

"Until I sell it."

His response brought a brightness to her insides, but her eyes were already catching on an anomaly in the leaves by her feet. Henry slowed to a pause as she did, crouching as her body lowered to examine the black movement against the brilliant remains of fallen birch and maple. She lifted a leaf with her fingers, the bushy caterpillar revealed.

Linnea tilted her head, thinking of Henry's eyes as she spoke, of darkness where some color should have existed. "Wooly bear. Have you ever seen one all black?"

His head shook, just the once, in her periphery. "No."

"I forget the folklore about the coloring and winter: if more brown, then something about winter..."

"Typically, they have black on either end with brown in the middle. The brown represents mild, and black harsh, so the ratio will tell you how the winter will be. Folklore, as you said."

"Autumn still has some time," she whispered as she stood, careful not to step on the little creature. "And I don't mind the snow." Not with two garages...

It wasn't long before she arrived at her SUV, reluctant to end the morning.

"What are you doing later?" He asked.

"Work."

"What time?"

"Two O'clock," she replied, though her shift didn't start until three. "Evenings at Morland Medical."

"Doctor?"

"Nurse."

"More flexible?"

"It is in my experience... I can't imagine being a doctor. I feel like the docs are always there, or in the office, or on call. I work just enough to get health and retirement benefits."

She'd just dropped her hours officially the week before, cutting down to three evenings a week. She'd been feeling the pull for some time, to focus more on her ceramics in search of a balance. It had been about five years since her last artistic breakthrough, and there'd been a sense of waiting for the next step, waiting that bordered on restlessness.

"What made you choose nursing? Your mom?"

"Yeah," She smiled. "I thought for sure I'd be an operating room or a PACU nurse so I could do medical missions, like she does... but I started on a medical surgical floor to gain experience... then I moved," she sighed.

"And here you are. What are you doing in the morning?"

"I've got a couple friends from work coming over for brunch: tea in the back garden, or maybe inside if it's chilly."

"What are you doing right now?"

Linnea shrugged. She'd probably take a shower, eat, work in the studio a bit... Her thoughts trailed off as she took note of the only other vehicle parked there: a mini cooper with roof racks and about forty bumper stickers on the back.

"Where are you parked?"

"Off the East Boulder trail."

Linnea's eyes went wide as she drew in a sharp breath. "That's on the other side. You said-"

"Nothing untrue. I enjoyed walking with you, I'd like to see you again, and I'd rather not wait."

Her heart began to pound with a blooming sensation. Henry's directness, proximity... his eye contact. It was altogether on the cusp of unsettling. His reluctance to end their time together, she understood it. As soon as they separated the dream would begin to wear off.

"What did you have in mind?"

9.

Berkshires, October 2014

"I didn't hear you," Henry said, the anomaly still seeming to please him.

Sitting across from each other in the bed of his truck with the tailgate down, they sipped hot drinks outside of Dee Dee's Coffee Bar. His was coffee, hers chai, both sweetened with maple. She hadn't been there since Erik had made it too uncomfortable, but with Henry, sitting outside, the experience was refreshing. Their legs were stretched out, pants touching. She still wore the clothes she'd run in, some blanket he'd pulled from the cab soft beneath her.

"I can't believe I didn't notice you until I heard you taking a leak from your stand," Linnea grinned, bringing the paper cup to her mouth.

"I've had years of experience…" he trailed off. "Believe me, it's your stealth that's remarkable," he smiled with dimples she hadn't noticed before. "I heard squirrels, birds, and chipmunks. I heard leaves and acorns falling, but I didn't hear your footsteps. Or maybe I did, but they just blended in. It wasn't until your breath…"

"You are some kind of brave going running alone again," Alex said, grabbing a modest supply of alcohol swabs, flushes, and red caps to stock his workstation pockets. Linnea leaned against the counter beside him in the supply room, trying not to fade back into her memories from that morning.

"But I'm not surprised," he carried on. "Because that's who you are. What's that saying? Speak softly and carry a big stick?"

"I think that was a comment on foreign policy, and the stick was carried as a deterrent."

"The part of you that carries the stick is quiet," he said with slow sincerity as he held her eyes with his. "There's something *fuck around and find out* about you, but you don't wear it loud. Like you don't want anyone to see what you're holding."

"I used to carry a stick when I ran," Linnea said with a light laugh to her voice, letting the accuracy of Alex's observation roll off her shoulders. "I played field hockey in high school and the coach told us to take it so we'd get used to the weight. I'm not quite sure why I stopped," she added, holding the door for Alex as she thought it over. The main reason she'd stopped was that she'd finished with the sport when school had ended…

"Because a girl is resourceful, and you had better things to do with your hands."

There was that also.

"So, I met someone while I was out this morning…" she said, following Alex into the hall. "He and I had coffee together after. We were there so long I didn't have time to shower. Had lunch in the car on the way here."

She was blushing when Alex spun around.

"You *what?* Girl, get back in that stock room," he said, walking her back toward the door.

"Oh my *god*, Alex… We just had coffee at Dee Dee's," She laughed, his body pushing against hers. "I need to find Gabby and get report!"

"Not until *I* get a report!" He laughed, ushering her inside.

*

When Linnea and Alex got to the nurses' station, Gabby and Steph were already seated at computers, looking over the shift assignments.

"There's an Alex A. and an Alex D. on today," Gabby started. "Which one are you?"

"Alex A., but you can call me *Alexa* on double Alex days."

"Management approval pending," Steph added.

"Girl, this is evenings," he said, leaning against Linnea's shoulder. "When we worked twelve-hour nights. We could have worn Snuggies and roller skates so long as we kept folks alive."

"I can only imagine," Gabby smiled. "I feel like I get a taste of it after about nine o'clock."

"It tastes good though, right?" Alex asked, then turning to Linnea he mouthed the word, *brunch,* with a hint of a whisper. He'd been after her to invite Gabby for a few days, but Linnea had been on the fence.

"Gabby, I'm having these two over for brunch tomorrow," Linnea started. "About ten o'clock, tea and coffee, fruit, and… probably some type of cookie or tart or something. Steph will bring a sandwich situation; Alex is on protein, or maybe it's the other way around?"

"Oh, that sounds nice," Gabby said, her voice a little high, eyes wide and unsure.

"She's inviting you," Alex said. "That's what this is."

"I honestly wasn't sure," Gabby laughed with a little sigh at the end. "I *thought* you were, but it could have been you guys just sharing your plans and I didn't want to assume."

"You should come," Linnea said. "You're training with Tai tomorrow evening, but you'll have time to get home and change, or wear your scrubs to my house. It's really nothing fancy, just a chance to get together outside of work."

"Don't be fooled when she says *nothing fancy*. It's teapots and china and all that."

"Okay, that's not intimidating or anything. What can I bring? I've made biscotti before."

"Can't go wrong with that," Steph said.

"Excellent," Linnea smiled. Turning to Alex, she asked, "Do you still have plans with Graham?"

"Yes, ma'am," he smiled. He's taking me to a movie after he makes us dinner, and girl, he can *cook*..."

Linnea looked up as Allie, their unit secretary, entered the back room waving sticker sheets like they were lottery tickets.

"Halloween stickers from pediatrics; what do you guys want?"

"Pumpkin," Steph said after a brief inspection, peeling off a jack-o-lantern. "They have witches, Linn. Gabby, don't be shy, get some stickers for your badge."

Linnea looked over Steph's suggestion. "I don't like the green faces."

"You don't need some cartoon witch on your ID," Alex winked.

"Black cat," Linnea beamed as he peeled one from the paper for her. She extended her badge from the retractable carabiner holding all the plastic cards deemed necessary to have on display. They'd been told not to crowd their photo or identification, and she already had a moon and a couple flowers stickers from summer on there, so the cat landed on the edge of a bar code card peeking out from underneath.

"So, when are you going to see Henry again?" He asked.

"*Who* is *Henry*?" Steph asked without missing a beat, biting fiercely at the bait Alex had cast out.

Linnea sighed.

"A girl has been naughty," Alex smiled.

"You are *such* a troublemaker," Linnea said, rolling her eyes as she turned to Steph. "I was going to tell you but we *just* got here. I pre-gamed with Alex in the stock room, and I just, I was excited and it came out, and then he needed all the details..."

Steph's eyes were waiting, Gabby discretely listening in.

"I went running this morning."

Steph's eyes went wide, her head tilting.

"Yes, in the woods, and yes, I *know*," Linnea continued.

"I can't believe you went back there! Killers return to the scene of the crime, Linn, it's a thing."

And Linn understood. It wasn't to kill someone else in the same place, it was to listen to the whispers of what had already happened, still feeling the echoes.

Linnea caught Alex dipping his chin, eyeing her. "Simmer down, Steph," she started. "Even if they did return, the killer is too busy having a post-coital moment to kill anyone else right now. It's like recovering from a seizure. It's their quiet time."

"Was the area… *disturbed*," Gabby asked. "Could you still tell?"

Linnea rolled her eyes. "I went to run, not to lie down where the body fell." Though she would have, if she'd thought of it. "I didn't take my usual route anyway. It was fine."

"It was more than that," Alex smirked.

Linnea smiled back at him. "You just can't help yourself." Then to Steph she said, "I met a guy named Henry on my run. He was bowhunting, but he called it an early day and walked me out."

"He could be the guy," Steph gasped.

"He's *not* the guy…" Linn protested.

"They spent the morning in bed together." Alex blurted.

"In the bed *of his truck*. Oh my *god*, Alex!" Linnea's cheeks were on fire, from both blushing and smiling so hard. She took a few breaths, miraculously without interruption. "We got coffee and the place was busy, so we went back out and sat in the bed of his truck. Right outside the front of the shop, in plain sight. It was *safe*… We were there for hours. I even got a little cold, so he grabbed me a sweater he had up front… It smelled so good," she sighed, remembering how her chemistry had changed as she'd wrapped the garment around her and inhaled. What she could see of Henry's eyes had remained the same, his dark irises not giving anything away, but Linnea imagined her pupils had spread like ink in water.

"So…" Steph sighed. "This guy doesn't seem like a psycho?"

"You can't always tell…" Gabby said, scrunching up her nose.

Rabbit, Linnea thought, then scowled. "No, he's not a *psycho*, Steph… Not so far anyways. In real life, though, it's highly unlikely, not the kind you're thinking of anyway. Just regular, every day, manageable derangement like the rest of us."

Steph shook her head. "I am frustrated by your dangerous choices, Linn, but I am also married with two kids, one of them a weaning toddler, so I'm going to need frequent, detailed updates that I may live through your experience. When are you seeing him again?"

"You live in Morland?" Henry had asked.

"Smithfield. It's a cute little house with two garages-"

"Two?" His eyes went wide with interest.

Linnea smiled and nodded, "My papa could build anything, and Grandma Grace needed her studio in the first garage, so he conceded the original, put in skylights… The second garage came when they got tired of cleaning off their cars in winter. It didn't take long… The back yard is nice, surrounded by trees, private. My neighbors, Cap and Missy, have a small farm next door, but they're retired."

She'd wanted to invite him over then. Him, a stranger.

"I don't know," Linnea said, color flushing her cheeks again. "We exchanged numbers, and he knows I'm at work, so I'm not expecting to hear from him yet. We said we'd get in touch tomorrow morning and make a plan to meet up."

"Whatever you do, don't make him a coffee, not until we know for sure he isn't the killer," Steph teased, then slowly her expression shifted to one more serious. "The woman who died was a barista at Dee Dee's named Rosalia Morales. Apparently, she liked to run in the morning too. Drew said her identity is being released today, but he couldn't talk about the details. The FBI is getting involved… Whatever they found, it was weird, and the FBI says they've seen something like it before."

The name of the coffee shop sent a prickle of ice through Linnea's chest, sweat pinching under her arms. She hadn't made mention of DeeDee's at the nurses' station when recounting her time with Henry. She'd told Alex though, and his eyes were boring a hole in the side of her head. She turned, not surprised to see the vivid concern on his face. She gave her head a subtle shake to the side, her mind whispering, *Don't.*

Some part of her exhaled when she turned back to Steph and asked, "How weird?"

"He wouldn't say, but probably because I was already freaking out about how you run there… Did you notice anything… when you found her?"

Of course. She'd seen the position of the woman, the folded clothes, the missing fabric, the smell, unless she'd imagined it.

"She may have been posed, but I was mostly focused on calling the police and getting safe, and I honestly think its fine to run there now, Steph."

"Drew said you should be fine," she conceded. "Whoever did it, it wasn't their first time. It's the kind of thing they'll keep doing, but he says in this case, it isn't likely the same location will be hit again. Still makes me uncomfortable though."

Linnea was uncomfortable as well, but for different reasons. She didn't like that they knew she'd been there, didn't care for the way the incident had come into her workplace, like water seeping through fine cracks in a vessel, or perhaps condensation clinging to the outer surface, moisture manifesting not from within, but from all around. She could feel the beads of mist forming along her exposed skin, water gathering that it might collect into a stream enough to drink. But what an unexpected fortune she'd had in changing course earlier that morning, a chance meeting, like new breath…

"You're just worried you'll miss out on all the brunches and wine nights if Linn ends up having herself a close encounter," Alex teased, giving Linnea a wink. His words were intentionally bright, pulling attention away from the dark cloud.

"There's a wine night?" Gabby asked, her eyes lit by the shining distraction. *Thank you, Alex.*

*

Just before dinner, Allie, the unit secretary, walked over to where Linn and Gabby stood in the hall, and handed Gabby a report sheet. "PACU is calling on this guy."

"Thanks, Allie," Gabby smiled as the secretary went back to her post. Looking over the description of her incoming patient's surgery, she said, "ALIF with cage? Dr. Norton, that's neurosurgery, and Dr. Giacometti is general and vascular… A *cage*? Is that… is it like a brace?" She asked, gesturing around her torso.

"No," Linnea smiled. "It's internal. Listen, I'll grab Alex to help turn the CMO while you call for report. Have the patient pulled up on your computer, and remember to ask lots of questions. I'll have you give me report after, and we'll check with PACU about anything you missed when they bring your guy up. Sound good?"

"Thank you, *yes*," Gabby sighed, already looking overwhelmed. "Oh, but before you go in, Catherine is the proxy for the CMO. She's got short, dark hair. Definitely dyes it… And a green sweater, long with a belt, and I'm not sure what her pants-"

"That's more than enough to identify her, Gabby, though if I walk in and find all the patient's family members to be identical, I can just ask," she smiled. "Go ahead and call PACU, they need to get patient's out to keep the flow going."

"Right. Okay, thanks Linn."

About a half hour later, Linnea stood with Gabby as PACU wheeled their new post-op into room six when Marie, one of the nursing assistants, approached holding up a glucometer.

"The guy in nine, it's fifty-one. He's awake. Looks okay, but tired. His friend said he would give him a candy."

Anything less than seventy meant low blood sugar, and a protocol kicked in.

"I'll grab some juice and the other glucometer for a recheck," Linnea said to Gabby. "Get your patient situated then meet me down in Pete's room."

Gabby nodded, *"Thank you."*

Pete grinned as she walked in, hard candy clacking against his teeth. "I'm eating candy while I'm playing Candy Crush," he said, beaming with satisfaction as he held up his phone for her to see.

"Impressive," she smiled. "Pete, I'm Linn, one of your nurses this evening, and I saw your blood sugar was a little low. Hi William," she added as Pete's cousin looked up from his laptop, a tall stack of paper beside him on the extra bedside table.

He gave her a warm nod, then looked back down, the sleeve of his jacket covering the scratches she'd seen. Linn wondered where his skin had disappeared to. Under claws? Fingernails? He seemed so calm, sitting with his work, breathing easy, relaxed in his shirt and blazer, behind his glasses. Was she so different, after what she'd done?

"I came in to sweeten you up a little bit," she added. "But it looks like you got a head start."

She peeled the lid back from a cranberry juice and handed it to Pete. "I know you like your Shirly Temples, but I need you to gobble this down and we'll mix you up a drink in a little bit."

"You got it, doc," he said, pushing the candy into his cheek and following her instructions.

Linnea began collecting the Styrofoam cups from his bedside table as he drank. They contained varying levels of cranberry juice and diet ginger ale that, even with the soda being diet, left her wondering how his sugar had ended up so low.

She glanced up as she tidied, catching sight of the muted television, feeling a rush of deja vu along with it. A press conference about the woman in the woods silently aired, now with the FBI present. A uniformed officer spoke at a podium, another in uniform beside him, and men in suits. *All men,* she thought.

"I felt guilty giving him candy," William smiled sheepishly, "like I was interfering, but I didn't know how long it would take for someone to come back. The bag of butterscotch is in the bottom drawer." Then he whispered, "I don't think he remembers it's there."

"Probably not, and I would have done the same thing. Sorry if I'm cramping your style, but I need to recheck his sugar in a few minutes, and it's just easier if I stick around. Once I go into the hall, someone will grab me for something..."

"Oh, no worries, Linn. I'm glad for the company."

She nodded her head at the papers on the table. "What are you working on?"

"A manuscript update I received last night."

The sandy crunch coming from Pete's mouth, his hard candy nearly gone.

"Are you enjoying the read?" She asked.

"Oh yes, and not just for the content, but… well there's something special about working with a piece when its untouched, for both the beauty and the flaws in it."

Linnea glanced back up to the press conference as William spoke, one of the men in suits catching her eye. He was off to the side, barely on camera. His face reminded her of Henry's. He was clean shaven, but the brows and hairline were similar, the shape of his eyes and his stature as well, but this guy was leaner. She couldn't quite say what it was, but she combed over his features in an attempt to pinpoint… Then the man reached into his pocket, pulled out his phone and put it to his ear, turned his back to the camera, and stepped out of view.

"How was your morning?" William asked.

"Got a few miles in this morning, trail running," she smiled, unable to keep from slipping into her thoughts. The sweet smell of moist leaves filled her next breath in, crisp, her body working to warm the air as she inhaled. Her feet pounded on the earth, her heart matching their pace, not from exertion alone, but from the flickering fantasy of what, of who, might be out there. An idea far more invigorating than the wind passing over her body, than the shadows of trees alone.

"I run in the morning as well," William said. "Early, depending on one's perspective, I suppose."

"Oh," she said, letting out her breath. "Right, I remember you mentioned triathlons."

"I try to run or cycle every day. I swim a few times a week and, since swimming outdoors is best, I keep an outdoor pool open year-round."

Linnea's eyes widened.

"Joking," he smiled. "I go to a health club. It keeps me out of the greenhouse, so to speak. I allow myself a deep dive into my passion now and then, but I can't live in there."

Linnea glanced at the wall clock, then to the clock on her computer. "Okay Pete, time to recheck that blood sugar."

She brought the glucometer over, noticing the prompt to scan herself first after the machine rejected his bracelet. She'd forgotten which went first… Usually, a nursing assistant did the sugars.

"Just a second, Pete," she said, flipping through her badge and the cards behind it. She found the barcode she needed, but it was partially obstructed…

"Darn *cat sticker* is covering the bar code," she explained, taking off her badge. "I just need to scrape it off, but it's smearing a little," she grumbled, attempting to scan her badge again but knowing the machine wouldn't take it. It didn't, of course.

"Billy doesn't like cats."

Maybe that's where the scratches came from… She thought.

"Stickers pose no threat, Pete," William said as he stood up. "Need a hand?"

Linnea peeled and scraped at the cat, leaving steaks of gummy paper over what she needed to access. "No… *Ugh.* Probably. There's a sticker over the barcode I need to scan. Unfortunately, I have to scan myself before I can do Pete."

William stood beside her, testing the adhesive with his finger. "Have you tried rubbing alcohol?"

"Good thinking," she said, opening a drawer in her computer station. "And I swear I've seen adhesive removal pads around here, like the alcohol swabs, but some other chemical. I should just flag down a CNA or another nurse if this doesn't work."

Linnea tore open the little package, taking her badge from William as he slowly handed it back to her. His eyebrows came together slightly into a puzzled expression.

"I thought your name was Lynn," he said.

"Linn, short for Linnea," she offered absently as she rubbed the mess on her badge.

"Linnaea borealis," he said.

She nodded, well aware of her namesake. The low-growing plant had leaves at the base with a long, slender stem, bifurcating to support two flowers hanging like pale pink lamp shades, a favorite of Carl Linnaeus.

"Twinflower is the common name," she said. "I think a lot of kids go through a thing where they want to know more about their name, read into its meaning. I used to wonder if I was like the flower, having two parts of myself."

I am, she whispered within, a reminder of what God had told Moses. She'd long since known it was true. She was all things, but the symbolism of the twinflower was strong, pulling at her sometimes.

"You're not a *Gemini,* are you?" William asked, a bit of humor in his voice.

"No, a Taurus," she smiled. "Too stubborn to believe in astrology."

William lifted his left hand, resting his first two fingers at his temple, the third drifting toward his mouth as he considered her, his sleeve exposing three bracelets. The bracelets had a trendy unisex style she'd seen some men wear, adjustable leather cords. Instead of metal or wood, the beads appeared to be fabric of some kind, three to five spheres on each cord, but she couldn't be sure of the number or material without staring... but the shock of bright pink on one of the spheres sent a rush of ice to her fingers, heat in her chest. She knew the color couldn't only have existed on a lifeless woman she'd discovered in the woods, but the coincidence was remarkable, so much so that her body reacted.

"Are you alright?" He asked, tilting his head.

"Oh, yes, I just noticed your jewelry," Linnea said, her voice calm. "Your jacket covered them up earlier. I don't want to come across as intrusive, but they look… unique."

"They are," he said with a smile. "Each one represents an impactful experience. I know you're an artist, so you'll have to excuse the amateur construction," he continued, humility in his voice as he raised his arm to expose his work.

Impactful. Was each bead a person? She had them for her father, but this… Was it different from her work? Her *other* work.

"The beads are wooden underneath," he continued. "I generously apply a scented liquid, then overlay the swatch of fabric, tucking the excess into the hole. I'm not much of a *crafter*," he admitted, pushing up tortoiseshell glasses and lowering his hand.

"I've heard of people doing something similar with lava beads," she smiled while her insides twisted. The woman had been a barista at Dee Dee's. He must have gone there and chosen her. Linn reflected on how she'd frequented the coffee shop until recently, that she may have come to his attention instead, if Erik hadn't been intolerable. "I *think* they're some kind of lava," she continued. "The stone is super porous, so the essential oil sinks in."

Their exchange was interrupted as Gabby breezed through the door.

"Hey, Linn?" She asked.

"Take this thing," Linnea said, holding out the glucometer. "The cat sticker is all over my barcode so it won't read. We've rubbed it with alcohol swabs, but I'm done. Pete looks fine but he needs a recheck and some crackers."

"Got it," Gabby smiled, but she seemed to have something else on her mind. "I just… My CMO just passed," she whispered. "The family came out."

"You checked her?"

Gabby nodded, already scanning the unobstructed barcode on her badge with the glucometer. "I waited a *while*. No respirations. I disconnected her from the PCA and had Allie page the in-house doctor."

"You did all the right things. There's nothing for us to do now until she's pronounced, and the family leaves. Go ahead and scan Pete."

"Another thing about Twinflowers," William said. "They're highly fragrant, more so at dusk. A member of the honeysuckle family, if I'm remembering correctly."

"That I *didn't* know," she smiled, uneasy beneath her skin, unsure if he might be molding her into his next target, some dance she unknowingly participated in. Was that how it worked? Wouldn't it be too soon, though? "I have honeysuckle growing on an arbor in my back garden. Some summer days I can smell it from *inside* the house."

"Yes, but *unlike* honeysuckle, flouncing over trellises and releasing its perfume for the wind to carry, Twinflower prefers the soil of old forests. Her scent is a gift one must work for."

A breath of laughter came through Linnea's nose.

"Eighty-four," Gabby said, patting her patient on the arm, flipping her hair as she looked over her shoulder. If Linnea hadn't cleaned up Pete's old cups, Gabby would have swept them off the tray table. *Did* they have a hair policy?

Pete looked up to Gabby, then to Linnea. "Hey…" He started, eyes wide, phone lowering in his lap. "Are you guys sisters?"

"If you think we look alike now, imagine her hair down," Gabby said with flirty exuberance. "She always wears it up at work, but I saw it out for the first time yesterday. Linn, you have the most *gorgeous* hair."

"Honeysuckle," Linnea whispered over her shoulder, aware that she was either playing a dangerous game or completely manifesting an absurd scenario, assigning meaning where there was none based on her own experiences…

"Exactly," William said, digging back into his reading with a tame smile.

"We are absolutely not sisters," Linnea said, her focus returning to Pete. "Just two lucky nurses. And it looks like the sweets did their job, so I'm going to leave you in Gabby's capable hands."

She was just turning her computer around as William said, "Speaking of leaving, I need to head home shortly after dinner today, and I'm not sure I can resist looking into your namesake, though the flower might be too rare for my library. Are you back in tomorrow?"

"No," Linnea cringed, almost feeling guilty for the reduced hours she worked. "I'm not on again until Wednesday…"

"Oh, that's a shame. You'll have to wait to see what I dig up."

"Looking forward to it," she smiled, while something inside her darkened.

William was an abomination, having twisted his divine depth into something vile. But still, she would care for him as a member of Pete's family, as she had countless others who'd walked through the hospital's doors. It was a place of immunity from the external world, with exception of justice for the patient, and William only seemed to do right by his cousin.

Outside, though. Outside was fair game.

*

Linnea ate dinner in the back room going over Gabby's documentation. She'd stuffed an unopened box of granola and a plastic bowl in her bag before leaving the house, right after she'd assembled a hodgepodge of apple slices, snap peas, nuts, and cheese to be eaten in the car on the way to work. To use the word *assembled* is perhaps a stretch, as she'd piled them together in a pie plate haphazardly, figuring the dish was wide and deep enough that she could reach blindly and drop freely without making a mess of herself.

As going over Gabby's work became monotonous, Linn started reading through Pete's History and Physical report again. She thought of William and his words, his scratches, the bracelet. With a few clicks she found Pete's address. Ten Magnolia Lane.

Her cell phone began to vibrate. Lars.

"Hi," she answered.

"Hey, you at work?"

"Yeah, but I'm in the back, it's fine. When are you coming over?"

"You need me to come over now?"

"No, but when can you come over without moving things around? I think…" she lowered her voice to a whisper. "A patient's family member has a bracelet like…" she sighed. "We need to talk in person. I'm getting a strong *may have been the one who offed the girl in the woods* vibe from him."

"Are you safe?"

"Yeah, I'm good, just preoccupied with my thoughts and… and a little curious maybe?"

"Channel it in the studio. Use it. Can you make it 'til Friday for a visit?"

"Yes! I'm doing a wine night. Come and stay over?"

"Wouldn't miss it. Is Alex going?"

Linn paused and shook her head, a little smile playing at her mouth. "Not bringing Teagan then?"

"I'm just feeling things out," he nearly laughed. "Might be a good night for her and I to make separate plans."

"You guys are so weird," she grinned.

"*You're* so weird. We're honest with each other, and we know what works for us. Sometimes that means getting a piece of something strange once in a while."

It had been like that since before they married, and likely why they'd agreed to marry, that and joint tax filing. While it was a lifestyle *way* outside Linnea's comfort zone, she respected his choice, and applauded his and Teagan's bravery and honesty in pursuing it together.

"Yeah, he'll be there."

"Did you run today?

"Sure did."

"I bet it felt great, too. Did you bring a stick?"

"Don't need a stick," she said, mouth curving into a small smile. "Met a guy in the woods. He's cute. We had coffee."

"Of course you met a guy in the woods," he said, and she knew he was smiling too. "Have you told Erik?"

"Ugh. I'm trying not to initiate interactions with him."

"Might help shut things down. So, what's Woods Guy all about?"

"Reminds me of Barny a little."

"Hairy? *Please* tell me he has a vestigial tail."

"He's quiet, dark eyes. A hunter."

"Deer?"

"Linn?" Allie said, her wide eyes peeking into the back room.

"Gotta go, Lars."

"K. See you Friday. Love you."

"Love you."

"Just a heads up," Allie said. "Dr. Grayer called to ask if you were on."

*

When her shift ended, Linnea lingered in the back room a moment after pulling a sweatshirt on, rereading the message on her phone.

Running again tomorrow?

Her phone had buzzed with his words while she gave report, and she'd been hearing his voice in her mind since, undecided on what to write back. She had Alex, Steph, and now *Gabby* coming over for brunch… She'd told Henry about her plans. Was he asking because he wanted to meet her on the trail? She could squeeze in a short run, but she actually had to make things before her friends came over…

"Wanna walk out together?" Gabby asked, catching Linnea with a goofy grin on her face.

"Yeah, let's go."

They found Erik waiting by the elevators with a grey hoodie over his scrubs. Linnea's stomach didn't sink upon seeing him, but her end-of-shift relief dissipated, replaced by the weighted sensation of having more work to do.

"Gabby, have you met Erik?"

"Dr. Grayer, yes," Gabby started, something star-struck in the way she spoke. "Well, only, we spoke on the phone once. Hi."

"Late night, huh?" He said, eyes lingering a moment on Gabby as he pushed the elevator button. "I kept popping over to see if I'd missed you. Didn't stick around, though," he continued, his voice lowering. "I didn't want you to see me and take the stairs instead…"

Linnea detached from his words, and typed a response to Henry.

Reluctantly skipping my time in the forest to bake… I'm not sure what yet. Are we still on for the afternoon?

"My fault," Gabby readily confessed with a blush as they entered the elevator. "It took me forever to finish documenting, then I was the last to give report with everyone."

"I'm sure Linny had her phone to keep her busy," he remarked.

Linnea thought it best not to respond, but she couldn't restrain her eyes from rolling.

"It's super thoughtful of you to walk us out, Dr. Grayer," Gabby said, turning to Linnea as the elevator doors opened. "Is that what's happening?"

"Yeah, that's what's happening," Linnea sighed.

Silence surrounded them, save for their footsteps in the empty hall until they'd just reached the exit, and Gabby gasped. Linnea turned to see the young nurse had stopped, eyes wide, mouth parted. Gabby pulled her hand from her pocket, and held up what looked like a stretchy spiral bracelet with a key dangling down from it. The PCA key. Each unit had only one, and they needed it to lock and secure machines that held large syringes of narcotics.

"You have to run it back up," Linnea said, thinking, *there's no way I'm going with you.*

Gabby groaned.

"Be thankful you didn't find it when you got home. See you Friday?"

"Yeah," she sighed, heading back down the hall. "I'll probably text you from a liquor store tomorrow."

"Wine night?" Erik asked, holding the door open as Linnea passed through.

She nodded.

"She should probably ask Steph," he chuckled, then paused before interrupting the silence again. "Hey, has Drew heard anything new about the woman from the woods?"

There was a cool mist in the air, soft but crisp, refreshing. If she'd been alone, it would have been quiet, like walking through a cloud.

"The FBI is doing their thing, apparently" she sighed, relieved at seeing how close they were to her car.

"Did he say anything else?"

"Like what?" She asked, hinting at a smile. "Like does he have any leads on a suspect?"

"Like when will it be safe for you to get out there and go running again, or have you thought about my offer?"

"Oh," she said, both of them turning in toward the driver's side of her vehicle. "It's fine, Erik. Thank you, but I'm good."

"Linny-"

"I've already been out, and if it helps you to sleep better, Drew told Steph it's not the kind of thing that would happen twice in the same location. So, the trail is safe," she said, tired, volume escalating. "I'm fine, and you can back off-"

"Linnea," a male voice interrupted. "Everything alright?"

She turned quickly to see a familiar face, hearing the footsteps she must not have noticed before as he approached.

"Oh, hey William," she said, too thankful for the relief from Erik's concentrated attention to be wary of what she suspected William was capable of. "Yeah, I'm fine. This is Dr. Grayer. He's an overnight colleague who offered to walk me to my car." Of course, she'd not needed, or *wanted* him too…

Erik narrowed his eyes in William's direction.

"Late night for you, huh William?" She continued. "Pete was okay when I left…"

"Charger," he said, holding up a long, thin cord. "I wasn't sure when I'd be in tomorrow, and he's much less likely to become anxious if his device is well charged. The one he's got in there now looked a little fragile. I won't wake him if he's asleep, and if he's awake…"

"If he's awake, they could use the help." Pete had a history of becoming anxious at night, disoriented. "Good thinking. Did you do any digging when you got home?" She smiled.

"I may have, but you'll have to wait until Wednesday."

"Fair enough. Just head in through the ER entrance. If they give you any trouble, ask them to call up."

"Will do. You have a good night, Linnea."

"You too."

As William walked toward the building, Linnea opened her car door, sliding a bit of her body behind it. With a parting glance toward a visibly irritated Erik, she said, "Have a good shift," and climbed in.

Ruffled and tired, she looked at her phone, smiling as it buzzed again.

Do you like kayaking?

10.

Berkshires, October 2014

White powder poured from the glass jar in Linnea's hand until she'd emptied it, and the tiny bowl on the scale was nearly three quarters full. She replaced the glass stopper, then poured from a second jar until the bowl had been adequately topped off. With dawn still hours away, and the moon offering no light from behind the earth's shadow, she'd needed the dull, golden hue of the desk lamp to illuminate her work. It didn't reach much farther, though, leaving the rest of the room like a cocoon around her, cozy and deep. She wrote the weight down and divided it in half to find the figure she'd use for weighing out the kaolin and Cornish stone. Once mixed, she added water, and the clay would soak for a day or two before she'd pour the slip into molds.

This work, it's in our history, Grandma Grace had told her more than once. *It's in our generations. Your ancestor, some eight grandmothers ago, was the first to add bone ash in a new way, making the porcelain strong, into something different.* She loved telling that story, wishing she'd known more. *It was a time when things could be written down, but so too could ink be spilled, and paper burned.*

Did William sit illuminated in some bespoke workshop with wooden desk and a magnifying lamp, toiling over what he'd salvaged from the masterpiece he'd had to leave behind? What he chose to do in the woods was abhorrent, there was no doubt in her heart, but she understood it. The difference between them, perhaps, was where grey became black. The coyote, West… they had drawn first blood and become fair game when Linnea had ushed life from their bodies and memorialized their remains. The women William wore on his wrist… there was an inherent wrongness to their ignorance of what had been expected of them, no choice on their behalf until the struggle for survival was thrust upon them.

He was a monster.

And was there any moral obligation on her behalf to… interfere? And what would that look like, exactly. Tracking him down? And then what? Watch him? The idea of challenging him to interact with *knowing* player on the gameboard did amuse, but… the grey came dangerously close to black for her, and while she thirsted for the next step, she'd find another way.

Linnea placed the two glass jars back on the shelf with the others, their little labels facing out to display not words, but the silhouettes of animals: a vole, an owl, a deer. With that done, she opened the small tin on her desk, and peered in at the tiny red leaf, feather, and dragonfly wing.

With a sigh, Linnea rolled her shoulders. She just had a few more things to do before heading out for some fresh air.

*

The sky was all ink and stars, but close to that time when a hint of something blue would blush beyond the black lace of the trees, cool light on the cusp of lifting secrets from the shadow draped over her garden. The chill in the air had left frost on the grass and fallen leaves, but Linnea remained warm where she sat beneath the grape vines on the pergola. In the sweatpants and knitted booties, wide-necked t-shirt, sweater, and blanket wrapped around her, she was well insulated.

The dawn chorus of summer had dwindled with the changing of the seasons, and so, while the sun reached for the horizon, Linnea's surroundings remained quiet. Autumn affected the cycles of animals, instincts driving behavior that they might not have a conscious awareness of, but remained subject to as if by compulsion. Birds nested in spring, mated in June… Deer in October… *But what of humans*, she thought. Humans were animals, yes, without tether to seasonal changes, driven by instinct, but also something more. *We're driven by pleasure*, she thought, *and the need to create, whether with our bodies or our minds. The timeline is of our own making, but the need is just as compelling.*

She thought of her work in the studio, of the clay in water, waiting, of how she sourced her materials. Using the remains of animals Cap had taken sufficed for supplementation, but Linnea needed more. She'd practiced with the bow all summer so he could take her out, so she could have a go at being the hunter, engaging with an animal that existed as part of the food chain, embedded with instinct, that would render the exchange fair.

She hoped it would be enough.

Her phone buzzed beneath the blanket, tucked in her apron pocket. Henry.

You awake?

A zing raced through her, cheeks aching, heart smiling somewhere in her chest. She hadn't been expecting to hear from him so early, from anyone for that matter, while the sun was still a whisper.

Yes.

She could have gone running with time to spare before dawn rose, had she left shortly after waking… The problem was with acceptable norms regarding when daytime started. After five o'clock, while perhaps early to most and still dark in autumn, was perceived as *morning*. Earlier than that, however, one ran the risk of triggering alarm. Were her car to be seen parked outside a trail entrance, someone might be tempted to phone-in the plates out of concern, cause a fuss.

Can I call you?

Yes.

The screen remained the same; the one word she'd written hanging beneath his question as if in open air. Her phone darkened, and then came to life.

"Hello?" She whispered, the device to her ear and her voice respectably low, as not to create too great a disturbance to the atmosphere.

"Linnea," he said, and she liked the way it sounded, her name in his voice.

"Hi, Henry."

"I'd hoped to get together later, but there's a work obligation I need to spend some time with this afternoon. Any chance you'd like an early coffee?"

It was possible. She could do a lot in an hour or two if she was industrious and kept things simple. She'd have at least that long until a coffee shop opened.

Linnea stood, holding the phone to one ear and securing her blanket with the other. She needed to preheat the oven while she decided, quickly, what to bake.

"How early?"

"Now?"

Now? She thought. *Is anything even open?* "Where were you thinking?" She asked, cutting through the kitchen and setting the blanket down in the living room.

"Your place. I don't want to impose, only offer what might be most convenient. I know you have friends coming. This would save you travel and transition time."

Linnea noticed the white noise surrounding Henry's voice, a rhythm to it.

"Are you driving?" The thought made her uneasy. Almost.

"Yeah," he said, chuckling a little under his breath. "I knew Smithfield, that your house has two garages, and is either next to or across from a farm… enough to point me in the right direction, but an address would be ideal. That and, with the sun being as low as it is, and us knowing each other being so new, I figured a call was necessary."

"Lipton Road," she breathed, feeling as though she were floating, carried by the momentum of the conversation, trusting she'd travel on their words until solid ground rose to her feet. "Twenty-seven."

The white noise changed; rhythm slower. "I'm just pulling over to put your address in my phone," he said. "I could have attempted without, but I'd rather spend the time drinking coffee with you, instead of wasting it in my truck looking for Lipton… Here we go. Oh," he paused. "I'm close."

"…How close?"

"Four minutes."

Linnea could almost see him wince through the phone. *Four minutes?*

"Okay," she started calmly, still standing in her living room for some reason. She was awake, and her house wasn't a disaster. "I just need to brush my teeth and throw some jeans on." *Should put some lights on as well.*

"I'll pull in the driveway and stay put until you give me a wave. Take your time… Three minutes," he added, a little laugh under his breath.

"Okay," she said, smiling bright.

Linnea heard the truck before she saw it; wheels slowing down, taking the turn, grinding on what dirt and small bits of rock had collected atop the asphalt over time. She came downstairs to the sound of his engine idling and wondered if Henry would still smell like the woods, or if that had been incidental when they'd first met with the length of a tree between them.

Seeing that he'd parked in the empty studio driveway, Linnea made her way through the dark hall and kitchen, opening the front door to a porch that spanned half the house.

The engine cut off as she stepped out, then she watched as Henry approached with a large, silver thermos in hand.

"I came prepared," his deep voice whispered as he came up the steps toward her.

A light flicked on over at Cap and Missy's. When Linnea turned, she saw Cap standing casually on his porch, mug in his hand. She smiled. He was checking up on her, what with a strange vehicle pulling in before dawn. Cap was an early riser, too, and he noticed things. One time he called over because she'd turned on more than one light in the house after coming home from work. He called first, but when she didn't pick up the phone, he came right over. She'd dropped a glass and cut her finger pretty deep. He cleaned up the glass in the kitchen, then disinfected, steri-stripped and derma bonded her wound, which they'd both agreed she would have been perfectly capable of doing, had she possessed a third functioning hand.

Cap nodded, then she gave him a wave. He nodded again, and headed back inside.

Henry hadn't missed the interaction, and Linnea hadn't missed his observation, that his face, however subtle the change, seemed to briefly express approval.

Henry brushed against her on his way into the kitchen. Then, when she turned after locking the door, she found herself nearly obstructed. He stood a little to the side, enough for her to know she had safe passage should she choose it, but she did not. Instead, she tilted her head upward, placed a palm to his chest.

She could have pushed, but she didn't.

The thermos hung down by his side as his other hand rose to her neck, making contact, gently, moving up so his thumb rested along her jaw. He glanced at her mouth, then to her eyes.

"I didn't want to wait. Though, we can still kiss when I leave, if that's alright?"

Linnea nodded, losing focus on the details of his darkened face as he leaned in further. His mouth against hers sent a flurry of electric sparkles melting though her chest, tingling down to her fingertips and toes.

Henry smiled against her lips, his beard against her cheek as he nuzzled down to her neck. He smelled like skin and fresh air, like the space between trees, not from scented soap, but from having been there.

"What a missed opportunity waiting would have been," she said, corners of her mouth curving upward.

Henry traced the wide collar of her t-shirt, her cloud-like sweater loose, and open.

"*Unknown Pleasures*," he said, somehow able to read the bottom of her T-shirt in the almost absent light from the window. He pulled back a little to look at her face, then tilted his head toward the darkened kitchen.

"You sure I didn't wake you up?" He asked with humor in his voice, his body still against hers.

"Shit. No," she said with a huff of laughter, stepping away to reach for a switch under one of the cabinets, activating an illuminating glow over the countertops. "I was outside when you called, then I just ran upstairs. I don't turn the lights on much."

"Is that an eco-thing?" He asked, all honesty and no judgment.

"No," she started reaching for a pair of mugs. She pulled down a rounded grey one for herself. Half the cup, including the handle, looked as though ink had exploded over it, like the vessel had been dipped in darkness. From this black came a small set of footprints terminating in the silhouette of a black cat. "I was afraid of the dark when I was little," she continued, and Henry set the thermos down as she went up on her toes to reach the second cup. "My Grandma Grace helped me get over it… Would you mind grabbing that one?" she asked, pointing to a mug with the top quarter a light blue-grey housing a small, full, white moon. The rest was matte black, save for a thin ring of white at the bottom, like snow. Similar to the bowl she often went to for soup, this cup had etchings, but it wasn't the outline of a coyote drawn in the clay or added as ash to the glaze, this vessel had evergreen trees.

Henry examined the mug as he pulled it from the shelf.

I'll tell you what," Linnea said, turning on the stove to heat the tea kettle. "Why don't I drink a cup of the coffee you brought, and you drink a cup of mine?"

"I won't insult your hospitality by saying no, so long as it doesn't put you out."

"No trouble, five minutes for the kettle, seven in the French press and it'll be done. Besides, my mom would kill me if she found out I had someone over for coffee and didn't offer. She gets these beans from Ecuador; we just refer to them as *the good beans*..."

"Wouldn't want to disappoint," he said, putting down the tree mug and picking up the one with the cat. "So, you were afraid of the dark?" He asked, examining her work.

"It started when I was four, not being afraid, but GG noticing. From then on, when I came to visit, she had me working with her in the studio at night... with the lights off."

Henry nodded, looking off to the side, toward a memory. "My dad had an anaphylactic allergy to aspirin. He went through a desensitization protocol in the hospital, and now he takes it every day. Routinely puts something into his body that had almost killed him once."

Linnea inhaled deep, sighed. "Yes..." she said, with a bit of a pause. "Very much like that. What do you take in your coffee?" She remembered he'd taken maple at Dee Dee's, but it seemed polite to ask.

"A little sweet, a little cream or milk."

"I have almond milk or cream."

"Almond."

"Sugar, maple syrup?"

"Oh, maple all the way," he said as she opened the fridge. "Do you work in the dark, here? Your artwork?" He asked.

Linnea nodded, leaning against the counter. "Sometimes. It depends what I'm working on, and how much of the moon is visible through the skylights in the studio."

"I'd like to see this place where you make things," he said. His voice couldn't have been more than a whisper, but it was loud enough to echo inside her. Henry's curiosity was palpable, almost a taste in her mouth.

Linnea's heart beat with more intensity as she scooped grounds into the press. Just as the kettle began to pucker its lips, Linnea turned off the heat and poured the steaming water.

"I can give you a tour while your coffee brews," she smiled, patting him on the arm. "Come on."

Passing through the studio door, Linnea's fingers had just reached the light switch when Henry's hand slid beneath hers, intercepting her intention.

"What light does this turn on?"

"The overheads," she said, gesturing with a nod to the ceiling. "But there's a lamp on my desk."

"I think we can make it."

And they did, with ambient light coming through the glass, there was enough silver among the shadows to see, though she could have navigated safely had it been absent entirely.

Down the steps and to the right, Henry's hand stayed on Linnea's hip as though *he* were guiding *her*.

"It's warm," he said, looking around as she transferred his hand to the back of the old couch. "A woodstove… and those?"

"Two kilns; I have a third outside, it's *huge*. I fired up the woodstove a few hours ago," she said, turning on the small desk lamp, his inhale discretely audible. "I mixed some clay for slip casting," she continued, gesturing to the bucket below the workbench. "That'll soak for a bit before I use it…"

"And this," he whispered, trancelike as he approached another table where the light barely reached.

"Paper," she replied as she came to stand beside him. Small rectangles of damp paper laid drying on a sheet of glass. "I blended the pulp earlier, a mix of paper towels, meaningful fibers…" Her eyes closed and she was at her desk, hours earlier, writing secrets on a napkin and dropping it in the water, then another she lit on fire above the surface, ash falling into the murky contents, to carry her intentions through the transformation. "I'll use it for a project. A book…" she trailed off as Henry turned, his hand grounding him to her body as it rested at her hip. His eyes bored into her, then slipped over her shoulder, and she guided him back to her desk.

He was hungry to explore the dark folds his eyes could not see, to feel where the light didn't reach. Linnea watched him, fascinated as he studied her through the objects she kept. The creases by his eyes flexed and deepened, his breath slow and steady, almost inaudible. If they'd been standing waist deep in water, very few ripples would have been made with what care he took in his movements.

When his attention seemed to catch, Linnea spoke a few words of explanation.

When his fingers hovered over a knob that would open one of the apothecary drawers, he turned his head toward her, eyes asking permission. And she nodded.

His thumb rested against the knob a moment, and as if there were nerves threaded in the wood, connecting to her somehow, Linnea felt the light pressure of his skin against hers.

He took hold, and slowly opened.

"Bits of glass Lars and I found over time while digging out back as children," she whispered.

He stared for a breath, then closed the drawer, opened another.

"Earrings," she said, then as he turned to look at her, Linnea nodded, and he reached in. "I've lost the matches to them, but they were each so special." Henry held one that looked like lichen carved into a teardrop. Henry rubbed the stone between his thumb and forefinger, then returned it, gently, to its home.

He opened another. A single prosthetic eye, glass reflecting what little light reached in, though not enough to discern the blue of the iris.

Henry paused, considered, closed the drawer… opened another.

"Honey bees," she whispered as he looked into a drawer about three quarters full with their little golden bodies. She had a whole jar of them on a nearby shelf, and another of their ash in the glass cabinet. "The Ostrowski's down the street, Marisol and Diane, they have hives…" She made honey pots for them to sell along with their jars at the farmer's market and the stand by their house.

"Sisters?" He asked.

"Married."

"I feel like I'm in a dream," he rumbled softly, tucking the bees back into their tomb. And he was right, in a sense. He was inside her while in that space, her dream.

The lamp on her desk illuminated his profile in shades of caramel against the blue light leaking in from outside.

"Coffee," she said, her words like breath, "to remind us we're awake."

11.

Berkshires, October 2014

Outside at the wooden table under the pergola, each with a blanket wrapped around them, Linnea and Henry watched the sun rise through the trees. She'd offered the dining or living room as alternatives, but he'd waved off her concern that he might get cold, reminding her that his mornings in the tree stand started early.

Linnea eyed the large kiln toward the back of the yard, the outdoor cook stove beside it, both covered by a roof. Her gaze drifted to where leaves rested on the ground, frosted edges glistening as shadow met light, crisp water not yet melted. Henry had given her a leaf when they'd met, they'd spent the morning together, she'd been in a *tree*... And then he'd come to her house in the dark, with a thermos... She sighed, taking a sip from her coffee, feeling warmth flood... her thoughts drifting further.

"The look on your face," Henry said, his voice drawing Linnea back to where they sat. "I don't know what thoughts are behind it, and I don't need to, they're yours to keep, but I'm thankful for them."

The air might have been cold, but Linnea was warm with his words, her memories, and the blanket wrapped around her. If her cheeks hadn't already been pink…

"I was thinking of when we met in the woods…" she said. "And when we kissed in the kitchen…"

Henry put down his cup and leaned forward, his eyes connecting with hers, expression sincere. "I'm not romantically involved with anyone else, nor do I plan to be; that's not how I do things," he started. His hand remained wrapped around his mug, thumb tapping at the side. "It feels like you're interested…"

"I'm interested," she smiled, cheeks aching. "And same, with seeing other people. That's not my thing either." Linnea took a long drink from her coffee, eyes still on Henry. "So, you want to spend more time together?"

He nodded.

Henry had called and come over because his work schedule had changed, but Linnea still didn't know what exactly he *did* for work.

"Somehow we've managed to cover what I do, the occupations of both our parents, and my grandparents," she observed, pausing to take another sip as she raised her eyebrows. "But what do *you* do?"

Linnea knew well that a person was more than their place of employment, that one could be many things, be *all* the things and wholly themselves, but work was part of that story.

"You want to know more about me," he smirked, making no effort to mute how pleased with himself he was.

"Yes, I do. I know you like good coffee, urinate from trees, and have a poor sense of your surroundings if you didn't notice me crunching my way around the woods," she teased. "And wouldn't the deer be deterred by you scenting the ground like that?"

"I don't know where to start," he chuckled. "First, there's nothing wrong with my hearing. I admit, though, I may have been distracted in the moment by my *process*... And the deer are curious, much like yourself..."

"And work?"

"Convallaria..." he said, pausing to look into his cup, then out to the trees.

"That sounds like a constellation, or an illness..." she said with a tilt of her head.

"Working for a constellation sounds intriguing," he started. "Convallaria is a risk management firm. Private sector and government contract work; logistics, consulting, and training, abroad and in the States.

"So, how do you help with the company's efforts to manage risk? HR department?"

Henry almost spit out his drink, clearing his throat after swallowing, followed by a full and satisfying laugh.

"Not everyone is cut out for Human Resources," Linnea shrugged with an exaggerated sigh.

"No, I have more of a senior leadership role."

"Suits?"

"Suits," Henry nodded. "Suits and clean hands."

"Cuff links?" She asked, using all her strength to keep a straight face.

"Cufflinks?" His eyebrows lifted.

"Hey, I wear functional pajamas to my job, and they're usually garnished with body fluid in some capacity by the time I get home. Allow me to indulge a little in this fantasy of what it must be like to dress-up for work."

"Cufflinks," he confirmed with a nod, then raised his wrist and pulled back on his sleeve, revealing a rugged, well-made watch. "And timepieces," he smiled, then readjusted his sleeve. "It's all a costume, though, isn't it… even the clean hands."

Linnea thought of the creases in her palms after working in the studio, sitting in the snow watching a truck catch fire, the acquisition of material left beneath her fingernails even after water, and soap...

Henry sighed; his thoughts having continued silently along as she'd had hers. "I suppose it's all part of who I am, whether I'm in a suit, or a shadow against a tree. I feel very much in my own skin, smiling while I shake hands with those who have no idea what's observing from behind the pressed shirt. Though, there have been times I've felt… *impatient*."

The id, she thought. *A beast best kept well fed.*

"My Grandma Grace would say, *Idle dog worry sheep*. Meaning, you need to keep the dog, or the wolf, busy, or it might start to look to the sheep for entertainment. She'd mention it when Lars and I were causing trouble, or when she told stories about my dad as a kid," she smiled. "But I think it very much applies to the parts of ourselves that become restless."

"And do you find yourself restless?" He asked.

Very.

"The balance between all the things I am, it's exactly that, a balance. There are times, though, when what might be considered my *hobby* creeps into my thoughts while I'm at work, creeps under my skin. Sometimes I become so focused on a project, or a concept for a piece that it just *haunts* me. And my mind, of course, is compelled in these pursuits, much preferring them to nurse-life." The need for more had been building, begging, left unanswered, but she was trying. There'd been a progression over time, footsteps on a path she couldn't see until her feet touched down. William's work in the woods had sent her on a wave of inspiration, and she just needed to hold on until the stone took its place beneath her foot. The next step would come.

"Ceramics is your hobby? Or maybe I should say art… I saw a lot more than clay in your studio. The space is large. Do you work with others?"

"No, not typically. I can't get deep into my work unless I'm alone. Well, that's not completely true, I suppose. I've worked with others around, like in classes, but I didn't have the same freedom I have when I'm working by myself. I do have friends over sometimes for wine and clay, but that's just for fun, no risk of depth there."

"So, if I wanted you to teach me how to make a bowl or something…"

"Oh, that I can do. I can instruct, churn out teacups all day, no problem. It's technical, and there is skill in that, but there's another side to art, to crafting something from raw materials, in sensing the story in the bones. Creating is meditative for me. It's personal, and private. I'd feel more exposed being observed while creating deep art than, say, if I were caught walking around the house in my underwear. I suppose I could try to tune a person out… no, if I knew they were there, I think I'd be too distracted."

"And if you didn't know they were there?"

Her eyes snapped to his, train of thought pushed outward to the background like a bubble surrounding them.

And if you didn't know they were there?

Some words carried darkness with them from their place of origin, and this, this was a dark question. Though they sat under a sky of powders, of dusty blue with a lemon sherbet haze seeping up from the horizon, Henry's voice carried the weight of shadows over them. And he sat still, patient, waiting for her to respond. Waiting for permission.

"When I'm hunting," Henry continued, saving Linnea from what her answer may have been. "It's very much about my state of mind while in pursuit, feeling my environment. There's a progressive heightening of awareness as time moves forward; sounds, smells… and then it's about my relationship with the animal. There's a transcendent intimacy in the ending of another being's life, and I don't think I'd feel as much if someone else were there. As you said, the technical aspects, I could give instruction, but it isn't the same."

The rapid pace of her heart seemed to fade from Linnea's mind as her muscles melted, as she relaxed into the feeling of being understood.

"I never considered…" she started, unable to picture Cap having an experience like that. Most likely he didn't. Lars, though…

"The hunt is primal," Henry continued. "And it takes as long as it needs to."

Linnea felt the change in him as he spoke, a part of her thrumming as she listened.

"Sometimes when I work," she said, "it's like a trance, and the idea of stopping before I'm finished is excruciating, like letting an itch go unscratched. Of course, so many projects take time to evolve, and what I've been working on becomes a persistent daydream I'm happily haunted by."

"Mmm," he rumbled in agreement. "The overlay of another reality-"

A soft sound progressed toward them from beyond the yard, footsteps on leaves and grass wet with dew and frost.

"Hello," a familiar female voice called out, then Missy appeared under the arch of honeysuckle. She stood a moment beneath the mass of green leaves and several persistent blooms not ready to give way to the cold. She held something in her hands.

"Hey Missy," Linnea smiled as her neighbor set her offerings on the table. "This is Henry. Henry, this is Missy from next door."

"Good morning, Ma'am."

"Nice to meet you Henry, but I'm not staying," Missy started, and Linnea thought for sure the woman was going to wink at her. "Cap said you had *company*, so when I heard the back door and some voices out here, I thought I'd bring some treats over. Cap should be coming along... So, anyways, I baked pumpkin bread earlier this morning," she said as Linnea rested a hand on the form wrapped in a tea towel, fragrant with spice and still warm. "The recipe makes two loaves, and we'd risk wasting it or gorging ourselves if we'd kept both. And here's some bacon," she continued, tapping the plate she'd set down with a generous stack of crisp meat piled in the center. "Because who doesn't love bacon."

"I know I do," came Cap's voice as he appeared with a mug in hand. "Especially with my coffee.

"And you had some with your first cup hours ago," Missy said playfully. Then to Linnea and Henry she added, "We're both early risers, though I don't know how he does it when he stays up past midnight. I'm in bed by eight thirty these days."

"The second cup helps," Cap smiled, raising his mug to take a sip.

"You missed introductions," Missy said. "This is Linnea's friend Henry. Henry, this is my husband, Cap. Retired navy, semi-retired farmer."

"Fully retired, and able to speak for himself…" Cap smiled, and planted a kiss on Missy's cheek.

"Didn't you mention yesterday that you'd been in the military?" Linnea asked Henry. He hadn't said what branch, though. They'd been in the bed of his truck, and he'd mentioned it briefly before the subject had changed.

"Yes," he nodded with a smile. "Though it might disappoint you to hear it was the army I served in. Love the water, but couldn't risk getting stuck living on a boat. Settled into special forces for a bit, did a little government work after that."

Linnea broke a strip of bacon in half, holding one piece waiting while she worked on the other, wondering for a moment what *government work* meant. The town clerk could say they did government work, same as someone employed by the department of agriculture.

"I was in a tree at the time," Henry laughed when Cap asked where they'd met. Linnea joined in, and the story rolled off both their tongues, Cap listening as their smiles grew warmer.

"I promised Missy I'd never get up in a stand," Cap said. "Wouldn't mind reading a book up there while I wait for the deer to come around, but I've done alright on the ground. I haven't hunted bow in, this'd make fourteen years this season, but that's from the arthritis."

"Have you tried crossbow?"

"I've thought about it, but, and don't tell my wife because I'll get an earful, but it can be hard starting new things."

Missy rolled her eyes.

"I'd be more than happy to bring one over. Probably won't get you out this season, but you can see if it's the right fit and get your paperwork in order for next year."

"That sounds like fun," Cap smiled. "We could do some target shooting in the back here or over on my side. What are you two doing later on?

"I have a couple friends coming over for brunch at ten," Linnea started. "The pumpkin bread means one less thing I'll need to whip up. I'm not sure how long Henry is sticking around, he has work…" she said, eyeing him.

"Depends… How many aprons do you have?"

She smiled, pausing long enough that it was Cap who spoke next.

"We'll leave you to it, then." Cap started, then he turned to Henry. "Have Linn get in touch, or you can just come around next time you're over. I'm looking forward to that crossbow lesson."

*

"I'm disappointed our afternoon was cancelled, but I can't complain about how the morning started," Henry said, leaning against the counter in Linnea's spare apron.

"Same," she smiled, pulling a pan of shortbread out of the oven. "This morning was unexpected, just like meeting you, and I'm into it. The woods, the kiss hello, the baking assist," she went on, flourishing her hand toward him, highlighting his apparel. "The list is not all inclusive, obviously."

"Mmm," he smiled. "I could add to it, but it would be like naming grains of sand, and would take up more time than I'd care to… What are you doing tomorrow?"

Linnea's phone buzzed on the counter, buzzed again, a call not a text. She eyed the screen, planning to ignore it, but it was her mom…

"Hey, what's up?" She answered.

"Do you have Grace's cookie molds for Halloween? You know, the fancy ones for the teacake recipe, the ones that look like carved cameo brooches-"

"The skeleton ones? We used those for last year. I didn't leave them at your house?"

"I can't find them. I've got bats, black cats…"

"That we never use because no one wants to bite into a layer of black icing at a party. I'll look, just… hold on a sec."

Linnea opened the cabinet above the stove, went up on her tiptoes, then turned to Henry.

"Can you reach up there?" she asked.

He raised his hand to demonstrate that he could touch the ceiling if she needed him to. Of *course* he could reach, but there were at least seven freezer bags of cookie decorating paraphernalia up there.

"Never mind," she said, rubbing his shoulder briskly.

She put the phone on speaker and placed it on the counter.

"Who were you talking to, Linn? Is that Alex?"

"Oh my god, Mom…" Linnea sighed, lifting a knee onto the warm, glass-top stove and climbing up. "*No.* His name is Henry. He's a friend who came over for coffee this morning, and you're on speaker, so don't be weird."

She pulled out two bags, glanced at the contents, then put them down on the stove and reached in for another.

"Well, I wasn't *planning* on being weird… But *now…*"

"Mom!"

Henry didn't say a word, but his breath vibrated with suppressed laughter behind her.

Linnea smiled, in part from hearing Henry's joy, but also because the third bag had the cookie molds.

"Did you use the good beans?" her mother asked.

Linnea turned to see Henry grinning, his arms coming out to assist her in getting down from the stovetop.

"The Ecuadorian coffee was wonderful, Ma'am," he said, turning his head toward the phone while keeping one arm around Linnea. "I'm thankful for the opportunity to have tried it."

"I'm so glad you enjoyed it! Don and I stock up whenever we go down. Linn, send him home with some. And please, Henry, call me Viv."

"Simmer down, Mom. Henry and I will come to our own arrangement as far as the beans are concerned. And I found the cookie molds."

"Excellent. Before I let you go, I need to know what weekend you're coming out for the Orphans, and if it's just you coming out…"

Henry raised an eyebrow, though she wasn't sure if it was due to the unexplained mention of orphans, or the comment about Linnea potentially bringing someone with her.

"I'm taking you off speaker," she said, picking up the phone.

"No, you enjoy your company. Just call me later. I need dates."

"Okay. Love you, Mom."

"Love you too, Hon."

Linnea put the phone down on the counter and smiled. "So, that was my *mom*."

Henry stood close, silent, then raised his eyebrows. "Orphans?"

"Yeah," she sighed. "There'd be something wrong if you didn't ask about that. The Gold Dust Orphans are a theatrical group that put on a few plays throughout the year in Boston. They're amazing. My parents try to see every one of their productions, but since I moved out here, I've just been making it to the Christmas shows. This year they're doing *Jesus Christ, it's Christmas!* Last year was *It's a Horrible Life.* They're adaptations of plays or films, musicals, have local humor. There's always drag, full frontal if you're lucky. The production quality is outstanding."

"And your mother asked how many tickets."

"She did," Linnea blushed.

"She thinks you might ask me to go."

"Yes, I believe that's the direction that was headed in."

"I'd like to join, but I don't think you should decide now. Later, if you're comfortable. Don't worry about dates. If you get me a ticket, I'll make time."

Linnea's phone buzzed on the counter, nearly stopping her heart. She reached over and glanced at the screen.

Call me when he leaves and tell me EVERYTHING. Love you.

Henry placed a hand on her hip as he followed her into the dining room to set the table. Once a tablecloth, runner, and placemats were down, Linnea began passing him china. With a stack of four saucers in hand, she turned to see him still holding two of the teacups.

"Each one is unique, but so obviously related," he said, examining the details.

"I painted a black cat into each of the animal cups in that set. She's meant to be in the background, but it's her story, really."

Henry's body seemed not to move, only his gaze flicking upward from Linnea's work to her eyes. "You made these," he said without surprise, but a sense of awe in his voice.

Linnea nodded.

"They're perfect," he said, holding one up to the light to see his fingers in silhouette through the wall of the cup. "So thin… *delicate*."

"Quite resilient, actually. The bone gives them strength, glasslike beauty, and translucency."

"Bone?"

"Yes. *Bone* china. Bovine bone ash is commercially available, but you can buy the clay mixture premade. I prefer to create my own: fifty percent bone ash, then a quarter each of kaolin clay and Cornish stone."

"You use bone ash from cows?" He asked, his eyes clever and his body still with palpable curiosity, like Barny, observing from the shadows.

"Only when I practice," she said, offering a taste of truth.

"These weren't practice," he said, cups still in his hands.

"No."

They held each other's eyes a moment, until his gaze drifted up to the molding above the doorway beside her. Small items were nestled there, like the treasures in her apothecary drawers, but his eyes settled on something larger, out in the open, left to breathe.

"Did you make those too?" He asked, nodding to the three pear-shaped clay sculptures at the center of the passage to the living room.

"Oh," she said. "No, those are tsa tsas from a trip my brother took to Bhutan…"

His eyebrows lifted slightly.

"He travels on medical missions with my parents, usually to Ecuador, but Bhutan was a special site visit. It's a long story, but he brought back the two on the left."

"And the third one?"

Linnea paused for a breath, remembering how her hands had worked the moistened dirt, clay, and ash, what she'd written…. "That one I made."

12.

Berkshires, October 2014

"Oh my *goodness*," Gabby gasped, eyes wide as she looked over the tea service laid out on Linnea's dining room table. Four seats had been set, each with a plate, silverware, teacup and saucer. A teapot, sugar bowl, milk, honey, and maple were all housed in works of fine china, and then there was the rest...

Linnea integrated Gabby's biscotti amongst the shortbread on a three-tiered stand beside a generous bouquet of bacon standing ready in a tumbler, Missy's pumpkin bread, and a bowl of berries. Linnea liked to play down the effort, but it was rather elegant looking.

As Gabby went on about the table-scaping, Linnea observed her guest's clothes, having only seen the young woman in scrubs thus far. She wore a bright pink knee-length skirt and a green sweater, hair pulled back into a ponytail with some wrapped around the elastic, as if the hair held itself. Linnea smiled, seeing that the ensemble bore the likeness of an upside-down tulip. In contrast, Linnea wore a blue silk camisole and wool trousers in deep brown that fit snug from her waist through her hips then stayed wide down to the floor.

"I love those pants on you," Alex said as he came in from the kitchen with the tiny sandwiches he'd brought, beautifully arranged on a three-tiered stand. "I want to say they make your ass look good," he continued, "but we both know it's not the pants."

"Ohhhh, a *bunny*," Gabby cooed at the cup in her hands. The wash of grey and black watercolor formed a rabbit peacefully standing in a field while, on the other side, a black cat sat patiently in the distance. Barny had looked absolutely vicious with pride when she'd sauntered over and dropped the limp creature at Linn's feet. Rabbits were rare among Barny's offerings.

"And my name is on this little tag. I get the bunny?" Gabby asked excitedly. Looking to Alex and Steph, who'd already poured hot water into their cups, she asked, "Did you guys get bunnies too?"

The whole of the tea service had the same theme of backyard creatures in a serene moment before the wildlife turned prey to Barny's instincts.

"Snake," Alex replied from where he sat.

"Birds," Steph smiled, reaching for the shortbread. Steph had her brown and auburn hair pulled over one shoulder, black shirt, dark jeans, and a long, leopard print duster. Steph loved that sweater, frequently describing it as her *fancy robe*. "We get the same ones every time. I asked Alex if he wanted to switch once, but neither one of us was really into it."

There were only so many teacups to choose from, but the animals suited her friends, Alex a snake, clever, graceful and venomous. Steph, like a bird, made her own path when she flew, tending her nest upon return. Eyes that didn't miss anything.

Gabby looked to Linnea, the question obvious, but Linnea waited, reached for the teapot and poured.

"What's on yours, Linn?" Gabby asked. "Butterflies?"

Linnea's lip curved into a little smirk, but only just. "No, no insects in this set."

"You stick around until spring though," Alex said, gesturing to the center of the table with a piece of bacon. "She's got a whole spread like this but with dragonflies, butterflies, ladybugs and grasshoppers, all that. There's a mouse cup with this set, but your girl doesn't drink from that one," he smiled.

The kitchen door opened in the distance, and everyone at the table paused, looking to Linn for answers.

"Am I late," a male voice called out. Lars. *Lars.*

Alex blanched, then flushed as Linn sprang from her seat.

"You said Wednesday!" she shouted, bursting into the kitchen and barreling into her brother with open arms.

His curly hair was cut short, face clean shaven, and his arms were solid beneath his blazer, sweater, and collared shirt. Linn stood back, making a show of squeezing his bicep.

"You're not juicing are you…" She teased.

He snorted and rolled his eyes. "I knew you were off, so I thought I'd come early."

"You're the fucking best, Lars," she sighed, then whispered, "Steph and Alex are in the dining room, and Gabby, she's a nurse I'm training. The table's set for four, but I'll make you a place."

"Just don't make a *fuss*," he said, grabbing a mug from the cabinet, then following her into the dining room.

"Guys, my brother, Lars," she said, pulling up a chair, as he took a plate from the cabinet.

"Nice to see you again Alex, Steph." His eyes lingered on Alex a slow moment before turning to the guest he didn't know. "Gabby, is it?" She nodded with glowing enthusiasm. "Don't let me interrupt," he continued, pouring himself a cup of tea and selecting a slice of bacon.

"We were just discussing our teacups," Alex offered. "Linn was explaining why she doesn't have a little creature on hers."

"I just have a preference…" she said, lifting her teacup, slowly turning it for Gabby to see. Black started at the rim and seeped down like ink in water, leaving the bottom third white as powdered bone. Nestled in the darkness was a waxing crescent moon, lined in gold. "It's a night scene," she said. I only made two… "

"I have the other," Lars winked.

"You *made* these," Gabby gushed, marveling at the teapot as she finally poured herself some hot water.

Linnea tilted her head to the side and nodded.

"She even made the clay" Lars said.

"You can *make* clay?" Gabby squinted. "I don't know anything about pottery, but I thought clay gets dug up, like dirt. Isn't it a special kind of river-dirt or something? How do you *make* it?"

"This type of clay, china, has a specific composition: Kaolin clay, Cornish stone, etcetera. Instead of buying ready-made clay, I acquire the components, and prepare it myself."

"Wow," Gabby said, taking a shortbread from one of the stands. "Are you working on anything now?"

"I am…" Linnea sighed. "The project is, well it's both conceptual and functional, like the tea service here," she said with a nod toward the table. "It's a bit to do with the idea of hunting, of sustenance, what the act of hunting provides, what it means to be sustained. I'm incredibly enthusiastic about the *concept*, but I'm a little underwhelmed with where I'm at… It's been rather slow going, which can be rewarding during the moments when I'm immersed in the studio, or excruciating, but," she paused, choosing her words as she picked up the teapot. Steaming liquid heated both her cup and its story, lighting a fire somewhere inside her that smelled like blood and remorseless clarity.

"What do you need?" Lars asked, and for a moment, it felt like just the two of them.

"I don't know," she said honestly. "I'm in a moment of inspiration, I just, I need a little something more, but I don't yet know what it is. Sourcing materials for the clay is part of the process," she added, turning back to Gabby. "It can be challenging. If I were passionate about creating my own paint, for example, harvesting my own cochineal beetles and Kermes insects for crimson… these things take time." The deer would be a milestone if she could manage it. That *had* to be it. It certainly wouldn't be anything to do with William.

Linnea's thoughts were drifting into her words like water, massive, threatening depth and porosity. Gabby's unsure expression was not unexpected, nor was the amusement Alex wore.

"Again, I'm not a pottery person," Gabby recovered with diplomacy, "but Linn, this is, this is like, *professional* quality. Like this could be in a museum gift shop, or at some fancy Downton Abbey event at an Estate."

Alex's smile radiated, matching Lars's as he put his hand on Linnea's shoulder. "Linn is under no obligation to get commercial with her creations… And I don't mind her being a well-kept secret, because I'm first in line for a commissioned tea set."

Linnea tilted her head down, giving him the eye, a little smile. "Someone would have their tea set already, if they could decide what they wanted me to paint on it."

"Motion to change the subject," Alex called out as he dropped a sugar cube in his cup.

"Second," Linnea said.

"Approved," Steph added, taking a bite of bacon. "This is so good."

"I can't take credit for the bacon or the pumpkin bread…" Linnea started. "My neighbor Missy brought them over this morning. I couldn't serve it to guests without trying some first, though… That's why there was a bit of the bread missing."

"That is a large chunk that's gone …" Alex said from behind his tea, painted snake slithering out from beneath his fingers.

"Henry was over, so I had help eating…"

"The woods guy?" Lars grinned.

Alex closed his eyes and swallowed, exhaling slowly as he placed his cup down on its saucer. "Ladies, take a moment to thank the deity of your choice that you are not wearing my tea, because I almost just spit it out. Girl. *Girl.* He stayed for breakfast… I might need you to open the door a crack, Steph, because it is heating up in here."

"Sleepover status?" Lars teased.

"He didn't *stay* for breakfast so much as he came over for breakfast, and it wasn't even breakfast."

"… This is the best brunch we've ever had." Alex sighed.

"Facts," Steph said, laying a hand down on the table.

Gabby's cheeks were nearly pink, eyes wide, expression like she suspected the conversation was stumbling into a place she wouldn't have been invited to under other circumstances, but she was happy to be there.

"Well, it was for coffee, really," Linnea started, trying to balance her joy for having had the experience and her protective urge to give as little as possible. "Then Missy brought the bread and bacon."

"We thank you for not eating all the bacon," Lars said, crunching into another piece.

"Indeed," Alex nodded. "And we would also thank you to circle back to the man you had in your home this morning. Start at the beginning, and please include as many details as you're willing to offer. I can't speak for Lars, or young Gabby here, but Steph and I need this…"

"We do," Steph confirmed with dignity, reaching for a sandwich.

The idea of recounting her time with Henry that morning, the whole of it, seemed too intimate, not because Lars was there, but more so with Gabby present. If she'd been alone with Alex, Steph, or her brother, it would be sharing, her words cradled and kept once passed. With too many ears, Linnea felt rather like she'd be giving a performance, to be consumed with absent-minded greed like theater popcorn. Linnea would decide who she would become food for, and it certainly wouldn't be Gabby…

"He texted first, to see if I was up," she began.

"Which you were," Lars said.

"Obviously," she smiled. "Then he asked if he could call, and did I want to get coffee… We'd had plans for later today, but he had a thing with work come up in the afternoon. I had our brunch mid-morning, and he didn't want to miss an opportunity to get together, so he asked if I wanted to get coffee *early*…" Linnea continued, slowly pulling back, reducing the encounter to bullet points.

As she paused to take a few bites, Alex inhaled dramatically, on the verge of an inevitable request for a more colorful account of the moments just prior to Henry's departure. Linnea had no desire for divulging more than what she'd given, though, especially not at that table, in the open, with others.

"Alex," Lars said. "Did you make these cucumber sandwiches?

"I did."

"They're deliciously refreshing."

Alex leaned into his chair, smoothed an eyebrow with his ring finger, and turned to Gabby. "Go on and try one, Gabs. I won't let the praise go to my head."

"Well, this is my first cucumber sandwich experience, so I have no comparison, but it's delicious," she smiled wide, white teeth on display. "Speaking of delicious… What's up with Dr. Grayer… Like, what's his *deal*?"

"Erik Grayer is an arrogant *tool*, and a mediocre surgeon," Lars said flatly before sipping from his mug.

"Let me tell you a little bit about Dr. Grayer," Steph started. Holding up a thumb, she said, "He likes skiing," then adding her forefinger, "he likes anything to do with the *history* of bourbon… What else?"

"Dabbles in indoor gardening," Lars nodded.

"I told you about that?" Linnea smiled. "Of course I did. Yeah, he has a whole setup."

"Right," Steph said, adding her middle finger to the tally. "Dabbles in indoor gardening, and then there's the home gym."

"That man stays in shape," Alex chimed in.

"He does stay in shape," Lars agreed. "One does have to excel at something…"

"Gabby," Alex continued. "You were not wrong in your use of the word *delicious*. Physical observation only. Go ahead, Steph."

"That's four things he likes," Steph continued, now holding out four fingers with her thumb tucked in. "I was hoping to hit five… Oh, I've got one: Dr. Grayer likes to think he and Linn will get back together, so he *accidentally* runs into her at the grocery store, like, three times a month, no matter how random she tries to make her shopping schedule."

"He stopped going to the coffee shop, though," Alex added.

"No, *I* stopped going to the coffee shop…" Linnea shot back with a laugh, enjoying where Steph had ended up with her list. She'd known there would be a punch line, and Steph had hit the nail on the head. "For all I know he's still sitting there every morning, waiting to see if I'll show up."

"Was he there when you went with Henry?" Steph asked.

Linn shook her head. "Not that I saw."

"So, you guys dated?" Gabby asked.

"Yes," Linnea said. "For less than a year. Nine months, maybe, depending on what one considers a start date."

"Or an end date," Lars said with a tilt of his head.

"Why did you break up?"

"You heard the part about his stalky tendencies?" Alex said with raised brows.

"Yeah, but that was *after*," Gabby countered.

"It wasn't one thing, really," Linnea said. "He began to express a desire for me to move in with him, but on my end…" The relationship had started to feel like a coat she just couldn't get her arms out of. "I didn't have those feelings, and suspected I never would. We ended things last winter after-"

"Winter?" Alex asked playfully.

Lars cleared his throat, but Linn knew perfectly well there was nothing in there.

"There was a transition period that ran into spring…" she amended. They'd had some sporadic interludes… Then he'd made it clear he wanted to get back together, and she'd made it clear she'd stop interluding with him if he couldn't handle it. "I haven't seen him outside of work *intentionally* since May, though he's started asking to talk…"

"Don't you dare," Steph started.

"Oh, I don't plan to. No communication outside of work."

"Thank god," Steph sighed, then, with a grin, she said, "Speaking of work, what does Henry do?"

"Oh, he told me this morning. Some risk management firm, but I'm not one hundred percent on what that means."

"Like finance?" Gabby asked.

"Right?" Linnea said. "That's what I thought too, but it doesn't seem to fit. Though, he did mention wearing suits to work."

Alex tilted his head. "Public relations?"

"I honestly don't know more than what I told you. The conversation drifted a bit before we got into what he does, though we established that he *doesn't* work in HR," she smiled. "He told me the name of his company. It made me think of a constellation or something… Tip of my tongue… Calvarium? No, that's the top of the skull… Convallaria," she smiled. "I think that was it."

Lars popped a blueberry into his mouth. "We need to do research."

"*Immediately,*" Lars agreed.

"I'm on it," Steph said, phone already in hand. "Okay, Its bringing up flowers, what the hell is this… Flowers, *more* flowers… Okay, here. Webpage is sophisticated, dark with a clean look." She paused speaking, then began whispering fragments of content as her eyes scanned the screen. "… *global risk management services… logistics, intelligence, security… infrastructure… experience… to anticipate, prevent, and adapt… tactical-* Wait, *what* did he say he does?"

"Risk management. I assumed it was some consulting service…" Linnea said, glancing over at Lars, then back to Steph. "Maybe finance."

"This does *not* present like a finance company, Linn." Steph looked up from her phone and into Linnea's eyes. "This looks like it might be some kind of private military situation."

"Yikes," Gabby cringed.

"Yikes?" Lars said, eying Gabby.

Alex put down his shortbread and turned his focus on Gabby. "I love a man in uniform. And I challenge you ladies to tell me you don't look for excuses to run into the firefighters when that alarm goes off. Know your truth, girls."

Gabby flexed an uneasy smile that quickly fell. "There was a man in the woods where a murder happened," she started, glancing around the table, settling on Linnea. "It's not the military work that leaves a bad taste in my mouth, it's that he wasn't truthful about it. Like he's keeping things from you. I mean, *risk management*… His company isn't exactly finance, is it?"

Linnea soured at the overreach, the *intrusion*. Gabby's commentary came from a place of concern most likely, but it also felt incendiary.

"He never said it was finance," Linnea started, not defensively, but with assertion, like a wave forming. "And of *course* he's keeping things from me, Gabby, as I keep things from him. I've known Henry fewer days than I have fingers on one hand, and there's only so much of one's life that can be revealed at a time. This unfolding of each other, it's part of meeting someone, petals opening of their own accord, not under forced interrogation." She closed her eyes a moment. "Depth too vast for echoes to sound, and yet intimate... A world in a drop of water," she sighed, reluctantly opening her eyes, a different kind of waking.

"There she *is*, "Alex started with enthusiasm.

"That's my sister," Lars preened.

"Linnea, you magnificent fucking songstress," Alex continued. "I love when you come out. It's like a waterfall of poetry just flowing out of your face and all over my body." He gestured with undulating fingers in front of his face and down his chest. "Showering over me, girl. Steph, I know you felt that. Gabs?"

Gabby nodded, mortification dissipating.

"Oh, I felt it," Steph said, tilting her head as she picked up a sandwich.

"I didn't mean to offend you, Linn," Gabby started uncomfortably.

"I know," she said. "I appreciate your opinion and your honesty, and while I don't think you meant to be offensive, I think you meant to stir something. The honesty was good, the stirring, not so much. And I did wax poetic a bit," she added. Reaching for the teapot, she glanced up at Gabby again. "More tea?"

"Sure," Gabby nodded, hesitantly loosening a bit.

Linnea poured until the pot was empty, filling the cup about halfway. "Well, that's not nearly enough," she said with a smile. "Why don't you guys start telling Gabby about wine night while I put the kettle back on."

"Oh, *hell* yes," Alex started. "Do you like to get your hands dirty, Gabs?"

Their conversation flowed through the hall and into the kitchen as Linnea flipped on the kettle and used the bathroom. When she returned to the dining room with a refreshed teapot, Steph had already breezed through all the ceramics-related activities to preach about the wine aspect of wine night. She was using words like vintage, body, and *fruit forward*…

"Just bring what you like," Linnea said with a smile, filling Gabby's cup the rest of the way. "You drinking this time, Steph?"

"I *think* so," she grinned. "I might be able to get Drew to pick me up if my mother-in-law is over. Oh," she went on, her lips falling as she continued. "He told me some of the details… from that girl's body."

"The one from the woods?" Lars asked.

Alex raised his eyebrows. "Steph, you've been sitting here eating bacon and drinking tea from a china cup like you don't have a dirty little bomb about to explode? Spill. It."

"I didn't know if it was the right time!" Steph flushed. "Everything was bunnies, clay, and *Henry*. Then I thought, you know, mixed company…" she shrugged, gesturing around the table, lingering on Lars and Gabby.

"Spill," Lars said, echoing Alex.

Steph sighed, tilted her head back to shake the brown and auburn strands away from her face. "So, the woman, the *victim*, she wasn't beaten up, or bludgeoned. It's not like she got hit on the head or anything, neck didn't look banged up. She'd had some of her hair cut, like from the back underneath, but not messy." Steph paused a moment. "Part of her bra was removed, like over the nipple, but her nipples were fine. And her underwear," she said, scrunching up her nose. "The crotch was, like, *cut out*."

Exactly as Linnea recalled, though she'd not noticed the hair, though it had been fanned out over her shoulders and upward, like it had been reaching for the absent sun.

Gabby cringed. "She wasn't…"

Steph shook her head, "Doesn't look like anything *internal* happened. But the weirdest thing is, they found an object in her mouth. They thought it was a stone at first, but then they analyzed it or whatever… Guys, it was whale vomit."

Alex held up a hand and closed his eyes.

Linnea casually picked up the teapot, refilling her cup. "I think I speak for all of us," she started, "when I say this detail has taken us in a direction not anticipated."

She'd known something had been in there…

Alex lowered his hand and pursed his lips, nodding as he opened his eyes.

"Drew explained a little, but I did some research too," Steph went on. "Apparently this stuff, ambergris, had been used historically in potions and medicines, but it's also an ingredient in really high-end perfume, even today. And while it sounds like it should be liquid, it's not. People find it on the beach, these little, waxy rocks, sometimes big chunks too. And it's *expensive*."

"Why would he put that in there?" Gabby asked, face contorted like she'd smelled something foul.

"We don't *know* it was a man," Linnea said, sipping her tea about halfway down.

"Please…" Alex huffed, rolling his eyes. "It was a man."

"Drew said these kinds of killers either do things to send a message to the people who find the body," Steph continued. "Or, as part of a fantasy…"

"The things her killer took," Linnea began, catching Lars's eyes, the depth between them. "Think of them like souvenirs, but a little more than that I suppose… They're kept to remember more than a place, but an experience, and a product."

"Drew used the word *trophy*," Steph said. "Not like a gold medal so much as what a hunter might have mounted on their wall."

"Mmmm," Lars hummed, lifting the corner of her lip with understanding.

Linn's eyes flicked down to the cup in her hand, her thumb moving over the waxing crescent moon, toward the darkness. More than a memento, but something earned by blood, sweat, tears, and *grit*. A trophy.

"That's exactly what it is, isn't it," Linn said softly. "A piece of the demon slayed worn suspended from one's neck. A bear claw, a shark's tooth, a head on the wall or a rug on the floor," she continued, bringing the cup to her lips. "That whale-stone in the woman's mouth, though… that was left because it belonged there."

Lars remained silent, but his eyes widened a bit with delight.

"He felt she needed that nugget of whale vomit in her mouth?" Steph questioned. "That's so fucked up. What can that even mean? That she was sick and he needed to ancient-medicine her? He *killed* her. What's the point of healing her if he killed her?"

"Art isn't always literal," Linnea shrugged. "It means something to someone, though… enough to have put it there. Didn't you say the FBI was involved now?"

Steph nodded. "Apparently what this girl had done to her is similar to some things they've seen before, that it might be the same guy, or, *person*," she added with a glance toward Alex.

"Thank you," Alex nodded. "Women have fought too hard not to be given equal consideration, even with creepy woodland murders."

"I can't believe something like this has happened before," Gabby said absently as she picked over the shortbread.

"Oh, you *better* believe it," Alex started. "Shit like this happens every day. There's some strange people out there, and sooner or later they all get sick. Then *we* end up with them."

How true, Linnea thought, picturing William in his blazer and glasses at his laptop, his bashful reverence when talking about his bracelets…

After Steph and Gabby left, Lars lingered in the mudroom with Alex before the door finally closed.

Her brother sauntered back in, sloughing off the remains of his careless flirtation as he advanced, and said, "Tell me everything."

13.

Berkshires, October 2014

A log snapped in the fire pit, the rhythmic crackle soothing, having long since lulled them beyond the boundaries of sunlit conversation.

"To clarify," Lars started. "You suspect him because of the scratches, the pink on his *special times* bracelet… You could run it by Drew, but if you're not comfortable with that, the FBI takes anonymous tips, don't they?"

"Right, I'll just call and tell them, anonymously, that I was the woman who found the body, and because I'm so good at matching color swatches, I think my patient's cousin has been crafting with women's underwear."

"It's got you all hopped up, that's for sure. Is it just the scratches and the bracelet?"

Linn rolled her eyes. "You'd have to just, you'd need to have been there, gotten a sense of this guy. Gardening is a metaphor to him, and he delights in flaunting his secret, part of him hoping someone will bite, see how clever he is."

"Is that what you need?"

"To be seen?" she asked.

Lars nodded.

"You see me."

"I always have, but it's healthy to want that… with someone else."

She thought of Henry, quiet as they walked in the woods, dimples when he smiled, their kiss hello in the kitchen, his face and fingers as they explored in her studio.

"Wait, do you think I want *William* to see me?"

"He left that woman for you in the woods, and provided you with quite the inspiration."

"Lars, he's a *monster*, and that woman wasn't mine. I don't even think she was his, which makes the whole thing so abhorrent."

She paused and he waited, watching her think, knowing something was growing worth patience.

"I've thought…" she continued. "I've wanted to be Barny, with my work. The one hunting. I'm supposed to go out with Cap, and I thought for a minute, maybe William…"

"Like be his helper, do the elf work?" He grinned.

"Oh my god, *no*, Lars!" she laughed. "He's…"

"You want to do this like the coyote."

She nodded. If she were to intercept him somehow. "I'd have to know… And I think he'd have to make the first move."

"You want to go to this man's house. You know where he lives?"

"Maybe?" she cringed. "It's Pete's house, that's where William said he was. The greenhouse is probably his garage, and the roses are women. The whole thing is distracting, like a song in my head. I just want to get eyes on it and go from there, so I can move forward, or move on."

"I've always supported you, but I'm not going to let you *Murder She Wrote* this thing."

"*Let* me?" She started.

Lars cut her off, holding up a finger. "We do it like *Hardy Boys*. Together."

"Seriously?"

"Yes," he said, standing up. "Let's go."

"Now?"

"Yes, Linn. I have to go back to work at some point; I can't just stay out here with you, brunching and scheming, and I don't feel comfortable leaving you curious and hungry enough to do something dangerous, like go over there alone with naught but a hockey stick."

Within the hour they'd parked on the street several houses down from Pete's home address. The air was cool, crisp, but not quite so much that she could see her breath. It was enough for her to wear a sweater under a down vest. Her brother wore a shearling lined flannel over a white thermal, and a knit hat, fashionably slouched in the back.

Two stories and an attic, dark windows, dim porch light, and a two-story garage waited, but they weren't interested in the house. Linn wanted to see the back garden.

"Front looks like it was nice once," Lars whispered from beside her on the sidewalk.

There was shape to the plant-life, where things had been plotted out before becoming overgrown. A path wove from the driveway to the front door, branching off through an arbor leading to the back. They'd have to thread that needle if they wanted to uncover the truth behind William's supposed greenhouse.

"Are you sure?" Lars asked, breaking the silence with another whisper.

"He visits in the evening; comes around dinnertime and has been staying later and later. The patient gets anxious at night. Sometimes he wakes up and forgets where he is. He's not here. Let's go."

They advanced, and thankfully there were no motion lights to flick on as they passed through the front, and into a grander version of what she'd seen out front, a neglected wonderland that reminded her of The Secret Garden before the children tended to and revived it. Through the shapes and shadows, Linn could see the potential William must have known once. She imagined the calling he felt to meet his hands with soil was stronger than just the need for the property's resale value.

Through the stone scaping, and wet decorative grasses, the trees growing over rotten fruit, sour and sweet on the air, she saw the greenhouse. Cold glass reflected the white moon, the structure roughly the size of a garage and dark within.

"His story checks out so far," Lars breathed.

"Mmm. Could still be a lie wrapped in truth," she whispered. "We need to get in there."

Without question, Lars walked beside her on the winding path, until her hand reached for the door handle, and she saw the lock.

"Shit," she huffed, cupping her hands around her eyes as she tried to see through the glass. "Can you see roses?"

"It's hard to see color, but yeah, I think there's flowers. Who locks a greenhouse?"

A mechanical hum groaned behind them, stirring Linn's heart into a frenzy as her head whipped around.

Lars's hand gripped her wrist. "Garage door."

Swiftly, they crept to the back tree line until they stood just behind the trees, the street appeared a little brighter to the side of the house, lights within shining out. They couldn't leave the way they'd come, and the neighbor's on that side had a high fence extending far, and on the other side of a dense network of prickers. So, it was in the other direction, and further from their car that Lars and Linn traversed the woods, exiting onto the street several houses down.

"Should we cross?" she asked.

"Yeah. Here," he said, taking off his hat. "Stuff your hair in this."

They still needed to pass in front of the house. She couldn't disguise her face, but the length and texture of her hair wouldn't be identifiable.

They took a few steps, then a scraping noise sounded and her arm shot out, grabbing Lars and pulling him toward her, into a shadow. The noise sounded familiar, like something heavy being dragged over asphalt.

"Trashcan." Lars whispered.

She saw what she assumed was William's Volvo parked in Pete's driveway two houses down, and sure enough, a figure appeared with a barrel. When he turned back toward the house, Linn and Lars moved forward at a steady pace, like they were uninterested in the mundane maintenance some stranger was performing. They walked like they belonged there.

The garage door began to close as they passed. Linn turned as the rectangle of light slowly winked, an empty bay on one side, and a pickup on the other. Heart in her throat, she put her hands to Lars's face and turned his head, to the logo for a nursery on the side of the truck, the name West clear as a comet in the night sky.

The nursery. West's sister had run that side of the business. Missy's friend Sarah, who'd just died.

Lars sucked in a breath and froze a moment as her hands fell from his face. Then he wrapped an arm around her, tight, and they became one body over four legs, a fawn stumbling away.

Their breath filled the car, Linn grabbing for Lars's hand and squeezing before releasing him to the steering wheel.

"I'm moving the car," he said, and she nodded as both their seatbelts clicked in.

There was too much to say while driving, too heavy, too many wheels spinning. So, they steeped in their thoughts, Linn periodically instructing him where to turn. He remembered, she was sure of it, but there was something in her direction they both needed.

It wasn't until they sat under the arbor, that they spoke of what they'd seen, what it meant, what parts of them had been left tender and open. They wrapped blankets around themselves, Linn's hair loose, Lars with his knit hat. Cool air on their faces, in their lungs, darkness all around them, soothing what their thoughts and voices left raw.

William had been the boy; the one West had left with his sister Sarah when he went to prison. William hadn't visited when his father got out, but he'd helped with the nursery, and Sarah's son, *Pete*. The gardens, the greenhouse, the flowers... Linn saw how it all could have been exactly what it was, exactly what someone needed after so much trauma...

"Do you still think..." Lars whispered.

Linn's eyes drifted out into the night, somewhere between the past and present.

"I don't know.

14.

Berkshires, October 2014

Trees moved on either side of her, or, rather, Linnea moved through them in her vehicle on a long, unpopulated road. The foliage and evergreens seemed muted, though, by the brilliance of a pensive sky. Like the underside of a massive quilt undulating over her, the clouds tufted down, still illuminated, but dark like a bruise spreading over swollen skin, heavy with rain and the unknown.

Linnea reached forward to her phone on the dash, placing it on speaker as she attempted to reestablish a call with her mother.

"Linn?"

"Yeah, sorry. Reception is less than ideal. I've been on this road for a few minutes with nothing but trees. Oh wait, there's some blue on the GPS."

"If you pull up to his truck and don't see kayaks, just get the hell out of there."

"Mom!"

"I'm kidding, Honey. Missy called and told me and mentioned she and Cap had met him. It would hardly be a sound plan for him to disappear you at this point."

"Right? My thoughts exactly. Okay, I think this is my turn," she said, slowing her vehicle as she approached a break in the trees. "There's a mailbox…"

Linnea's chest sent out a low and steady zing of excitement.

"Like a driveway?"

"It feels more like a driveway than a road, especially with the mailbox. It's paved, though." Linnea thought back to her communications with Henry.

"What lake is it?" Her mother asked.

"Baxter Lake," she said, continuing down the drive, or perhaps it was a private way?

"Huh."

"I hadn't heard of it, either." He'd mentioned that he and his brothers called it Moon Lake when they were kids, because it reflected- Oh my god, there's a house."

As the drive curved, the view opened up, revealing several structures, Henry's truck, the lake… The house was dark, slate grey, mid-century modern, definitely built on since first constructed. It was attached by a hallway of sorts to a large garage, two bays but room for a third, though there was no door there. Another house stood off on its own though the trees, small, one level, same color as the main house and garage.

"Is it *his* house?" Her mother asked.

"I don't know, I think he mentioned something about a lake house; I guess it didn't stick for some reason. I see his truck, and there are definitely kayaks down at the dock. I gotta let you go, Mom."

"Have a good time, Honey. Oh! Look for otters! Take a video if you see one."

"Okay," She smiled. "Love you."

"Love you, too."

Linnea ended the call and pulled in beside Henry, though he wasn't in his truck… He strolled out from behind the garage wearing a black jacket, knit cap, grey athletic shorts, rugged, closed-toe sandals… and smiling. Her chest and cheeks began to warm, limbs electric.

She opened the door a crack. "Okay to park here?" She asked.

Henry nodded and leaned against the garage, in no hurry as Linnea assessed what she would take and what she would leave in the car. She'd packed an *in case I fall in* bag, which she left, but she put on the small cross body bag that one might have called a fanny-pack if she'd worn it over her waist, which she didn't.

"Socks and sandals?" He asked with dry humor as she got out of the car.

She looked down, and rolled her eyes as he moved slowly toward her. They were *hiking* sandals…

"I didn't want my toes to be cold… But I also didn't want water dripping inside my hiking boots, and rain boots felt too… tall?"

She wore loose jeans rolled up, t-shirt, thermal, and a rain shell over. She had gloves in her pocket, a knit hat on her head, and Henry's hand on her back under the jacket, the other behind her neck, his mouth warm against hers.

"We've got maybe an hour before the sky opens up on us," he said as their lips parted. "It would be best if we're not on the lake when it starts coming down. Are you still ok with going out?"

It wasn't as if they were going down river in some remote location. They were at someone's house…

Linnea looked out to the water, the sky, and nodded.

"Just need to grab a couple vests," he said, leading Linnea toward the hall of windows that connected the house and garage structure. "I used to keep them in the boat house with the paddles, but there was an incident last summer with my nieces and nephew… My brothers and their families visited for the Fourth of July, and the kids got an idea to launch all the life jackets out onto the lake with sparklers…" he sighed and shook his head, a little smile forming. "I just meant to move them while the kids were visiting, but I find fewer spiders on them now."

"This is your house," Linnea said as they entered the hall.

Henry had closed the outside door and turned toward her. He nodded, then looked out the large windows, out to the water.

"Yes. The house, the lake, three hundred twenty acres, and about five miles of trails."

Her eyebrows raised, but only slightly, to her credit. *The whole lake.*

"It was a family house. I grew up coming here during the summer, long weekends. It looked a bit different then. My parents signed the place over about fifteen years ago and I did some renovations. It suits my needs," he said, opening the garage door. "It suits *all* our needs, to have me here."

The back wall of the garage was half lined with doors, like one long closet. The other half was shelving of equal depth. As Henry opened one of the closet doors, Linnea looked around the space, noting the empty garage bay where his truck could have pulled in, the bay beside it with ATVs and plow attachment, a few pieces of equipment. The wall at the end acted as the backstop for a long workbench that terminated at a door with an electronic panel beside it. A keypad?

"What room is that?" she asked.

Henry paused.

Holding the life jackets in his hand, he remained silent a moment, then ticked his head toward the door that had sparked her interest. She followed as he led her over, placed the vests on the workbench beside several bundles of tools wrapped in canvas, and a small wooden dish. It reminded her of the bowl she kept in the mudroom, for her keys and things.

"Do you empty your pockets in this?" she asked, tapping the dish.

"My watch," he said, lifting his wrist. He wore what looked like a diving watch with a case made of brass or copper, a patina over the metal, like it had seen many years, or been pulled from the depths.

She tilted her head in question. "Why your watch?"

"Because I don't keep time here," he said, and opened the door.

Linnea's fingers and cheeks felt the freezing cold air first as they entered, her eyes overwhelmed by the white tile walls. A keypad, a thermostat of some kind, was mounted to her immediate left. A large, black hose coiled on the wall to the right, beside a long, clean, stainless-steel workbench. Across from her, far on the other side, a metal door led not to the outside world, but to a metal room within the one where they stood, another panel on the outside.

"What's in there?" she asked, her mind conjuring a nesting-doll situation.

"Meat," he said, and she nodded with understanding. Storage.

This other room couldn't hold her attention, though, because, above the drain in the center of the concrete floor, chains hung from the ceiling, and from the chains, the skinned carcass of a large quadruped, split down the middle, absent of internal organs. Hair frayed around the animal's hooves, but he was otherwise free from fur, except for the head. From the neck up, the deer was intact, wearing a magnificent crown of antlers.

Linnea's feet tapped against the wet floor as she took a few steps toward the mass of muscle and bone, coming close enough to have felt warmth had the creature been alive.

Skilled hands had worked on the body hanging before her, and would continue to do so, carefully, as they had many times before. Her eyes darted to the workbench, imagining Henry's tools laid out, then she glanced back to the material suspended like uncut marble.

Acts of purpose and precision, she thought.

Linnea's mind wandered a bit with her eyes as she further reflected on what it meant for a thing to be a labor of love, how engaging thusly is sustaining. It was not lost on her that, by ending life and carving food from it, Henry provided himself with nourishment, but also met the needs of some other thing, something Linnea felt in herself as well.

A sensation like darkness loomed behind her, wide and open like the night sky, heavy with potential. She turned, watching Henry as he watched her. Contentedness and curiosity shaped his expression, and there was perhaps something hungry about it, but in his characteristic stillness, he seemed thoughtful and savoring.

Linnea moved toward him, his arms receiving her, a warm hand on her back beneath the jacket steering her body toward his.

"You work here," she said, feeling his beard against her hair.

"I do."

She wanted to explore, wanted to find what he kept, to dip her fingers into the apothecary drawers of *his* workspace. *What are his honeybees,* she wondered. What would she find instead of glass fragments, earrings, and an eye. What bits of bone did he keep?

"Take as long as you need, if you want to look more."

"The sky won't wait," she said.

He nodded against her hair, then pulled away to reach for the door. "The room will still be here."

*

"Blueberries," Henry said, gesturing from his kayak to the bushes along the edge of the small island, their branches reaching out above the water. "Early August, you can just pull alongside and eat berries in the shade without leaving your kayak."

They'd been quiet for some time, gliding through the surface of the water as the sky darkened over them.

"I bet it really comes alive when the sun shines."

"Indeed. The birds… I've closed my eyes while out here, just drifting and listening."

Linnea thought back to how she felt in the tree stand, moving with the breeze, surrounded by birdsong.

"Tranquil," she said.

"Mmm."

"Otters," she gasped, the thought flying into her brain suddenly. "Do you have otters here?"

Henry cocked his head slightly, smiling. "We do, though I'm not sure we'll see them now."

"Because of the rain coming?"

"No, they're just as likely to come out in the rain as the sun. They have their own agenda, though. You can go looking for them, and find not a trace but their smell, then one of their little heads will pop up right next to the dock as I'm hauling up the kayak."

"My mom *loves* otters."

"What's not to love?"

"I think it started as something else for her, though. Her birthday is in early February, she's an Aquarius, and the otter is her *animal* apparently. She doesn't believe in astrology by any stretch of the imagination, she just made a connection to something, found a piece of herself," she continued, paddle in her lap as she and Henry drifted beside the island. Her thoughts drifted as well, from her mother… "I've often looked, too much maybe, into my own name, as if it were prescriptive of who I would become…" she whispered. "Whatever the root, I feel like I'm two things, and this other part of myself isn't fed enough…"

"Mmm," Henry hummed, head moving with a slight nod, a thoughtful look on his face as he leaned back into his seat. "You are not two things, but one. And you deserve an environment that nurtures the whole of you."

Yes, Linnea thought, and her face relaxed, body warm beneath chilled cheeks, then there was a sound… a sound, like someone flicking her jacket. She looked down at her sleeve, seeing the splattered water dribbling through a wrinkle in the fabric, then saw another strike her boat. All around her, muted silver reflected in black glass. The lake only rippled around their kayaks, remaining ghostly still throughout the rest of its body's expanse. There was no great turbulence, no wind ruffling up the lake into chop and swell. Linnea marveled longingly at the way the water waited. This was not a place where water leaked in, but welcomed, called out to the sky. With each large drop, a tiny part of the lake rose up to meet the clouds, only making it an inch or two in the air before falling back.

Henry put his paddle in the water, pushing just enough to draw nearer. He reached out, touching a raindrop on her face, dragging the liquid across her skin, then he pushed past her, away from the island.

Linnea followed, thinking Henry was heading for the dock, but he tucked his paddle up and leaned back. She was unable to see his face, but it was tilted upward, toward the rain. Knowing she was behind him, out of sight, she did the same. She paddled out a few strokes, then drifted, leaning back with her head tilted upward. Rain fell like tiny fingers tapping all over her body, their icy impact on her skin not quite numbing. Then, almost suddenly, the sky's song changed, and the rain came down hard.

Linnea straightened in her kayak to see Henry's head whip around toward her. He pointed to the shore by his house in the distance, and waited for her to begin paddling. He continued to hold until she'd almost reached him, then he sped onward, the space between them becoming grey and warped with falling water.

With his kayak on the dock, Henry knelt at the edge, arm outstretched. He stabilized her boat as she climbed out onto the wooden planks. Her hands shook, teeth beginning to chatter, though there was an excited grin on her face as she took in the extent of their soaking wet clothes.

"Head to the house," Henry shouted as he hauled her kayak up onto the dock, water streaming from his hood and over the shadow of his face.

Linnea took off toward the house, laughing, feet moving faster than she seemed to have control over, but still they kept moving… There was something primal in running. She'd read that if the self were a map, the id would be the basement, a deep place, where metaphor and dreams and who we *are* live. Running, running from Henry, had that same primal spark, a deep thrill, racing through her. She didn't dare look back, didn't have to, because as her foot caught a stone, his arms were around her torso. He towered over her, holding her off the ground where she would have hit hard had he not caught her.

His mouth was cold, but his tongue was warm, as was his breath against her cheek when he said, "Shower. You're freezing."

Linnea nodded, and for a moment she thought he might try to carry her, but instead they ran together, hand in hand. Up the stairs to the deck overlooking the lake, toward the glass wall of windows, and the door to the adjoining house, Linnea saw through to a living room with brown leather couches, white walls, and a long wooden table. Henry turned, bringing her not to the glass door, but to a thick gate about head taller than him. He opened it, ushered her in, and turned a knob on one of the wooden walls that enclosed them.

She was in an outdoor shower, and one of the walls included a frosted glass door to Henry's house, secured with a keypad lock.

Once hot water sprayed at them from the showerhead, he tapped the small bag she wore.

"The hooks," he said, ticking his head toward the back wall.

Linnea unlatched her bag and hung it up, then her coat beside his. She started to remove her shirt, then his hands moved to her waist, and she put her arms up. After the fabric passed over her eyes, she saw his torso, chest, tattoos.

"Bathroom is just inside," he said. "There are towels."

She nodded, and attempted to remove her sport bra, which had become adhered to her, apparently.

"Off?" Henry asked as he drew nearer.

"Yes," She nodded again, teeth still chattering. "It's plastered on."

"I got it," he smiled, his hands against her ribs, her arms up again.

The rest of their clothes stayed on the floor of the shower. Cold rain from the sky fell with hot water over their skin, and Linnea's teeth stopped chattering.

*

Stretching her limbs across sheets no longer cold, Linnea thought back to the whirlwind of excitement that had carried her from the lake to the shower, and into the house. She replayed the moments, both fluid and pieced together, pausing as her mind's eye flashed to a white wall covered in skulls and antlers… water, stairs, a bedroom overlooking the lake, sheets, and Henry's tattoos. There were many on his right arm, all sorts. Trees reached up from dark bands and dots encircling his wrist, seeping into pools of greyscale water, sketches of a human heart straight out of a DaVinci notebook, backwards writing, a honeybee, scales, a pattern working its way across his chest.

"Honeybees," she whispered, remembering his reaction to the drawer in her studio.

"Mmm. I was doing some contract work overseas…" He started, looking off toward the rain, toward something else. "Just before Convallaria started up. I was working a job alone, and the work resulted in an unexpected stay in a remote village. I was there several weeks. Two women took me in. They could have been sixty or eighty years old with the way one ages when life is hard, add in sun and open fire cooking… They were sisters, one widowed and caring for her husband's disabled brother, the other never married." He paused, turning toward Linnea. "They kept bees," he smiled, and Linnea smiled back, seeing the memory twinkling in his eyes. "I'd been stung before, and knew I didn't have an allergy, but still…" he said with a laugh.

"You were scared." She teased.

"I was," he laughed, "and I have no shame in admitting it. Getting stung just *once* hurts… But I watched them; they were so calm. I knew peacefulness there, for a time."

He could have said more, as with any moment, with any memory. Not sharing didn't imply that one was unworthy of being shared with… It just demonstrated an appreciation for pauses, for silence, for allowing what has been said to bear weight.

On the back of his arm, above his elbow, was a flower, or rather six flowers hanging like bells from one stem, two unopened blossoms toward the tip, long leaves at the base reaching upward.

"My sister, Lily," he said, as Linnea's fingers grazed over the surface of the image. "Her death was unexpected… She was fifteen. My brothers and I had the flowers tattooed after her service; we had a guy come here, to the lake house. Marcus was only seventeen." His hand found Linnea's resting over the memorial. "I can't see her, but I know she's there."

"I have beads that I make to remember my dad. I make one every summer, but I don't often wear them now. He and my papa died when I was little, then my Grandmother, GG, five years ago…" she trailed off. "I've come to appreciate how trauma can cause something to take root, and grow in unexpected ways. I was overcoming my fear of the dark when my dad and papa died…" she sighed. "My brother, Lars, was with me through everything. Do your brothers live close by?"

"Jon and Phil both travel for work. Mostly just Phil now; Jon does more work at the desk. Jon is my older brother by two years, Phil younger by two. Jon is FBI and Phil a marshal."

"Like a cop?"

"The United States Marshal Service…" he smiled. "It's *federal* law enforcement. They don't stop at town or state lines."

"And your younger brother, Marcus? Is he employed as a hero as well?"

"Don't let Jon and Phil hear you say that. Their proficiency in preening exceeds their on-the-job skillset… *Especially* Phil," he added with a sigh and a smile. "But Marcus, no. He had asthma as a kid. They thought he'd grow out of it, but it stuck around. He made out alright, though. Practices law. Costs an arm and a leg to keep him on at Convallaria, even with the sibling discount."

"Oh, I forgot to tell you," Linnea started, a laugh bubbling up with her words. "Your *finance* company became quite the hot topic at brunch."

"You discussed me over brunch?" He asked, amused, lying on his side with his head propped up.

"Well, the missing pumpkin bread was noticeable, and I may have mentioned that I had help eating it. When I told them who assisted me… They became relentless."

"*Vultures*," he smirked.

"That's how it felt! I felt like I was *feeding* you to them, though it doesn't feel as uncomfortable when it's just my brother, Steph or Alex. I think it was Gabby being there, that threw off the vibe, made things feel impersonal."

"Which teacup did you give her."

"Rabbit."

"Mmm."

"So, the curious vultures asked what you did for work."

"And you told them I was in *finance*?"

"I said risk management, which none of us really knew anything about. I am absolutely guilty of making assumptions, but in my defense, I wasn't really concerned with what you do and hadn't given it much thought. So, we speculated finance, but that wasn't enough for Steph, who googled the company you work for."

"Not finance."

"Private military?"

Henry nodded.

"You like it?"

"Yes. I'm not in the field much now, but I take time off for hunting every year so I can stretch my legs. Takes the edge off until October comes around again," he said, leaning back, folding his arms above his head.

"*Lily of the Valley,*" Linnea said as Henry's tattoo became visible again. "A beautiful choice."

"The other Lilies weren't her style," he smiled, brightening slightly. "She was more subtle."

"Were they a favorite of your parents, or did they just like the name?"

"My mother's grandmother, Lillian."

Linnea nodded. "I think my parent's liked that Linnaeus was a Swedish scientist, and my family on my mom's side are from there. I don't think they considered the flower aspect until they were already serious about the name."

"Your name is a flower?"

"No one ever realizes. Though, the other day, a patient's family member knew as soon as he heard it. He'd thought my name was just *Lynn*, but when he saw my badge he went into full botanist-mode."

"Speaking of work… when are you going in again?" He asked.

"Tomorrow," she groaned. "And Friday, then I'm off the weekend. I usually work less, but I picked up a day. I don't know how they're still letting me train someone when I'm never there," she chuckled. When are *you* working again?"

"Not today," he sighed pleasantly.

"And no hunting today, what with the deer in your garage and the rain coming down."

"Mmm," he rumbled, pausing for a moment with his thoughts. "Hunting is more than a day. It's a season, sometimes longer…" he trailed off, his body shifting as the back of his hand followed the curve of her hip.

"What do you do with the remains of the deer," she asked.

Henry propped himself up on his arm, free hand scooping her hair up onto the pillow where she rested her head, exposing her neck where his fingers found a curl.

"Freeze the meat, mount the skull. Forest takes the rest."

"And the bones?"

"Fertile soil makes surprisingly quick work of them. What's your experience with butchering?"

"I've never…" Linnea started. "Missy usually handles what Cap brings home, out in the barn. I planned to have her show me, if I have success hunting deer with Cap."

"Mmm," Henry nodded. You'll need to learn how to do it on your own."

"I mean to; that's part of it, really," she sighed. "Do you remember the tea service you helped me set out for brunch?"

"Mmm," he hummed, the corners of his lips lifting as he ran a hand over her back. "Beautiful work, the unsuspecting creatures: bird, snake, and rabbit, all unaware of the predator watching. There was another, the moon…"

"I mixed the clay from powder for each piece. Bone china is fifty percent animal bone, and I acquired the materials myself."

"From a butcher?"

She gave a faint shake of her head. "No. Snake for the snake, rabbit for the rabbit, bird for bird."

"Their bones are so small. That must have taken an *incredible* amount of work. Traps?"

Linnea shook her head.

Henry inhaled with thought. "The cat. Are *you* the cat?"

"No," she said, smiling as she admitted, "No, they were offerings from my old cat, Barny. Boiled and cleaned the bones, fired them in the kiln because you can't just dry them out and grind them up, they need to be calcined to eliminate the remaining organic matter…"

"The piece you're working on now… Without your cat, what is in the clay you were pouring?"

"Mouse or vole bones… from owl pellets."

"So, you're telling the owl's story now," he smiled. "And you'd rather tell your own?"

"I had a taste twice… The first," she sighed, shaking her head. "There was an incident with a coyote…"

"I'm listening," he said, something of a sparkle to his eyes, a waiting smile.

"It was in the backyard going for Barny or GG, I intervened… and the animal perished at my hand," she said dramatically. "Lars was there, standing by in case I needed help. It's a story best told by my mom, honestly, even though she wasn't there. She *loves* to tell people how I choked that thing out."

"We're calling your mother immediately."

"Oh, she would delight in laying that story out for you."

"So, did you use the animal's bones? Were you concerned with the risk for rabies?"

"Not bones… I hadn't started with bones yet. There was blood from the animal on my shirt… I, well, Lars, trimmed the collar off, and we burned it. Then I used the ash to make glaze for a couple bowls."

"*Unknown Pleasures*," he whispered, apparently remembering the band shirt she'd worn… the one with the wide collar…

"And what of the moon?" He asked. "There were no animals that I could see featured on your cup. What bones were used there?"

Her eyes flicked up to meet his, feeling the weight of a crossroads, and the longing for release from it. She wanted him to know. She wanted him to understand what type of creature she was, both in the light and in the dark. She wanted him to know… just not yet.

15.

Berkshires, October 2014

Sheets and blankets, both crisp and warm, felt lovely on Linnea's skin as she moved between them. Stretching, she felt radiating heat against her fingers.

"You slept," he said.

She opened her eyes. White, grey, and the persistent sound of rain.

Rain felt like a place between day and night, a time when the sky was called down.

Henry sat beside her in bed, laptop over his thighs. She *had* fallen asleep. And Henry was wearing sunglasses.

"Explain," she sighed, gesturing to her eyes, then to his.

"The computer is bright."

"Doesn't your device have a function to decrease brightness?"

Linnea glanced at the screen and saw what looked like footage from security cameras. One image showed tables, a counter from different angles, all black, white, and grey. It looked like… It was the coffee shop, Dee Dee's, where they'd gone after first meeting in the woods. The other image had footage of what looked like a hospital hallway.

Henry closed the laptop and placed it on the nightstand, then turned back to Linnea as he reclined on his side, head propped up by one hand.

"Then you wouldn't have woken to me wearing these shades," he said with a straight face, maybe a twitch of his lips, probably a wink behind the glasses…

She couldn't help but chuckle a little. "How long was I out for?"

"Long enough for me to take a quick shower and grab a couple things from my office. Maybe an hour and a half? I'd wondered if maybe you'd join me in the shower, but the thought of you sleeping was… pleasant."

Henry had showered, and was still very much nude, except for the glasses. He'd walked throughout his house naked and slid back in next to her.

"An indoor shower sounds nice," she said, turning her head to the wall opposite the giant window, where a sliding door remained open enough for her to see the white tiled floor of a bathroom. "And food," she added, stretching again as she twisted back toward Henry. "I was told a meal would be provided."

Henry laughed deep and loud, joy dimpling his cheeks. The exposure of his amusement swept through her, vibrating and warm.

"And provide I will," he said, setting the sunglasses down on the laptop beside him. "I've got a whole bird down there. Well, the head and feathers are absent."

"Feet?"

"No feet. It's a store-bought chicken I roasted. We could pick at that, put chicken on a salad, make a sandwich, soft tacos… What?" He asked in response to Linnea's evolving expression.

"Look at you, roasting birds."

"That's right. I'm a grown man. I made it Monday, though. Should still be good, right?"

"Yeah, it's good. I think there's a three-day rule, but that might be for pot roast. My mom would know, but we're not calling her again," she smiled, remembering her mother's eagerness to tell the coyote story, Henry's delight in hearing it.

Henry smiled softly, seemingly distracted, or perhaps very focused as his eyes wandered. He inhaled deep, then there was a pleasant stillness about him, about them, the rain, the room.

"Chicken soup," he said.

"Yes. That sounds *really* good… Cozy," she breathed as his arm came around her. She was unclothed, what she'd been wearing presumably still outside. "We came in rather rushed," she smiled. "I don't have a problem with nudity, but I think I'll get cold. I have some clothes in the car, but I'm not enthused about going out for them. I might need a robe, or a long sweater…"

"You can use the sheet; I think I have some safety pins."

"I wouldn't want to put you out."

He paused another moment before responding, his full focus on her.

"I have sweatpants with a drawstring that will work, t-shirt, and a sweatshirt. I'll start on the soup while you shower," he said, his face nearing hers until their lips grazed, pressed against each other.

Another thirty-five minutes or so passed before she stood beside Henry in the bathroom, his hand halting at the switch on the wall.

"You'd prefer the light off," he said.

Linnea studied his shadowed face, and nodded.

Filtered sun came in grey through the bathroom window, enough to see her way around. She often showered in near complete darkness at home, depending on the state of the moon, but her bathroom was familiar.

Henry stayed a few minutes before leaving to start lunch, watching her through the glass door until she slid it open, and he observed unobstructed a moment longer.

The water was hot, relaxing, and she was thankful he'd had conditioner she could use to detangle her curls.

As she turned off the water, Linnea heard a sound like a door closing, then Henry speaking downstairs. No, there were *two* male voices, then they abruptly stopped. Had it been just Henry, perhaps talking on the phone?

She dressed in his loose sweatpants pulled tight at her waist, his t-shirt, and hoodie.

"No."

She startled at the depth and finality in Henry's voice, though it had come from downstairs.

Listening in earnest, she heard an exhale follow, then throaty noises accompanied by rustling fabric, repetitive sounds of movement, and another, quiet exhale.

Henry wasn't alone down there.

She crept slowly from the bathroom to the bedroom, pausing as the rustling below turned to sudden silence.

"And then I come back to an unknown vehicle in the driveway and deerskin in the compost," the unknown male said. "I thought you might have been in the cold room, but your watch wasn't there. Instead, I found *clothes* in the shower outside. You brought a woman to the *lake house?*"

More of that sound, like movement, skin.

"There's only so much Phil and I can do. We need you focused, Henry."

"*Focused?*"

"There's no need to get gravelly…"

More muted sounds, a bit of a growl, then something was placed firmly on a table or countertop.

Linnea moved softly on bare feet across the stone tiles, the wood floor, to an open window overlooking the downstairs level. She saw the living room: wide plank floors, brown leather couches, and white walls, the largest of which was covered in deer skulls, mounted in neat, even rows. Part of the kitchen was visible as well, a roasting pan with the remains of a chicken, cutting board, carrots, and two men standing on either side of the counter. Their hands and arms moved in a heated exchange of gestures, what looked like American Sign

Language… Henry wore loose black sweatpants and a fitted black t-shirt. The other man struck her as familiar, as she'd seen on television while at work the day before, the one who looked like a leaner version of Henry without the facial hair. She'd been unable to gauge his height at the press conference, as he seemed tall compared to the men he stood with, but next to Henry he appeared a touch shorter.

Henry put his hands down and sighed, "It's a flower, apparently."

"…Fuck," the man whispered, drawn out and slow.

Henry's hands and fingers flew once more, the other man silently speaking back.

"Or you wouldn't have brought her to the fucking lake house," the other man said. "I suppose she's seen your dimples then."

Henry looked at him with a stern expression that broke into… a smile.

"There they are," the other man grinned. "Has she seen them?"

Henry's smile persisted as his hands moved once more, the other man laughing and signing back.

"ASL?" Linnea called down, projecting her voice through the open air.

The two men looked up. A flicker of tension passed over Henry's face, cast out by a wave of something like warmth Linn felt move through her at the sight of his smile.

"Thank *Christ*," the other man said, picking a hunk of cold breast meat from the chicken. "Now I can use my hands to eat."

"My brother Jonathan," Henry said, tilting his head. "Jon, meet Linnea."

"I'm going to come down," She said tentatively.

"Yes," Henry smiled, "please."

Henry stood at the bottom of the steps as she descended. When she put an arm over his shoulder, he slid his hand around her waist, blocking her path with his body. She felt very clearly it was not his intention to stand as an obstacle in her way, but rather as a barrier between her and the kitchen, until she was ready.

"My brother is visiting from out of town," he whispered in her ear. "He's been staying in the guest house, though I wasn't expecting him to be here so early today. Are you comfortable?" He asked, running his hands over her. "I brought your bag in."

"I'm more than comfortable in your sweats, and have no plans on changing until I leave," she smiled. "So, do you two sign often?"

"My mother is hearing impaired, so we grew up with an advantage, able to communicate in mixed company, and at a distance without shouting. I didn't want our talking to disturb your shower; thought you might feel vulnerable with unexpected voices," he said, then ticked his head toward the end of the hall, checking without words if she was ready.

"It was a bit of a surprise to hear the two of you down there," she said as they walked into the kitchen, where she was once again struck by how bright and neutral the space felt, what with the white walls, cabinets, countertops, faded wood floors, and steel. The kitchen was a giant alcove with a long island separating the business side of things from the rest of the living space where a vaulted ceiling, brown leather furniture, and grey landscape through giant windows accented even more white. Then there were the skulls on the wall…

"Need any help?" She asked.

"No, the soup is off to a good start, I've got the carrots, and potatoes simmering in stock. I was about to cut up the chicken when this one showed up…"

She sat down at the counter where Jonathan remained standing. Henry walked around to the other side, and opened a cabinet, pulling out a mug and a glass.

"Hot or cold," he asked.

Tea was tempting, what with the rain outside, but she'd be having soup, and she was thirsty.

"Water."

Henry nodded, filled a glass at the cooler, set it down in front of her, then removed a hunk of chicken breast from the roasting pan and started in on cutting it to pieces.

"Pleasure to meet you, Linnea," Jonathan smiled, extending a hand toward her. "Sorry about the greasy fingers… I've been trying to tear into this bird since I got here, but Henry insisted on signing." After popping another piece of chicken in his mouth, he asked, "Do you sign?"

"No," she said with a brief shake of her head as she took a long sip of water. "Not much more than *eat*, *drink*, and *more*. My friend, Steph, has been teaching her littles a few things; helps before they're verbal, apparently."

Henry poured the chicken off his board into the soup, then tore off another piece, and began to chop again.

Jonathan turned to his brother and made a short series of gestures. His fingers fanned out as they circled round his face, before he reached for another piece of chicken and walked over to the sink to wash his hands.

"Jon thinks you're beautiful," Henry announced flatly as he continued cutting. Then, with menacing stillness he glanced toward his brother and said, "Don't sign in front of her again. It's rude."

Jonathan released a frustrated sigh as he opened a cabinet and selected a drinking glass. "I *also* said I wasn't surprised, as there are very few things that can get Henry out of a tree once he's started hunting."

"Not even using the bathroom, apparently," Linnea smiled as Henry added the rest of the chopped chicken to the soup. "You told him how we met?"

"Mmm. Briefly."

Jon peeked into the roasting pan, deciding not to take another piece, then got up, taking a glass from the cabinet. "He mentioned your uncanny ability to see him before he saw you, though he must have left something out of the story…"

"I *heard* him before I saw him," she offered.

"I don't believe it," Jonathan said, filling his glass at the watercooler in the corner. "No one hears Henry first. The *last* sound they hear, maybe…"

"I was taking a piss," Henry clarified, adding a bag of frozen peas to the pot.

"On the ground or from the tree?"

"Tree," he said, bringing a brown paper bag over to the cutting board. "The variation in height makes no difference; no sense getting down."

"You got the *good* bread," Jonathan sighed as his brother revealed the bag's contents.

"So, Jonathan," Linnea started with curiosity as she watched Henry select a knife, his brother bringing plates and butter over. "You work for the FBI?"

Jon glanced at her, then Henry, his eyes probably asking what he'd rather articulate with his hands.

"Yes."

"I recognized you from a press conference I saw on television yesterday. What do you make of the ambergris?"

Henry looked at Jonathan, a touch of admonishment in his eyes as he cut through the crust of a round loaf, his gaze on his brother, slices flawless.

Jonathan, to his credit, maintained a calm demeanor. "That's not something we're advertising."

"My friend Steph's husband is local police. They're not spreading details around; I think they're just concerned because I trail run alone real early where the murder took place… Though, I honestly don't feel any more at risk now than I did before."

Henry held an apple in one hand and a small, curved knife in the other, segmenting the fruit with precision, fingers in no danger as his eyes flicked between Linnea and his brother.

"I wouldn't single out that location as being of higher risk to the general population at this time... You're a nurse?"

She nodded. Henry had managed to mention quite a bit while she was in the shower.

"I'm sure you understand," he continued, "as you are unable to talk about specifics in regards to patients, I am prohibited from discussing information not ready to be made public, even if you have come to know about it through back channels. It's work, it's policy, I just can't talk about it."

Henry slid a plate of bread and apple slices in front of Linnea, then sat down beside her with another glass of water she hadn't seen him fill. He took an apple slice from the plate. They were sharing, apparently.

Swiveling in her seat to meet his eyes, Linnea felt the hairs on her arms lift, some anatomical awareness she was not consciously privy to. As her eyes changed focus, Henry's face began to blur, the skulls behind him crisp with clarity. Fifteen of them. *Fifteen*, she thought, *one for every year since the house has been his.*

"The bone is so white and the antlers so dark," she observed. Henry's eyes remained trained on her as she continued. In her periphery she noticed Jonathan spreading butter on his bread, his movements stalling as she spoke. "Cap has one in his den, but the color of the skull is more like butter. I've seen bone get this white after running it through the kiln, but they'd be brittle if you'd done that."

"After the meat and hair are removed, I treat the skull with a hydrogen peroxide solution. It can be brushed on, or added to water for the skull to boil in for an hour. I've done both."

"And the antlers?" Linnea continued, a series of images and movements playing in her mind: boiling bones, the work she'd done, Henry's hands holding each of the skulls, eyes and fingers working carefully, alone. "The antlers were never this dark," she said, her focus coming back to Henry's face, his eyes waiting for her.

"The contrast makes the antlers appear darker," he said slowly. "These on the wall, though, they've also been treated with a blood stain."

"The effect is impressive."

"Thank you. It's a labor of love, I suppose."

Linnea's heart pounded harder then, sending out threads of ice and sparks of heat with his words. Labor of love. Had he been listening to her thoughts?

"Each is a reminder of what was done, so it can hang there" he continued. "Each carries a story, whether or not one can read it. A snapshot to remember the process, rather than the process being about the product, if that makes sense."

She nodded, of course it made sense. "And you have fifteen of them."

"Mmm," he hummed. "I'm hoping the harvest I have hanging in the cold room makes sixteen on my wall."

"Why wouldn't it?" She asked.

With the corner of her eye, she saw Jonathan, visibly uncomfortable, knife hovering over the same piece of bread, untouched, in his hand.

"The conditions need to be right..." Henry said, his voice growing a little quieter. "There's a bit of timing to it."

"And focus," Jonathan added, face heavy with subtext she couldn't read. She'd heard him say something earlier, *We need you focused, Henry.*

"It's why I take time off from work to hunt," Henry said with an easy face, eyebrows raised as he buttered his own piece of bread. "What with the long hours and high stress nature of finance…"

Linnea smiled, her cheeks heating as he offered her the bread.

"Finance?" Jonathan asked.

Henry grinned.

Linnea sighed, something like joy bubbling inside her. "A couple friends and I thought *risk management* meant finance, until we googled Henry's company."

"I don't know of a finance firm with a training center in a Kentucky cedar swamp," Jonathan huffed.

"The compound is impressive," Henry admitted with a tilt of his head. "So are our personnel. We provide weapons training, hand to hand, tactical driving, marksmanship, and some other specialty training. We have a local facility, something of a corporate office and command center. We've also got what I like to call the *Toy Division*…" He smiled, sparking another wave of electric flutter through Linnea. The t-shirt, the one with the wide neck and coyote blood, was a Joy Division band shirt. "Yeah, I thought you'd get a kick out of that. Toy Division handles all the gear, equipment, gadgets."

A dull vibration sounded briefly, both their heads turning toward Jonathan, who pulled a phone from his pocket. His brows gathered as he examined the screen.

"Where's your cell?" He asked Henry.

"Silent and out of reach. I need undisturbed time and space, Jonathan, non-negotiable. That's the arrangement."

The arrangement, Linn thought, examining the exchange between the brothers.

The phone vibrated again, in longer, unrelenting bursts.

"It's Dad," Jonathan said, eyebrows raised with concern.

Henry released a textured sigh, extending his palm up as he stood. "I'll handle it."

He offered Linnea an apologetic look that lingered as the phone continued to convulse. "I'll just be a few minutes." Then he put the device to his ear. "It's Henry," he said, walking barefoot through the glass hall to the garage.

Linnea thought of her mother, who she spoke to almost every day. Yes, if she was honest with herself, there were times she rolled her eyes when she phoned at an inopportune moment, but this, this with Henry and Jonathan's father calling, there was more there. Jonathan looked troubled; Henry inconvenienced.

She took a bite of bread as Jonathan chased a heavy breath with a long drink of water. Her teeth scraped through creamy, salted butter, full of flavor... The bread was light and chewy, a yeasty aroma filling her nose.

"This is *really* good," she sighed.

"I can't keep bread like this in the house," Jonathan said, buttering another piece. "I'm trying to cut carbs. I tell myself I can drink as much coffee as I want if I lay off the bread and potatoes, but the math isn't perfect," he chuckled. "Then there's Henry, who has some twisted form of metabolism that turns gluten into muscle. Wait until you taste the soup; you'll swear he's snuck something else in there. He's always been good with his hands, though, in the kitchen or elsewhere. My expertise ends with sandwiches... Do you cook?"

"I bake," she said, with something of a wince and a grin. "Often."

"Christ..."

"Moderation," she said. "How long do you expect to be here for? I'm not prying into the case, just curious."

"It'd difficult to say. I'd like things to wrap up as quickly and smoothly as possible. Especially with things here being what they are," he said, something a little distant in his words. "Henry needs a particular atmosphere about the place when he's working."

"He said he's taking time off from," she always forgot that constellation name... "The company he works for. He *has* been working, at least I think he has, remotely anyway."

"The company he works for..." Jonathan grinned, ignoring the apple wedges and taking another slice of bread. "Henry started Convallaria. He's the brightest of all of us, though Marcus comes a close second. Don't get me wrong, none of us are *dim witted*, not even Philip, though he puts on a good performance..."

"Oh, wow. That's *massive*." He would have been in his twenties when he started it... Explained the suits he'd mentioned, not being in the field. She glanced down the glass hallway, then back to the kitchen, her eyes lingering over the skulls on the wall.

"Do you or your brothers hunt?" she asked.

"Not like Henry," he said, his gaze following hers. "He has his own way of doing things; we just leave him to it."

Linnea traced the mounted skulls with her eyes, white as snow contoured with shadow, antlers bold in contrast. She could almost feel the blood on her hands where it had been before, when she'd made the dark cup, her first cup. She imagined her fingers smoothing over the branched bone.

"It's the first time I've heard him talk about it," Jonathan said, following her gaze with a sense of calm honesty about him. "Or maybe it's that we don't ask out of respect for his privacy. We just see another skull on the wall… another number."

The door at the end of the hall opened. Henry's stern countenance warmed as he met Linn's eyes.

"Phil's on his way," he said, holding out the phone to his brother.

"Shit," Jonathan cursed. "Marcus?"

"Not yet," Henry sighed with a shake of his head as he approached the stove and stirred the soup. "I don't want to see either of you until…" He looked over the countertop, leaned slightly with a crooked smile. "You filled up on bread, didn't you?"

"I have no restraint," Jonathan confessed. "There's nothing but chickpeas and kale at the house. Jess purged everything to go plant based and gluten free."

"You're a grown man and you've been threatening to cut carbs for years," Henry chuckled. "You can't put all the blame on your wife. How's the change going over with management?"

"The kids are resilient. I heard from Luke they've been using their allowance to get pizza at school. They'll be alright."

"And you?" He asked, pulling a glass container with a lid from under the counter.

"I'm drinking more coffee."

Henry shook his head, dipping a ladle deep into the source of the fragrance filling the space around them. He pulled several generous portions, filling a container beside the stove.

"That's not sustainable, Jon. If you don't have balance, you'll lose control when you come off the leash."

His words resonated. Slowly chewing a bite of apple, Linnea felt the truth of what he said. Henry spoke from experience, but not with food. He knew the risk of not feeding the thing that lived inside a person, how a void could form, a void that could become a vacuum.

No one on this earth can stop that, her grandmother had said. *You'd find a way.*

And Henry had hunting.

He handed Jonathan the sealed container of soup and pointed to the door. "I don't want to hear any complaints about the rain. You've a jacket in the hall, and it kept you dry enough to walk the perimeter before you came in."

Both brothers walked toward the glass hall, Henry's hand on Jon's shoulder.

"I need space, Jonathan. Non-negotiable. Your being here doesn't change that."

"I'm not the only one going off script, Henry," he whispered with a glance back toward the kitchen.

"No, but I'm the only one of us who has the discipline to manage it. Think about that while you're eating your soup, and dreaming of bread."

Henry came back through the glass corridor with a smile that bordered on mischievous.

"Soup?"

"I'd love some."

She looked down at his arms as he approached the stove, at the stories in ink, her eyes catching on the honeybees.

"Would you want to go with me to visit Marisol and Diane sometime?"

Henry turned from the pot as he ladled out two bowls, and raised a brow.

"The couple down the street with the bees. The hives won't be open, but they have honey at the farm stand. It's hard to pin them down too long during the day right now, but they're usually game for a hot drink and a snack. We could swing by tomorrow before I go to work..."

"I'd like that, but not tomorrow," he said, pulling two spoons from a drawer. "Hunting."

"But..." She glanced toward the glass hall, the source of her confusion obvious. He had a deer hanging.

"I told you," He started, placing the bowls and spoons in front of them as he sat down. "It's not a day; it's a season.

16.

Berkshires, October 2014

The studio lights were bright, shadows remaining only beneath things, and in corners. The space felt entirely different when lit for company, facilitating a shift in mood, allowing Linnea to glide effortlessly over the surface of what was incredibly deep water. And though she could move thusly, laughing and giving instructions on how to use the materials, she still felt the hum of what secrets sat unshrouded on shelves and tucked into drawers in the room, the house, and within herself.

Linnea took a few long sips of Shiraz from her glass, then raised her voice to address the fourteen guests sitting at her studio tables with unfinished mugs.

"A few rules and guidelines before we start. First, do not drink your glaze, people," she said, pausing for the anticipated laughter. "Most of you guys have played the glazing game, but for first timers and friends who need a refresher, you're going to apply at least two coats of glaze coverage on your piece. No whining, it dries *super*-fast. Please note that putting it on thicker to avoid a second coat is not recommended. Also, you do not have to stick to one color, but your brushes do." Linnea held up a finger, holding their attention as she took another drink from her glass. Linnea wore a deep green dress that hit at the knee, navy cardigan, and warm tights in the same color. Her hair, she'd woven into two long braids, pinned up and crossing at her nape, curving upward. She'd accessorized the outfit with dangling silver earrings, and a faded apron with indigo block-printed paisley. She cherished the garment, wearing it when she baked, or worked dry in the studio, trying to avoid too much damage to the well-worn relic. The gathering seemed a safe event, provided people's wine stayed in their glasses…

"Also," she continued, "very important, do not glaze the bottom of your piece. You'll get some on there, it's fine, that's what the sponges in the water are for. When you're done and it's dry, just wipe off the bottom and a millimeter or so up over the edge. If you can estimate wound dimensions and pupillary dilation, you can ballpark how far up to go with the sponge. Oh, and the sponges are also for wiping up any glaze that drips on the table. Anything clay or glaze related in powder form is not your friend; you do not want to breathe it in. Ceramicists have their own lung disease called Potter's Rot, also known as Silicosis. For those of you eyeballing Carmen with concern, she's fine, we talked about risks ahead of time. Wipe your mess while it's still wet, and it won't be a problem. Raise your hand if you have a question or need a refill."

Steph and another nurse, Irene, both put their glasses into the air.

"That didn't take long," Alex laughed, downing the rest of his wine and holding up his glass as well.

"I'd better bring out a few more bottles," Linnea said to Lars beside her, surprised to see Gabby get up and join them in heading out to the kitchen.

"Thought you could use another hand," she shrugged, and smiled. "That, and my glass is empty too."

"Which wine tassel did you get?" Lars asked to Gabby's delight.

"Charm," Linn corrected. It wasn't the first time.

Gabby held up her glass, and the small ceramic disc attached to the stem like a keychain. Upon closer inspection, she gasped at the black silhouette of a rabbit.

"A bunny," she grinned. "Like my teacup."

"How very appropriate," he smiled, grabbing two bottles from the dining room table.

Linnea opened two more bottles, handed one to Gabby, then slipped a wine key into her apron pocket. "Let's get these guys topped off."

The three poured where necessary, mixing reds in a few glasses to no one's protest. When Gabby reached her own chair, she filled her vessel high, lifted it to her lips, then followed Linnea to her desk in the corner to drop off the empty. As Linnea opened another bottle, just to be ready, Gabby remained beside her, looking things over, examining, hovering in a way that carried many qualities similar to that of a fruit fly.

Linnea began observing Gabby's intrusion fully, following the woman's eyes where they'd landed on her shelf of powdered bone.

"These glass bottles…" Gabby started, tipsy with oblivion. "I feel like I'm in some old pharmacy where they mix up potions and remedies. And these labels are so cute," she continued, pointing, nearly *touching* as she referenced what remained of Linnea's avian bone ash, then the silhouette of a bird, a deer, the jar without an animal…

Her eyes were open, but Linn's mind saw the eye in her palm, the truck in flames, logo disappearing. She hadn't seen it in years, until a variation appeared in William's garage.

"This was on your cup," Gabby said, pointing to the crescent moon, not knowing the remains of a man's arm waited within. She interrupted herself with a sharp inhalation, holding up her wine glass, her charm at eye level. Turning to Linnea, she grinned with wonder. "It's the same bunny!"

Another jar, another offering marked with a silhouette.

"Indeed, it is," Lars said from behind Linn, her eyes catching his smile as she turned.

"Let's get you over to the glaze before the others finish and become hungry," Linna said. "Then we'll be alone in here, while they eat all the good cheese."

Well over an hour later, when the studio had emptied and time had become soft with drink, Linnea found herself leaning against a wall in the dining room, laughing over some nonsense about the night shift with Steph and Alex. Lars stood with them drinking a blend of cranberry juice and ginger flavored seltzer from a wine glass, his eyes spending more time on Alex than anywhere else.

"I want to table this discussion about our fast-food eating, blanket-wearing colleagues to ask Linn a very important question… "Steph smiled, her lips tinged purple. "How was your morning?"

"Morning was good," she started coyly. "missed my run, but got some kayaking in at Henry's."

"Like, *with* him? Is his house near a lake?"

"He… So, the lake-"

"Brace yourself," Alex advised.

"The lake where we kayaked, he has a house on the lake."

"Ooooh, lake house," Steph swooned.

Alex held up a hand. "What your girl is dancing around, Stephanie, is the fact that this man owns a lake."

Steph's eyes went wide and she took another sip. "I got a text that you were going kayaking and having lunch. Alex clearly got more details…"

Alex put his arm around Steph's shoulders. "Don't feel bad, Sweetie, I dug for them. And we should be sitting down."

The four of them left their places at the table for the living room, Alex and Steph each grabbing an open bottle of wine on the way while Linnea traded her shoes for slippers. Alex sat on one end of the couch, Steph in the middle, and then Linnea beside her, leaving space at the other end, the spot where GG had always nestled in and leaned back, dropping pencils against the wall. Lars dragged a chair closer to the coffee table, sipping his mocktail across from the other three.

Wine bottles were placed on the coffee table beside some books on the work of Damien Hirst and Christopher Marley, a soft grey bowl filled with ceramic beads, and a candle, flickering warm light through the tiny holes of a lantern Linnea had made.

Lars reached out and topped off Alex's and Steph's wine as Alex tilted his chin down, preparing to deliver his message.

"I'm just going to say *one hundred and thirty acres*, then let Linn tell the rest. Okay, go."

Linnea took a long drink and sighed, three sets of eyes on her, waiting, savoring the anticipation as much as they would delight in what she chose to share. Lars knew more than the others, as he'd greeted her with a grin when she'd come home.

"So, when I went to the lake yesterday, it turned out to be Henry's house. He had a deer hanging in the garage, kayaks on the dock. He lives there. And, yes, there's quite a bit of land with some trails. He invited me to run there in the morning if I want company and a change of scenery."

"Wait," Steph said, pausing to gather her thoughts. "He was hunting when you met him, yes?"

Linnea nodded, took a sip from her glass.

"He was hunting where you usually run, but he has a lake house on one hundred thirty acres of forest. Why would he go on public land to hunt when he lives in a private woodland paradise?"

"Variety?" Linnea offered.

"And he's going out again tomorrow," Steph continued, "after you saw a deer hanging in his garage?"

"You can take more than one per season," Lars said.

Linnea had thought Henry's plan to harvest another animal was odd, but when she'd talked with her brother later, he'd reassured her that there was a bag limit of two antlered deer annually, then he got into some particulars about antlerless deer and special tags.

"Okay," Steph said with a wave of her hand. *"Number* of deer aside, that he hunts on public land when he has that kind of acreage to himself… I'm deferring to your judgement here, Linn, your gut, because I'm looking in from the outside, with greater than four glasses of wine on my insides…" she smirked. "But, are you getting any feelings? Like, that something is off?"

Steph suspected something with Henry, but in all the years she'd known Linn, had never suspected she drank from the bones of a man who'd killed her family.

Linnea sighed, knowing… knowing she was in the dark, but uninterested in articulating how comfortable she was there. She and Henry had honesty between them where it was most important, and she never felt in danger, but there was no doubt in her mind that there were shadows they kept to themselves, some they'd invited one another into.

He'd just started to let her feel the unlit surface with her fingers.

"I can only tell you that he was in a tree stand, and he had gear when I met him. Maybe it's not good for the deer population to keep hunting in one place? I don't know, but he seems to be successful in his pursuits. He has a wall of…" Somehow she felt uncomfortable using the word *skull* at that moment, "…antlers. You're not thinking of trying to connect him to the woman that was killed…" Linnea said, a squint to one of her eyes.

She'd been so focused on William, but things were blurred now.

"I'm just, I'm *exploring*. I'm just exploring," Steph said, tipping back her glass, consuming the remaining wine. Then, she held it aloft, looked around the room, and called out, "Garçon."

"Oh my god," Alex laughed, Linnea and Steph along with him. "Get this girl a refill."

Lars lifted a bottle, checking the label before filling her glass halfway. "You either need to slow way down, or take ibuprofen with some Pedialyte before you go to sleep," he advised. "Should probably do that anyway."

"Give me your phone," Alex instructed. "I'm gonna text Drew. Don't worry, girl, we got you. I know there's got to be some Pedialyte stashed away in your house."

"It's probably expired," she sighed.

"Won't be the worst thing you've put in your body tonight," he said, still holding out his hand.

Steph surrendered her device. "Okay, but then you're pulling up a map."

Alex dipped his chin and raised his eyebrows. "I am *not* a cartographer."

"Pull up, not *draw* up… *Fine*… Linn?"

"What maps will I be pulling for you," Linnea smiled, noticing her glass was also in need of a refill. She drank the remains while grabbing the bottle with her free hand.

"That's a good one," Steph said, taking another sip. "Who brought that?"

"The maps, Steph," Linnea laughed. "You're all over the place."

"Right. Pull up a trail map of the place you run."

Alex returned Steph's phone. "Drew says he's leaving in about fifteen minutes to come get you."

Linnea took another sip and pulled the map up on her cell.

"I've got it," she announced, flashing the screen to Steph and Alex.

"Okay, print it," Steph said.

"What?"

"Print it out. Oh my *god*, it will be so quick. Just print it. I can't look at that tiny screen right now. Lars?"

"Just print it," Alex shrugged. "We're already locked into whatever journey she's trying to take us on."

"On it," Lars said, then took the phone from Linn's hand and headed to the study.

With a paper map on the table and pen in her hand, Linnea followed Steph's prompt to mark where she thought Henry's tree stand had been when they met.

"I was on this trail," Linnea said, running her pen along the path, pausing at the center of a deep curve. "Then somewhere around here there's a stone wall. I left the trail and followed until…" she drew a line, then an X. "Until I saw him."

"Now, show me where you usually come in… from before."

"Way over here. I wouldn't have even seen him on this trail," she said, thinking for a brief moment at the good fortune she'd had as a result of the woman's death. She'd chosen a different course as a result of the incident, and from that, something unpredictable had blossomed. She'd also been haunted by inspiration just out of reach.

"Would you be able to mark where the murder happened?"

"Where I… Where the woman was located?" Linnea asked.

Steph nodded.

Linnea traced the trail with her eyes, the fork where it branched. "There," she said, drawing a thin oval over a tiny section. Somewhere around here."

And then she saw it, how close the X was to the circle.

"I had a feeling," Steph said, leaning in. "I had a feeling, but I needed to see it."

"You had a feeling," Linnea asked, tone flat. "Now what's your assessment."

"It probably doesn't mean anything," Alex cut in. "This is an itty-bitty map, representing a huge amount of space in the real world. These two locations are not as close as they look on paper. Don't let yourself stress over this, Linn."

She hadn't noticed anything, any activity from the crime scene, not even when she'd been up in the tree. Had they wrapped up by then? Steph was right, though. It was close.

"Let's assume," Linnea began, "for the sake of argument, that Henry killed this woman."

She could deflect by mentioning her suspicions about William, but decided against divulging what she'd once thought of the scratches and the bracelets. The wine-fueled rabbit hole of nonsense didn't need to get any deeper, besides, her theory had become murky. William had been young when his father had killed hers, gone to jail. He'd likely had a renewed sense of purpose helping with Pete, love of a sober adult, gardens to tend, a greenhouse.

"We're doin' this?" Alex asked, both he and Steph still with wide eyes, Lars unmoved and observant.

Linnea nodded. "He did some premeditated whale-perfume murder things to her, returned to the scene to revel in memories, and now he and I are openly dating. Am I in danger? The woman who died wasn't dating her killer, and it's not the type of thing one does to one's established partner that they can easily be traced back to. So, are we still worried about my safety?"

"You don't shit where you eat," Lars said before taking another sip from his glass.

"I'm not worried about your safety, girl," Alex said. "Now I'm concerned you'll get your heart broken when the FBI comes and takes your man away."

Except the FBI was his *brother.*

"You don't honestly think, though," Steph started, her eyes narrowed, poised with enough ideas and alcohol to lean in any direction.

"Of course not," Linnea smiled, rolling her eyes. There was darkness there. He hunted animals for more than food, but he had ethics. She felt it in her bones.

Gabby entered the dining room, glancing over the wine bottles. Linnea found herself thankful she hadn't been present for the exploration Steph had led them on…

Gabby poured until her wine reached the rim.

"That is *full*…" Lars whispered.

Alex nodded. "She better cross her fingers it spills on her tights and not that French Vanilla skirt she has on."

Gabby brought her lips down and drank until the level was low enough for her to pick up the glass. She turned, waved, and sat down at the end of the couch beside Linnea. Steph and Alex both leaned forward with smiles and greetings. Lars remained as he was, nodding once as she sat.

Gabby turned away from the group as she settled, looking down, fingers dipping into the crevasse between the cushion and the arm rest.

Lars leaned forward, Linnea's eyes catching his. She knew what the young nurse had found.

Gabby swiveled her head slowly toward Linnea, lifting what she'd discovered in her hand, her expression one of a startled animal.

Rabbit, Linnea thought.

"What the fuck is this?"

The object was a two-foot long, stainless-steel wire with wooden grips at either end. Gabby's alarm was absolutely understandable.

"It's a tool for cutting clay," Linnea said with a sigh and a disarming smile, knowing more than earth lined the frays and grooves where wire met wood. "My Grandmother lived here before me; did I tell you that? She wore this apron when she was working in the studio. In and out of the house she had it on, and she kept whatever tools she'd been working with in her pockets…

"We pulled so many things out of the couch cushions as kids," Lars smiled.

"Coins, marbles, pocket knives, cough drops, glasses… and GG's tools. She sat in that corner all the time."

"There's something else down there," Gabby slurred.

Lars stilled.

"Leave it." Linnea said, the depth of her voice allowing for no misunderstanding.

"Put the wire thingy back, Gabs," Alex said lightly after trying desperately to instruct her with his eyes.

"They were the last things…" Linnea trailed off with a deep breath. "I like them to stay there, for sentiment."

"Linn, I am *so* sorry. It just," Gabby paused, mortified as she tucked the tool back where she'd found it, her skin defiling the object somehow the longer she maintained contact. "It looks like what they wrap around the person's neck." Whoever *they* were. "I didn't know something like this existed with a real purpose."

"Don't beat yourself up," Steph said, her words not slurring so much as relaxing. "You're not the first person to pull that thing out of there."

"You too?" Gabby grinned.

"And me," Alex admitted, taking a deep drink from his glass.

"Your house is so *lived* in," Gabby sighed, "but in a good way. You have all these little treasures hidden all over the place. You have…" She trailed off as she leaned forward to inspect something on the coffee table, the bowl, made of thick, woven cords of grey fiber. She took a deep drink from her glass, nearly draining it. "This is so unique, and the little beads. Did you make this?"

"Yes," Linnea said, voice flat, both willing her not to touch and daring her not to stop. "Did you drive yourself here, Gabby?"

"What? Yes, why?"

Alex let out a loud exhale. "Nobody told you to get a ride? You can't drive home after drinking a gallon of red, Gabs. Linn will call the police to breathalyze your ass before she'll let you get in that car. You need to make arrangements, girl. Where do you live?"

In an act of unnecessary generosity, Steph's husband drove Gabby home, leaving Linnea eternally grateful. She lounged on the couch with Alex while Lars puttered, putting away the perishable food. She was in that warm place where thoughts flow before the stopper can be put into place.

Alex rubbed his hands together. "Can I take your braids out? Girl, *please* let me get my fingers in there."

Linnea laughed and took the first of the pins out, sitting sideways and facing away from him as he did the rest, unbinding her tresses. As she worked out of her slippers and tucked her feet up under her body, she realized she still had her apron on.

"Oh, if I had hair like this…" he sighed, digging his fingers in as Linnea leaned her head against the back of the couch. "What does it feel like getting your hair pulled, for real?" He paused long enough for her to bring up a recent memory, but not long enough for her to share it. "If I had hair like this… I can just imagine his hands squeezing through here… Hey how's your new cup you're working on? Didn't you say you were starting a new tea-set with owls or something?"

Linnea groaned.

"It can't be that bad," Alex grinned.

Was it bad, though? Or was it work, without enough reward?

"It takes a great deal of digging, to work out the bones of a thing." The words drifted from her lips before she could stop them, slow as they were. "I've been inside an animal, extracted truth from their insides, and this project is just, it's good on paper, but, something's missing. Like it's not where I'm supposed to be."

Alex's hands slowed, but didn't stop. "When you say *bones*, is that figurative or literal?"

"Both."

Tentative but steady, he asked, "Why do you need bones, Sweetie."

"Because bone china is made from bones, Alex."

Neither of them spoke for a moment, her words hanging as Alex's fingers massaged her scalp, sliding through her hair, careful not to disturb the rippling curls.

"Foraging for bones is some weird shit," he smiled as she turned toward him. You know that, right?"

Linnea let her head slide onto Alex's shoulder. Maybe it was the wine, but she felt different than she had when telling Henry about her work. With Alex she felt safe, heard, but revealing herself to Henry had been intimate, and he'd *savored* it.

"I grew up protecting parts of who I am…" he continued, warm light from the luminaries causing parts of him to glow. "There are some things you wear, and some things you keep inside, because of your environment… Never hide who you are from yourself. You do you, girl. Go get your bones."

"Thanks Alex," she said, her smile dreamy.

"Lars knows, obviously. Does Steph?"

Linnea shook her head.

"Henry?"

Linnea smiled again soft and easy, then nodded.

"Good. You deserve a partner who sees all of you," he sighed.

"That's what I've been saying," Lars said, entering the room with a towel over one shoulder.

"And it doesn't hurt that your man is an *artistic* killer," Alex smirked. "Someone who'll understand your bony needs. If it doesn't work out, try an orthopedic surgeon."

"I'm done with surgeons," she said, rolling her eyes. Alex wasn't wrong about Henry understanding her. He knew his way around an animal, worked with intent, precision.

"Shit," Alex sighed. "I need to go to bed. I'm gonna help you clean this all up in the morning, though."

"Do you have a ride home?" Lars asked.

"No, I came prepared. Packed my toothbrush."

The two of them stood staring at each other; Alex loose from wine, Lars prowling.

"Would you like a ride home?" Lars asked.

Alex's eyes flitted to Linnea; her brother's unmoved.

Linn smiled, nodded.

"I'll go grab my bag," Alex said, blushing through dark skin and shadows as he headed upstairs.

Lars joined Linnea on the couch, sitting at one end and patting his lap for her to lift her legs up. He slid her slippers off and began kneading her feet with his hands.

"Your hands are trouble…" She sighed.

"You've got at least five minutes while Alex is primping."

Linn smiled. "He is one hundred percent brushing his teeth and reapplying eyeliner, and I am far too relaxed for the amount of tidying up that still needs to be done."

"I'll help you when I get back in the morning. What's happening in the studio?"

"Ugh. I need to load the mugs in the kiln. I'm not running it until I get off work tomorrow; I just need to get them off the tables."

"That's not what I mean, Linn. You're still working with the owl pellets after what happened?"

"I've already mixed the slip."

"You had inspiration laid at your feet."

"It was a crime scene, Lars. I couldn't take anything."

"That's not why."

"She wasn't mine," Linn whispered. "Not like what Barny left us, or West."

"What do you need?" He asked.

"I'm not a hunter," she sighed.

"Do you need to be?"

"I thought that was part of it, but now I'm not sure. I know… With the coyote, the creatures, Barny, West… The work was *sustaining*. It came from a place of depth and darkness. The work was profound, Lars."

"*You* are profound. You were the womb where tsa tsas blended with the death of a local girl, made a promise to *grind his bones to make your clay.*"

Footsteps upstairs signaled the tapering conversation like the bottom of a teacup.

"Have faith," Lars said, sliding the Linn's slippers back onto her feet. "You'll find what you need. You always have."

With her brother and Alex gone, Linnea blew out the remaining candles before switching off the garish studio lights, pausing to sigh before stepping down into moonlight and shadows. She left the brushes in water, but rinsed out the sponges after checking the bottom of each mug, wiped a couple with glaze still creeping a little too low.

Loose, warm, and a little tired, Linn loaded the mugs, one by one, into the kiln. She was standing by the glass garage door, arranging ceramic wares, when her phone buzzed. Pulling it from her apron, she read Henry's words on her screen.

What are you wearing?

Linnea smiled, and typed, *Green dress, blue sweater, tights, apron, slippers.*

During the pause, waiting for his response, she wondered if she should ask what he was wearing. Then the muscles of her face slackened as she read what he wrote next.

Moss and dark water with a hint of moonlight... and silver earrings.

Linnea turned, seeing only landscape on the other side of the glass, then she looked back down at her phone, time becoming heavy, thrilling, waking her cells. She couldn't see him, but she knew he was out there.

She wrote, *The rear kitchen door is unlocked.*

Then she heard it close.

Not for the first time, Linnea found herself waiting for what would manifest from darkness.

As she took her first steps forward, his silhouette appeared as a density of shadows at the top of the stairs, his form melding with his surroundings, a talent Barny had possessed. *Innate, or learned,* she wondered as her feet transported her closer. Was Henry's ability to camouflage his presence the result of education, or a display of some inborn instinct? Perhaps instinct, too, is a skill practiced and perfected over the lifetime of a successful predator, animal or otherwise. *Though we are all animals,* she supposed.

As Linnea rose up out of the studio, Henry moved back, allowing her in, away from the edge.

"You should keep your doors locked," he said, his arm sliding around her body, her hand against the back of his neck as he leaned in, and they kissed.

"You taste like wine, and honey," he murmured as they parted, one hand around her back, the other brushing down her arm.

"Excellent palate, though the wine would have been an easy guess," she teased with a tilt of her head toward the bottles she'd moved into the kitchen.

The smell of smoke from the extinguished luminaries became more noticeable as they entered the dining room where Henry's hand slid over her lower back, coming to rest on her hip.

"There are two cars in the driveway," he said, surveying the table.

Two that weren't hers.

"Alex. He was going to stay over, but my brother took him home."

Henry tilted his head.

"They have a history. Lars won't be back until morning."

Henry smiled and nodded. "And the other?"

"Gabby," she sighed. "She's a nurse I've been training, and she drank her bodyweight in Cabernet with no plan for transportation other than to drive home intoxicated. Steph's husband gave her a ride, for which I am immensely grateful."

Henry raised his eyebrows.

"She's… she's a little," Linnea rocked her head back and forth as she searched for the words, all the while aware that Henry was wholly focused on her. "Unintentionally intrusive, maybe? Timid, and maybe a little clingy. I don't know, but I was right to give her the rabbit teacup at brunch," she laughed.

"Mmm," Henry hummed, brushing a thumb over her cheek, his watch catching her attention before her eyes fluttered closed a moment. "We could get this handled in under twenty minutes," he said, turning toward the table with confidence. "I could stay, when we're done."

"Okay," she said, another burst of warmth flooding through her. "I just need to be up early. I want to get a run in before work."

"That won't be a problem."

"Tell me about this watch you've got on. It looks… "What's the circle and bead all about?"

"This?" he said, lifting his hand to display the object at his wrist: a black circle on a black band, though more grey than black, like gunmetal. "This is a timepiece."

"Yes, your *timepiece*…" She restated, making note of an absence of hands on the watch face, though there were raised lines where the numbers should have been, and a circular groove with a small metal sphere rolling freely along depending on the angle of his wrist.

"It's a braille watch," he started. "The grooved inner ring allows the small bead to travel, but it stops to rest at the hour," he said, with demonstration, then pointed to the other groove she hadn't seen, the one on the side that went round the circumference of the watch. "The outer ring tells the minutes. Close your eyes," he said.

And she did.

"Feel," he said, guiding her fingers to the watch face, where she felt the grooves, the number lines, the beads. "I don't need light," he continued. "I can tell the time in absolute darkness."

17.

Berkshires, October 2014

Linnea looked up from her computer and rolled her eyes as Gabby walked into the back room of the nurses' station.

"Christ on a cross," she muttered under her breath as Alex released a poorly restrained laugh beside her.

"Oh my *god*!" Gabby shouted, tossing her bag under the desk and rushing over. "*Twinning!*"

Grinning with delight, Gabby stood in green scrubs with a black, long sleeve shirt underneath. The very same thing Linnea wore. Their sneakers as well, Linnea realized for the first time, were both variations of grey.

Allie, the unit secretary, came out back, nearly all of her teeth flashing as her smile expanded.

"Not a word," Linnea started.

"I can't do braids right now," Gabby started, flipping a length of hair over her shoulder, "but I *could* put it in a bun, unless you take your braids out and we both do a pony or something."

Linnea had her hair in two braids like she'd done Friday, pinned up like a wreath at her nape. She had no intention of taking them out. Then she chanced a glance at Alex, who raised his eyebrows and whispered, "*Pony.*"

Linnea groaned. "I don't have an elastic."

Gabby held up an arm and pulled back her black sleeve, exposing two pink hairbands.

"Pony!" Alex exclaimed, clapping his hands. "Let me get my fingers in there, girl. You know how I feel about long hair at work, and Gabby, I do *not* care if you take offense, it's unsanitary, but this is the right choice. We're making some magic here."

With the fuss over their appearance over, everyone settled back into getting report.

"What's this letter C mean?" Gabby asked.

"Hmm?"

"This patient has a lowercase C beside her name. Is that a typo?"

"Oh, no, it means *confidential.* It's usually a safety issue, like if there's an abusive family member or an ex they're keeping distance from. If anyone outside of the care team calls to ask about the patient, you don't even acknowledge that the patient is here."

Linnea counted herself as fortunate that she hadn't known physical abuse, that she couldn't say from personal experience if such a development would progress slowly over time, or break through with a sudden snap. She'd wondered though, given some of Erik's loose ideas on relationship boundaries, of his difficulty with the word *no*… She wondered if he would be capable, if the conditions were right.

"*God.* I can't even imagine," Gabby said with a sympathetic tone.

"Mmm," Linnea hummed, breathing through Gabby's oblivion. "There was probably a time when the patient couldn't either."

*

Linnea stood in the hall next to the med room, mixing antibiotic powder into a bag of saline. Her heart felt light, watching Alex smile beside her.

"…He asked if I had cereal," Alex sighed.

"Which you don't."

"Of course not. Girl, your brother made us crepes. Like, as if that was the only option. And he had that recipe on mental file. Just went through the pantry."

"Shit. You love food.

"And he's so relaxed when he's cooking," Alex sighed.

"He's married," she warned, stating the obvious, but he clearly needed a cold splash of water.

"I know. I've always known what the deal is with Lars… And I want to see where things go with Graham when he's back."

Linn's pocket vibrated in one short burst, then again as she pulled her phone out. Missy. She'd sent pictures.

The smile on Linnea's face was nothing compared to the feeling like sparks bubbling in her chest. She opened the first image so it filled her screen. A picture of Missy's back yard taken from the porch. There, in the distance, Cap stood beside another man, Henry, aiming a crossbow at a target. She swiped to see the next image. This one was close up, Henry, Cap, and *Lars* standing beside the target with several arrows embedded within the rings, two in the center. Her brother looked content, and Cap grinned wide, looking directly at the camera, at Missy. Henry had a pleased look on his face, not gloating, but warm.

The memory of Henry's smell came on so strong; he could have been standing beside her in the hall by the med room. Closing her eyes, Linn felt the echo of his face against hers.

The phone vibrated again in her hands. Missy.

Henry stopped over earlier. He's an absolute love. He brought the crossbow, bolts (apparently that's what the arrows are called, news to me.) He even brought a target. Then Lars came by and joined us. Cap is so happy.

"Henry is at my neighbor's house… With Lars," she said, reviewing the photos Missy sent.

"Cap and Missy's? Shit, they're like three hunter-peas in a pod. Has he met Lars?"

Linnea shook her head. "Nope. He met Cap and Missy though, when she came over with the pumpkin bread and the bacon."

"And Cap came sniffing to make sure you didn't have a creep on your hands."

"Something like that," she said, smile persisting. "Henry offered to teach Cap how to use a crossbow. Cap has arthritis, bow hunting is hard, long story, but apparently Henry followed through. Look."

Linnea held the phone out for Alex and his eyes went wide, his chin dipped.

"I've seen Cap happy, but this is like some *puppy for Christmas, Good-old days*, joy. And while what he has going on deserves more of my attention," Alex said, his thumb and forefinger spreading across the screen. "D*amn*…"

"What?"

"*What?* Don't act slow, Linn; that's not you. I'm commenting on this man here with your neighbor, the one you coaxed out of a tree stand and have apparently wrapped around your little finger… Bringing you coffee before the sun came up… kiss *hello*… kayaking… I am head over heels for Graham, and had a *really* nice night with Lars…" he sighed. "But a girl can still swoon."

"He came over after you left with Lars last night."

"Shut. Up."

"Okay," Linnea laughed, reaching toward him. "Phone please."

"I can feel the magnetism coming off him through the screen. And now he's met your brother." He said, handing the device back.

"We ran early, then Henry had a work thing, but he did mention wanting to make it back over to Cap's."

Her phone buzzed again. "It's Missy," she said at Alex's interest.

"Please tell me she sent more pictures."

It was much later in her shift that Steph approached Linn, Alex, and Gabby with elated urgency.

"Linn," she said, hooking her friend's arm where they stood by the med room. "There is a man asking about you at the desk. I may have ovulated."

The man in question came around the corner, and Linnea's heart began pounding.

Steph hadn't seen the pictures.

"That's Henry," she whispered, her mouth working into a smile as he walked toward her holding a brown paper bag like a boy bringing his lunch to school. Grinning, she couldn't take her eyes off him, his smile mirroring hers.

"What are you doing here?" she asked, her words breathy against his ear as his body closed in.

"I brought you soup," he said, passing her the bag.

Linnea peaked inside, seeing what looked like a tall, plastic take-away container.

"Venison stew."

"When did you... Weren't you at Cap's?"

"Crock pot," he said, one side of his mouth turning up.

"Thank you," she blushed, putting the bag down on Gabby's computer station, feeling flustered, bubbling. "This is Alex, Steph, and Gabby."

"Nice to meet you," he said, shaking each of their hands.

"And this is Allie," Linnea started, seeing the secretary coming toward them, her expression grave. "Henry found me," she smiled, assuming the reason for her fluster.

Allie waved briefly, then got right to the point. "I was putting up an NPO sign outside room ten," she started, feeling no need to censor herself with civilian company. "When I walked back by nine," she continued, pausing to put her hand on her chest, as if to calm herself. "I walked right into the linen cart. The visitor was in there unbuttoning his shirt. Then he takes it off. Linn, this man is *ripped.* Is he single?"

"Allie," Linnea laughed, noting the amusement on Henry's face. William hadn't been in when she'd rounded on Pete earlier, but he was most certainly the subject of Allie's attention.

"Ok, ok, ok. What's he *like*, though…" Allie persisted.

Linnea took a breath, knowing what details she *could* give would only work the woman into a frenzy. Allie was a recently divorced bibliophile with an herb garden in her kitchen… But Linnea wasn't about to indulge her. She still hadn't ruled him out as, well, as *something.* She hadn't seen him since the other night with Lars, since seeing the gardens, the greenhouse, the garage…

"He's an editor," Gabby started.

Allie's eyes went wide, Linn's shot daggers.

"I don't know exactly what kind of books," Linn said, holding up a hand. "So, just slow yourself down."

"But he reads, and he's *good* at it," Allie sighed. "He gets paid to read. You *know* I always have at least two books going."

"I know…" Linn sighed, reassuring herself that nothing would come of this, that the buzz was good for morale.

"Okay, what else," Allie grinned.

"He gardens as a hobby," Gabby continued. "Like, *seriously* gardens. Got scratched up by his roses the other day."

"In October?"

"Greenhouse," Linn reluctantly added. It just slipped out.

The secretary paused, considering.

"There's a nursery nearby that I've been to a few times," Henry started. "They have lemon and tangerine trees inside. Full size."

"See?" Gabby said. "Not weird at all."

"Why is he so jacked, though?" Allie asked, eyeing Henry, then Alex. "Or do you all just walk around looking like that and I've never noticed?"

"CrossFit," Alex shrugged.

Would Linnea have described William as *jacked*? He was slim, and she assumed he was in good shape, but hadn't seen him without his jacket on.

"He mentioned triathlons," Linnea offered.

Allie shook her head. "I can't. I can't hear anymore until I know what his deal is."

That was a line Linnea wouldn't cross. She wasn't going to break the fourth wall of Allie's fantasy. It wasn't worth the risk, the risk of what if, but also… she wasn't sure how close she should get, knowing what he didn't about what connected them.

"We're about to go in and do Pete's insulin," Gabby announced. "I've had Pete a bunch of times, and William is always there. He's quiet, but he's not grouchy or anything. I'll ask right now."

"I'm gonna need to walk over there," Alex said with raised brows. "Because the words *unbuttoned* and *triathlon* have piqued a girl's interest."

Steph's phone rang. She answered, scowled, and sped off to the nurse's station.

"How about Alex and I walk you down to this room," Henry started. "Then he can get me back to the elevator." Leaning into Linnea's ear, he whispered, "Can I kiss you at work?"

"I think that would be acceptable," she said, bringing her lips to his. She could have been doing anything when he'd arrived: placing a catheter, checking Gabby's documentation, adjusting pillows, or responding to a code. Instead, she was in the hall, gossiping about a man undressing in her patient's room. "Come on," she said when their lips parted. "We'd better get down there before he gets his shirt back on."

"Woh," Pete exclaimed as Linn and Gabby entered his room. "Are you guys sisters?" He was sitting up in a big chair, phone in his hands, bedside table against the wall.

"Nope," Linnea smiled. "Just two lucky nurses."

The sound of running water pulled her attention to the left, to William. He stood in a very snug white t-shirt, washing his hands nearly up to his elbows. A look of surprise, then amusement worked into his features as he looked up from his task with something of a sparkle to his eyes.

Linn found herself staring, trying to see through him, into the boy he'd been. What had he been like with West? Had the brightness she saw in him existed then, before, or had it been like walking out from under a grey cloud when he moved in with Sarah and Pete? Had they saved him? His aunt and his cousin, the gardens, and chance… had they saved him from his father? What would he have become? In the balance of things, she supposed, the life of her dad, and her papa had been given, and perhaps something had been saved. William had been taken from West and been given a loving family, a chance at something meaningful, something beautiful.

"Oh my *God*," Gabby whispered in Linn's ear as she wheeled the computer around her.

William turned off the sink, glancing from one woman to the other.

"Is this some play on your namesake?" He asked Linn.

"*Twin*flower," she sighed, rolling her eyes. "Cute, William, but no, this was entirely unintentional… Now you. Explain. I've never seen you without full sleeves."

"The Shirley Temples got me," he said with humor and defeat. "You've seen how the cups pile up. Pete pushed the little table out of the way as I helped him to the chair, and over they went. Thankfully I hadn't pulled my laptop out yet. My shirt was not so lucky," he shrugged, head tilted toward the pile of white and pink fabric on the counter.

Linnea examined what he *was* wearing: white t-shirt with a wet patch, grey trousers, nice shoes, and his bracelets, the pink bead still slightly unnerving. She tried to lean on the rational thing inside her that knew a color could exist in two places, but somewhere else, somewhere deep and dark, she felt the weight of a glass eye, and made connections others couldn't see.

"Cosign," Gabby said, dispersing Linn's thoughts back into the ether.

"All set," she said, handing the pen to Gabby, who *winked*.

"So, William," Gabby started, swabbing the back of Pete's arm with alcohol. "A colleague of ours asked about you… She loves to *read*, and she's super *nice*. I told her I'd ask if you were single."

Linnea sucked in a breath, cheeks growing pink. "I'm so sorry, William. I thought it would be overstepping, but Gabby is persistent, apparently."

"It's perfectly alright, Linnea," he replied, pulling his jacket on, smile growing as he turned to Gabby. "I'm sure she's lovely, but the timing just isn't right," he said, glancing at Pete, and back. "Please be sure to mention that I declined without knowing who she is. I wouldn't want her feelings to be hurt."

"Linn," came Alex's voice from the door. "Surgical House is at the nurses' station asking for you." Then he turned his head. "Make that the hallway… *Erik*," he greeted with judgement and a tilt of his head.

Then a familiar man in blue surgical scrubs appeared.

"Linn, can I speak with you? It will just take a minute."

She turned back to William, his expression flat, perhaps with recognition from their encounter in the parking lot.

"Hi, Dr. Grayer," Gabby smiled.

Erik gave her a small nod, brought his focus back to Linn, then he squinted, looking between the two women. "Gabby, is it?" He asked, a slight grin forming as his charm unfurled.

"Was Alex wearing green, too?" Erik asked, following Linn out into the hall.

"No," she sighed with a scowl, leaning against the wall beside the linen cart. "This was an unfortunate accident."

"You never wear your hair out at work…" he smiled, flourishing a finger toward her ponytail that left her with a very *fuck around and find out* feeling as she waited for him to touch her. "Was that an accident too?"

Her scowl turned to a smile as he dropped his hand, because she just couldn't help herself. "Alex's doing. I had it braided, but he got excited when he saw us matching," she said, rolling her eyes. "I let him do my hair like Gabby's."

"That's the other nurse," he said, glancing back through the door.

Linnea nodded. "He loves any excuse to get his hands in there."

"Can't say I blame him."

"Erik…"

"You weren't here last night."

"Wine night."

"Right," he said with a lazy smile. "So, what are you doing after work?"

"Driving home."

"Wanna get donuts?"

"You're going to leave halfway through your shift to get donuts with me? At what shop, Erik?" She laughed.

"I brought in a couple dozen for the ED, but I bagged three when I found out you were working. Because foresight," he winked.

"Two for me, and?"

"*One* for you, Linny. Saving lives takes calories, and I'm a big boy. Big boys need their donuts."

Linnea couldn't help but laugh.

"Full disclosure," he continued, his face solemn, "the boxes had been picked over when I made my selection…"

"Oh god… What'd you get," she asked, still smiling.

"Blueberry glazed…"

"*Christ…*"

"Maple frosted, and a jelly."

"You can walk me to my car, but it is *not* a date, Erik. I'm seeing someone, and it's serious."

"Understood," he said without hesitation.

Linnea narrowed her eyes, knowing he perceived reality differently than she did. It should just be a donut and a walk to the car, but Erik would see it as more. They needed to find a way to coexist at work, as colleagues, as two people who had been *more than* colleagues, but still had a mutual respect for one another. Hadn't she been stern with him during their last encounter? If cold avoidance was what it took, she would do it, but a casual, friendly work relationship felt better, less dramatic. Perhaps walking to her car could be a start? She should be able to eat a donut and walk to her damn car with a person…

"We eat the donuts on the way to my car," she started, voice firm with no room for nonsense. "The interaction *ends* at my car, and I get the maple."

"Deal."

"What are you even doing here this early?"

"Those online learning modules. I've been getting the deadline emails…"

"Better hop to it. Just poke your head up here around midnight. Gabby hasn't mastered brevity with her handoffs. She'll get there."

Linn's phone buzzed in her pocket, and again. Her mother.

"I'll find you," he grinned as she took the call, then turned, heading off to whatever computer he'd been parked at.

"Hey, Mom."

"I was going to text because I know you're at work, then I thought I'd just leave a voicemail. Everything okay?"

"Yeah… Why, what's going on?" She would have been worried if she hadn't clearly heard the smile in her mother's voice.

"Missy sent me some pictures."

"Oh god, Mom…" She blushed.

"Don says he looks like the kind of man who understands the difference between a hatchet and an axe."

"I'd let him cook my steak," he said in the background, bringing a huff of laughter from Linn. Don was particular about his meat.

"He showed up a little while ago. Brought me soup," she smiled.

"Oh, he's got it bad," her mother squealed. "I still haven't heard from Lars. I texted him an hour ago that I want a full rundown. I didn't even realize he'd gone out for a visit, but I'm glad you have him, Sweetie. The whole woods thing must have been a lot. Still is, I bet."

"Sure is," Linn said, eyes lost in the hall, trees on the cusp of forming around her, rain on leaves, her skin. "Love you, Mom, but I've gotta go."

*

"He started getting agitated around nine thirty," Linn said, filling in where Gabby trailed off. "He'd fallen asleep, woke up, forgot where he was. William came in about an hour later and we set up the sleeper chair. Pete's been good since then. His cousin can do a few nights here and there, but we should plan on bringing him out to the nurse's station on eves tomorrow before he gets worked up, then a sitter for nights."

Gabby continued giving report, and Linn backed off, leaning against the nurses' station beside Alex.

"How much longer are you training her?" He whispered.

"It's not *that* bad. We were all new nurses once, and we all took forever. It was months before I started telling Tara she could look up normal lab values *after* report, and I wasn't fresh out of school."

"You'd be here 'til one o'clock if you answered all her questions. She's a damn good nurse though. Thorough as *fuck*."

"Just go, Alex, seriously. I'm supposed to walk out with Erik. He got doughnuts…"

"Watch yourself."

"It's fine. I just want things to be normal. Avoiding him is too weird."

"I know what *you* think is going on, but that man doesn't read signals right. I am not on team *she asked for it*. This shouldn't be on you, girl, but it is, and you need to watch yourself. Tonight, he's walking you to your car, and tomorrow, you're bumping into him at the grocery store again."

"It shouldn't be this hard," Linnea groaned.

"Pretty ain't easy," he said, tossing a mane of imaginary hair over his shoulder. "But there are worse things in this world, so count your blessings, and stop interacting with him. He's not worth the doughnuts. Now, what's good with Henry?" He smiled. "You seeing him again after work for another sleepover?"

"I'm not sure, though I'd probably know by now if he were coming by. We left things a little open ended, and he didn't mention anything at the soup drop off."

"That was an unexpected delight."

"Sure was. I should send him a message and see what his night is looking like. Have you heard from Graham?"

"We have a tentative thing for Saturday when he gets back from a work thing," he said, then yawned. "I need to get out of here and get some beauty rest, because I know I didn't get any last night…"

"See you tomorrow," she smiled, shaking her head.

Alex gave a wave, disappearing down the hall. Then she heard his condescending voice say, *"Erik."*

Gabby emerged from the back room as Surgical House came around the corner, grey hoodie over his scrubs, and a specimen bag dangling from his hand. When he spotted Linn, he smiled and held up his prize: the clear bag marked with an orange biohazard symbol, and three old donuts inside.

Shift over, headed to my car. Are you around tonight, or tomorrow? Linnea wrote to Henry. Then, figuring the presence of another human would act as a buffer, she said, "Punch out and let's go, Gabby. Doughnuts aren't going to eat themselves."

Erik barely masked his grumble, then ran his eyes over the third wheel, considering.

"These are a lot better than I expected," Gabby said as they exited the elevator. "It's like blueberry cake with icing." She took another bite from the half-eaten doughnut. "I don't think I'd *get* one, though, if there were other options."

"You and everyone else," Erik said, no longer looking at Gabby. As they neared the door, he put his hand on Linnea's arm. "I feel like we're not getting a chance to talk," he started. "Why don't you come by after your run in the morning, my shift will be over… Or we can go get coffee. I could meet you at Dee Dee's."

"We *have* talked, Erik," she said with a stern whisper. "Extensively. And, I just don't want things to be weird anymore. It's nice being able to say hi in the hall when you're up seeing patients, but I think it's sending the wrong message if I meet with you outside of work. And, if I'm honest, I don't *want* to spend time with you outside of work. Our lives out there have transitioned away from each other, and I'm not looking to change that."

A timely gasp from Gabby interrupted the tension, but not Erik's irritation. Linnea turned to see her trainee standing beside the exit door, holding up a key she'd undoubtably pulled from her scrubs. The PCA key.

"*Again?* Gabby, you've *got* to check your pockets upstairs," Linn said, holding out her hand, seizing the keys, and the opportunity. "I'll run it back, you two go ahead."

"But-" Erik protested as Gabby passed her the keys.

"You aren't going to let Gabby walk the rest of the way alone, are you? It's dangerous out there." Then Linnea turned without regrets, and took the stairs.

*

The air didn't waste time in slipping through the weave of Linnea's black shirt where it extended beyond her green scrubs. She'd finally made it out the door, jacket stowed away with an empty food container and a water bottle in the canvas bag over her shoulder. She'd foregone the added layer, choosing to feel what she could of the crisp surroundings, refreshingly absent of conversation.

Leaves moved under the wind's ministrations, both on branches and on the ground. Her footsteps pulsed over the asphalt, breath in the air, all pleasant sounds uninterrupted by the human voice. She'd missed walking alone to her car.

Then there was a buzz in her pocket, and a delightful thrill racing through her as she paused to read Henry's message.

Did you want some time alone in the studio tonight?

She *should*, but the push to continue with her current work wasn't strong. She'd felt so inspired recently, but wondered if maybe the woman in the woods had the opposite effect on her work.

I could come by in a few hours? He added.

That would bring her to, what, three? Four in the morning? She'd go home, shower, eat a snack, and work in the studio. That would be more than enough time to cast that cup while she waited for inspiration.

GG's words whispered through her: *It won't be my bones rising to meet your foot, Honey, but the next step will come, and you will be ready.* With what might have been faith, Linnea clung to her grandmother's words, to their timelessness.

I'd like that, she typed.

Phone screen black in her hand, Linnea stood well beyond the hospital's glow, buffered in a pocket of darkness among the remaining parked cars. She'd wear that cocoon home, until she met the moon in her studio.

A sensation that preceded knowing awakened within her suddenly, pausing her steps as they restarted. Hyperawareness and foreboding combined with curiosity, calling her to look for the source of the primal overture.

And then something caught her eye down low, like a painted egg nestled deep in the garden, treasure left for her to find. Linnea's discovery came in the form of a shadow on the ground, reaching beyond the space between cars, like… like dark hair spreading out through water.

Taking a step forward, Linnea swiveled her head slowly, seeing that it wasn't *like* hair, the shadow *was* hair… hair that she followed to a woman's form. Green scrubs, black shirt, grey shoes, a stethoscope by her neck, bag at her feet, distorted remains of a blueberry doughnut under her left leg.

18.

Berkshires, October 2014

Heat prickled under Linnea's arms, ice in her blood pumping outward as she dropped low to the pavement. Heart pounding, she scanned beneath the surrounding cars for feet, for movement, for what might remain still in the shadows.

Nothing.

Gabby dead in parking lot calling 911 I don't see anyone, she shot off rapidly before dialing the three numbers.

How long had Gabby been down? Before she had a chance to think it over, Linnea placed two fingers over the young woman's carotid artery as the call went through, feeling for a pulse she knew would be absent. She spoke to the dispatcher with breathy clarity while repeatedly forcing her weight down onto Gabby's sternum.

Her phone on the pavement buzzed, briefly displaying a message from Henry on the call screen.

We're coming.

Two words, and a deluge of relief.

With the dispatcher's calm reassurance fading from importance, with skin both numb and *awake*, Linnea compressed, allowed for recoil, and she observed. She looked for anything, anything that might reach out like hair from shadows, studying the crumbled doughnut, the stethoscope, contents of her pockets spilled, red caps, alcohol swabs, bandage scissors, penlights. *Such a new nurse*, Silk tape… bolt cutters? What the hell Did Gabby need bolt cutters for?

She met Gabby's eyes, their emptiness, the red where white had been, the marks on her neck. Scratches and petechiae peppered the skin under her jaw. Scratches, not from her attacker, but from Gabby, trying to free herself from what had stopped the blood and air from passing... The single ligature line. The assailant hadn't used their hands, but had they wanted to? What would keep someone from using their hands?

Thoughts of contaminating the crime scene were pressed back into the corners of Linnea's consciousness. Instead, she focused on her compressions, on the idea that perhaps her trainee had been an organ donor and CPR could help in some way. Could they harvest from a murder victim? Wouldn't the police need to take photographs? Would they find anything in Gabby's mouth?

Red, blue, and white lights flashed as a whirlwind of first responders arrived. Linnea was ushered to the side, given a blanket, and the world seemed to build up around her in time lapse.

She spoke to a woman in uniform, eyes wandering around the scene as she recounted what had transpired.

Hospital staff emerged from the main building, clustered together in the glow of the ambulance bay, though the nursing supervisor was allowed to pass through to speak with police.

Was Erik there among them, hovering by the door? Was William?

Another vehicle arrived, no colored lights, unmarked, familiar. Curiosity caught hold of her, and she found herself focused on the windshield, trying to see… Jonathan. Like shade and cool water after sustained exposure to a star, Jonathan stepped out, and with him the promise of respite.

The passenger door opened and another man emerged, though not Henry. He came around the car and stood half a head shorter than Jonathan. While Jon wore a suit, the other man had on cargo pants and a long sleeved, black thermal… and aviator sunglasses. At night. She hadn't checked the time, but it had to be one o'clock in the morning. No sooner had the thought crossed her mind, than the second man took off his shades, met her eyes, and smiled. *Phil.* She could see it in his face that he was another of Henry's brother's. But where was Henry?

Phil appeared to nudge his brother, who gave Linnea his attention. He raised one hand as if to say *hi*, then turned his palm inward and encircled his face. She'd seen that gesture before. Had he just said *hello beautiful* in American Sign Language? Jon smiled, seeing the wheels turn as he approached with his brother, pausing to give their credentials to a uniform.

Jon's arms came around her in a hug she hadn't been anticipating, but felt comforted by, while Phil began introductions with the officer who'd been interviewing her. The woman stated she'd just been wrapping up, and would get in touch should she have further questions.

"I bet you're ready to get out of here," Jonathan said, his hand briefly rubbing her back.

"Yes," she sighed as he pulled away, still jittery, exhausted but wired. "It's just… I…" she continued. After the clarity of speech with the dispatcher and the uniforms, she let herself relax enough for her words to come a little slower. "I could use a shower," she said with a heavy smile, then turning to the other man, she said, "You must be Phil."

"You know it," he grinned, leaning in toward her, then scowling as Jonathan swatted him away. He signed something to his brother, who shot back with a short burst of gestures.

"Hey, none of that," Linnea teased. "Where's Henry?"

"The situation required a prompt response," Jonathan answered without missing a beat. "He'll meet us at the house. Phil and I just need to take a look at the victim before we go. Gabby was her name?"

Linnea nodded, and the brothers made their way over to the body, Jonathan walking a step ahead. As soon as he came into range, his expression changed, and the word *shit* came flying out of his mouth. Linnea didn't have to hear to know what he said, there was no subtlety to it.

Phil paused beside his brother, and together they stared down at the victim, looked up at each other with concern on their faces, then turned toward Linnea, their actions synchronized.

Was it the manner of death that prompted the reaction, or the similarity in appearance shared by Linnea and the victim… down to the sneakers and hair style?

Her pocket buzzed long enough to register the vibration as a call, not a message. Henry.

"Hello?"

"I'd like you to head to the lake house with Jon and Phil."

"You're at the lake?"

"Jonathan will drive, and Phil will follow behind in your car. I'd like to say I'll be there shortly, but it could be a little while."

Linnea sighed. "I need a shower, and a snack… and to shut my brain off for a bit."

"Everything you need is there. Take a shower, grab some sweats and a t-shirt. Anything you find in the kitchen is fair game."

"Okay. I need to call Lars."

"Want me to handle it?"

"No… No, he'll want to hear from me."

"Alright," he said, then paused with a huff of breath, she could almost feel him smiling. "You're under no obligation to entertain my brothers, but they do make good company during a shitstorm."

When the call ended, Jonathan and Phil had returned from their viewing, and she held out her keys.

"I'm perfectly capable of driving," she started, feeling she had to at least make a show of asserting herself. "But I'm not complaining. Wait, can we even take my car out of the lot? What are the crime scene rules?"

"It's fine," Jonathan assured her. "I spoke to the officer in charge and located your vehicle. They'll allow it."

"Good," she sighed. "Just let me grab my flip flops."

"Your what?" Jon asked, Phil cracking a smile beside him.

"I like to switch into flip flops after work in the summer, and I still have a pair in that pocket behind the passenger's seat. These work sneakers aren't going anywhere near the lake house. They've walked through everything."

*

Showering helped. Linnea had put a light on in the bedroom and left the door open enough that she could see her way around in the bathroom, while still feeling buffered by darkness. Water fell over her, the sensation a distraction from the pulse that continued to travel from her hands and through her body, echoes of chest compressions. The tactile memory repeated, alternating and overlapping with the visual of Gabby's open eyes.

She hadn't felt like the woman in the woods, the coyote, West. She had been Linn's, but not. She'd been nearly warm.

Bunny, she thought, hearing Gabby's voice say the word in her mind, thinking of her oblivious joy upon seeing her totem. She'd last lit up for a blueberry donut and Erik's attention. He'd walked her to her car, hadn't he? She should have been safe.

Familiar with where to acquire what she needed, Linnea dressed in sweats, a t-shirt, and a hoodie.

Found Gabby dead in the parking lot, she wrote, texting her brother. *Call if you need to, but I'm okay.*

At work??? Where are you? Are you okay?

YES. Staying the night at Henry's. Talk in the morning. Love you.

After shooting a quick email to her mom, not wanting to risk waking her with a text, Linn typed out a group message to Alex and Steph.

Guys, I found Gabby dead in the parking lot.

I'm so glad you texted, Alex wrote. *I just heard, but Lars said not to message because you're safe and probably tired.*

I am. I'm safe and at Henry's. Exhausted. What happened to beauty sleep?

You get what you need, girl.

Steph is probably asleep. I'm going to get a snack then get some sleep. Tell Lars I said lights out. Love you guys.

No promises. Love you.

She headed downstairs without peeking through the open window overlooking the living space. Jon and Phil sat at the counter, each drinking some manner of hot beverage, the room rich with the bitter scent of freshly brewed coffee.

"Would you like a cup?" Phil offered, but Linnea shook her head as she approached.

She knew she needed *something* but wasn't quite sure what. Caffeine, though, didn't feel like the right idea, not with racing thoughts.

"Cards?" Jonathan asked.

She circled the counter to the kitchen side, checking her phone. "Have you heard from…"

"Henry's doing Henry right now…" Phil said gently. "It takes however long it needs to." He extended an arm, palm up. "Phone."

Linnea slowly pulled the device from her pocket, narrowing her eyes.

"I'm putting our numbers in there," he said, glancing down at her hesitant hand, then back at her eyes until she handed him the phone.

He swiped and typed while Jonathan sat quietly.

Glancing at the glass hall now and then, Linnea looked over their shoulders at the expanse of wall covered in bone. It was as her eyes traced the curves of the skulls, branching upward through the antlers, in the calm stillness of that moment, that she felt the hunger which had perhaps been present for quite some time.

"Do you think Henry has oats?"

"Like oatmeal?" Phil asked, still typing.

"Like Quaker Oats, for cookies…"

Phil took on a real thinking face as his eyes slid over the cabinets, perhaps imagining what was behind their doors. "Instant packets or steel cut. Check that one," he said, pointing to a pantry that spanned floor to ceiling beside the fridge.

There were no rolled oats, but she pulled out flour, sugar, and salt, placing them on the counter. She found a pie plate, butter, eggs, and gathered seven apples from the fruit bowl.

Phil handed the phone back to Linn, and she scrolled through the contacts, smiling enough for her teeth to show when she reached *Brother Jon* and *Brother Phil*. She clicked on Phil, and sure enough, there was a note at the bottom: Likes m&m's, grilled swordfish, all manner of food trucks, spicy fish tacos, long walks on the beach, falconry…

"Falconry?" She asked.

Phil grinned with a huff of laughter as he nodded.

Jonathan sighed, looked to his brother, and said, "It's an act of *god* you don't have a bird." Then to Linnea he added, "There's a place we bring him to once a year."

"I don't have a falcon because I don't have adequate space for a mews, Jonathan, and it's hardly a chore for you guys to *take* me." Then to Linnea, he asked, "Did you do Jon's yet?"

His brother looked on suspiciously.

"Brother Jon," she started. "Likes craft beer, World War Two documentaries, meat and bread when he's not home. Enjoys any type of puzzle: Sunday Times crossword, jigsaws if over a thousand pieces…"

"I bet you'd have made a good clockmaker, with all the little parts," Phil said from across the counter. "He could puzzle for hours,"

"I get in a zone," Jon shrugged.

"Well, I think I have something you can work on. Where are the knives?" She asked, placing the phone in her pocket and bowl of apples on the counter in front of them. She began opening drawers before either answered.

"Got them," she said, then handed one to each brother. "Peel, then slice. Doesn't have to be fancy."

She turned to preheat the oven, expecting questions, but instead she heard the sound of blades scraping between skin and flesh.

"Swedish apple crisp," she said, going back to the pantry to look for vanilla. The recipe lived in her heart; one she could execute easily. "I could make it in my sleep, and the ingredients are bare bones." And also, she was stress-baking, cousin to stress-cleaning, but with an edible byproduct.

"Christ, Phil," Jonathan whispered over the sound of chewing. "Leave some for the pie…"

Linnea looked up from stirring the sugar and melted butter to see Phil chomping on an apple, his brother scowling.

"The two of you are sharing that guest house while you're here?" she asked with just a hint of a smile gracing her face. "How's that working out?"

"We grew up together," Jon started. "We're family, a team. The bumps are just a part of it."

"Things would run smoother if Jon cleaned the sink after he used it," Phil said, popping another chunk of apple into his mouth, then continuing with his work.

Jonathan took a deep breath and exhaled, clearly restraining himself.

"Clean as you go," Phil continued, depositing the last apple peel into a refuse bowl Linnea had provided. "See, Linn knows what I mean, look at her workstation." Then, to her, he politely said, "There's a stainless compost bin under the sink, separate from the trash."

"I won't dispute your claim, Phil, nor will I counter by citing any of the *multitude* of your shortcomings," Jonathan quipped with dignity, perhaps internally holding onto his age and accolades for strength.

Linnea finished stirring the batter while the two brothers continued with their brand of bickering. The exchange was oddly refreshing, comforting, evoking in her a sense of nostalgia.

"I have a brother, Lars," she started, taking the bowl of scraps to the sink. "If anyone knows how to push my buttons, it's him. But it goes both ways..." she said, sliding the cores and peels into the compost. "He's also been beside me in the deepest trenches I've ever experienced. When I cut my teeth on something *questionable*, he supported me, every time. No questions."

Both Jon and Phil nodded to themselves, perhaps recalling questions they never asked. Phil combined cinnamon and sugar, then poured the mixture over the apples for Jonathan to stir, the space around them blooming with the scent of warm spice. They had been through so much together, the two men before her.

They'd survived the untimely loss of a sister, and who knows what else, but they were bonded by death, something she understood intimately. She knew how the roots of trauma could extend into the deepest, darkest parts of a person. She sensed something current bringing them together with Henry.

Jonathan was investigating the girl in the woods, but was Phil? And the police had just let them walk into Gabby's crime scene, though they were both reasonably credentialed, she supposed… Did Henry have something to do with it? For work or leisure? He took time off work for deer season, needed it, and yet Jonathan had said, *There's only so much Phil and I can do.*

Linnea felt the brothers' eyes on her. She glanced down at the bowl, and reached in, selecting a smaller piece of apple coated unevenly in brown goodness.

"Now *this* is the time to sneak a slice."

The others followed her lead without hesitation.

*

The pie had been out not ten minutes when a door opened in the glass entryway. Henry, wearing all black, his t-shirt snug under the jacket he took off. His eyes flashed toward the kitchen as he removed his boots, and it was all Linnea could do to wait, though a sigh came through with her breath.

Phil immediately got up and made for the exit. Passing Henry, he placed a lingering hand on his shoulder.

"I'll be waiting outside, Brother," he said, then walked out the door.

Linnea stood on the kitchen side of the counter, arms encircling Henry when he came into reach. He touched his forehead to hers, closed his eyes.

"Smells good in here," he whispered.

"We made a pie," she said, ushering in a long pause before either of them spoke again.

"It was a lot, yeah?" Henry finally said, Linnea nodding in response. "Tea?"

She moved her head again, up and down, so Henry turned and stepped toward the stove, eyes catching on the pie, surface golden and bespeckled with clumps of dark brown sugar. He looked back to Linnea, eyebrows raised.

"It's still pretty hot," she smiled. "But we could scoop out a couple portions to cool faster…"

The corner of Henry's lip curled up as he turned to face the stove again, lifting the kettle to check its weight, switching on the burner.

Jonathan, who'd remained seated on the other side of the counter, might as well have been a ghost, thus far unsuccessful in taking form.

"We need to talk about this, Henry," he finally said.

Henry reached for two mugs, his back toward the counter.

"Take a walk, Jon."

"I'd like to go to sleep," his brother replied, draining what residue remained in his cup as he stood. "Instead, I'm drinking coffee." He paused, his eyes pleading. "We're *tired*, Henry."

"It's what you agreed to. I'll be over in a few minutes," he said, eyes flicking to the stove. "With pie."

Jon nodded, then his attention fell on her. "Linn," he sighed, offering a single wave and a heavy smile. "Until next time."

Linnea held up a hand, watching as he turned and followed the path Phil took, exiting the house. She'd enjoyed her time with Henry's brothers, felt a sense of ease she couldn't attribute entirely to the shower. Baking had busied all of their hands, the company had pleasantly busied her emotions, and not once had either brother pressed her to talk about her experience in the parking lot. Would she have spilled her memories if they'd asked? Had she been waiting for an excuse to relieve herself? Perhaps, but not with them.

Henry prepared two mugs with tea, two small dishes of apple crisp, then walked the steaming cups and plates over to the coffee table. Tilting his head toward the couch, he stood with some variation of a white throw blanket cascading from his hands.

Linnea accepted his invitation, relaxing into the end of the sofa, her legs coming to rest over his lap as he arranged the blanket. The weave was both thick and billowing, as if the mist from the lake had been spun and woven to cover them instead of the water. She reached for her tea, fingers hesitant, thinking the vessel might still be too hot, never mind the liquid…

"I added quite a bit of milk," he said, low and with something of a smile. "It may have cooled down enough."

He reached for his cup, tested it, and nodded. Blowing gently, he took another, longer sip, and nodded again. She followed his movements with her own, the tea cooled *just* enough not to burn.

"Thank you," Linnea sighed, her thoughts drifting out the wall of glass and into the darkness beyond. "I was with Gabby just before," she started. "We were walking out together, she and I, and Erik."

Henry cocked his head.

"He's the overnight surgical house, the on-call, in-house surgeon during off hours."

Henry nodded in understanding, and for her to continue.

"We used to date. It was monogamous, but very casual, for me at least, and *temporary*. He felt something far more serious, and I thought it best to end things before it was too hard for him. So, we broke up. Then I started bumping into him outside of work. A *lot*. He'd just pop up at the grocery store, picking up takeout, showing up at Dee Dee's every morning after my run; It's why I stopped going..."

Henry listened, a forearm resting on her legs. He didn't become uncomfortable at the mention of a previous partner or his behavior. He drank his tea, occasionally squeezed her foot through the blanket, and he kept listening.

"I talked to Erik, the *accidental* meetings stopped, and we just saw each other at work now and then. But when this all happened with the girl in the woods, he texted. Then, when I didn't respond, he came up to the floor and said he was concerned about my safety. He started trying to walk me down to my car… Alex said I should have been more firm with him, but I thought I had been *absolutely* clear…" She continued to walk him through what had happened with the doughnuts and the PCA keys, returning to find Gabby on the ground.

"Hmm." Henry put down his mug, and took out his phone. He typed briefly, then tucked it away again.

"I should text him and ask where the hell he was," she whispered, fire in her words.

Henry shook his head, calm. "I think it's best if you maintain limited contact with him, given your history."

Linnea sighed. She wanted to give Erik a piece of her mind, but it probably wasn't worth the engagement.

"Gabby and the woman in the woods…" She started, thumb rubbing over the cup in her hands. Do you think it was the same person?"

He considered her silently for a moment, then asked, "What are your thoughts?"

"Well," she started, having played the scene over in her mind almost every time she closed her eyes. "I found the woman in the woods… she'd been posed, things taken and left behind. Gabby's clothes appeared intact. No pieces were taken that I could see. She'd been discarded." Linnea paused, closed her eyes, then opened them when she saw Gabby's. "I wish I'd looked into her mouth."

"You attempted to resuscitate her…" He said, citing details she hadn't given. He'd spoken to his brothers, and they to the police.

"I didn't give rescue breaths," she admitted. "I knew she was dead. I had to go through with compressions, but I knew, and I just couldn't breathe into her knowing she was gone."

"Nothing would have been found in her mouth," he said, picking up a plate of pie, offering to exchange it for Linnea' s mug.

She took the plate Henry offered, handing him her remaining tea to be put on the table.

"No ambergris, then," she said, questioning if Gabby's murder was incidental, entirely unrelated to the woman in the woods. She'd found two women dead, less than a week separating them. She'd thought William had been responsible for the first… The sweet smell of apples and cinnamon flooded into her, prelude to the bite she would take, easing her into what she was about to say.

"I've only told Lars, but" Linn paused, exhaled, shook her head, and smiled. "Remember the whole thing at work with that guy taking his shirt off? I thought it was him at first, assuming the assailant was a man."

"The one who took the woman's life, in the woods?"

Linn nodded.

"What led you to suspect him?" He asked, supportive with a hint of humor, and no judgement.

"The woman in the woods, she had swatches of fabric missing from her, her undergarments. And William has these beaded bracelets he wears…" She rolled her eyes, thinking it foolish but honest to say out loud. "One of the beads was the same bright pink as the woman's underwear. *I know*… probably a coincidence. But he had scratches on his arms. He said his aunt's gardens had been neglected, and the scratches were from roses in the greenhouse, but I would have sworn they were from an animal."

"Have you shared your thoughts with your friend, Steph, the one with the detective husband?"

"No. She would freak out, but also, eh." She shrugged. Steph already had a theory she liked playing with, she didn't need another about a patient's cousin with trophy beads. "I don't know if I want Drew thinking I'm at work profiling patients and their families."

Henry nodded, lifted his plate from the table, securing her legs with one hand as he leaned forward, then settled back into the couch. Linnea took her first bite as she watched him, his fork lifting upward, knowing what he would taste as soft apples bathed in sugar and spice melted over her tongue.

He sighed around the food, setting the plate and fork in his lap, the warmth from the dish passing through the blanket to her legs.

"For what it's worth, Gabby wouldn't have been killed for the same reason as the woman in the woods," he said, words gentle, but eyes *piercing* as he spoke "She didn't meet the right criteria… Perhaps she looked similar enough to someone who did, though."

She remembered his brothers in the parking lot, their reaction to Gabby's body, the way they'd turned back toward her, seeing the similarity. Was the death unrelated, or was Gabby denied the whale stone and posing because she was the wrong woman. Or perhaps a perfect substitute, to lengthen a process the killer knew would end, but was not yet ready. Or was he seeking to provoke a reaction from her?

"I went by Pete's," she started, "just to look, thinking if there were no signs of flowers, I'd know William was lying. But there were gardens, extensive and overgrown, and there was a greenhouse. I didn't get inside, though."

Henry's stance hadn't changed, but there was a flicker of something in his eyes. Concern, maybe. "You suspected this man to be a serial killer of women, and you went to his home?"

"In my defense, I brought Lars, and he *did* wrestle through college," she said, trying to weave in something light while feeling the weight of what she'd done, the risk she'd taken. In retrospect, it had turned out fine, but still foolish. William's greenhouse-flowers story checked out, though she didn't know if they were roses inside. Did that negate the possibility that he could have some unhealthy obsession with both flowers *and* women? He'd been at the hospital when Gabby was killed, could have slipped downstairs. But would he? She knew who he was, what he'd come from…

"And you're good with a stick, under pressure?" He teased, though she still sensed something deadly serious underneath.

"Right," she breathed, a smile peeking through. Then her features relaxed. "When Lars and I were there," she continued, memories slipping slow, the threat of a torrent looming. "He came home."

Henry maintained his predatory observation, listening, thirsty for every word.

"The moon was a waxing crescent the night my grandmother died. She was hit by a drunk driver, like my dad, and papa. The first accident was the fault of a man who owned a local landscaping business. *West*, his name was. He got out of the truck. There was so much fire and blood. Half his face was bloody, missing an eye… Lars and I were so young then, but we were grown when GG was taken. I was already a nurse, Lars an anesthesiologist. We came out for winter solstice. The three of us took a drive to get marshmallows and stopped to look for the moon. It was cold, crisp, and the truck was like darkness moving, swerving, until it pinned GG in a ditch. She was gone. I crawled under the front end, tried to get her, but I couldn't feel any life. I took some of her hair, the beads she wore, but I couldn't have pulled her free. The driver had survived, and I attempted to assist him while Lars called emergency services, but Lars saw something written on the truck, and he froze up. It was a sign for his Landscaping business. The man in the cab, reeking of gin, with a scar on his face and glass eye where I'd once seen an empty socket… The man in the cab was West."

"The eye," he whispered, with not a shred of disgust on his awestruck face.

Linn sighed, nodded, trusting that he could see all of her, and she continued. "I took the eye, and with Lars's help, I took an arm. We set the truck on fire and called for help."

"The teacup," he breathed, the room around them a blend of white and black, skulls and antlers fading to a rippled pattern until it was only him, and her, and the truth between them.

"Two cups, two saucers. One set for each of us."

Butterflies, uneasy within her, fluttered, waiting. Henry's mouth was silent, but he was wholly rapt, like a grown man seeing dawn for the first time.

"Lars and I passed the front of William's house on the street. He'd just returned home, the garage door was open, and we saw signage in there… for the West Nursery," she paused, taking a breath, eyes flitting up to the wall, then back to Henry, grounding her from sliding into her memories again. "West had the landscaping business, and his sister the nursery. When West was incarcerated for killing my dad and papa, his son went to live with her."

"*William.*"

She nodded. "William."

They sat in silence, surrounded by the sweet scent of apples and cinnamon, and Henry cradling her lower half. One strong hand massaged her leg, soothing, quiet, allowing her story to settle within them like water after a storm. giving the rain time to sink into the earth

His voice was smooth as it entered the room, warm and easy. "Do you feel misplaced guilt, for your piece in the shadows of his life?"

"No," she answered. "Nothing like that. Lars and I took liberties in a very grey place, crossed a line within ourselves, but not into the black. If anything, I wonder if, if it was more than Lars and I who were released when West burned. Maybe William felt relief as well, a weight released, like we'd freed him from a necrotic limb threatening to infect the rest of his body," she sighed, pausing a moment. "I saw the gardens, and the greenhouse. I've heard the way he speaks of them, the way he is with Pete. I had nothing to do with that, though, his moving there. That was West on his own after Dad and Papa."

"What you know now, this changes things? Your suspicion with the bracelet and the scratches?"

"We are all capable of being more than one thing, more than two…" she said, recalling GG's words to her when Linn had felt conflicted, feeling divided as her namesake.

"You took your grandmother's hair," Henry said softly, relaxed as he spoke. "Bone and hair, the eye… But nothing in the woods. Nothing tonight?"

The idea crawled like bugs on her skin. "Did you think I would have?"

He shook his head. "No. Didn't seem right. I wanted to ask, though. See how it felt to you."

"It feels revolting. She wasn't mine. I had a right to the coyote, and the other animals were offerings. My family is mine innately, and West…" There was no question. "He'd been mine since I was a child; I'd only been waiting… And now I think I'm waiting again, waiting for the next step, but not Gabby. I could have taken hair, glazed a rabbit from her ashes, but I don't…" Again, she felt the wrongness of it creeping along her skin and her insides. "I've thought maybe hunting would be my next step, but there's something about an offering. I was involved in an exchange with the coyote, with the driver… but they were still offerings of a sort, opportunities, forced encounters when I took what was mine, but I didn't go looking for them. I didn't hunt, and I don't think I'm meant to," she sighed.

She looked to Henry for a sense that he understood. It had been a dangerous thing to open to him thusly. Only Lars had been there through the whole of it with her, and she'd known Henry such a short time. As she looked at him, though, his eyes drifting up the wall of antler and bone, she knew she'd made the right choice.

Henry reached for his plate, and took another bite of pie, not looking at his phone when Linnea heard it hum briefly from beneath some pocket of fabric.

"It's tomorrow that you're working again?" He asked.

"Mmm," She nodded.

"I'm assuming you plan on staying here the rest of the night, which I will selfishly enjoy, but would you consider spending the day as well?"

"I'd like that," she smiled. "I'll just need to head out around lunch time to change for work, grab some food. Lars is probably still at the house; he and I should talk before he goes back home."

"Have you thought about not going in tomorrow?"

Of *course,* she had… but would that help her to move forward? She'd worked closest with Gabby, had her in her home, trained her… But others would feel the young woman's loss, and they would be there at the hospital, supporting one another, as they always did.

"I think going in would be good for me, for all of us. Alex and Steph will be there."

Henry nodded again, smiled and leaned in for a kiss before easing her legs down to the ground.

"My brothers are very likely still outside the front door, sulking. Jon at least, with Phil berating him."

Phil had seemed quite serious, and Jonathan… Deeply troubled.

Linnea stood and stretched, collecting half the dishes as Henry gathered the others. Together they cleaned up, his brothers still, perhaps, waiting in the cool October night.

She stood facing him in the entryway before he stepped out, a glass covered container of pie passing from her hands to his.

"Would you like the light left on?" He asked.

Linnea shook her head.

He lifted a free hand to her face, then reached for the switch as he turned for the door.

19.

Berkshires, October 2014

Linn woke as dawn crept in easy. Her body could have used more sleep, but she couldn't bring herself to ignore the soft, grey light flooding Henry's room like a whisper. She could have run with him through the network of trails threaded through the acres surrounding his home, but the idea of wearing her work sneakers in that context rested like a stagnant film over her skin. Instead, she sat beside Henry on the deck, wearing his sweats and the flip flops from her car. Blanket wrapped around her and tea in her hand, they welcomed the morning in relative silence.

He made her oats, and taught her how to play cribbage. They took the kayaks out, had lunch on the deck, then Henry followed her home so she could change for work. She spoke to her mom on the drive, feeling the more than gentle nudge to *come out and visit for a few days.*

The first half of her day had been full enough for Linn to maintain a sense of peace. The intrusive thoughts about dead women, William, fire, and flowers rested in her mind, but she still heard their steady breaths as they slept, felt the flicker of their eyes as they dreamed. And so, she left for work earlier than usual, wearing scrubs the color of wet sand, pockets stocked with alcohol pads and red caps, badge clipped to the V of her neckline. Instead of the hospital parking lot, she pulled alongside the sidewalk a few houses down from Pete's.

It wasn't that she still suspected William, but that she held some sense of curiosity she couldn't quite assign a name to, a curiosity that somehow still managed to peek around the corners of walls she'd been silently building since seeing the word *West* in Pete's garage.

She told herself she wouldn't get out if she saw William's car in the driveway, but it was absent, so she approached as she had before with Lars, over the stone path and under the arbor.

In the midday light, she saw so much more than she had under the moon, the way the gardens had been shaped, the way lilacs and rose of Sharon would have kept the perimeter blossoming from spring through early autumn. She imagined the thought that went into what plants flowered when, what nutrients they took from the soil, what life needed to be shaded to thrive by those who preferred sun around them.

She took slow, careful steps as her mind wandered, cautious not to trip on the overgrown remains of decorative grasses or stones fallen out of place.

A metallic click snapped Linn from her thoughts.

Heart pumping hard and fast, her eyes darted around, seeking the source of the unnatural noise: behind, to the back door, the greenhouse, then returning to the back door as it opened, and William stepped out.

His head turned toward her immediately, then tilted to the side. His eyes squinted slightly behind his glasses, a note of confusion, then the corner of his lip perked up into a still befuddled smile.

"Linnea?"

Her face had grown hot, heart still pounding, perhaps less from fear than embarrassment, until she thought of Gabby's body in the parking lot, and pictured William holding a phone charger around her neck, easing her to the ground. Linn shuddered, though waves of heat pulsed through her chest. Had he wished it was her? If it had been, would he have put a fucking whale stone in her mouth?

No, she thought, shaking her head. *It wasn't him.*

"I was, well, I was on my way in for my shift," she started, glancing down at her scrubs, strengthening the shell of confidence forming over a very unstable foundation of uncertainty and speculation. "I remembered Pete's address from his paperwork."

William let the door shut behind him and moved away from the house, slowly closing the distance between them. Linn tried not to make her surveillance of their surroundings too obvious. They were alone, the house, fence, and trees obstructing the view of any curious neighbors.

"I understand *how* you're here, but not why," he said. "Is everything alright?"

Of course she wasn't alright… But oh, he meant his cousin. "No, I mean, yes, Pete's fine, I just know how hard things were last night, and we're so thankful that you stayed over. I thought…" Her eyes wandered throughout the garden, landing on the greenhouse, then back to William. "You'd mentioned roses, and I thought maybe it would help if I brought some flowers in for him? Something familiar, something from home, and connected to you."

"Ah," he breathed with a nod of his head. Then, with equal parts scolding and teasing, he said, "While your heart is in the right place, this feels a little *tresspassy*, don't you think?"

"Yes, but, on the right side of tresspassy?" She cringed.

"*Just*," he smiled with the brightness in his eyes that she'd seen the day before, when he'd stood at the sink rinsing his shirt. "We're fortunate I was home, or you'd have found the greenhouse locked. Wait here while I grab my keys."

The colors appeared like an impressionist painting through the glass, coming into focus as William opened the door.

"It's beautiful," she whispered.

She took a few steps in, not wanting to miss anything during her initial observation. Roses. *Roses*, pink centered fading out to white tinted green, blush, magenta, ballet pink. She saw other flowers, too, and a worn wooden workbench stood stocked with tools, gloves, pots underneath, soil and fertilizer.

"They certainly are," he sighed behind her, his soft voice sending an alarm through her chest and over her skin, raising the tiny hairs over her body.

She'd forgotten him for a moment, amid the flowers and the glass. She'd left herself vulnerable, but to what? Frozen where she stood, Linn wasn't sure she was capable of turning. What color underwear had she put on? Cotton. Mauve with a soft lace border. Would he use the lace for his bracelet, or just a smooth portion from the center?

"Bone meal is a wonderful source of phosphorus," he said, "increases bloom development and seed production, the kelp meal helps release mineral in the soil, and-"

"What?" Fear slipped from Linn like silk as she twisted in place, following William's gaze to the bags on the bottom shelf of the workbench.

"It's all organic," he said, as if to reassure, to ease some concern that hadn't crossed her mind.

There are no bodies here, she thought, seeing the whole of the greenhouse again, retained weight leaving her with every breath. She saw the flowers, and she saw *him*, the boy who'd grown into a gardener, growing something beautiful out of the soil he'd come from.

Ignorant of her thoughts, William donned a glove on his left hand that just grazed the wrist, then selected a pair of pruners. A bit of guilt spread over her like wet clothes, uncomfortable, chafing as she watched him with his roses, calm and purposeful. She debated telling him who she was, who she was to *him* in their shared story. Maybe telling him would provide something of closure for her, closure she hadn't thought she'd needed until things had been stirred up. Maybe it would quell the curiosity that had brought her back to Pete's, because she couldn't use the woman in the woods as an excuse anymore, the beads and the flowers. William had a garden and a greenhouse there, she'd seen the roses, but that wasn't all she'd come back for.

What would she even say? She couldn't tell him about the eye or the arm, only that his father had killed three of her family members, but for what? Where would sharing that information leave him, a man who'd overcome the absence of two parents, a father who cared more for the bottle than his son? He'd found something bright from that awful mess, and he should be allowed that peace without the dust and bone she'd stir up.

"I'm partial to the Queen of Sweden," he said, brushing the back of his right hand over the blush pink petals of a bloom as he passed, pausing to dip his head down, inhaling. "Go ahead," he said, smiling like he held a secret, eyes flicking to the flower and back to Linn.

She leaned forward and brought the scent into herself, something less sweet than she'd expected, but no less intoxicating. "Smoldering," she murmured, breathing it in again to the point where she felt almost lightheaded.

"Myrrh," he said, giving a name to the scent still lingering inside her. "But I think something a little brighter would be more Peter's speed."

"If they're going to compete with the candy-colored games on his phone," she smiled.

"The Carina and Queen Elizabeth are these bold pinks here, and a yellow Casanova will pop," he said, pausing a moment to survey the blooms. "Oh, forgive me, why don't you put on that other glove there to protect your hands. You don't mind assisting?"

"I'd love to."

Linn glanced at her phone to be sure she wasn't running late, then turned back for the bench. Sliding into the right glove he'd left behind, her eyes caught on the bag of bone meal, and a little seed slipped into the soil of her mind.

An idea took shape as she took the stems he cut, slow and careful.

"What temperature do you think the bones get to, for bone meal," she asked.

"Now that's an interesting question, and I'm sorry to say I have no idea," he said, focus never straying from the flowers he worked over. "I just buy the bags, but I've heard of folks making their own, so I'd think a conventional oven must be enough." He handed her another stem, pink, then finally met her eyes again. "Do you have a butcher in the family?"

"A butcher? Oh, no… My neighbor hunts deer. It was just a thought."

"Thinking of making a kiln project of it?"

He remembered.

"I've worked with ceramics that require bone ash, but that's heated super high in the kiln. I wonder if that would do something to it; make the bone less helpful in the soil."

"It's possible," he yawned, then smiled. "Sorry, sleep was less than ideal last night. I'm not prone to difficulty sleeping, but between the reclining chair and all the noises in the hospital, then the commotion outside and the flashing lights. I found out this morning…" His words slowed as he clipped a yellow rose, Casanova, then his eyes searched her for something as he handed off the stem. Tentatively, he said, "I heard there was a death in the parking lot."

Linn pressed her lips together, thoughts somewhere between the flowers she held and the way Gabby's lifeless body moved as she pounded on her sternum, repeating on a loop in her mind like a song she didn't want to hear, over and over.

"The nurse I was training," she started, pressing in on her left thumb with her other fingers, on the cusp of transferring the thorned stems from her right hand and squeezing. "Gabby. It was Gabby in the parking lot."

William's face fell and his eyes went wide. "Linnea… Oh, I'm so very sorry. You must… What was…" he paused, taking care to choose his words, brows pinching with concern. "Are you sure you're up to your shift?"

Linn reflexively brightened, wanting to spare him the burden of his sympathy. "Keeping busy will help, and being with my work family. We support each other, we always do."

"Driving," he sighed, "the time alone with your thoughts… If you don't mind waiting, I could grab a vase from inside and we could carpool? You're welcome to leave your vehicle in the drive."

Linn shook her head, checked her watch, then passed the roses from her gloved hand to his. "No, my shift ends so late, and hopefully these flowers will do the trick and you can get some sleep at home," she smiled. "I should get going."

He nodded, his face gentle, so different than the man she'd seen bloodied with a gash through his eye, replaced with glass, shoulder socket hemorrhaging out onto the crusted winter snow.

With William at the workbench and her hand on the latch, Linn turned, and took a deep breath, inhaling the flowers, soaking in one last moment of filtered autumn sun. And that was it, wasn't it. The greenhouse was a filtered space, untouched by the raw world on the other side of the panes.

"William…" she started, one foot out the door, cool October air already kissing her skin. "I can see how a person could lose time in a place like this. Thank you for letting me in."

20.

Berkshires, October 2014

Linnea's breath remained suspended as the arms around her held firm, though the faint smell of cologne persisted, having coated the last bit of air she'd brought in. They weren't supposed to wear perfume to work, but scent had a way of binding itself to fibers, of marking a person as theirs.

"The parking lot is a shit show," Alex said into her ear, finally releasing his grip. They stood together for a moment in the ambulance bay, looking out to the row of news vans and reporters. "I'm surprised Henry didn't drop you off with an escort. Didn't Drew offer to bring you with Steph?"

Linnea had talked with both Alex and Steph *extensively* that morning, retelling the story of how she'd not wanted to give Erik the wrong idea again, the donuts, the PCA keys...

"Yeah, but I said I was fine," she sighed as they headed in, snaking through halls and into the elevator. "Henry's at Cap's with Lars, then he has who knows what, who knows where. He'll be back at the house when I get home from work, so I won't have any of that pesky *alone time* everyone's worried about."

"Except when you're driving."

"Or walking out to my car."

"No one's walking out to their car alone. They have a security thing going into place, chaperones. I heard they were getting a golf cart, but don't ask how I know."

She looked past his words for a moment, seeing his face, the eyeliner that did nothing to hide his tired eyes. "What happened to that beauty rest you were supposed to get?"

"You know what they say, *you can't always get what you want*," Alex sighed, pursed his lips, fighting a blush. "I got what I needed last night, though."

"Oh my god," she grinned, swatting his shoulder.

"What? It was a waste having your brother all alone in that big house with you at Henry's."

The smile on her face lasted until they rounded the nurse's station. Allie stood from her desk and followed them into the back room, where it seemed like everyone was waiting.

Alex's arm came around her shoulders, Steph wrapping around both of them, then Allie. Linnea's heart swelled like a cloud suddenly turned grey, saturated with rain ready to fall. An unmistakable blonde bob and pink glasses wobbled through the water coating her eyes, until she blinked the tears away to see Cheryl's face clearly.

"I can't believe they didn't call and cancel you," Cheryl started, voice sharp. Steph and Alex stepped back so the charge nurse could go in for a hug. "Night supervisor had a lot on her plate, but Honey, you shouldn't be here. We're going to get you out early, mark my words."

There were times when eight-hour evening staff were offered the opportunity to leave at seven if patient census was low. Linnea looked up at the board listing all the patients on the floor, then to the assignment sheet. Every bed was accounted for, every nurse at capacity once the post-ops arrived. There was no way. But if anyone could make it happen…

After nodding and smiling through a flurry of sympathy and support from her coworkers, Linnea sat with Alex and Steph, gathering information on her patients before report started.

"I don't want to be disrespectful," Alex said, looking to Linnea, then back to his work, "but you dodged a bullet. And I'm glad it was you that brought those keys back."

"Alex," Steph gasped.

"I'm not ashamed to say what I'm thinking. I'm thankful."

Linn couldn't help but align her thoughts with Alex, wondering what would have happened if she'd let Gabby take the keys up. Had Erik not walked Gabby to her car? Maybe he would have stayed with Linn longer, a deterrent. Or maybe it was as Henry thought, about them looking similar. Was Gabby an appetizer of sorts? Perhaps Linn would have been safe, too precious to take too soon.

"Drew says it's not the same guy," Steph whispered, still looking at her computer.

Henry had said the same.

"Totally different," Linnea agreed, combing through a patient's labs. "When I found Gabby, what was done to her... It was quick and clean, not... reverent."

"*Reverent?*" Alex repeated, his voice playful but she felt the opposition in it. "As opposed to the woman in the woods?"

She nodded.

"You think that woman was worshipped so hard she got killed?"

Linnea sighed, choosing her words carefully. It was a dangerous thing to attempt explaining that some people don't have the same innate sense of where lines are drawn, that they know where boundaries exist for others, but have what feels like a biological need superseding whatever man-made laws have been put in place around them. They feel with depth, and create with compulsive intensity...

"The woman in the woods was posed with intention," Linnea breathed, speaking slow, careful. "Samples were taken. She was clearly a piece of something bigger, venerated for the part she played." Gabby had been an entirely different situation, an animal killed for sport or out of frustration, pelt left in-tact. Worthless. "Erik should have been there," she added, her train of thought drifting, then she shook her head. "No, I take that back. It wasn't his responsibility. We should be able to walk to our cars and run in the woods alone without being attacked."

Alex raised his brows and pursed his lips, said nothing, but glared, obviously, at Steph.

Steph's eyes widened, then she sighed, loud, and whispered, "Erik might be a person of interest…"

Linnea's head snapped to the side, her focus on Steph.

"This morning, I told Drew about how he's been escalating with you again, and I may have mentioned the resemblance… *I'm* not saying she looked like you, but people commented. Drew told me a few things, but he isn't supposed to talk about work anymore, and they hadn't brought him in yet when he dropped me off… Alex, you are in the biggest tattle-tale trouble *ever.*"

"I didn't say anything…" he shrugged.

"Please," Steph huffed, rolling her eyes before her smile broke through. "Your eyes are as loud as a glitter-coated freight train."

"She should know Erik is a suspect," he shot back with an edge of something serious. Then Linnea saw something flash in his eyes, a switch flipping. "And you should have that glitter-train comment put on a t- shirt. I might know someone who would wear that, under the right circumstances."

The three of them smiled and got back to work, warm under a blanket of comic relief.

The roses were on the windowsill by Pete's bed, shades of pink dotted with yellow opening in the sunlight. William had chosen a clear vase, bubbles speckling the thick glass like water. The scent wafted into her, a gentle flood floating on the back of her memories or the air, perhaps both. Sweet, maybe a hint of lemon, but none of the myrrh she'd inhaled from that blush bloom in the greenhouse.

William greeted her with a solemn nod and a heavy smile as she entered, and Pete, she'd never seen him less interested in his phone. She listened to his breathing with her stethoscope as the game remained paused, and he stared at her unabashedly. She couldn't fault his innocent curiosity, but still, his attention was irregular.

After checking his wound sites, she lowered his shirt, and, finally, he blurted, "Did you have a sister?"

The shock to her heart was sudden, setting it to beat faster, sweat prickling.

"No," she smiled, her voice thready, cool. "You might be remembering the nurse I've been training."

Pete looked toward the door expectantly, and Linnea looked to his cousin.

"She's not in today," William said, closing his laptop. "And I think it's been a few hours since you've been up for a walk, Pete. What do you think about taking a stroll while Linnea fixes you a Shirly Temple?"

"I like the sound of that!" Pete grinned, swinging his feet over the edge of the bed.

"Thank you," Linnea mouthed, tension in her face and body relaxing as she tossed a small stack of Pete's empty cups in the trash on her way out.

She nearly collided with Cheryl.

"You want to take off early tonight?"

Linn's answer was a sigh through pursed lips, tears welling in her eyes.

Cheryl put an arm around her. "Staffing shuffled a couple float nurses and got Sue from nights to come in at seven. Someone's got to go home or you'll all have three patient's each, and that's not going to fly with management. You're all set."

"It can't be my turn…" They rotated through who was offered cancels, and Linnea had taken one just two weeks prior…

Cheryl paused her steps, looked down her nose and over her glasses before lifting them into her hair like a hot pink headband. "No one else will take it."

"Well, yes, then, obviously," Linn laughed, sniffling, reawakening the tears that had threatened her eyes just a minute before.

The rest of her shift had been good, the work demanding enough to get lost in for a while, finishing a shift's worth of documentation done by seven was a feat in itself. With the promise of starting another stretch of days off a few hours early, what with everything that had happened, she didn't mind one bit. The bonus she hadn't anticipated was how good it would feel to linger after clocking out.

"Technically it's his aunt's greenhouse," Linn said, leaning over Allie's desk as she explained where William had sourced the roses he'd brought in.

"He's an absolute dream," Allie sighed. "When's he coming back?"

"He didn't give a time, just that he was running home to grab his noise cancelling headphones and a better pillow. I don't blame him."

"I'll buy you dinner if you stay," Allie blurted.

"Oh my god…"

"I need you here so you can accidentally introduce us. It might not be a good time for him now, but if I lay a foundation… I know at least three nurses who would order out if we get the ball rolling," she said, picking up an incoming call. Phone to her ear, Allie's face seemed to melt as she looked up at Linn. "No, she got cancelled at seven," she answered, eye's going wide before she hung up.

Linn went still, waiting for more information, her insides a breath away from tumbling. Who was calling to ask if… "Erik?"

"And he did *not* seem pleased to have missed you," Allie nodded, a little smile on her face as she pulled a binder of menus from her desk.

"I should skip food and get out of here," Linn sighed. If anyone on the floor needed surgical house, she'd have to see Erik. She wanted to know how things had gone at the police station, but not enough to speak to him. Must have gone smooth if he was on time for his shift.

Alex walked Linnea downstairs, but only to the exit. Then, to her delight, she received an escort to her car via golf cart. When the car door closed, though, she had a contradiction of feelings. Night and the soothing calm that came with it tried to settle in, but the bright lights of the parking lot persisted, relentless.

She sat in the driver's seat with the phone in her hands, car idling with the doors locked and radio on low, and sent off a message to Henry.

Got out of work early. Security escort and staggered floodlights, each with the power of an exploding star, to brighten the way.

Everything looked different outside, like she'd parked on a baseball field during a night game. The sky was black beyond, but she couldn't feel the hovering blanket of the sun's absence.

Where are you? He asked.

In my car, haven't pulled out yet.

Meet at the lake house? Phil will be there when you arrive, I'll be along soon.

Linnea sighed, very aware of what she had on. Her scrubs had only put in a half shift, but her shoes… She suspected there was a microscopic jungle of pathogens thriving there that could only be purged with fire, and she hadn't put the flip flops back in her car. And the idea of wearing Henry's clothes again was nice, more than nice, but she felt a little like she'd be wearing pajamas the whole time she was there. Was that terrible, though? If she had some basics… She figured if she drove home, she could scoop up some jeans, underwear, a sweater, boots, then rinse off and change at the lake house

Sounds good, see you in a bit.

She dropped the phone in her pocket, feeling it buzz before she had a chance to put her car in gear. She picked it up, thinking Henry must have made a mistake when she read the message.

Where are you?

But it was Erik.

Linnea looked up, out the windows, thankful for the bright lights, but not how they illuminated her. She felt exposed.

Scowling, she typed, *Cancelled, headed home,* then dropped the phone in her pocket again. It wasn't long before the flood lights of the parking lot were behind her and the buzzing of what she presumed were Erik's messages faded, but the feeling of quiet didn't come until she closed the car door in her driveway.

And she could *breathe*.

The moment stretched from seconds to minutes, the atmosphere different than if she'd arrived after midnight, but still soothing.

Until her pocket buzzed again, and again. A call. Henry.

Linnea unlocked her door, put the phone to her ear, and stepped inside.

"Hi," she whispered, not out of fear, but courtesy. It felt odd to use her full voice when her surroundings were so peaceful.

"Phil said he hasn't seen you yet."

"Yeah," she signed with a smile. "I stopped at home to grab some clothes, not that I don't like wearing yours."

She kicked off her shoes, put her keys in the bowl by the door along with alcohol swabs, red caps, a couple gauze packets, roll of silk tape… they added up, but she'd use them to restock her pockets before her next shift.

"Linnea…"

"Where are you?" she asked.

Then the darkness moved.

The shadow was fast, fast like Barny but larger, fast like a truck speeding under a hidden moon with no headlights. Arms banded around her from behind, and she heaved herself upward. One foot kicked out, reaching for the table by the door, pushing them both backward into the wall, her attacker's body cushioning the impact, but holding firm.

The mudroom light went on, and she saw the beads around his wrist, his skin speckled with healing scratches. *Not roses.* The thought flashed quickly as her body burned, struggling against muscle and intention, against an unrelenting grip, against the fabric gathered around her mouth and nose that had started to dampen with a sweet, antiseptic smell, traces of citrus and cut grass pinching as she inhaled.

Linnea's legs began to give out, dragging more than stepping as her feet moved ineffectively beneath her. Another light went on, too bright, as she was brought, still upright, into the living room. She began to feel weightless, dizzy, the floor absent as arms lifted her. Then, the whole of her body settled into the familiarity of her couch.

Linnea's eyes were uncooperative as she attempted to use them, lids like leaded curtains slipping down into her field of vision. Her muscles were too relaxed, and those lights on the other side of her eyelids…

Should I be unconscious? Her thoughts were difficult to gather, fleeting and disorganized as her coordination. *Should I pretend to be?*

She felt her socks slide off, but nothing more, then, through what opening she could manage by lifting her eyelids, Linnea watched William stand, and switch off the mudroom light. She observed him walking to the bathroom, and turning on the light there. Because isn't that where someone would go when they got home from work?

William sat across from her in a high-backed chair she never used. He appeared pleased with himself, but controlled, one leg crossed over the other, one hand raised, fingers working at something in his palm.

"Roses," she said, her garbled voice stronger than she'd anticipated.

William smiled, almost wistful. "More than my work in the greenhouse," he sighed, closing his eyes a moment, moving an object from his palm to his fingers, holding it beneath his nose, inhaling. A stone?

"Rosalia," he whispered, almost wistful. "We met at the coffee shop where she worked, developed a connection."

"Flowers," she said, beginning to move the hands at her sides, her limbs feeling too far away, but not as heavy as she'd expected. Shouldn't she be more… affected? He'd given her something, ether or chloroform, she suspected, but Linnea knew nothing of them, really. The bulk of her pharmaceutical knowledge ended at what was available in the machine at work. *He expects me to be impaired*, she thought, deciding it was safest for her to maintain her limp, drowsy appearance. If she sprang up to run, he'd catch her before she reached the door. That's if her legs were strong enough.

Another idea, then… Slowly, Linnea began working her right elbow, folding her wrist as she slid the corresponding hand against the deep seam along the cushions.

"Flowers," William smiled in agreement, lifting a beaded wrist and inhaling. "I had the good fortune of spending the latter half of my boyhood years living with Pete and my aunt, Sarah. She had the most *beautiful* garden, worked in a botanical nursery," he sighed. "I can't imagine what would have become of me had I stayed with my father. Fate," he breathed. "Fate and alcohol chose his path after the sun set."

Linnea steadied her breathing, thoughts racing alongside her heart.

William brought the stone in his fingers up toward his mouth. Then, he tilted his head so the beads at his wrist brushed his lips. "Flowers. Beautiful, but temporary. I've managed a method of preservation, but the process requires sacrifice of the blossom so the *essence* may continue on as it was in that moment..." He held his wrist on display to her, beads visible. "Each bracelet is a bouquet, each sphere covered in fabric procured from a different flower, and each flower with its own fragrance, with perfume I've distilled." William's other hand came up, a finger resting on each bead as he recited their names. "Rose, Heather, Holly, Magnolia, who had introduced herself as Maggie," he winked, a nod to Linnea's name having been hidden from him briefly. Had he been waiting for her in the parking lot, and found Gabby instead? Would he have killed her then, if they'd been alone together? Would he have used his hands, then slipped a stone in her mouth?

"Another Rose," he continued, "then another Heather, though each specimen is different. Jasmine, and *Lily*. She knew exactly what type of flower she was: Lily of the Valley," he whispered. "Not one of those heavy-blooms with their loose pollen. *Convallaria majalis*... We'd met over the summer; we were both so young," he trailed off, drifting into a memory, carried by a scent that crept up from the beads and through time.

Convallaria, Linn repeated to herself, thankful that William didn't possess enhanced hearing, because her heart thundered, and the effort it took to maintain the gentle appearance of eyes barely kept open... Linn had been fifteen when a local girl was found dead, surrounded by flower petals. Henry's *sister*.

Linn's hand passed between her body and old leather, fingers coated in sweat, collecting unknown grit as they slid down into the depths of the crease at the armrest where GG used to sit.

"You were not a flower I'd been expecting, *Linnaea borealis*... I thought we'd have more time, then you came to the greenhouse," William continued, his voice little louder than a whisper as he approached. "You're on the cusp of something immense, Linnea. You're peaking, and positively *laden* with depth in this moment. I couldn't wait any longer, you understand."

She kept her eyes half lidded, no longer seeing the stone he'd had in his hand. Instead, William clutched something new, a thick, blue pen with orange details and... a white tag. No, that was a patient label from the hospital's pharmacy. Pete's missing insulin.

Linnea's hand gripped wood, wove wire through her fingers. *Not yet.*

"This will take some time," William continued, placing his free hand on the arm rest and his lower leg on the back of her knees, pressing into her. "The insulin will pull nectar from your blood... You will wilt, of course, but this is necessary." He leaned in, his weight shifting to his supporting arm as he brought his face in close, inhaling deep from around her neck.

Linnea's body bloomed with repugnance at the invasive proximity, at the idea that parts of herself more tangible than an idea entered him without her consent. With each breath, he drew her in, and the heat of his exhalation reached beneath the collar of her shirt, down the valley of her spine.

His mouth or his nose made contact, warm, brushing against the skin at her hairline...

Linnea exploded. Pushing her body with all she had, Linnea twisted, thrusting her hand and the fettling knife upward, sinking the blade into the soft space of William's underarm.

He clenched inward, pulling his knee from the couch reflexively and losing his balance, sliding to the floor.

Linnea had wanted his neck, but with his weight on her legs and the arrangement of their bodies, she'd done what she could. She'd struck an artery at best, but at the very least, she'd injured him enough to buy her the instant she needed.

Wire unwound from her fingers as she launched off the leather cushions, mounting William's back as he attempted to right himself. With advantage enough to wrap the frayed metal thread around his throat and thrust downward, Linnea gripped the wooden handles with all the ferocity of a woman who had been made to pretend she was lethargic under a man's breath.

His head lurched forward, then shot back as he attempted to strike her with his skull, but Linnea squeezed his flanks between her thighs and ground her face into his hair, maintaining pressure on his neck while she desperately tried to avoid being bludgeoned.

A burst of color-coated darkness shrouded her vision as her ribs felt the impact of the coffee table's edge. With all her effort, she was unable to avoid blows to her body, though she held strong, even as he managed to brace himself on the table's surface with his good hand, standing as she clung to his waist with her legs. He grabbed at her, reached back for her hair and her legs as he rounded to the other side of the table. Linnea felt the impact of elbows to her midsection repeatedly, though she never let up on the wire. She wouldn't. So long as she could decide, Linnea would not let go.

Blood seeped from around the old, frayed wire as he stood to his full height. Then he leaned forward, propping himself on the coffee table once more, her father and Papa's beads tipping from the bowl made of GG's hair.

He's going down, she repeated to herself. *He's doing down.*

The kitchen door swung open, and despite having one hand on the table, William stumbled beneath her as Henry rushed toward them. His movements were smooth and without hesitation as he grabbed her assailant's head between his hands and forced it downward, bringing his knee up to meet William's face.

Linnea collapsed onto William as he fell, adjusting her grip to account for the loss of gravity. Eyes wide and breath heavy, she held on.

Henry knelt down beside her, his moments unhurried as he coaxed her fingers to loosen the wire around William's neck. With his hand on her back, Linnea's breaths began to slow to match his. She closed her eyes as he leaned in, tears welling up like a spring long waiting.

"He still has a pulse," Henry began, his words calm, smooth. "I'd like to speak to him if he rouses, but we need to bring him outside, or we'll get a great deal of blood on the floor."

Linnea started to nod, the room silent but for their breath, their hearts... then the sudden rhythmic pulse of buzzing that came from the mudroom.

Both she and Henry stilled as they caught the sound, then it stopped abruptly before starting again, louder, closer.

Henry's eyes met hers, his head tilting slightly as he reached for his front pocket, one hand remaining at her back as he put the phone to his ear.

"Cap," he said. "She's safe, but there was a break-in."

Linnea still straddled the unconscious man's back, tears streaking her face, red from emotion and physical trauma. The wire down by her fingers remained wrapped loosely around the man's neck, a ring of blood oozing from his skin.

Was that the blood Henry was concerned about getting on the floor? No, he was bleeding where she'd stabbed him.

William's body began to feel wrong beneath her, like a warm meal gone cold. The momentum that brought them together had stopped and, with Henry on a call, there was a pause long enough to sense the strangeness, to be repulsed by it.

Linnea tilted; her legs stiff as she tried to climb off. Her hands started to shake, the tremor moving upward as she leaned into Henry. His arm slid around, pulling her toward him as he stood. Had standing ever felt so good? He walked her to the dining room table where she sat down, his hand gliding up to her shoulder, down her back in a slow, circular motion.

"I'd rather not," Henry said into the phone. "Of course, she's right here."

Linnea took the device from Henry, put it to her ear, rested her arm on the table, head on her arm.

"Cap?"

"Are you alright?"

"A little banged up, but I'll be fine," she smiled weakly, feeling jittery and awake, head throbbing, like she needed to breathe, to come down. The sensations were exhausting.

Henry's hand fell away as she spoke, leaving her safe with her conversation while he turned off all the offending lights. He went to the kitchen next, perhaps beyond, as she heard the studio door open.

"I saw too many lights on," Cap started, "then Henry pulled up and ran in before I could get out the door. The guy who broke in, did he run off? I couldn't see out back."

"No," she said, glancing down to the breathing body on her living room floor. "He's still here, just not conscious."

Cap paused, his voice a little slower, a little quieter. "Henry said he doesn't want to call the police."

"No," she breathed, ribs sore. She heard footsteps again in the kitchen, the refrigerator door open and close, the sound of a plate set down on the countertop. "He wants to talk to him, he says, but I don't think... Do you know what Henry does for work?"

"I know enough."

"This *person*, the man who broke in, he told me things before I fought him off," she sighed. "He killed that young woman in the woods... and others. I think he killed Henry's sister," she whispered.

"Shit," Cap sighed.

Linnea heard the fridge open and close again, footsteps as Henry came in, felt his hand, heavy, pleasant on her back. She closed her eyes for a moment, then opened them to find him holding a glass of water. He'd placed a roll of duct tape and a rag from her studio on the table, and tapped the rim of a plate he'd set down in front of her, laden with two oatmeal cookies, a cut up apple, and a few slices of cheese.

He took a bite of apple and held the water out toward her. She needed no encouragement to drink.

"You understand he means to do more than talk to him," Cap asked.

She drank, sips then gulps. When her mouth parted from the cup, and she steadied her breath, watching Henry finish his slice of apple, pick up the rag and duct tape, then set off toward William.

"I do," she said, as Henry approached the body on the floor.

William's eyes were fully open once his mouth had been sealed over, his response to the application unsettling in that he didn't scream. He made no attempt at vocalization, that Henry might remove the hindrance to hear his plea, that he might stop binding his ankles, his wrists. He seemed not to panic at all. Instead, William took on a state of alert, though perhaps slightly impaired, observation.

"Is that…" Cap started, then lowered his voice to whisper. "Is that something you can live with?" He asked, with not a hint of judgement in his voice. It was an offer, one last opportunity, should she want it. But, did she? Could she live, *knowing?*

Henry returned to the table, taking a piece of cheese from the plate as he sat down, his other hand reaching for hers, a smile as he brushed her fingers and squeezed gently.

"Yes," she whispered.

"Alright then," Cap sighed. "You'd better hand him the phone."

She did.

"Mmm," Henry hummed with the device to his ear.

My phone. Linnea remembered when they'd first heard the buzzing of Cap's call, it had been…

"I dropped my cell," she said absently, turning to the mudroom and attempting to stand.

Henry held up a hand, encouraging her to pause, to let him get what she needed, but Linnea raised her palm to mirror his. She stood, and carried on, aware, but not looking directly at the body in the living room.

She breathed in deep, surveyed the mudroom mess, somehow finding her phone undamaged. Little pieces of her life littered the floor, things she'd emptied out of her pockets every night: red caps and alcohol swabs, keys and pens, her disgusting shoes. They stoked memories of the struggle to pulse through her, kindling for some fire burning on embers decades in the making, coals that had never quite gone out.

Linnea found Henry still seated at the table, call ended, phone presumably in his pocket once again.

"Don't you need to…" her words trailed off as she glanced at William, the work that needed to be done.

"Yes."

She sensed his awareness of a timeline, but also his concern for her. She imagined her face, her hair… but he didn't fuss over her, wasn't escalated in any way. He'd brought her food and water. He was so… *calm*. Linnea closed her eyes, took a breath, a sweet smell from the plate rousing her curiosity.

"Where did you get the cookies?" she asked.

"Missy baked them earlier while Cap, Lars and I were out with the crossbow. Lars took at least half a dozen home, but I managed to tuck some away for you."

Henry took another apple from the plate, assessing her with each bite, then he glanced over to the living room, stood, and walked to the sliding glass door. He opened it wide, wide enough for a man to pass through while carrying another. His form remained there, in the darkness between two places, inhaling the young night air.

"I'll get him situated out in Cap's barn," he started as she came to stand beside him, his voice slow and full. "Then you and I can talk before I get started."

He leaned in with a kiss, soft and considerate, the smell of his skin a welcome antidote to everything else she'd breathed in.

"The barn…" Linnea whispered as their bodies parted. Cap had given him permission.

Henry nodded, and she held his eyes with hers.

She saw him then, a man in two places, both present and retreating to another world.

"I need to be separate for this… to work," he said, relief and gravel in his voice. "I had thought to take him back to the lake, but…" he paused, looking out, connecting, settling in. "The kiln."

Linnea didn't need to follow his gaze to know it rested on a cream-colored chimney growing up out of the shadows. His eyes flicked to hers, a serious question in them, carrying the weight of life, death, and after.

Linnea nodded. "Once it's loaded it'll take a little over two days to get to temperature. The fire will need to be fed around the clock."

"Can it burn everything?"

"Yes."

Henry nodded and returned to the living room.

"Could you call Jonathan?" He asked, dragging the muted man up onto his feet. "I need my tools. He and Phil will bring you what I need, then they'll find and move this one's car," he continued, tilting his head toward the yard, the honeysuckle, the barn beyond. "Just knock on the door and wait. Don't open it."

She nodded, recalling her own collaboration with darkness, when inspiration moved through her, deep and delicate.

Henry hoisted his harvest, limp body molding to his shoulder as he carried William through the dining room, to the open door.

Then He paused once more, a man between two dark places.

"Tell him I have Sixteen."

21.

Berkshires, October 2014

Sixteen, she thought, his voice lingering in her mind as he passed over the threshold, and melted into the night.

Linnea closed the door, dialed Henry's older brother, and took a bite of cheese, wondering if William could fathom what she suspected, what she was words-away from knowing…

What it meant for him to be a number.

Henry had fifteen skulls on his wall, and she'd seen the next in his garage, mere hours before he'd boiled flesh from bone. She imagined the skull bleached white, antlers waiting, not yet dark enough to mount.

"Linn," Jon answered.

"Henry's here. He has Sixteen."

"Sixteen is *there?*"

"He was just in my living room."

"Phil," Jonathan said, curt and clear. "Do you need transport? Medical? Are you both okay?"

"I think I'm okay." Though she wondered what color she'd find her skin changing to beneath her shirt, if her face looked as raw as it felt. "Henry is fine, but he, no, he didn't mention *our* transport. He needs his tools, and a car moved. Henry's bringing him, *Sixteen*, out to my neighbor's barn."

"*Shit*," Phil said on their end. She was on speaker. "Shit. I'm on it."

"And I think," she started, questioning whether she should ask Henry first, but his brother would know… "He didn't mention it, but should you bring the other sixteen? The antlers?"

Silence. Breath.

"I don't know," Jonathan finally sighed. "We're not… present, for that part of it."

It. It, because there had been fifteen others. This was Henry doing Henry. This is why he took time off from work. This was hunting. Were the other's like William?

"Hold on," Linnea said, moving quickly, her bare feet on rug, wood, then cold grass. Over dirt and leaves, through the honeysuckle she swiftly bounded, phone still in her hand. A two-headed opacity in the shadows took form by the barn, then one body split from the other as she drew closer.

"Does he have a change of clothes at your house?" Jon asked.

"No."

"He'll need that too then. Christ."

Henry came out from the barn's side door, alone, a calm shadow existing between two worlds.

"Jonathan," she said, handing him the phone.

"Mmm," Henry hummed against the device at his ear, the vocalization low, deep. Then he listened. "One," he said. "And get Marcus moving. Good. Canvas. Drop off my tools with Linnea, then I need you to move a vehicle. Right. Ten Magnolia Lane." He paused, his eyes catching Linnea's. "Bring it," he said, then ended the call.

"The teacup…" he whispered, his low voice deep, resonant. "The one with the crescent. You made *two* with what you took?"

"Yes."

Henry nodded. "You'll have more than enough."

His hands came together in front of him, fingers moving, then he held out his braille watch, and lowered it into her palm.

Because I don't keep time here.

Intention moved through the words she remembered and into her body, spreading out through the air with his breath, and into the night as he turned back toward the barn.

Linnea's hand shot up to his shoulder, and he paused, waiting.

"Is he awake?" she asked.

"Mmm."

"I'd like a moment."

Much passed between them in the next breath. Henry considered, then held open the door.

He stayed there as she entered, the smell of hay and musk surrounding her. The barn had been emptied of livestock for a lifetime, but the scent of feed and animals remained embedded in the wood, lingering, ghosts of another time.

To her surprise, William stood upright, casually leaning backward in a shadow beside a stream of moonlight. Then she saw the ladder rising up from behind him, that he was expertly tied to it, and, of course, there was the covering over his mouth. Gripping Henry's watch, she moved forward slowly, not with fear in her heart, but something akin to the savoring of a moment. The wood under her feet felt smooth against her skin, deep grooves partially packed with dirt meeting each step. The image of Barny's paws touching down filled her mind briefly, the way he'd stalk slow, soft, deliberate.

William's fingers extended away from the ladder, then curled back toward it, the ropes snug at his wrists. *His beads must be digging in*, she thought, knowing what they'd been made from. Then her eyes ran the length of his arms. It had been one of his father's arms that she drank from at tea.

"I'm going to grind your bones to make my clay," she whispered in his ear, a promise fulfilled. Then she turned, weightless, toward Henry, and out, under the ink and moon.

Through the walls, Linnea felt Henry still, felt darkness on either side of the door he'd closed, washing over her. She stood for as long a moment as she could spare, her heart a drum the night could surely hear, each calling to the other.

He would have let her stay. She'd felt it in Henry's quiet observation, and while Linnea had every right, she was sure of the path she set out on. Henry had his work, and she had hers.

Linnea passed over grass and dirt on her way back to the house, and though her soles were near numb from the cold earth, she felt stone rising to meet her feet with every step she took.

*

From the kitchen, Linnea caught a brief flash of headlights in her driveway. She'd changed into sweats, which had been both painful and slow, then she'd cleaned up the mudroom, gathered what large pots she could find, and turned out the lights in the time it took Henry's brothers to arrive.

Without words, she led Jon and Phil around the house to the table under the grape arbor where they unburdened their arms, and converged around her.

Linnea winced as Phil pulled her against his chest, the pain easing as he backed off, concern on his shadowed face.

"Jesus, Phil," Jon scolded, then took out his phone and shined the light over Linnea's face, his hand cupping her cheek, fingers tracing her neck before the light dropped, and the phone slid back in his pocket.

"That's enough of that," Phil said, and Jonathan backed away, though only for Phil to take his place. His arms raised to come around her neck instead of her torso. "Has Henry seen your ribs?"

She shook her head. "No. It looks a lot worse than it feels though."

"And it feels like shit, I bet."

She nodded with something of a smile. "I can keep going though, really. Even if they're broken, the treatment is just time and deep breaths."

Phil nodded and looked to Jonathan.

"This pack has clothes and shoes, it goes in the house," Jon started, his hand touching each item on the table as he spoke. "This bag has two canvas drop cloths; this one has his tools. Can you carry all this with what you've got going on?" He asked, glancing down to her torso.

Linnea nodded, demonstrating her ability by loading up, then placing the items back down.

"Good," Phil started. We need to get going for a bit to find and move the vehicle. Marcus might be here before we get back, but just keep him at the house. We should all go in the barn together, let Henry alone until then," he sighed.

"When you bring his tools," Jon added, then paused a beat, the brothers maintaining the solemn stillness they'd carried since their arrival. "Don't open the door."

Linnea nodded. "He asked me to knock and wait."

Phil nodded. "As long as you have an understanding..."

Jonathan tapped a finger on the table, eyeing the expanse of yard, trees, privacy, the barn's roof over on Cap's side. "Did he mention anything regarding what to expect... when he's finished working?"

"The outdoor kiln." She said with an even whisper. "I'll get it up to twelve-hundred Celsius, which is adequate. A crematory maxes out at just under a thousand." She needed the higher temperature to assure the bones had been properly calcined, that she could mill them to ash.

Moonlight illuminated their faces enough for Linn to see traces of bewilderment beneath the surface of their expressions, though it was brief.

Henry had papered the windows, or applied some similar covering to the glass by the time Linnea approached the barn again. Not much more than a dull glow could be seen, an illumination not nearly strong enough to draw the interest of insect, or human. With bags over each arm and an antlered bundle in her hands, she was the only moth it seemed, though not drawn by the light.

She knocked. She waited. And then the door began to move.

Henry appeared as a black figure silhouetted in lantern light, any color gracing his clothes or skin masked in shadow. No sound came from behind him, and no words left his mouth, only breath, ethereal as it left his body for air. He reached out, relieving her of the bags pulling at her aching arms, placing the burden just inside the door. She passed the skull into his hands, time standing still around them, because time didn't exist in that moment. He'd carved out some moment like magic when his watch had come off.

She became enveloped in the totality of his eclipse as he stepped forward, one hand reaching for her neck, fingers sliding back beneath her hair, his thumb at her jaw as his lips came in to meet hers. He smelled like sweat, evergreens, and iron, inhaling along her skin after releasing her mouth. His hand remained a moment longer, then slid slowly back to cradling the bones in his hand.

She felt his eyes lingering on her as she turned, until darkness swallowed her shadow as the barn door closed, and time began to move once again.

*

Linnea lit a small fire to warm the kiln's chimney, not quite knowing when Henry would finish; wanting to be ready when the time came.

It was maybe forty-minutes later that Phil and Jonathan returned, walking out back to where she sat by the kiln.

"How can we help?" Jonathan asked. "We have about a half hour until Marcus arrives."

"Well," she started, surveying the large pots of water ready at the stove, the fire she had going to warm the chimney. "It's waiting at this point, really. I'll need assistance later, for you to take shifts running the kiln."

Phil tilted his head. "Are you bleeding?" He asked, stepping to her side, then reaching up to her jaw, running his fingers over her neck.

"Oh... I don't think... No," she said, fire and shadow hiding the blush on her cheeks. "It must be from when I dropped off the bags and the antlers."

Phil smiled and shook his head.

"So," she restarted breathing in composure, "it will be easier to teach you how to run the kiln if we go over it in the moment, so you can feel and hear what I'm talking about as far as keeping the fire fed properly." *Fed*, she repeated to herself... "Have you eaten?"

They shook their heads, something boyish in the act, like schoolchildren confronted by their mother about chores left unfinished.

"I don't have anything made; I haven't really been home. I've got granola bars, cheese, bananas, probably snap peas, apples and carrots. Bread maybe? Just poke around. Oh, and my neighbor Missy made some oatmeal cookies. You could start there."

"Apples?" Phil grinned.

"Yeah, at least three or four," she said, pausing a moment. "No, I've probably got six in there."

"That's enough for a pie, right? Not now, though, obviously." Then to Jon, he said. "We don't touch the eggs or the apples."

Linnea huffed a little laugh, smiling as the two took off walking toward the house, the same warmth in her heart when three came out a while later. Marcus was with them. Slim and tall, hair long enough to tuck behind his ears, color undefined under the moon. He seemed youthful, and he held something, lifted it up toward his face as they neared.

"You must be Marcus," she said with a low voice and smile, noting it was a sandwich in his hand.

His eyes sparkled, chewing quickly as he could. "Grilled cheese," he smirked. "I double checked that we turned the stove off. Thank you, by the way. And it's, I want to say it's a pleasure to meet you, but standard greetings seem a little…"

"He *triple*-checked the stove," Phil interrupted. "And I told him the grilled cheese would be too heavy."

"I was hungry, Phil. I didn't pack food, or stop."

"I said saltines or toast, Marcus. At least until after."

"I saw what you ate, Phil."

"My gut has been battle-tested. I'm just looking out for you, Marc."

"Things are ready here, then?" Jonathan asked her. His attention thus far had been on the barn, and hers on the other two. Linnea thought of days spent at GG's with Lars, finding herself thankful for the company.

"Ready to go," she said.

"We are as well, I suppose," he sighed.

Marcus looked down at the remainder of his sandwich, not more than a moment passing before Phil took it from his hand and finished it off, relieving his brother of carrying any additional weight within.

Jon paused for a moment beside her as if he had something to say, but it was just a moment, and no words were spoken. Then he followed his brothers through the honeysuckle to the barn.

Linnea listened, heard the knock, the door open and close, but there were no voices, not even when she heard the door open again. She only heard footsteps, and retching.

Jonathan came through the arbor first, followed by Phil, his arm around Marcus, supporting him.

"Do you have any ginger ale?" Jon asked.

"Too sweet," Phil said.

"I have some seltzer, and lemons."

Marcus nodded, and the three brothers moved on toward the house.

Linnea sat for a time, tending to her fire in the not-quite silence, what with the wood feeding flames. The act was meditative: her movement, her stillness, and in her awareness, the way she could feel both her surroundings and what continued within. Heart pumping, Linnea knew a whole world carried on inside her, a symphony of timing, of life happening, of sparks in the darkness.

Then a new sound, the opening and closing of the barn door breaking through the rhythmic crackling of the cookfire and the flames warming the kiln chimney. Linnea's heart beat harder, her breath deeper, unable to see the barn through the trees or hear the footsteps she anticipated.   Then, there he was, coming through the honeysuckle, his arms filled with a dark mass, branches extending outward.

As Henry drew closer, she estimated he held three parcels, each neatly wrapped as though they'd arrived in the post or from a local butcher. His pile was crowned with the white skull cradled in his arms; antlers dark as the night behind him.

When he stood close enough for their breath to reach one another, for the fire to light some parts of him, Linnea reached out to what he held, feeling canvas, not paper, folded into oblong packages. She didn't dare touch the bone.

"Do you have enough water?" He asked.

Linnea nodded, glancing over to several pots she'd brought to a gentle boil. She had the hose if she needed to top them off.

He placed his offering down on the two tables beside her, then tilted his head as she'd seen Phil do earlier. She exposed her cheek and neck as his hand and eyes examined her. He must not have seen or noticed the blood as he transferred it.

A low hum sounded from his chest as his hand slid down her arm. Linnea found herself imagining the radius and ulna that had once terminated in a hand, now waiting in a parcel on her table. And the wrist encircled in beads… what had become of them, she wondered. It wasn't likely that Henry had delivered hands or feet, what with the small bones… He'd have separated those, and there'd not been a sound from the barn…

"I didn't hear…" she started with a cautious whisper, wanting her words to fall like breath on water, rather than ripple.

Henry tapped his throat, his voice smooth and cavernous as he whispered back.

"Vocal cords."

Linnea stared up at the shadow where his eyes were kept, until he turned such that the moon and fire caught enough to define his lashes and the outer ring of his irises. He seemed calm as stone and gentle as still water, half melted into the night behind him. He didn't appear to have much blood on his person, considering, though he must have had some on his hand earlier. Linnea's mind flashed to the room in his garage, the cold room, with the deer hanging above a drain, hose coiled on the wall.

"I'd like to leave this here with you," he said, glancing down at the antlers, the vulnerability in his voice a song to her heart. "I have some finishing up in the barn…"

Linnea nodded, overwhelmed by his face, her surroundings. Glistening water coated her eyes. "Of course," she started, her palms tilted up, "Do I just…"

"Yes," he said, expression warm. "Try not to touch the antlers… Some parts may still be damp."

This offering she received into her hands, and while not much more than their fingers touched, the transfer was profoundly intimate. It felt not unlike the moment they'd shared in her darkened studio, as he opened wooden drawers filled with tokens of memory, like they were existing in a shared dream.

Henry smiled soft and melted back into the shadows. Linnea worked by the fire until flesh began to fall from bone, and the kitchen door opened again. Phil exited the house, followed by Lars and Jon. They looked to her, waiting. She nodded, permission for them to return inside, but only Phil went.

Her brother advanced with Jon at his side. She understood the apprehension Henry's brothers must have felt, what with a dismembered body boiling beside her, and they must have only just met. She imagined it had been quite the surprise…

"This is my brother, Lars," she said, bringing an arm around her brother's waist, one of his coming resting across her neck as they turned toward Jon. "You met Jon, Phil, and Marcus inside."

"Briefly," he said.

"We'd seen his picture, but there was still a little confusion before we saw his face when he arrived… He pulled in, then he made to go around back, so," Jonathan shrugged.

"The other one tackled me," Lars grumbled.

"Phil," Jon clarified.

"Yeah, well I figured it wasn't Marcus," Linn smiled, shaking her head. "You can head inside, Jon, really."

Jon's eyes flicked to the open fire stove behind her, to what boiled in the water, to the honeysuckle that separated her yard from Cap's. He tilted his head.

"Lars was with me the first time I used this kiln, Jonathan. And we weren't firing clay."

Jon nodded, albeit reluctantly. "It might be best if he heads inside before Henry comes out, though. Just… to keep things smooth."

He retreated through the kitchen door, leaving Linnea and Lars alone, together, echoes of where they'd been only five years prior, a portrait of two children trying to make things right.

"I thought you'd have gone back home," She smiled, heart melting at his unexpected presence. He'd been a part of her journey since they drank from raw clay that first night, marked with blood.

"Tomorrow," he said. "I thought to meet you when you got off work."

She hadn't told him about getting cancelled, about getting home early, being attacked, or what had come after.

Lars's eyes wandered to the boiling pots, the waiting kiln, the antlers. And he *smiled.*

"I knew…" he whispered, then released a lungful of air. He took another breath and blew out, wiped tears from his eyes. "The inspiration had been there, you just needed something that was yours to take."

Something inside her seemed to open at witnessing his catharsis, opening as much as coming together. Her brother had supported her during the growing pains of her soul, the raw birth that was her most poignant work, but he'd been transforming alongside her, through her. His need had been as great as hers, through providing what she needed, whether tools, space, or permission.

Something within her stilled, cooling, shifting, but not yet clear.

"Lars…" she started, unsure what she was asking.

His eyes held hers, then drifted back to the pots. "What did you take?"

There was no way he could have known about William. Could he? Could he have somehow led him to her home? No, he wouldn't have put her in that situation. It wouldn't have been worth the risk. Maybe if he'd been there to assist should she have needed him, but even then, to ambush her… He wouldn't. *You just needed something that was yours to take*, he'd said, and she'd had no connection to the woman in the woods, but…

"Lars…" she whispered. "It wasn't me."

"I know, Linn."

His eyes found hers again, illuminated by more than what burned beside them, glowing with a history, a fire of their making, and the shadows they'd cast. Those weren't the words, their way to reassure each other they'd not strayed from a path drawn with hard lines. A path they'd agreed upon.

Linnea felt warm as the flames yet her fingers were like ice against his hand as he took hers. His hands, his wrists, unblemished by roses. Hands he worked with, and couldn't risk.

"Gabby," she said, her voice becoming firm as her pounding heart. "It wasn't me, Lars. I need to hear you say it."

"I won't tell you what isn't true."

She sucked in a breath and released her grip on his hand, bringing her fingers to her mouth, circling them round her face as her heart fluttered and pounded. Her eyes wandered, settling on the antlers, Sixteen. Henry was still in the barn.

"She had no part in any of this," Linn started, emotion vibrating down to her shaking fingers. "We had no right to her, Lars. She was good, she had a future, a *family*."

"I watched you with her, Linn. She was yours as much as anything Barny brought home to us. Tell me you didn't see her as the rabbit."

God help her, she did, but she would never have crossed that line. She'd only taken those who'd engaged her, and Henry hunted those that couldn't see the boundaries as they were. He hunted men like William… and Lars.

"I gave you what you needed, Linn. I always have," he said, glancing again toward the pots of boiling water. "What did you take?"

"I did compressions," she grimaced, nauseated as her panic rose, hearing the memory of Marcus vomiting upon his exit from the barn, feeling again the metronome thrumming up her arms. The red where the whites of Gabby's eyes had been, William's breath on her neck. "Lars, you need to go," she pleaded, breathy, trying to steady herself as she looked to the barn again, back to the house.

"If you need space to work, I'll head inside for a bit. Where's Henry, and why do you have so many pots? How much did you take?" Concern wrinkled his brow, concern for her as he looked into one pot, another. "Linn." His eyes went wide, his face falling like her insides, in fear, and panic. "Linn, this is too much. This is more than… I left bolt cutters for you to take a few fingers, Christ, Linn. Radius, tibia, another tib... God, how did you manage this on your own?"

"It's not Gabby," she said, eyes and nose pinching with tears emerging. "It's William. He was waiting for me in the house when I got home."

Her brother's face became laced with a different kind of fear as she told the story, his features budding with interest, then bespeckled with pleasure as she described overtaking her attacker, then his expression evened out as she continued with Henry's arrival and Cap's call, sparing the history behind the skulls on Henry's wall. Those were his secrets, and she wouldn't release them.

"His brothers know," Lars whispered.

Linn nodded. "Jon is FBI, Phil is a marshal, and Marcus is a lawyer, apparently. Henry's still out in the barn, cleaning up I imagine."

"Shit," he whispered, glancing over to the honeysuckle. "I should give him a hand. We can't leave a mess for Cap and Missy, for *anyone* to find."

"Lars, I need you to listen to me," she said, lowering her voice. "You need to leave. Go spend the night at Alex's."

Her brother's face recoiled slightly, contorting. "Why would you have me leave? This is ours, Linn. We've been together through everything. You have strangers in your home and in the barn, bones over the fire and blood on your cheek, and you're asking *me* to leave?"

She blew out a breath. She was fully aware of how quickly things had escalated with Henry, how unexpectedly deep they'd become, the state of irreversibility and trust in which they existed. She couldn't tell him about Henry, the other fifteen, what put him at risk.

"Lars, you need to understand that what you did with Gabby was wrong. We had no right to her. And," she blew out a breath, her nose wet, sniffling, lungs filling fast. "It was this type of loss that shaped us as children, that twisted William into a monster. Do you know who his father was? West. He grew up warped and murdering women, he rattled off so many names, all flowers." She paused, gasping for breath, she put a palm to each of his cheeks, forcing their eyes to hold. "I'm fucking terrified that you can't see the lines anymore, that you'll only see what you think I need, and that you won't stop until someone makes you."

"Shhh," he hushed, her hands sliding away as his arms came around her shoulders, her body warring between urgency and the comfort he provided. "It's going to be okay."

Behind Lars, darkness took form beneath the honeysuckle. Henry, carrying a large canvas bag, Absolutely menacing. His approaching presence calmed her breaths until they became steady as his silence. Fire and shadow played over his features as he drew close, nearly upon them when her brother finally turned.

"Lars. Your plan was to head home for work in the morning," Henry said, resting his bag and clapping her brother on the shoulder. "Now we have another set of experienced hands."

"I can spare a few hours. Do you need help with the barn?"

"Barn's all set, but I imagine the kiln is another story. Linnea mentioned it takes a couple days."

Linn nodded. "We can take shifts once everyone knows what to do."

"I really shouldn't stay more than a few hours," Lars said, hand brushing over Linn's arm as he spoke, hearing, she hoped, the pleading in her eyes to *go*. "I have work tomorrow."

"Mmm, you have that obligation," Henry nodded beside them. "I understand. Though sometimes, in extreme circumstances, we make exceptions for family."

His words hung in the air as the kiln was loaded, as Linn stood beside Lars, unable or unwilling to leave, as Henry's arm brought her in to rest against him. Together with his brothers, they looked on as flames licked up through the dark sky like dragon's breath from the chimney.

22.

Berkshires, October 2014

The morning light was silver, sun barely peeking over the horizon somewhere beyond the trees and smoke scented air. It was a time when voices were still kept low and, though a new day had long since arrived, a pensive mood still carried over, perhaps in wait for coffee, time, or the sky to turn warm.

Together with Lars, Henry's brothers had taken turns running the kiln under her supervision, each impressive in their attention to detail and willingness to follow directions, watching the temperature, listening for changes.

Linnea leaned against Henry, and he against a wood pillar holding up the structure around the kiln. It was, perhaps, the first time she'd seen him visibly tired. With the radiating heat from the fire, and warmth from his body, Linnea began to test her eyelids, or at least that's what she told herself as she let them fall for several seconds at a time.

"Mmm," Henry hummed, agreeing with something someone had said. His chin nodded against her head, his beard catching her hair. Then, with his lips to her ear, he said, "Let's get some sleep."

Her first thought was to protest, but why should she? Their brothers could take the helm for a couple hours, and a world of difference could be made with a nap and a shower. She had concerns that the shower might be too invigorating, such that it would keep her awake, but the cocoon of steam had the opposite effect. To Henry's credit, he remained on task as they undressed, and waited until she was thoroughly saturated with warmth before inspecting her injuries.

Crouching beside her, Henry sprawled his hands over the bruised skin of her torso.

"Take a deep breath," he instructed, his eyes closing as she inhaled.

She was quite sore beneath his fingers, but the pain was manageable, and without any clicking, or crunching.

He looked at her expectantly.

"I don't feel anything suspicious of a concerning break, but it would take imaging to be sure."

"I could bring you in…"

"No," she said, guiding him up beside her. She could have gone down for her stethoscope in the mudroom to get a better listen, but what would she do with the information she ascertained? "The treatment for broken ribs is just pain management, that and deep breathing to prevent pneumonia."

Henry acquiesced, understanding as she did, the risks and inconvenience a woman with her manner of injuries would encounter during a trip to the emergency room, especially were she to be accompanied by a man.

A kiss beneath the water settled things, the heat and spiced soap soothing, leaving her relaxed under the weight of both her blanket and Henry's arm, not a trace of blood or smoke on their skin as they drifted off to sleep.

*

Late morning glowed from the edges of the blackout blinds covering her bedroom windows. The sun had risen in earnest, calling for Linnea to embrace the day, her path lit with daylight and kiln fire.

They'd both been awake, she and Henry, for some time, though they'd been silent. His body leaned against hers, or perhaps she leaned into him, likely both, and their thoughts, though formed and housed separately, seemed just as entwined. Linnea had gone boneless as his fingers gently massaged their way through her hair and trickled over her back, information and images coming together like a dream as they replayed and reformed in her mind.

"You knew…" she whispered, barely audible.

"Hmm?" he hummed, his fingers continuing.

"You knew it was William… That he'd killed the girl in the woods. You came to the hospital while I was working."

"I suspected. I recognized at the hospital, he'd been on security footage from Dee Dee's, where the victim was employed."

"The coffee shop we went to."

"Mmm," he nodded. "His frequency there, and his behavior toward you… It was enough for me to start looking into both him and Peter."

"You looked into his family as well," she asked, the scent of rosemary and gasoline seeping into her memories with such ease that it wouldn't have surprised her if Henry could smell it on her skin.

"No siblings, mother disappeared when he was a kid. Father was a local landscaper and habitual drunk driver who apparently incinerated himself after crashing his vehicle. William went to live with his aunt and cousin, Peter, after an earlier incident that resulted in jail time."

"He had a glass eye," she said, feeling the phantom weight of it in her palm like a small, smooth stone.

Henry paused, adapting effortlessly to the change in course.

"Hmm?"

The moment became both slow and clear between them. Henry's body remained relaxed against hers, but his senses had suddenly awakened, sharp, poised to detect a beating heart through brush and snow, the dilation of pupils, the fine edge of nuance.

"William's father," she said, easing her words into the silence. "I took it, before I took his arm."

She watched Henry's face as he traveled somewhere internally, through landscapes of memory until he reached a dark room lit just enough…

"In the drawer," he said, drawing in a breath, "by the earrings and the honeybees."

Linnea nodded, the movement just enough to acknowledge, but not enough to disturb the wonder and astonishment on his face.

"When did you know?" he asked, perhaps realizing that Linnea could have long been aware of the connection, but been unable to make mention of it because of patient privacy laws. Discussing information pertaining to William's identity would have compromised Pete's, and therefore unacceptable content for discussion, however desperate she might have been to share the burden of her revelation. This was not the case, of course, as she had not assembled those particular pieces of the puzzle until she was kept captive on her own couch.

"Yesterday," she started. "It's too late to be upset, so just let it go, but I stopped at Pete's before work yesterday. I just wanted to get in the greenhouse and see if there were roses."

"Henry grumbled, narrowing his eyes.

"There were, of course. He was there, and the garage was open. I saw some signage for the landscaping company his father owned."

What an unexpected snare she'd walked into when she arrived home that night, one she could have avoided by meeting Henry at the lake.

He hadn't wanted her in her house without him there…

"When did *you* know," she asked, not with malicious suspicion but curiosity, needing to comprehend his decision making. "When did you know I wasn't safe? And why…" she paused, carefully seeking to avoid any accidental undertones of accusation in her wording.

"Why did I let you go to work?" Henry asked, picking up on her trajectory, continuing as Linnea nodded. "We discussed the idea of you taking a day to recover from Gabby's death, but you wanted to go in. You're a grown woman, Linnea; I'm not your gatekeeper."

"I was grossly uninformed," she said, her voice powerfully flat and steady.

"I was supposed to be there with you," Henry breathed, his voice slow and heavy. Guilt lived there, in his chest, his fingertips, his eyes. She saw his trauma, his loss, and fear, what had been taken from him, what he'd relived, how close he'd come.

"You weren't sure, and you weren't ready to tell me everything," she sighed, her feet finding his reassuringly under the blankets. "You did what you could, though. We both did. And we're still here…"

Henry reached over to her; the back of his arm visible enough for the lily to catch her eye. She'd seen the same on his brothers with the exception of Marcus, but she knew it was there.

Linnea gently rested her hand over the inked flower.

"Convallaria," she whispered. "You named it for her."

"Not a constellation," he smiled softly. "I'm surprised you'd not made the connection earlier. When you put Convallaria into a search engine, lilies are the first thing to come up."

"It was Steph who did the search at brunch. It wasn't until last night," she started, holding Henry's dark eyes with hers, watching for any cue that she should stop. "He mentioned others," she said softly, waiting, but Henry's face was open, his breath steady. "Their names were all flowers. The first was Lily. When he whispered the Latin… I knew it was her."

"Mmm." Henry drew breath, deep and slow, then let it out before he spoke. "Her death awakened a purpose, set pieces into motion. She was the seed it all grew from." He closed his eyes, breathed again, deep. The corners of his lips moved, she thought it a wince, but no, it was with the hint of… almost a smile. "I've hunted him since the day life left her body. I've known for a long time that nothing can bring her back, or even out the loss, but there's a piece of me that can rest easier knowing he departed this world by my hand."

Lily's death may have started Henry's hunt for William, but the living room at the lake house was lined with trophies… with others. And his brothers had known, they'd known when she called and said *Sixteen* like it was a name instead of a number. *We don't ask…* Jonathan had said at the lake house. *Some parts of what he does are just kept private. We just see another skull on the wall, another number.*

They knew, and they supported him, as her brother had supported her, every time.

His fingers stroked the back of her neck, swirling around the sensitive hairs at her nape, soothing, cradling her such that the burden in her heart eased out.

"Lars," she whispered, chest needing release from the knowledge and the fear suckling at her from within. "It wasn't William who killed Gabby, it was Lars."

She exhaled then, and as much as oxygen, carbon dioxide, nitrogen, trace elements, water, as much as they dispersed into her surroundings, so did some of the weight of what she held, entering Henry's body with every breath.

"I know," he whispered, fingers still moving, twining with the hidden tendrils of her hair.

She wanted to know how, she wanted to know when, she wanted to know if he thought Lars was beyond rehabilitation, or if it was as she suspected, that he didn't see the boundaries as she did… But would he act again if she asked him not to, if he'd done it for her, if he knew she no longer needed his help in that capacity?

Silence hung between them, a silence of delayed questions, of *just one more moment of this.*

"A web of connections best left undetected, that a spider can survive to hunt again unseen," Henry started. "Too many bodies, or I would have taken him. Sometimes, in extreme circumstances, we make exceptions for family." He'd made the same statement to Lars by the kiln, knowing. "Measures will be taken, though. Every act plants a seed, and we need to be careful what we grow."

They were living proof of that truth, each of them impacted, the ripple affecting the rings of their years as they lived on.

"Will you stop hunting," she asked.

"No," he said with a subtle shake of his head, but not hesitation. "I won't stop bringing deer home in October, nor will I stop darkening their antlers."

He saw it as a service, but it sustained him.

If you don't have balance, you'll lose control when you come off the leash. Henry had said those words to Jonathan at the lake house. They'd been regarding Jon's lack of restraint with bread, but the truth could be applied elsewhere. Henry could have been speaking of the balance he kept by allowing himself a hunting season. He could have been speaking of her need…

"My Grandma Grace used to say that god created all things, but pieces of the divine made their way into us, into humans. She believed that's what it meant for us to be made in god's image. She thought the piece I had was powerful, why I need to create."

Henry nodded in understanding. "It is a need, isn't it."

"She asked me once, what would happen if I was made to stop. I said I'd find a way."

Henry smiled, pleased.

"She believed there were some people, though, whose piece of god was twisted," Linnea continued, recalling the moment she and GG shared out under the grapes, reflecting on the girl who'd been found dead in the woods. "But, how do we know," she whispered, working the skin at the base of her thumbnail with her forefinger, working the words up from the knot in her chest, replaying a flurry of William's words mixed with Lars's in her mind. "How do we know if someone can come back from what they've done? Lars… After what happened with West and GG, the visceral, poetic intensity of it, we agreed not to cross certain lines, not to take what wasn't *ours*. I never thought he would… That he'd have been the one." She took a breath, shook her head, trying to steady herself. "I thought it would be me who lost the path, but how do I know it isn't? With Lars as my gauge for morality…" She inhaled, nose stinging, tears lining the edge of her eyes. "How do I know *my* piece isn't twisted?"

"Do you feel weighted by what you've done?" He asked, head turning on his pillow, his eyes finding hers.

"No," she answered honestly, terrified. She'd not asked him out of guilt, but for lack of it. "There's nothing I've done that wasn't part of a fair encounter between animals. And I've made nothing that wasn't composed of materials obtained justly." Linnea sighed, thinking back to the beginning, then back further still, when she'd poured slip guided by GG's hands, when her own hands began to mold clay, the bloody handprint that marked her first cup, how torn she'd once felt about who she was, GG's words of guidance, encouragement, reining her in… "I almost dug up a dead coyote once," she smiled, cheeks warming as she huffed a breath of laughter, pulled Henry's hand with hers to cover her eyes.

"The one you put under the ground?" He asked, his smile audible.

Linnea nodded.

"GG absolutely forbade it; said she had to draw a line."

Henry moved his shoulder against her, a shrug. "Depends on how much time passed, I suppose. How long had the animal been dead?"

"Years," she winced.

"*Gross*," Henry chuckled, pulling her hand back toward him, resting it on his chest. He pressed his thumb into her palm, over the mounded flesh at the base, then back toward the center, where the lines and wrinkles told stories. "I agree with your grandmother about the coyote," he continued, his smile relaxing as his thoughts shifted behind his eyes. "And I agree with her existential insights. By god, evolution, or chaos, there are monsters among us, whether I can count myself as one, I'm not certain, but my calling has been to hunt them. We can only act according to our nature, stay inside the parameters of our instinct," he went on, pausing for a deep, slow breath. "I'm not concerned so much with the hereafter as I am with the here and the now, I suppose, but when I stand before the judgement of god or my own conscience, I'll do it without a heavy heart."

His palm wrapped around the back of her hand, his thumb pressing at the base of her fingers, bringing them up to his chin, his cheek. Linnea continued to move her fingers through his beard, considering what she knew, and finding herself content with what she didn't.

*

In the empty kitchen, Linnea and Henry found a plate resting atop a large bowl on the counter, hiding its contents. Henry lifted the lid, smiled, and pulled out a slice of apple, brown with cinnamon and sugar.

"I missed this last time," he grinned, crunching into his prize, braille *timepiece* once again in place around his wrist.

Linnea leaned against the sink beside him, looking out the window, through the grape arbor, to the four figures by the kiln.

"Do your brothers help?" she asked, still looking through the glass, again recalling something Jonathan had said. *There's only so much Phil and I can do,* Jon had said. *We need you focused.*

"Mmm," he hummed after a second apple disappearing quickly into his mouth, freeing his hand to take another.

"I have what resources I need through Convallaria, but Phil and Jonathan are invaluable in an intelligence capacity, as well as with rerouting attention. They also assist with target identification."

"Marcus?"

Henry shook his head. Sleighing monsters wasn't for the faint of heart.

"Both Marcus and my father know, but their involvement is limited. William was a special circumstance. My father expressed wanting to be here, but was unable."

"Perhaps you can enjoy a cup of tea together, when the work is done," she offered. Henry was right, there would be more than enough material…

A knowing smile pushed at Henry's cheeks, coaxing his dimples. He took another apple from the bowl, and brought it to Linnea's mouth. The fruit was sweet and grainy between her lips when he held it there, crisp and tart when she bit down. His fingers traced the wide neck of her dark t-shirt, traveled over her left shoulder as the flavors blended in her mouth.

"Unknown pleasures," he said, giving voice to the faded words she wore.

"Mmm," she hummed, reaching up for a kiss. "Why don't you get the egg and a couple sticks of butter while I get the rest from the cabinet?"

Henry let his fingers run over Linnea's right shoulder, and together they gathered the ingredients for an apple crisp, their movements fluid, their smiles easy.

*

Linnea's eyes flicked up toward Henry with his brothers and Lars at the kiln as she began to set the table under the grape arbor, laying out a sage runner over an oatmeal-colored tablecloth. She arranged the tea service, flatware, and plates in the center, each tea cup and saucer in front of a chair, one place absent a teacup, as Lars preferred a mug. All were made with more than just love, sweat, and clay. Thinking Henry and his brothers might prefer coffee over tea, and to drink it from a larger vessel, she set a mug down for each of them as well. It was about the gesture, really, with the teacups, though the mugs were each special in their own way.

Linnea went straight to the fire once the pie had been put in the oven, leaving Henry to grind *the good beans*. She'd been eager to check the temperature, the sounds, the feeling the flames had taken on. Unsurprisingly, Henry's brothers had done an excellent job at the helm in her absence under Lars's guidance, which she gratefully told them. And though her praise brightened their faces, the promise of coffee brought visible relief to their collective countenance, their facial muscles relaxing, shoulders drooping slightly.

Morning light filtered through the wood and leaves overhead, leaving Linnea, Lars, Henry, and his brothers bespeckled in shadow and light at the table. Linnea took a deep drink from her tea, the liquid on the hot side of warm, the bergamot and maple *just right*.

"I have to admit," she started, scrunching up her nose, "after Gabby, there was more than a moment or two when I thought it could have been Erik. And I wonder what happened with him. He was about to walk Gabby out to her car when I left. I didn't hear from him at all that night or the next day, until I was leaving work early… Then his messages were relentless."

Lars caught her eyes, still unaware that Henry, and likely a brother or two, knew it was by his hand that the young woman's life was taken. The sweat and restrained panic were less than what he deserved, but he needed to feel something.

"Erik Grayer was a suspect, briefly," Henry said. "Derailed us a bit."

Linn tilted her head. "Really?"

"Who's Erik?" Marcus asked, diluting his coffee with a generous amount of milk.

"A surgeon at the hospital," Linnea sighed. "We dated a while ago, and the breakup has continued to be challenging for him. He'd been walking Gabby and I out to the parking lot the night she was killed. Then I went back in to return some keys to the unit…"

"Surveillance from the parking lot would have been nice," Phil added, stirring sugar into his coffee.

The outdoor cameras, it turned out, had evolved into a *display only* capacity over the years.

"The police would have known who'd killed her, though," Linnea said, realizing that surveillance from the garage would have led officials directly to her brother.

"Backup," Marcus started, his head tilted to one side. "If there was no surveillance from the parking lot, how did you clear the doctor?"

"The indoor cameras function perfectly," Jonathan said, pausing to drink from his mug. "Erik Grayer took two steps out the door, turned around, and went back inside claiming he had a work obligation."

"They have audio?" Linnea asked.

"No," Henry smirked behind his coffee. "Jon and Phil interrogated him."

"You *didn't*," Linnea smiled, eyes wide.

Lars beamed from his seat. "Before or after you saw the video?"

"After," Phil grinned.

"I'm surprised he attempted contact with you afterwards, Linnea, considering…" Henry commented, leaning back in his chair, mug cradled in his hands.

"I'll prioritize a meet for follow-up questioning," Jonathan started. "What with the two active investigations, I'll still be here."

"You don't mind?" Linnea asked.

Phil huffed a short laugh. "I'd say we both enjoyed putting him through the wringer."

"I'm sure you did," she said. "But I mean, with work. You'll have your name on two unsolved cases. Won't that… look bad?"

Jonathan took a sip of his coffee and winked. "My reputation can afford it."

Two unsolved murder cases… and fifteen skulls on Henry's wall. Linnea had painted with Bill West's blood as a child, taken his eye and his arm. She knew what it felt like to be the hand that delivered justice that was hers to take, and there was no doubt Henry was entitled to Sixteen, but there were others, others that wouldn't have the kind of closure knowing can bring.

"The families," she started. "Gabby's family, the girl in the woods, the others. They'll never know," she sighed. Wasn't it worth it, though?

The table went still, Henry's brother's regarding him as he gently put his coffee down on the table, and spoke.

"Five, Seven, Eight, Ten and Thirteen," He said. "Their families know, but we couldn't risk it with the others. We know what it's like. We've had fifteen years of not knowing, the torture of it, and that's a word I don't use lightly. A great deal of effort goes into screening families for communication. In most cases, we couldn't take the risk."

Linnea nodded.

"And a great deal of effort goes into selecting the next number," Jonathan added, looking up as Missy's figure came through the honeysuckle, her hands full as her smile. Cap walked a few paces behind her, alert, though his expression relaxed as he took in what warmth there was at the table.

"Hey," Linnea greeted. "Perfect timing; grab a seat."

"Oh no, we don't want to impose," Missy said politely. "Cap said you had some company staying over last night, so I thought I'd bring by some treats. They're just savories," she shrugged, adding a platter of bacon and a basket of scones to the table. She even brought softened butter…

"First of all, I'm thankful for anything you bring," Linnea started. "Second… I have an apple crisp in the oven, so the savory delights will make a perfect addition. Pie will be done in five or ten minutes."

All three of Henry's brothers perked up, then a concerned look came over Phil's face as he worked out the reduction in portion size were two additional people to stay and share it.

"Guys, this is Missy and her husband, Cap. They live next door. And you know Henry, these are his brothers: Jonathan, Phil, and Marcus."

Those named reached across to each other, shaking hands and exchanging pleasantries, Lars getting up to hug Missy, and share a pat on the back with Cap. Then, when Linnea claimed a slice of bacon, the others followed suit, reaching toward the gifts at the center of the table. Jonathan, she noted with a smile, didn't restrain himself in the slightest.

"This smells *wonderful,*" Marcus said, inhaling a scone he'd selected. "What have you baked into them?"

"Just some herbs," Missy said casually, but not dismissive. "And I've chopped the rosemary very small. No one wants to bite into sticks with their breakfast…" she said, directing her comment to Cap. Then, to Linnea she asked, "Did you have a chance to eat some of those cookies?"

"I did," Linnea said. "They were delicious."

"That hint of orange," Phil said.

Missy, of course, brightened. "Yes!" She beamed. "I added some orange zest and coriander, and the dark chocolate chunks, of course… the recipe practically writes itself."

Cap came around to Linnea as his wife spoke to Phil, then Henry and his brothers.

"I needed to see you were okay," he whispered, placing an arm, thankfully, over her shoulder instead of her waist. "I fell asleep in my chair early last night; woke up and went out to the porch, saw too many lights on over your place," he said, letting out a long breath. "Then I saw Henry pull in and tear off running to the front door, and when he couldn't get in, he raced out back… I went out to the barn this morning… it's spotless." Easing away from her, Cap found her eyes with his. "You okay?" he asked, keeping his voice low.

She nodded. It was a lot, what she'd experienced. Heavy. Not heavy like iron, but heavy like vastness, like space that goes on to a place one can't see.

"I was so excited when I saw the outdoor kiln running," Missy said, pulling Linnea's attention. Cap sat down beside his wife, and she put an arm around him. "I remember when Grace had those college kids building it. They'd stay over in tents when it came time to run the thing. And I want to say it was like a clown car when they finally pulled their work out, cups, plates, vases, and bowls, they just kept coming. But it is rather big, isn't it? What do you have cooking in there?"

"Henry had success with hunting, and it seemed like too much for the studio kilns." She said, not missing the way Cap's eyes widened, knowing more than his wife on what the contents might be...

Missy's smile changed to one of memories shared, stories to tell.

"Do they know about your work..." Missy started, tilting a head toward Henry and his brothers, "about how you've been making your teacups?"

"Henry knows quite a bit, but you might as well share. I'm sure they'd enjoy whatever it is you've got bubbling up in there."

Missy did look about ready to burst.

"This girl had us out here all night one summer, picking boiled bones out of birds and snakes and rabbits... mice," she added, Linnea warming with memory.

"I had a good time," Missy went on, "I always had a good time with you and Grace, and I knew you were capable in the studio, but that china was *beautiful*. And what you did with Barny..." she said, admiring the tea service laid out. "The *creativity* and the *skill*... Your GG was so proud of you. I know she still is."

Missy reached across the table and took Linnea's hand, warmth wrapping around her fingers and flooding through her, a feeling of home.

"Thank you," she said softly, Henry's hand coming to rest on the small of her back as she took a breath. "Let me go get you guys a cup and something to put your pie on," she smiled. "Coffee or tea?"

"Better make it tea for us both…" Missy started with a look toward Cap. "He's been in rare form this morning. Met his coffee quota twice over."

"You got it."

Henry stood alongside Linnea, his hand finding its way back to her. "Do you need any help inside?"

"Sure. You can help me get the teacups."

Linnea closed her eyes a moment as they entered the kitchen, inhaling a smell that was nothing short of heavenly. When she opened them again, her eyes met Henry's, a content, if not slightly mischievous look on his face.

"Snake and the bird?" he asked.

Linnea nodded. "Perfect."

Wearing oven mitts and a paisley apron, Linnea set the hot pie outside under the grape arbor as Henry set a place for Cap and Missy. The smell of home, of woodsmoke, spiced apples, and the *good* coffee surrounded her

A sense of rightness settled into her bones as they sat and ate, talked, and smiled. If memory could be stored in locks of hair, this was embedded in a place far deeper, a substance that could be transformed by fire, to hold secrets that one day her daughters might drink from them.

Henry tipped his mug up, draining it, then seemed to catch Phil's eye, and a subtle gesture passed between them, like a whisper with hands.

"Cap," Henry started. "Do you have a table saw?"

"Yeah, she's out in the Garage."

"I was thinking about that target project we discussed. I've got some wood in the back of my truck. Want to head over and get her fired up? We're planning on sticking around this weekend; there's no rush."

A twinkle of joy broke through Cap's face in a smile. "Sure," he said, rising from his seat, resting a hand on his wife's shoulder. "See you in a bit. If we're not back by lunch…"

"I'll make sure you eat," she laughed. "I know what happens when you get in the garage with a project."

Henry stood, and Phil. Then Henry looked at her brother.

"Lars," he started. "Come give us a hand."

Linn didn't think it would go as far as the entire hand, but she knew her brother wouldn't leave the garage with all his fingers. He seemed oblivious to the impending lesson. The food, surroundings, company, or conversation must have dulled his senses, because he finished his coffee and rose without question. Or perhaps it wasn't that he was dull, but that Henry was sharp.

Missy, Marc, and Jon remained at the table; their discussion focused on baking.

"I don't know how you and Cap manage with all the bacon and pastries in the house."

"Oh, don't kid yourself," Missy smirked. "That man has no willpower when it comes to food. I keep Linn fully stocked with leftovers."

"And I don't mind one bit," Linn smiled, rising from her seat. "I'm just going to check the kiln,"

She paused a moment as she stepped out from under the grape arbor, breathing deep.

To the eye, darkness might manifest as the absence of light, but as a word, it had come to mean so much more. Linnea was profoundly aware in that moment, that she could walk, illuminated by the haze filtered sun on her shoulders, while carrying unfathomable darkness inside her, a womb with divine potential.

The kiln radiated before her; the ground below cool with clarity. Though she wore shoes, Linnea could feel that it wasn't one stone that had risen beneath her feet, but the path itself, long, wide, and with no end in sight.

Epilogue

Manhattan, May 2019

Everything in the gallery had been beautifully arranged, the space filled with Linnea's work, filled with bodies. Pedestals of varying widths rose from the wooden floor, all of them topped with her creations. Large bowls with lacelike details carved into their rims, teapots, cups and saucers, pieces that blurred the lines between sculpture and function. Each display had a corresponding card giving the work's title, maker, date of manifestation, and a list of materials used. All of the ceramics had been made with bone china. All of them made by Linnea's hands.

Instead of a barren expanse of white, the gallery walls carried her work as well. Twelve large-scale black and white photographs enhancing the atmosphere. Some of the images were of work displayed in the gallery, photographed to demonstrate the beauty of their translucence, others told the story of Linnea's process, of how her ceramic pieces were made. Kiln fire devoured wood on a wall to her left, beside it a photograph of the grape arbor, set with plates, steaming teacups, tiered serving dishes, a teapot, the landscape beyond blanketed in snow. A third image depicted a deer skull, white surrounded by darkness, antlers stained with the blood of Eighteen disappearing into shadow.

Carolanne, the gallery owner, widened her eyes and raised a hand to Linnea from across the room, an effortless signal that it was time for the artist to speak. Linnea made her way over, thanked the owner for her introduction, took a breath, and spoke.

"Sustain/Sustenance is a body of work that explores what it means to sustain, to nourish, to be nourished," she started. "But also, as it pertains to ending, the ceasing of a thing, and in the case of my work, procured from the bones of hunted animals, their lives were ended to create these pieces, provided food for our bodies, figurative fuel and quite literally material for the creative process, to form vessels for offering sustenance. In transforming these creatures, we have, in a sense, become their caretakers. How will we choose to memorialize them? What will we take into our selves through these vessels crafted from their bones? There's also something to be said about the act of creation… For me, as I'm sure is true for many makers, the act of creation itself is sustaining."

Linnea took a breath, cheeks warm as she saw her mother approach Henry and Jon, Linnea's nearly three-year-old daughter beside her with arms outstretched toward Henry as she said, "Daddy, *uppa.*"

They hadn't planned on a child, but life is unexpected. And she hadn't been the reason Linn and Henry had married. They'd paid homage to her parents when they'd announced their decision, claiming taxes and health insurance as persuasive factors. Marriage on paper was the least of what bonded them.

A few heads swiveled toward the little girl, their attention returning to Linnea as she continued.

"Humans have long understood that there is power in the way we make something, what purpose we infuse into it. And we love our secrets too, don't we? Even if we are unaware of what it is, there's something about knowing the esoteric exists, like indecipherable whispers we can hear but not understand. I like to think there are stories in the bones I use, from the life of the animal, from how they were taken, embedded with the overt and subliminal intentions of the maker, the creator. It is my hope that the work I've presented carries this sense of mystery, and that their whispers call to you. Thank you."

Those with free hands clapped, while others raised a glass. Carolanne leaned in for a social embrace, then raised her arm to regain the attention of those present.

"Can you tell us what you're working on presently in the studio?" She asked with a smile.

Linnea nodded. "No secrets there, Carolanne. I plan to continue working with themes of offering and sacrifice."

"Oh, I know I'm not the only one who likes the sound of that," Carolanne grinned.

And with those words, more applause ensued, and Linnea began the mingling process.

A blonde woman in her early sixties wasn't the first, nor the last in a string of attendees wishing to greet her, to ask questions. The woman introduced herself, letting Linnea know which hospital board she was a member of, then politely rested a few fingers on Linnea's shoulder, gesturing to the card beside the closest pedestal, an enormous white cube the size of a table, which was set with an elaborate tea service for six. Each of the cups were delicately painted in greyscale, displaying moments between a hunter and a deer, between two animals. Each handle in the collection was marked with a red thumbprint. Lily's. Her small fingers had been the perfect size, and she'd delighted in helping with Mummy's work.

"This one says, *Hand painted glaze on bone china. Bone ash Odocoileus virginianus, Nineteen.* I saw another that listed Seventeen and Twenty. What do the numbers mean?"

Several people standing close enough to hear turned to listen, hors d'oeuvre plates and wine glasses in hand. There'd been a magazine article and a few blogs on Linnea's work that had come out recently, creating quite a buzz. That she was so involved in the acquisition of her bone ash should have been well known to those in the gallery, though the depth of her intimacy was knowledge for fewer than she could count on two hands, unless she included those embedded in the clay.

"I process my own bone ash from animals hunted and harvested by my spouse, Henry. The genus and species you see references the deer, and the number corresponds to a bone blend unique to each season," Linnea smiled.

Another woman approached, dark red hair to her shoulders with a chunk of grey at the front as if she'd been struck by lightning. *Rogue,* Linnea thought, or… she searched the crowd, finding her brother. He winked, then his eyes went wide as Linn tilted her head toward the red headed woman. Lars lifted a disfigured right hand toward his face, evidence of the five-year-old lesson Henry had administered with a table saw.

With his thumb and only remaining finger, Lars gestured down from his brow like a curl of hair as he mouthed, *Bonnie Raitt!*

I know, she mouthed back with excitement, then returned her focus on the woman patiently waiting to speak with her.

"Do you grind all your bone into powder by hand?" She asked, turning toward the photograph depicting pieces of Seventeen being crushed with a pestle and mortar.

"I *start* them all by hand, but finish them off in a grain mill," Linnea said, scrunching her nose comically at the admission. "The process is incredibly important to me, but so is the product. A mill ensures the powder arrives at the necessary consistency, and it works *so* much faster than I can," she laughed.

The woman's eyes sparkled, relishing in her presence at the event, at the knowledge she'd received, at being seen.

In that moment of calm between the smiles and questions, a large finger gently traced the flesh beneath the neckline of Linnea's dress, wide, like her favorite t-shirt. With no sleeves, the frock left almost the entirety of her shoulders exposed.

Henry wore no tie, and the long sleeves of his white shirt had been rolled up, cufflinks in his pocket, jacket back in the truck parked outside. The ink on Henry's forearm detailed a twinflower, one bloom on either side of where his thumb met his hand. The stem coiled tight around his wrist, rippling out into dark water. There, floating on the lake over his flesh, were waterlilies, as if Monet had taken black and grey to his arm. The watch he chose to wear, a *timepiece,* he'd call it, had no numbers. His braille watch. She liked that one.

Henry had mentioned something to her once when they first met, about the way he dressed at work, when he wore expensive suits instead of tactical clothing. *I feel very much in my own skin,* he'd said, *smiling while I shake hands with those who have no idea what's observing from behind the pressed shirt.* Linnea felt it too, in the interviews, in the gallery, with her knee-length black dress, heels, and ornate earrings. She wasn't suppressing any parts of herself, she was whole, fully present, relishing in the private joy of having a secret in the blood, bone, and clay beneath her fingernails.

I am, she thought as Henry kissed her, as Lily asked to see the cups with her fingerprints again. *I am.*

Acknowledgements

First, Thank you to whatever form of divine intervention keeping me from being investigated by the authorities while I researched for this novel. I had a fair amount of prior knowledge, but digging deeper has no doubt left my browser history more colorful than ever before.

To my three parents, I love you. To my first dad, if you have any post-mortem sentience, thank you for having had a glass eye that continues to inspire me, for leaving a deer's head hanging from a tree in the woods out back, for boiling the bones, and for the skull mount that lives in my house. Thank you, Mom for your medical insight, for mementos brought home from your travels, in your hands and in your stories. To my second dad, thank you for your insight, for taking this endeavor seriously, and for co-renovating my kitchen. The new space is one of my favorite places to write.

Thank you to my spouse, Damien, for all the things. I love you. You support my artistic whimsy while keeping me tethered. You supply me with the good chai and Momofuku noodles. You build shelves for my moth specimens, and place your Transformers action figures around the house (finding them brings me joy.) I continue to feel grateful for these services, and for your presence alone. And also, the kitchen. That peninsula is clutch.

Thank you to my daughters, for enriching my life and keeping things beautiful, interesting, and sometimes a little bit gross. Never stop bringing things in from the woods; never stop reaching for the pestle and mortar. I love you.

Massive thank you to Kerry, Mel, and Colleen. You are my original champions, betas, and editors. So much more than a book club. Thank you, Caroline, for ignoring life to tear through this novel in a weekend, and for telling me it felt like reading a real book (ultimate praise.) Shout out to my Fight Club moms. You are my found family, and a lifeline. And finally, The Rock, who, by way of my book club, kept me going when I got in my own way. The memes have been invaluable. Thank you.

About the Author

Kristen Cornwall is a writer, an artist, and a great many other things. She likes maple in her tea when she wants it sweet, enjoys the seasons in New England, croissants, and listening to birds (though it's a little love/hate when days are longest and they are awake before she really wants to get started.) She likes being in the woods and by the ocean, and reads often. She occasionally makes crepes.